KILL
AGAIN

Also by Neal Baer and Jonathan Greene

Kill Switch

KILL
AGAIN

NEAL BAER
AND
JONATHAN GREENE

KENSINGTON BOOKS
www.kensingtonbooks.com

KENSINGTON BOOKS are published by

Kensington Publishing Corp.
119 West 40th Street
New York, NY 10018

All Kensington titles, imprints and distributed lines are available at special quantity discounts for bulk purchases for sales promotion, premiums, fund-raising, educational or institutional use. Special book excerpts or customized printings can also be created to fit specific needs. For details, write or phone the office of the Kensington Special Sales Manager: Kensington Publishing Corp., 119 West 40th Street, New York, NY, 10018. Attn. Special Sales Department. Phone: 1-800-221-2647.

Kensington and the K logo Reg. U.S. Pat. & TM Off.

Library of Congress Card Catalogue Number: 2015934128

ISBN-13: 978-0-7582-6687-3
ISBN-10: 0-7582-6687-1
First Kensington Hardcover Edition: July 2015

eISBN-13: 978- 07582-8629-1
eISBN-10: 0-7582-8629-5
First Kensington Electronic Edition: July 2015

10 9 8 7 6 5 4 3 2 1

Printed in the United States of America

For Alan Downs and Marc Levitt, who listen.
To the next generation: Mara, Josh, Zach, Matt, Jacob, Shayna,
Noah, Sophie, Adin, Michael and Matthew.

PROLOGUE

He'd chosen the studio apartment not only for its location in the basement of a brownstone, but also for its own private entrance from the sidewalk, away from prying eyes. The apartment was shaped like a perfect square—a large, starkly furnished, windowless room. If you happened to enter, the first thing you'd see was the white-framed Ikea bed wedged into one corner against the rear and left-hand walls, situated such that he'd need only to turn his head to see the front door. Hugging the bed's headboard sat an unstained pine dresser, drawers facing the right-hand wall. At first glance, perhaps it would appear a feeble attempt at feng shui. But he had no interest in such folly.

Walk a bit further in and, across the room and opposite the bed to your right, you'd see the small porcelain sink and two-burner gas stove that passed for the kitchen. You might also notice the place was spotless, as if he sprayed, rinsed, and wiped clean every inch daily. In the bathroom, the toilet gleamed like he scrubbed it after each use. Gone was the original antique claw-foot tub the brownstone's builder originally had installed; in its place stood a cookie-cutter fiberglass bathtub/shower unit. To the tenant, the presence of this . . . thing . . . in such a place reeked of a rush job by a miserly charlatan, a glaring imperfection in what was otherwise the perfect place for his needs. But right now, it was just one more sin committed by one more sinner in a world filled with too many of both.

Beside the bathroom stood the door to the apartment's lone closet, which, if you opened it, would appear as modest as that in most prewar buildings. Each article of clothing hung from the same type of light-wood hanger, each hanger evenly spaced from the next. The tenant's wardrobe consisted of crisply pressed white oxford shirts, khaki pants, and one black suit. You might guess the occupant as someone who coveted simplicity, who didn't want the added pressure of deciding what to wear every day. Who didn't care about worldly possessions or creature comforts.

And you'd be correct. Because what interested him—and at times drove him mad—were the thoughts running through his mind.

He took the apartment under the condition that the landlord never enter without a day's advance notice. He actually insisted it be written into the lease, which of course made the landlord instantly suspicious—until his prospective tenant handed over three months' rent and two months' security without blinking an eye. Which brought the landlord's immediate signature on the document and ensured that the tenant's clause protecting him from prying, unwelcome eyes would be respected.

He was counting on it. He had to. After all, who would possibly comprehend a grown man writing words on his wall? The cops found words written on the walls of the apartment of David Berkowitz, the notorious Son of Sam serial killer—and they didn't understand.

No cop would ever see his writings. At least, not while he was alive. Of that he was certain. He swore to himself he would protect this, his creation, at all costs. Even if it meant painting over it.

Now, alone in his sanctuary, he finished the latest addition to his work, taking a sniff of the black Magic Marker before capping it. He loved the intoxicating smell. He'd collected Magic Markers as a child, and had one of each color: brown, blue, red, orange, purple, green—even yellow. The yellow one was his prize. He never saw anyone use a yellow Magic Marker. Then one day, when he was twelve, his mother threw them out because he'd drawn "nasty, sick, perverted" pictures on his bedroom wall. He smiled, remembering. He used the yellow marker for their private parts. His mother painted over the pictures of the women he'd drawn because Magic Marker can never be washed off.

It's permanent, *he thought,* stepping back to admire what he'd done. He added two words, fictions chaperone, *to the dozens of pairs of words already written, neatly, one pair above the next, on one wall. He smiled, looking at* infections poacher, octopi enfranchise, *and* Pinocchio fastener *at the top of the list. Though the combinations of words would've appeared nonsensical to others, they calmed him because only he knew what they meant.*

They did make sense, didn't they? It was the alphabet itself that made no sense. It was just a long train of letters, waiting to be made into words and sentences and thoughts. Individual letters could be coupled, with more letters added like a delicious recipe, to make words. He loved to cook too, to add assorted ingredients together to make a savory stew or a delicately crusted pie. Just like the letters of the alphabet, the ingredients alone weren't satisfying. But the right combinations of letters or ingredients brought order to the chaos of his life. The words on his wall and the cinnamon aroma of the apple pie he had baked earlier in the day eased his mind, bringing even more perfection to an emerging, flawless world of his own making.

Order. Perfection. Flawlessness. He mused on these words, as he often did, because they were exactly what he strived to find in the randomness of his own life, and they had always, for one reason or another, eluded him.

Until now.

He grabbed his favorite yellow Magic Marker and wrote two words atop the other pairs, outlining the letters in brown so that they almost sparkled like gold in the glint of the one bare bulb that lit the room: GATHER STAMINA. *Those words meant more to him than just a motto; they were his mantra. They represented who he was. Who he wanted to be. His very being. And only he knew why.*

He turned to the wall to the left. Again, he admired his work: a grid of fifteen neatly drawn boxes running across and down. To anyone else, it would look like an empty crossword puzzle. Using a ruler, he neatly finished the final box, in black Magic Marker, in the lower right-hand corner. He'd waited for this day longer than he realized. When the grid was full of those random letters, finally ordered into words, it would be his masterpiece. His life's work, completed. And with those last strokes of the Magic Marker, he knew it was time to begin.

He walked across the room to his small kitchen and picked up a manila envelope he'd left on the stove. He turned on the gas burner, watching the blue and yellow flame dance before him, luring him. He opened the envelope and poured its contents into his hand— perfectly cut up half-inch squares from a photograph—which he dropped over the flame. The fire licked the pieces, an eye, an upper lip, a nose, consuming them until all that remained was a small pile of gray ash.

Satisfied, he turned off the burner and removed two large pots from a lower cabinet. Then, from a drawer, he took a rolled-up piece of cloth, from which the handles of knives, a cleaver, and shears protruded like spires. From his closet's top shelf, he removed a sleeping bag, small canvas tent, and deflated air mattress, all neatly folded. He'd always loved the outdoors, and tonight he would sleep under the stars.

After he had finished what he was compelled to do. Which he knew, beyond any doubt, would relieve the unbearable anxiety he'd felt all his life.

At least for now.

CHAPTER 1

Claire Waters sat bolt upright in bed, one hand covering her mouth to muffle the scream that otherwise would have escaped, the other hand throwing aside the sky blue comforter covering her. Claire loved this time of year in New York City: early May, still cool at night in these minutes before sunrise. If you could tune out the perpetual noise from the street below in the City That Never Sleeps, it was perfect sleeping weather with the open window, at least for her.

As far back as she could remember, even in the frigid winters of her childhood home upstate in Rochester, Claire had always preferred a cold night's rest and could never sleep in a warm room, which for her was anything over sixty-five degrees. After all, she reasoned, you could always pile on more blankets (which she relished) when it was cold. You couldn't rip off your skin if it was too hot.

Right now, Claire wanted to rip off her skin. She was sweating profusely, and not because of the temperature. Her nightmares were becoming more frequent. And this one—a man in the shadows, holding a small knife and lunging at Claire just as she woke up—was the most vivid yet.

She tried to shake off the anxiety but her pounding heart wouldn't cooperate. She reached for the drawer in the night table beside her bed and the bottle of Xanax she kept there, but changed her mind, realizing that a quick fix wouldn't make the churning in her stomach go away. When it came back tomorrow night, and the night after, and the night after that, what then? Pop Xanax until it went away? The last thing she needed right now was to become dependent on benzodiazepines, among the most addicting substances on the planet. The nightmares were hellish, but benzo withdrawal could kill you. Literally.

As the anxiety lingered, she tried to count how many consecutive days she'd relied on the drug after one of these nightmares. When she lost count, she realized she'd already been on it too long. Had she counseled a patient to use it as she'd been doing, she'd lose not just her board certification as a forensic psychiatrist but likely her license to practice medicine as well.

Physician, heal thyself. Yeah, right. Whoever wrote the Bible had never tried benzos.

Claire realized she needed to follow the advice she'd give her patients.

She had to talk about it.

She had to *feel* it.

But all Claire could feel was emptiness.

Feeling is still too painful, she thought. And then came the thought that always followed: she'd suffered enough emotional pain to fill several lifetimes.

So she did what she'd always done when her emotions overtook her brain: shut them down.

She grabbed her iPod, put in the ear buds, and blasted Led Zeppelin's "Stairway to Heaven" as loud as she could stand. Music had always been Claire's therapy, especially through the worst times, of which she'd had more than her fair share in the past year.

She felt the soft guitar melody begin to ease her tension, a drug of its own. As a research scientist, she knew that buried in her own brain, in the amygdala, the most primitive neural structure, was a switch that reacted to danger. When she began swirling into the abyss, her amygdala, her own neural makeup, sensed a mortal threat. But what? She'd had the nightmares since she was a child. They'd gone away three months after the horror of last year. And, though she'd made steady progress since then, they'd suddenly returned two weeks earlier. Why had they come back?

She turned to look at the clock on her nightstand. 5:29 a.m. Perfect. She set the alarm every night as a precaution, but never had to shut it off; she'd always woken minutes before it sounded. Even the mornings after those seemingly endless thirty-hour shifts as an intern and resident, when she'd come home and collapse into bed, sleep deprived, her only desire was to nod off and escape from the world.

Now, she threw her legs over the side of the mattress, turned off her iPod, removed the ear buds, and flipped on the light. The boxy dresser, nightstands, and headboard for the queen-sized bed were all made of beige wood and laminate, bought from one of those generic stores where you can pick furniture for every room of your apartment and have a completely furnished place the next day. She took in her surroundings: the parquet floors, rectangular, ordinary bedroom in a standard, stark, cookie-cutter, one-bedroom box on the twenty-eighth floor of a contemporary glass tower. About as nondescript as one could get in Manhattan.

Perhaps as nondescript as Claire wanted to be right now.

She looked at the framed photo of Ian, her fiancé, the image she woke to every morning, on the nightstand behind her clock. The apartment they'd shared had been cozily furnished with antiques and memorabilia, most of which Claire had sold or given away.

"Can you believe I actually live in a place like this?" Claire said to the photo.

As if he might somehow answer her.

Claire showered, ran a brush through her shoulder-length brown hair (no time for the blow-dryer), and pulled a sharp navy blue Donna Karan suit, a white blouse, and a pair of black Louboutin pumps from her closet. A year ago, when she'd entered the Forensic Psychiatry Fellowship at Manhattan State University Hospital, wearing this "costume" every day was unthinkable to her. She'd come there from research work in a lab at the National Institutes of Health, where nobody cared what one wore under their white coat.

But that was before the trouble started. In the months since she returned to the program following some much-needed time off, she found herself filling her closet with suits, shoes, and scarves. And actually enjoying wearing them. She wondered if her sudden interest in fashion was a way of filling the emptiness, the void in her life, with material instant gratification.

She was about to slip on her shoes when she remembered the guest sleeping in the other room. She picked up the pumps in one hand, carefully opened the door to her bedroom, and tiptoed toward the front door. She picked up her Coach purse and brown, soft leather briefcase and took a quick look into the living room. The sight of the man sleeping on the sofa bed brought the day's first smile to her face. Her father.

Frank Waters had begun spending more time with his daughter after she'd returned to the family's home in Rochester, New York, for a leave of absence from her Forensic Psychiatry Fellowship last fall. Frank, a physicist specializing in fiber optics, had worked his way up to vice president of his company, which built computer networks and the devices to run them. His new position freed him to step away from the office during the day, allowing for late breakfasts and early lunches between father and daughter, giving Claire time to enjoy the dad she had barely seen as a child.

Then one morning at home in Rochester, Frank was in the kitchen brewing a pot of coffee when Claire came in and announced it was time for her to go back to Manhattan and resume her life.

"I can't stay here forever sponging off you and Mom," she'd joked.

Frank had thrown his arms around Claire, his pride and joy, telling her he was ready to help her move.

Claire had called her mentor, Doctor Lois Fairborn.

"Sweetheart!" she'd exclaimed, just one of the many terms of endearment Fairborn used on a constant basis. "Please tell me you're coming back."

"I'm ready," Claire had said. "But I want to make sure it's what's best for the program."

"Having you here is what's best for the program," Fairborn had interjected, assuring her that she'd shoehorn her star student right back in whenever Claire thought she'd return to New York.

They agreed she'd appear at Manhattan State two weeks from the following Monday. Claire knew she'd need every second of the time before then to get herself settled.

Father and daughter had left Rochester early the next morning, a Friday, flying to La Guardia and renting a car to begin the always arduous task of finding a Manhattan apartment. In Claire's case it had to be one she could afford on the meager salary of a medical fellow. She and her late fiancé, Ian, had split the rent on their shared flat, a beautiful second-story floor-through in a small, secure building in Chelsea. Claire knew going it alone would mean a step down from that. She was hoping she wouldn't have to accept a one-room studio.

After grabbing bagels at Daniel's on Third Avenue, they were walking down Fortieth Street toward the East River. Just past the ancient firehouse, Frank steered her into a high-rise, luxury, doorman building with a sign outside announcing there were apartments available within.

"Are you kidding me?" Claire whispered as she looked at the rich furnishings in the lobby. "This place is way out of my league."

"Indulge the old guy, okay?" Frank had replied, not bothering to slow down.

The building's rental agent took them to the nicest one-bedroom she had. On the twenty-eighth floor, facing east toward Second Avenue, with views over the East River to Long Island City and the rest of Queens beyond. And a terrace from which one could enjoy them.

Claire was about to thank the agent for her time and make a graceful exit when Frank had asked, "How soon can she move in?"

"Monday," the agent had replied.

"Do you accept cosigners on the lease?" asked Frank, patting his pockets for his checkbook.

"As long as you pass the credit check," the agent had responded.

"Dad," Claire had pleaded, "I still can't afford this."

Frank was already writing out a check and handing it to the agent, whose eyes, when she saw the amount, grew as wide as saucers.

"That should cover one month's security and half a year's rent," Frank assured her with the click of his ballpoint pen.

An hour later, with the paperwork all signed and credit approved, they'd walked through the building's ornate marble lobby and out onto Fortieth Street. Claire's head was still spinning. Her father had always been such a meticulous, careful man, especially when it came to money.

"Dad," she'd said, "you didn't have to do that."

Frank walked with purpose, the stride of a man well satisfied with himself. "All your life, even as a child, you never asked for anything. Not a toy, not a book, not a cent. Nothing."

It was the first time he'd said anything like that to her.

"Are you telling me or asking me why?" she'd asked him.

Frank continued as if he hadn't heard her. "Everything you've achieved, everything . . ." He'd drifted off, as if having the conversation with himself. "You did it all yourself." He'd seemed to realize she was right beside him. "We saved so much money for your education," he'd said. "Enough to pay for everything, in full, no loans. And you kept getting full scholarships so we never had to use any of it. It's been sitting there, in a trust account with your name on it, all these years. I just thought it was time we put some of that cash to good use."

He looked up at the apartment tower that was soon to become Claire's new home and raised his arm, palm upward, as if holding a new world in his hand. "It's time you let yourself live a little," he'd smiled. "Just a little."

Now she was about to open the door when a wide-awake voice came from behind her.

"You look beautiful."

Claire turned. Her father was sitting up. Frank Waters was tall, thin, sporting a full shock of thick gray hair and the piercing green eyes his daughter had inherited. His devotion to the gym made him look and move like a man who was a decade younger than his sixty-six years. He lifted the comforter, revealing blue silk pajamas a shade lighter than Claire's suit.

"Thought I was being quiet," Claire said, heading into the living room.

"You didn't wake me," her father assured her.

She gave him a kiss on the cheek. "Go back to sleep," she said.

"Nah," Frank replied. "Gotta hit the gym and then I have a day full of meetings. What time do you think you'll be home?"

Claire knew it was his way of being protective. "Probably around eight," Claire replied. "My day's loaded too."

"That why you're so rattled?" Frank asked.

Claire thought she'd given away nothing. *How did he know?*

"I could always tell when you were upset," he said, "even before you knew."

"It's nothing," Claire replied, slipping her pumps on. "I had a nightmare."

"You had those as a child too," said Frank, trying to find his slippers with his feet. "You'd wake up in the middle of the night and tell me all about them."

"I'd tell you about this one. But I can't remember it." She pretended to adjust her skirt so she wouldn't have to look at him. She didn't want to talk about the dream lest it make her late and open the anxiety floodgates.

"Maybe I can jog your memory," Frank offered through a yawn as he opened the drapes, not waiting for Claire to refuse. "Do you remember how you woke up?"

"I sat up in bed with my hand over my mouth," Claire answered, checking her watch to give her father the hint that she didn't have time for this.

It didn't work. "So I wouldn't hear you scream?" Frank asked as he folded the comforter. "Why would you think to do that in a nightmare?"

Claire smiled at the irony of having her head shrunk by a physicist. "So I wouldn't wake you up?" she asked playfully.

Now her father smiled. "Maybe the nightmare was about me."

"I don't think so," Claire said.

"But you said you don't remember," he reminded her, folding the bed back into the sofa. "So how can you be sure?"

Checkmate. The conversation ended where it always did—at a brick wall. Frank, in perpetual motion, replacing the couch pillows, tried another tactic.

"You know," Frank began, plopping down on the sofa, "when you were a child you used to talk to someone who wasn't there."

"Yes, Dad," Claire said, sighing. "That I do remember."

"We were worried about you. Your mom and I."

"It's common for children to have invisible playmates," she said in her official psychiatrist's voice.

Frank knew that tone; he'd heard it from his daughter many times and was no stranger to what it meant: I've gotta go. He'd used a similar tone with her many times—something he didn't like to admit to himself—and knew when to stop pressing her.

"It's okay. Don't be late," he said as he rose from the sofa.

"Thanks, Dad."

He came over, gave her a kiss. "Have a good day, puppy," he said.

Claire smiled over his shoulder as he hugged her; he'd called her that pet name for as long as she could remember and she loved it each time. She kissed his cheek again and turned to head for the door, feeling just a little more secure.

* * *

He didn't want to be late. He gathered all the items he would need: the pots, the rolled up cloth with the razor-sharp chef's knives and shears. He felt a pounding in his head. A rhythm almost like a drumbeat that drowned out any thoughts that would stop him from what he was compelled to do. He grabbed the tent along with the pots and knives and left his apartment, stepping out into the cool, early morning sunlight that promised a beautiful day.

CHAPTER 2

"Bet you didn't think you'd be talking about brain science here," said Claire, hoping she could stimulate the brains of the seven people sitting before her as opposed to putting them to sleep. "But there's a lot of new evidence out there that's helping us explain why people turn to a life of crime."

"Because they're psychos," murmured Miguel Colon, twenty-five, a serious-looking, hard-bodied Latino with a tattoo of a dagger adorning his oversized right bicep. His Hispanic-Bronx accented comment brought snickers and smiles to the others in the room, including Claire.

"Not all of them," Claire corrected. "But you're not wrong either, Miguel. It's just a bit more complicated than that."

Miguel and his five young colleagues who sat at a modern, graphite-colored table before her were students at Manhattan State University's renowned School of Criminal Justice and Forensic Science.

Claire turned to the dry-erase board behind her and in large block letters wrote a single word—*EPIGENETICS*—which she underlined and then turned back to the group.

"Anyone know what epigenetics is?" she asked.

Not surprisingly, not one hand went up. And the one man in the room over the age of forty, Professor Walt McClure, knew better than to raise his.

McClure was a "friend" of Claire's mentor, Lois Fairborn, and speculation was that they were a lot more than just friends. He taught the class in which Claire now sat, a senior seminar in criminal profiling, and had asked Fairborn (perhaps during pillow talk) whether Claire would be up for coteaching the class with him, enlightening his students on recent advances in psychiatry and genetics, especially the emerging field of epigenetics, and how it might apply to criminal behavior. Fairborn had approached Claire with the request shortly after she returned to work two months earlier. At the time it was the last thing Claire had wanted to do. But she owed Fairborn for her compassion, understanding, and flexibility in arranging her leave from the fellowship and found it impossible to refuse. Believing it would be a one-time deal, Claire figured she'd do it, get it over with, and hope it didn't hurt too much.

Fortunately, it wasn't what she'd expected or even feared. There were only six students in the class plus Professor McClure, in a small but far from claustrophobic seminar room. To her surprise she'd lit up the moment she began talking, as if telling a story to a bunch of friends at a dinner party, engaging the students in a lively discussion of her experience tracking a serial killer the previous year. They'd listened raptly and asked numerous questions. McClure was ecstatic, and the way they'd tag-teamed the class proved to both of them they worked well together. Claire, for her part, was shocked she'd taken to teaching in the way she had and, hesitant though she was, enjoyed the distraction.

This was session number two. From the looks on the students' faces, she wasn't off to the same gangbusters start as last time. Epigenetics was dry material for people *with* medical backgrounds, and these kids were all headed into law enforcement—as either cops, federal agents, or forensic investigators. Not that any of this marked them as unintelligent or underachievers. She knew Miguel Colon, for one, had somehow managed to survive being raised by gang-member parents without getting killed or hurt and minus a criminal record. A straight A student all through college, Miguel wanted to go to law school after graduation and then into the FBI. Rough around the edges though he was, Miguel was Claire's hero. What he'd overcome made medical school look like a piece of cake. But still, he and the other students were laymen and women. She'd better find a way to make it interesting.

So she looked Miguel in the eye. "Epigenetics is the study of how genes change permanently over time without the DNA changing as well—and what causes those changes."

"You mean, like how animals adapt to changes in their environment," said Kara Wallace, a petite blonde from Alpine, New Jersey, who, to the horror of her wealthy family, had dreams of joining the NYPD.

"How their genes adapt—and ours as well," answered Claire. "And the environment doesn't just include the air we breathe, water, food . . ."

"And all the toxic chemical shit in them," smirked Wesley Phelps, a funny, smart, and handsomely dark-haired, slate-eyed, future prosecutor—or so he'd written in his profile on Facebook. "We are what we eat."

"Speak for yourself," said Justine Yu, a hot twenty-four-year-old forensic science major with long black hair, heavy mascara, and red lipstick one shade over the line of tasteful to Claire. Before Miguel could weigh in on how Wesley's answer might apply to Justine's sex life with her live-in girlfriend, Claire did a preemptive strike.

"That's correct, Wes, but it's not the whole story. We also are where we're from. Where we've lived and with whom. How we were raised. Whether we were victims of trauma—physical or emotional—during our lives. All of these life-cycle factors cause reactions in our body and brain chemistry that leave marks—chemical marks—on our genes. So if you think of the DNA in those genes as computer hardware, the mechanisms of epigenesis are like software directing or affecting how the genes work over time."

"When you say 'over time' do you mean the time we're alive?" asked Leslie Carmichael, a pretty, lithe, African-American woman with long dreadlocks pulled back into a ponytail, who'd just returned to finish college at the age of thirty after a six-year interruption to care for her chronically ill mother who'd recently died.

"Yes," Claire said, "though there's new evidence that epigenetic changes to our genes can be passed down to future generations. One study followed a group of infants who were born grossly underweight because their mothers were pregnant during a famine. Makes sense, right? These kids grew up with as much to eat as they needed. Anyone wanna guess what happened when they gave birth to their own kids?"

Cory Matthis, a lanky twenty-five-year-old from Staten Island who still had acne, had his hand up before Claire had even finished. "The babies had low birth weight too."

"Enough of them to show a trend," Claire affirmed. "So let's circle back to where we started—"

"Whoa, whoa, whoa," Miguel interrupted, holding a hand up. "You saying I was in a gang 'cause my parents were and my kids'll be too? 'Cause I'll kill 'em."

"But your kids will be born to a parent with a responsible job and they'll grow up in a positive atmosphere," Claire reminded him.

"First you gotta find someone who can stand you enough to make 'em with you," muttered Justine, who had a love-hate relationship with Miguel.

"You volunteering?" Miguel shot back, a wicked grin crossing his face.

Professor McClure covered his urge to laugh but knew it was time to step in. "Maybe one of you clowns could speculate on why this has anything to do with criminal behavior," he said, quieting the room and bringing the seminar back into focus. Claire shot him a look of thanks, reminding herself that teaching was more than just imparting information. It was an exercise in managing the personal dynamics of some very different people.

"Okay," she said after silently taking a deep breath. "Any thoughts?"

"It's sort of what Miguel said," offered Kara Wallace, "isn't it? That if you grow up in a family of crooks you become one by osmosis. Like Tony Soprano," she finished, referring to the popular TV character and proud of herself for it.

"He's a fictional character," Leslie Carmichael shot back in a tone of voice that said, "What kind of idiot are you?"

Claire felt a burst of inspiration. "Hold on, Leslie," she said. "There's a lot of examples of this in pop culture. Let's go with Kara's example. What else do we know about Tony Soprano's background?"

She could almost feel the heat from their brains churning for an answer. Claire didn't watch a lot of television but her late fiancé, Ian, had been a *Sopranos* fan.

"Well, his father and his uncle were both mobsters, weren't they?" asked Justine.

"And his mother was a raving bitch," argued Miguel.

Claire's hand pointed Miguel's way. "Tell us more about that," she encouraged him.

"Like, she was cold. She'd say something and then say she never said it. She put Tony down. She'd be calling him a good son one minute and screaming that he's a *puto* the next, for not being as tough as his father. She even tried to get him whacked."

He said it without his signature bravado, evenly, as if it were fact. For Claire it was a glimpse of how perhaps Miguel might overcome what his parents' epigenetics passed down to him.

"Miguel's right on the money," said Claire. "What happens when a pregnant mother uses cocaine or heroin?"

"The baby's born a junkie," said Wesley, who'd kept mostly silent until now.

"Okay, so let's say you had a mother like Tony's," Claire continued, reading the students' faces, seeing in their eyes real interest and focus. "What do you think could happen?"

"I'd spend the rest of my life on a shrink's couch when I wasn't popping Prozac," Wesley responded. "Just like him."

"Or his son," offered Cory. "Who turned into a real whacko."

Claire nodded. "Exactly, and there's science to back that up. A study published four years ago linked abuse in childhood—sexual, physical, or even verbal like the kind Tony Soprano's mother subjected him to—with stunting the activity of a gene that regulates the hormones we release when we're under intense stress."

"So if your parents yell at you all the time, you don't have a chance," said Kara.

"They don't even have to do that. Another study, from three years ago, found that the children of parents who were under severe stress during the first three years of parenthood had epigenetic markers on certain genes that were still there when the kids were fifteen."

"By then the kid's probably already gotten into trouble and it's too late," offered Wesley as Professor McClure subtly gestured to his watch that time was up.

"Exactly," said Claire. "And that's where we'll stop for today."

The students closed their laptops and gathered their belongings, thanking Claire as they headed off to their next classes. "Great work, Claire," McClure said, quiet excitement in his voice. "You really had them."

"Kara kind of saved my ass," Claire responded. "I wish I'd thought of the *Sopranos* thing myself."

"Can I give you some advice?" asked McClure in a way that reminded Claire of her father.

"I'll take whatever you've got," she answered.

"Don't stress yourself out about this," McClure suggested gently, donning an ancient plaid sport coat with lapels of a width that had long ago gone out of style. "The first thing you think when you start teaching is that you have to know everything. But when you really become a teacher is when you discover the secret—that there's more you can learn from your students than any book can ever teach you. Or them."

She couldn't help but grin as she pushed a wisp of hair away from her face. Her former mentor had said something similar to her on his deathbed—that he'd learned so much from her—and she hadn't thought about it until just now. It made her feel closer to McClure and, as she left the room, proud of herself.

Manhattan State University's medical complex spanned a long city block between First and Second avenues in Kips Bay, a sprawling mix of old and new buildings encompassing the hospital and house staff offices, medical school, research buildings, and student residences. Normally it was just a five-minute walk from the college campus, but Claire could barely move down the crowded sidewalk as a police-escorted motorcade sped up First Avenue, no doubt headed for the United Nations. She silently cursed herself for forgetting the president was in town speaking to the General Assembly today; how dare he bring the city to a standstill when she had a patient waiting? It took her an extra five minutes just to cross the street, guaranteeing she'd be late.

Finally reaching MSU Hospital, Claire rushed out of the elevator, hoping she'd make it to her office before Fairborn noticed she wasn't there. But she'd gone just a few steps when the voice she dreaded came from behind her.

"Good morning, dear."

Its sincerity made Claire feel even guiltier. Doctor Lois Fairborn had run MSU's Department of Psychiatry for more than a decade and was now doing double duty after inheriting the reins of the Forensic Psychiatry Fellowship in which Claire was about to begin her second year. Fairborn was trim, in her early sixties, with silver hair she had recently stopped dying auburn. Today she wore a charcoal Armani suit and several strands of pearls. She showed not a care in the world on her face.

"Sorry I'm late," Claire answered, catching her breath.

"No worries," Fairborn said. "I just assumed you'd be in class this morning. How's it going?"

"Better than I thought," Claire replied. "The students seem to like me. But you already know that."

"Busted," Fairborn said with a smile. "How are you holding up?"

"Good. I'm good," Claire replied.

"Think I saw Rosa Sanchez waiting by your door," Fairborn said.

Claire smiled and checked her watch. "My model patient," she said. "Early as usual." But she hadn't even rounded on her other, hospitalized, patients yet.

Fairborn seemed to read her mind. "I'll take care of your inpatients."

"Thanks," said Claire, grateful not to have to keep Rosa waiting.

"You're welcome, dear," Fairborn replied, making no move to walk away. Her expression signaled to Claire their conversation wasn't over.

"Doctor Fairborn, is there something else?"

"You seem preoccupied lately. Is everything okay?"

Claire took another breath and decided to tell her the truth. "I've been having nightmares."

"What's your day like?" Fairborn asked, concerned.

"Packed," Claire replied.

"Come see me when you're free," Fairborn suggested.

"Thanks," Claire said, again grateful. "I will."

He maneuvered the car through the bumper-to-bumper traffic that was morning rush hour in Manhattan. He'd looked all over for just the right car, for just the purpose to which he was dedicated this day. Owning a car was prohibitively expensive in Manhattan, and a pain in the ass to park. And though he was glad he'd be getting rid of it soon, he couldn't help but feel the irony. Driving soothed him, especially here, for it too was a way of constructing order from chaos. So many vehicles, jockeying for position, honking, wheels screeching, then each arriving at its proper destination. His was just a few blocks away now. He glanced at the clock on the dashboard and smiled. He'd be on time after all.

Rosa Sanchez stood at the door to Claire's office. As Claire approached, she saw that her pretty, petite, twenty-four-year-old patient with dark brown hair and bangs almost covering her walnut-shaped eyes had the weight of the world on her shoulders.

"What is it, Rosa?" Claire asked, concerned, as she unlocked and opened her office door. She noticed Rosa shaking as they entered together.

"The ACS says I still can't see my babies," Rosa replied, plopping down on the soft, comfortable, dark green, velour sofa. That and the brown leather chair in which Claire sat across from her were the only items of color in the otherwise institutionally furnished office. Nothing hung on the wall, not even Claire's diplomas. She'd changed offices after returning from her leave, and told herself she'd get around to warming the place up. And then she'd gotten busy. Or couldn't bring herself to do it. She couldn't decide which.

"Tell me everything that happened, from the beginning," Claire urged Rosa.

Claire already knew most of it. Six months earlier, Rosa had been on top of her world. Working nights cleaning office buildings, she did such an excellent job that she caught the attention of the company's owner, Larry Merchant, who promoted her to shift supervisor at one of his most important clients' office towers. The extra pay that came with the promotion allowed Rosa, her husband, Franco (a New York City sanitation worker), and their two children, Pablo, four, and Adelina, six, to move from their cramped one-bedroom apartment in the South Bronx to a clean, three-bedroom place on the Grand Concourse in the borough's Fordham Manor section.

Life was good until one night, shortly after starting her supervisory job, when Rosa saw Larry Merchant heading toward her, smiling. Pleased that the place was immaculate, he pulled Rosa into the CEO's office and, without ceremony, put his hands all over her. When Rosa refused to satisfy him and pushed him away, Larry threatened not only to fire her, but also to report her to Immigration. Rosa, no shrinking violet, replied that she was born at Lincoln Hospital in the Bronx, which made her just as American as he was, and that if giving him a blow job was what it took to keep her job, then he could take it and shove it. Then she walked out the door.

At the nearest police precinct, she filed a complaint against Larry Merchant for sexually assaulting her.

When the cops arrested Larry the next morning, he had a different story to tell. He claimed Rosa put the moves on *him*, and when he refused her advances, she threatened to tell his wife that they'd been having an affair and that was the reason he promoted her in the first place.

In the police world, this was the classic "he said, she said" sexual assault complaint. It was Rosa's word against Larry's. There were no witnesses. Rosa didn't have a mark on her.

The Special Victims Unit detective who heard Rosa's story presented the case to an assistant district attorney assigned to Sex Crimes, who decided it was a loser from the get-go. She ordered the SVU detective to void Larry Merchant's arrest and cut him loose.

Larry walked. Rosa was disgusted, bolstered only by the knowledge that at least the bastard couldn't fire her because she had already quit. She was sure she and Franco could make ends meet—at least for a while—on his salary.

What she didn't know was that her troubles were only beginning.

A week later, Franco came home from work one night and announced to Rosa that their marriage was over. He was leaving her for a woman with whom he'd been having an affair for nearly a year. When Rosa asked him for child support, Franco told her she should have slept with her boss to keep her job, and that if she wanted a cent out of him she'd have to take him to court.

Rosa went to a neighborhood check-cashing place she used many times and cashed two checks, each for five thousand dollars. The owners were reluctant to hand over so much to her, but they knew and liked Rosa and felt bad when she explained her situation to them. They had never liked Franco. So they gave her the money, which she used to pay three months' rent on her apartment.

Unfortunately, Franco had already emptied out their checking and savings accounts.

When Rosa's checks bounced, the owners of the check-cashing place called the police.

Rosa tearfully explained to the detective who arrested her that she had no idea her bank account was empty, and that she was sorry.

The detective took pity on her and recommended to an ADA in the Bronx district attorney's office that there was no intent and therefore no crime. But the ADA saw the case as an easy win and arraigned Rosa on two counts of grand larceny in the third degree.

Suddenly, Rosa, never in an ounce of trouble in her life, faced seven years in jail. She was tried and found guilty and transported to the Singer Center, the lone women's facility among the ten houses of detention making up Rikers Island, New York City's notorious jail, to serve out her sentence. Her mother, Maria, promised to bring her two children to visit as often as possible. She'd kept her word as long as she could, but eventually Maria had to go back to working six days a week to support herself and the kids.

Then things went from really bad to a whole lot worse.

Rosa was assigned to mess hall duty, where she helped prepare, cook, and serve meals to her fellow inmates. Though all the corrections officers who dealt with females in the living quarters were women themselves, the CO who supervised the mess hall and its workers was a man—Jack Storm—aptly named considering his raging temper.

Storm took a liking to petite, pretty, twenty-four-year-old Rosa.

One night, not long after Rosa was assigned to the mess hall, she was on after-dinner cleanup duty, exiting a supply closet with a broom, when Storm pushed her back inside, shut the door, and groped her.

Rosa told him to stop. Storm replied with a blow to Rosa's head.

Then he pulled down her pants, bent her over, and forced himself inside her.

When he was done, Storm told Rosa that should she consider telling anyone about their encounter, the next blow to her head would be fatal.

The women on mess-hall duty who found Rosa bleeding in the closet warned her not to report what happened. She wasn't Storm's first victim, and the rest of them knew that the best way to get along with this man was to give him what he wanted. They assured Rosa her time would pass more smoothly. Rosa nodded and said she understood.

The next day she called her legal aid attorney, who in turn called the Queens Special Victims Unit of the NYPD.

It was only a few hours before the attorney showed up with a teddy bear of a detective named Vito and a warrant, signed by a judge, ordering Rosa's release into protective custody.

Rosa was taken to Elmhurst Hospital, where a sexual assault nurse examiner performed a "rape kit," gathering forensic evidence from Rosa's body. Rosa was then brought to the Queens SVU office at the 112th Precinct in Forest Hills, where she gave Detective Vito a statement.

Vito told her he had an informant in Rikers who corroborated Rosa's story. He was going to put Rosa in a hotel under twenty-four-hour guard while the lab at the city's medical examiner's office rushed the DNA from her rape kit through the process. He'd been trying to get Jack Storm for years, but not one of the CO's victims had ever been willing to testify. Detective Vito asked Rosa whether she would step up and testify against this monster in court, to put him away so he could never victimize another woman.

Rosa said yes. And what came next all but made her head spin.

Storm was arrested and a sample of his DNA was taken for comparison with the DNA of the semen found in Rosa's body. It was a match.

When word spread among the female inmates, more than a dozen women came forward claiming they were victimized in much the same way as Rosa. Like Rosa, all of them were first-time offenders convicted of nonviolent crimes, serving short sentences.

Storm was charged with forty-two counts of rape and sexual assault. The evidence against him was bulletproof.

The city contacted Doctor Fairborn, asking if her psychiatric fellows would be available to evaluate Storm's victims to see if they were suited for early release, and counsel them as sexual assault victims who no doubt suffered from post-traumatic stress disorder.

Fairborn agreed and assigned Rosa Sanchez to Claire, knowing that Claire had the skill to help Rosa find her way back through the trauma she had suffered.

Claire determined not only that Rosa was a candidate for early release, but that she had never belonged in jail in the first place. She and her colleagues in the fellowship program returned similar conclusions for every one of the seventeen other victims of Jack Storm, recommending their immediate release from Rikers and probation if deemed necessary.

Rosa and her fellow victims were all sprung from jail and on probation within a week. None of them ever had to testify, however, against the corrections officer who'd attacked them, for on the eve of his trial Jack Storm took a nine-millimeter Glock, sat in a reclining chair in his den, and blew his brains all over the seventies-style wood paneling.

Now Claire was helping Rosa cope with having been raped and putting her shattered life back together. Every conversation began and ended with the two things most important to her in life: her children.

"The ACS lady said I had to be off probation before I could see them," Rosa told Claire.

"That's absurd," Claire replied, meaning it. "You've never done anything to those kids but love them. I'll talk to her and see if I can work something out."

Rosa relaxed a bit. "I thought it would be great to get out of jail," she said, "but now I'm scared."

"What are you afraid of?" Claire asked her.

"That I won't be able to be a good mother to my kids. That I'll always be their mother who went to jail."

Claire hated to see this young woman, who had already been through so much that wasn't her fault, lapse into such self-doubt. "Rosa," Claire said, "you're a survivor." It's as far as Claire got before tears started to fall from Rosa's eyes. She handed Rosa a tissue as she continued. "All your kids know or need to know is that you're their mother. You love them. And believe me, your kids know that now because everything you did, you did for them."

Rosa wiped her eyes, nodding, but wasn't convinced. "It's just that, you think your life is going the way you want it to and then suddenly something bad happens. And then you're not free anymore because you're always waiting for the next bad thing to happen, you know?"

Yes, Claire thought. *I know more than you ever could imagine.*

Aloud she said, "I know exactly what you mean. But life is a journey. I'm here to help you. If you continue to be the model patient you've been, there's no reason you can't get your life back."

"All of it?" Rosa asked.

Claire smiled. "And then some," she said encouragingly. "Now, are you still having nightmares?"

"Less and less," Rosa said. She described them—a man chasing her and almost catching her—but Claire was drifting. She couldn't help but think she was a kind of soul sister to Rosa; that in many ways she and this undereducated but nevertheless poised young woman were living parallel lives.

Why can't I be at peace? Why am I not feeling free to live my life? What is it that's holding me back?

"Doctor Waters?" Rosa asked. "Are you okay?"

Claire tried to regain her composure. In the past, she'd try to cover. But she'd come to realize that with her patients, honesty was the best policy.

"Sorry, Rosa, I guess I went off into la-la land," she said, rising from the chair and holding out her hand. "Come on, I'll walk you out to the lobby."

He parked the car at the curb in a delivery zone on the street, making sure to put the plastic card on the dashboard to prevent it from being ticketed and towed. That card, the equipment he'd placed inside between the two front seats, and the make and model of the nondescript sedan itself would guarantee this car he'd searched for and bought for just this purpose would remain where it was until he came back.

He then walked quickly—but without attracting attention— around the corner, to a spot across the street from the monolithic building. He looked like any of the other millions of suit-clad businesspeople walking through the chaos of Manhattan. Though he knew he was different from everyone else and prided himself on it, today he was satisfied to just blend in. Anonymity was what he

needed now. He knew he'd arrived on time. His wait would only be
a few more minutes.

Claire and Rosa walked through the main lobby, mostly in silence.
The serious look on Rosa's face made Claire feel like she'd insulted
her patient by drifting off during their session. She stopped and
turned to the young woman.

"Rosa, what I did upstairs is inexcusable," she said. "I shouldn't
have allowed my mind to wander. I promise it won't happen again."

This seemed to make Rosa even more uncomfortable. "Doctor, I
don't want to step into someone else's business. But please don't say
you're sorry. You've done so much to help me. . . ." She trailed off.

"You're amazing, Rosa," she said. "Thanks for asking, but I'll be
okay."

"I'll see you on Thursday?" Rosa asked tentatively, as if she expected Claire to say no.

"Of course," Claire replied. "Call me if you need anything."

Rosa walked through the doors out to the street, as Claire turned
and hurried for the elevator. She always spent a little extra time in
her sessions with Rosa. She had a half hour until her next appoint-
ment, and had hoped to check on her inpatients in that short window of time.

She bolted into an open elevator car and checked herself in the
mirror. *Dammit. I forgot my stethoscope.*

She punched the button for the third floor. When the doors
opened, she ran to her office, unlocked the door, grabbed her
stethoscope, slipped on the flats she always wore on rounds (since
slipping in heels on a patient's bodily fluids one day), and was
about to run back out when a flash of lightning drew her attention
to the spring storm brewing outside. Something on the street
caught her eye.

She hurried over to the window, which had an expansive view of
Second Avenue.

A man in a dark suit was leading Rosa down the street.

In *handcuffs.*

"No!" Claire exclaimed, rushing out the door.

She ran down two flights of stairs, burst through the metal door into the lobby, and sprinted to the hospital entrance and out into the street. She looked in the direction she'd seen the suited man leading Rosa.

But all she saw was the already thick traffic on Second Avenue coming to a dead stop and the sea of black umbrellas opening almost all at once as the downpour began.

Rosa and the man with her were gone.

CHAPTER 3

"I don't understand," Claire barked into the phone on the desk in her office. "How could there be no record of her?"

An hour after she'd watched the man in the suit lead Rosa Sanchez away in handcuffs, Claire was no closer to finding out where her patient was or why she'd been arrested.

If she'd been arrested.

Claire kept looking out the window onto Second Avenue, where both the rain and the traffic had subsided, as she waited for the police officer on the other end of the line to answer her question, hoping she was finally talking to the right person.

This hadn't been her first call. After canceling her remaining patients for the day, she'd started trying to track down Rosa's whereabouts. The events of the previous year had given Claire an unexpected but fast and thorough education on the inner workings of the New York City Police Department. It had also given her entrée with the cops; there were few who didn't know her name and how she'd helped them apprehend a killer.

When a rookie cop at the local precinct had told her Rosa hadn't been brought there, she tried the detective squad in the Bronx that had arrested Rosa for the bad check. To no avail. The detective had suggested she try the NYPD's central booking facility in Lower Manhattan.

She did, and was now on the phone with a friendly enough but no doubt bored police sergeant whose name she couldn't remember.

"Probably hasn't been booked yet," he said. "Until your Rosa

Sanchez is in the system and being transported here, we don't know she exists. Make sense, Doc?"

Claire took a breath. Whatever had happened to Rosa, she knew, wasn't this guy's fault.

"Yes," Claire answered, "it makes sense. Sorry to give you a hard time."

The sergeant chuckled. "Lady, you wanna see a hard time, spend a few hours in this hellhole. This was a piece of cake. See ya."

The line went dead. At least the guy had a sense of humor. But as she hung up the nondescript institutional phone on her nondescript institutional desk, that was little comfort.

She rose from her chair and went to the window, staring, searching, as if Rosa would suddenly, magically appear among the hordes of people walking the street. It was wishful thinking and she knew it.

Did I miss something? Was her humility an act that I either didn't see or didn't want to? Did she commit another crime she didn't tell me about?

As quickly as she was flooded with questions, Claire dismissed them. She knew she'd always been an excellent judge of character. Her ability to read people upon meeting them had served her well throughout her life. Rosa, Claire decided, was exactly who Claire thought she was: a hardworking young woman who got swallowed up and victimized by circumstances out of her control.

Just as the city outside had swallowed her up an hour earlier.

Claire vowed she'd do whatever it took to find Rosa.

She went back to her desk, on which Rosa's file still sat. She opened it and rummaged through, looking for something, anything she hadn't thought of. She was only a few pages in when her cell rang. She eyed the phone's display, which read *Cecil Ward*: Rosa's probation officer. Her mind formed a picture of him, a lanky black man in his forties with a "been there before" demeanor, and she answered the call.

"Cecil," she said. "Thanks for getting back to me so fast."

"You said it was urgent, and you never once left a message like that," said Cecil. "What's wrong? Our girl didn't show up or something?"

"She showed up all right, but as soon as she left some suit took her away in cuffs."

"Seriously?" Cecil exclaimed, sounding as stumped as she was.

"I thought you might know who it was or at least why."

"Hell, that woman's a Swiss watch," Cecil said. "I don't have one violation on her and any warrant to pick her up would've come straight to my desk."

"Is there anyone you can call?" Claire pressed.

Cecil, a twenty-two-year veteran of the Probation Department, knew as well as Claire that Rosa wasn't one of his most likely clients to take a powder. He liked Rosa, felt almost as bad for her as Claire did. And he trusted Claire. Rosa was the third "probie" they'd shared; he knew Claire wouldn't sound the alarm needlessly.

"Wait a minute, let's start at the beginning," Cecil said. "Did you actually see this happen?"

"Yes," Claire answered, "from the window of my office."

"Your office on the third floor of the hospital."

"They were across Second Avenue."

"So there's no way you saw the guy's face."

Claire struggled to remember. But she'd seen nothing but the man's back. "All I saw was the dark suit and the handcuffs."

"Any chance it was a fed? Immigration catching up with her or something?"

"You know damn well that Rosa was born in the Bronx, Cecil," she said, rising from her chair and moving toward the window again.

"Sorry, Doc," Cecil said. "Sometimes Immigration arrests first and asks questions later. I'll call the detectives who arrested her in the Bronx and the Queens SVU guy who handled her rape case for starters; how's that?"

"Vito over at SVU was my next call," Claire said, treading lightly. "I already tried the other two. But I'm afraid this is some bullshit complaint her ex-husband made and I don't want her getting into any trouble over this."

Now it was Cecil's turn to be concerned. "Sounds like she's already in trouble," he said. "You're not pulling my chain, are you?"

"Why would I do that?" Claire asked, struggling to hear him over the blaring siren of a fire department ambulance passing on the street below.

"You know, like Rosa didn't really show today and you 'think you saw' some guy take her away in handcuffs because you don't want me to send her back to Rikers for violating her parole."

"Cecil, if I were lying to protect her, why would I have even called you?" Claire said, her voice rising. "Rosa hasn't missed a session in the two months she's been out of jail. She always gets here early."

"Relax, Doc, you don't have to sell me. I'll check around on the down-low and let you know what I find out. That is, if I can find anything."

"Thanks, Cecil." She hung up, not wanting to wait however many hours—or even days—it might take Cecil to call her back.

She looked down at Rosa's open file on her desk. Everything she needed to know about her patient's life was right in front of her. With purpose, she picked up the folder, crossed the room, sat down, and began reading where she'd left off.

It was just before noon when Claire hurried down the immaculate hallway and around a corner to Doctor Fairborn's office. Almost as soon as she knocked, Fairborn was standing in front of her, knowing from the look on Claire's face something was terribly wrong.

"What happened?" she asked, ushering Claire into her spacious office, comfortably furnished in earth tones and tasteful but nondistracting prints and paintings. She was about to sit in her usual spot, a high-backed chair across from the sofa, when Claire started telling her about Rosa and what she'd done to track down her vanished patient.

"I called her cell phone half a dozen times," Claire said, "and when she didn't pick up, I left messages. I've already called her probation officer. He's looking into it."

Fairborn listened, but knew something was missing, something Claire wasn't telling her. She prodded: "You think something happened to her."

Claire nodded, though she didn't want to say it out loud. "I don't know why, but yes, I do," she admitted.

"Well," Fairborn said, "there could be a reasonable explanation for this." Claire looked up sharply, as if the notion of anything about this being reasonable was nonsense. But Fairborn pressed on. "I know

Rosa's been conscientious, but even the most forthcoming patients don't tell us everything," she said.

"Rosa's been seeing me twice a week for a month," Claire replied, taking the edge off her voice. "If she were trying to hide something, I'd know it by now."

Fairborn gestured Claire to the sofa, but Claire stood where she was, way too wired to sit. So Fairborn tried another tack. "Still, we all have secrets, and some of us are much better at keeping them than others," she said. "It's possible, as good as you are—and you're the best I have here—that Rosa did something she was too ashamed to tell you about, and she got arrested for it."

"Then what should I do?" Claire asked.

Fairborn knew what Claire wanted: her blessing to search for Rosa. It was the last thing Fairborn was about to give her.

"It sounds like you've done everything you can for right now," she said to Claire in that calming, soothing voice on which Claire had come to depend. "So now it's time to just wait and see."

Claire had been staring at a watercolor on a far wall of a cityscape with rain coming down. When she looked at Fairborn, her mentor's eyes were locked with hers, as if trying to burn a message into her brain. Gentle though it was, she'd been given a direct order by her supervisor; the general telling the private to stand down. Claire knew better than to argue her case.

"Okay," Claire replied, heading for the door. "I understand."

"Please let me know if you hear anything," Fairborn said as Claire walked out, barely finishing the sentence before the door closed.

In the hallway, Claire stopped and leaned against the wall, questioning. She had tremendous respect for her mentor—the woman had been like a second mother to her over the last year. But Claire couldn't shake the feeling that Rosa was in more than just legal trouble. The thought gave her the jitters, and she knew that sensation well. To her it had always come, even as a child, after being told no.

Right then, she decided she wasn't willing to rely on or wait for the police or anyone else to learn Rosa's fate.

She knew it was up to her. She'd find Rosa herself.

*   *   *

The graffiti-ridden, run-down, four-story tenement in the Sound-view section of the Bronx was a throwback, a dinosaur living out its final days before extinction in the form of gentrification spread to even the toughest neighborhoods. Claire opened the building's battered front door and was welcomed by an overpowering stench of stale urine invading her nostrils, forcing her to breathe through her mouth so she wouldn't gag.

She climbed the decayed wooden stairs as a number 6 train rumbled over the Westchester Avenue elevated subway, known as "the el," half a block away, fighting for attention with the din of cars battling rush hour on the Bronx River Parkway. Claire wondered how anyone could live in such a place and think straight or get a night's sleep. She hoped the cacophony masked the groaning and creaking of every step she took.

She reached the second-floor landing, found the apartment, and knocked on the beat-up plywood door. She heard footsteps and a female voice.

"Who is it?"

"I'm looking for Franco Sanchez," Claire said.

The door opened as far as the security chain would allow. A young woman with dark complexion and hair made no effort to hide the lavender bra and matching panties she wore as she peered through the slit. Claire figured her to be no more than twenty.

"You a cop?" asked the woman, presumably Franco's girlfriend.

"I need to talk to him," Claire stated, deciding not to answer the question. "About his wife."

The young woman closed the door. For a second, Claire thought she'd walked away. But then Claire heard the chain slide across its latch and the door opened again. The young woman stood there, blocking the entrance. She didn't want to let Claire in but she couldn't think of a good reason to refuse.

"Franco, cops are here about Rosa," she shouted, then disappeared through an inner door that presumably led to a bedroom.

"Thank you," Claire called after her, looking around. The place was a dump. A railroad flat with windows that faced another building, too close to allow any good natural light into the apartment. What passed for a living room was nothing more than a battered wood floor on top of which sat dinged-up furniture that looked like it had been picked up on the street. She could hear conversations and clanking dishes from the coffee shop below as if it were in the next room.

Two more trains rumbled past outside, a minor earthquake that shook the building. Claire wondered why Franco would have left the comfortable apartment he and Rosa had shared with their kids for this hellhole.

As the din from the passing trains subsided, Claire heard an angry Spanish exchange behind the door through which the girlfriend had gone. All at once, the shouting ended, the door opened, and Franco Sanchez scowled at the sight of Claire.

"She's not a cop," he shouted behind him before slamming the door.

Then he focused his ire on Claire. "Why'd you lie to my girl-friend?" he demanded, pulling on a soiled T-shirt over his solid body. He had green-and-red sleeve tattoos of the Virgin Mary and Harleys on both arms. His kneecaps stared at her through large holes in the disintegrating pajama bottoms he wore.

"I didn't lie to her," Claire said with defiance. "She asked and I didn't answer."

Their first meeting had been just as adversarial. Claire had to in-terview Franco as part of the custody process for his and Rosa's two children. She'd quickly pegged Franco as a man with a serious anger disorder, a diagnosis her lengthy interviews with their two children confirmed. Franco wanted the kids to live with him; Rosa, of course, wanted them to live with her. Rosa won out, based on Claire's rec-ommendation to a family court judge, forcing Franco to pay child support to his soon-to-be ex-mother-in-law and pissing him off to no end.

"The hell you want?" Franco asked.

"Tell me where Rosa is," Claire demanded, matching Franco's anger. That made Franco grin.

"Aw, what happened, mama? She take off on you?" he taunted, en-joying himself.

Claire wasn't about to tell him anything, so Franco assumed he was right. "Toldja you shouldn'ta bet the farm on her," he leered, get-ting in her face. "And you came here to tell me this why?"

"Because," said Claire, not backing away a millimeter, "you'd know where she might go if she wanted to drop out of sight."

Franco saw that he wasn't intimidating Claire and turned away, picking up a half-empty Coke bottle off a rickety table and taking a swig. "Why do you think I'd know that?"

Claire saw her opportunity. "You were married to her once," she said forcefully, but not so much that she sounded like she was trying to threaten his manhood.

"So what?" Franco retorted.

"So you're still a father," Claire fired back. "Whether you want to be with her or not, she's still the mother of your children and those kids need her. More than they need you or any of this," she finished, gesturing around at the dumpy apartment.

For some reason—and to Claire's surprise—her words actually affected Franco. He looked at her, and then looked at the floor, with what Claire could tell was shame. Then he looked back at Claire and gestured toward the closed bedroom door.

"Sometimes you make mistakes, you know what I mean? You know, like guys do, thinking with the wrong head?"

His self-awareness almost made Claire begin to like Franco. It also gave her the opening she needed. She forced a sympathetic look and spoke in an approving tone.

"Nobody's perfect, Franco," Claire said. "And it takes a big man to look at himself and realize that."

Franco sat down on the stained sofa. "I screwed up, Doc," he said. "Believe me, I know it. And I miss the kids. Two days a week ain't enough."

Claire was starting to feel sorry for him. "You really don't know where Rosa might be?" she asked him.

"I swear," Franco said, "I don't. But no way she just leaves the kids behind. I'll ask around, okay? And if I hear anything, you're my first call."

Claire believed him. It was the most cooperation she had ever gotten from this man, and she couldn't let it go without saying something. "If I hear anything, Franco, I'll call you too."

Franco got up and opened the front door. "You should ask her mother. She always knows what's going on with Rosa."

"My next stop," Claire assured him, walking out. "Thanks."

She hurried down the stairs, holding her breath until she burst outside and gulped down a lungful of humid, gritty, Bronx air. Claire looked up at the puffy white clouds looming above, their bottoms bulging with streaks of dark gray. She cursed herself for leaving her umbrella behind and walked briskly to the subway station, hoping she'd get there before the rain fell again.

The day's second downpour was in full force when Claire exited the subway at the Southern Boulevard stop a few minutes later. She ran for the cover of the stairs down to the street, hoping to find a cab to take her the rest of the way to Rosa's mother's place, which was seven long blocks away. And then she remembered where she was. Yellow cabs usually only came to the South Bronx when they had to drop off a fare picked up in Manhattan.

She ducked under the awning of a storefront insurance agency and scanned the streets for a livery cab. There were none to be found, far from surprising in this weather. She was scouring the stores for one that might sell umbrellas when she spotted a city bus whose sign said it was heading for Hunts Point. Claire sprinted as best she could in heels across the slippery street, the rain penetrating her stockings, barely making it on board before the doors closed.

Fortunately, it was a short walk from the bus stop to Rosa's mother's apartment, which couldn't have been more different from the dilapidated building Franco lived in. Maria Lopez, as petite as her daughter, her hair still naturally dark in her late forties, embraced Claire as if she were another one of her children.

"I'm so glad you came by," Maria said to her, drawing her inside and closing the door. Claire gazed around at the photos of Maria with Rosa and her two grandchildren, a four-year-old boy and six-year-old girl, both with the dark eyes and complexion of their parents. In the living room, old but well-kept furniture, including an aging plush sofa, beckoned her. A crucifix hung on one wall, above a table with photos of Rosa, her mother, her grandchildren. In the center of the table was the largest picture: Rosa in her white confirmation dress.

As Claire sank into the sofa's soft cushions, she couldn't help compare Maria's clean, warm, inviting home to Franco's disgusting rat hole.

"It's always good to see you, Maria," Claire replied, meaning it.

Rosa's mother had been a pillar of strength throughout her daughter's ordeal. When Rosa had been arrested, Maria dipped into her savings to take care of her grandchildren. Even though she was hurt that Rosa didn't ask her for help and money when Franco left, she also respected her daughter for trying to do it on her own. Maria always believed that Rosa had never done anything wrong, even when the justice system said otherwise and sentenced her to jail.

Claire thought Maria, like Rosa, deserved a break after all that had happened. She dreaded having to deliver her news.

"Have you spoken to Rosa today?" Claire asked.

To Claire's surprise, Maria's face lit up. "Yes, and isn't it wonderful?" Maria said.

Her exuberance faded when Claire seemed confused. "Did Rosa not tell you what happened?" Maria went on.

Claire knew she had to be careful here. "You know I'm not allowed to discuss what Rosa and I talk about."

"Well, she must have . . ." Maria replied—and then stopped, as if catching herself.

"Must have what, Maria?" Claire asked.

Maria glanced over to the table with the photos of her daughter. "It's just that . . . well, I don't want her to get in any trouble."

"If Rosa's done something wrong," Claire said, her voice full of empathy, "I need to know about it because I can help her, even if she committed a crime."

"My daughter did nothing wrong," Maria hastened to say. "All she's trying to do is make life better for her and her children."

"Then how could she possibly get in trouble?" asked Claire, her voice soothing.

Maria looked down, seeming ashamed she'd raised her voice. "She went to Connecticut," Maria said. Claire understood Maria's fear. Rosa would have needed permission from her probation officer to leave New York State for any reason, and she clearly didn't get it.

But that's the least of Rosa's troubles. Rosa's not in Connecticut. I just saw her this morning. In handcuffs. This doesn't make sense. Wait. Think.

Claire needed more information. "Rosa knows she's supposed to stay in New York," she said to Maria.

"But it was for a job!" Maria cried out to Claire in frustration. "A good job! I was so excited when the man called."

Claire's inner alarm went off. She shifted in her seat to keep her composure. "What man, Maria?" she asked.

"The man from the cleaning company. In Hartford," Maria answered. She stood and walked over to an aging, beaten-up, red, upright piano that Claire could only imagine would sound as bad as it looked.

"Tell me what the man told you," Claire urged Maria, knowing she had to be careful here.

Maria's words spilled over themselves, barely containing her excitement. "He said that his company wanted to offer my Rosa a job as a supervisor, cleaning the office building of a big insurance company. He was calling to make sure Rosa left to catch the train up to Hartford for the interview."

"Maria, did Rosa say anything about this before she left this morning?"

"No, she said she was going to see you first. But when the man called I knew Rosa didn't tell me so I wouldn't get my hopes up. Or stop her from going."

"What else did this man say to you?"

"That they were going to pay Rosa a lot of money. Enough for her to move to Hartford and buy a house. And for me to live with her and take care of the children."

It took Claire everything she had to contain her own anxiety.

"Did you ask to speak to Rosa?"

"Of course," Maria said, "but the man said she was busy filling out paperwork. And then he said they might keep Rosa in a hotel in Connecticut overnight."

"Did this man give you his name?"

"Yes, and I wrote it down. Thomas Smith."

"So his number is in your cell phone."

"No, he used Rosa's phone. He said his had run out of juice."

This confirmed Claire's worst suspicions: she now knew Rosa was in terrible danger. Still, she held back, knowing that causing Maria more worry would be needlessly cruel.

Claire rose from the couch. She moved as softly as she could, sneaking a peek at herself in an oval mirror hanging from the wall to make sure there was nothing but compassion on her face. She put her hand on Maria's shoulder and spoke in a calm voice, though she felt anything but calm. "Maria, you need to do something very important for me. Rosa will call to check on the kids, won't she?"

"Of course," Maria answered, "and to tell them good night."

"When she does, you must tell her to call me. Right away. She won't want to do it, but she has to. And after she calls you—or if she doesn't—either way, you need to call me as well. Okay?"

"Yes. Okay. Is something wrong?"

Claire headed for the door. "Well, I wish she had told me where she was going. I need to know everything. From her. So I can keep her out of trouble."

"I understand," Maria said. "Thank you." She threw her arms around Claire, grateful she wasn't the only one watching out for her daughter.

"Say hello to the kids for me," Claire said, releasing her own embrace of Maria and walking out the door and down the hallway, until she heard it close behind her.

She stopped, her heart heavy, and grabbed the wall for support. She knew Rosa wouldn't call her mother or anyone else. Rosa wasn't in Hartford, Connecticut, in any hotel or in any law enforcement facility.

She didn't know why she knew this. She just felt it. The fact that Rosa's so-called employer used Rosa's phone convinced Claire she was right.

Rosa's been kidnapped. And I'm terrified for her.

A clap of thunder woke Claire from her temporary paralysis. She steadied herself as she walked to the stairs, then grabbed the splintered railing with her right hand. She'd hated thunderstorms since she was a child. Bad things seemed always to happen in her world during thunderstorms. And no doubt something bad was happening to Rosa.

If it hasn't happened already . . . Concentrate. Focus.

She took a breath, slowly let it out, her thoughts shifting from raw emotion to the logic she needed right now.

If Rosa had in fact been kidnapped by someone impersonating a law enforcement officer, Claire knew that she herself was probably the only witness who mattered. There was no way she could walk into a police station and make such an accusation.

Claire strode out onto the sidewalk. The downpour had slowed to a trickle and there was even a patch of blue clearing in the sky.

She was in over her head on this. She needed help. Now. From the last person she wanted to ask.

But she knew she had to. Both she and Rosa had no choice.

CHAPTER 4

Claire dashed from the cab and ran through the rain toward the brownstone, a newspaper over her head replacing the umbrella that had blown apart in a gust of wind, as a man in a raincoat unlocked the building's front door. He held it open for her and smiled as Claire ran right through and inside. She was grateful the man didn't ask any questions about who she was and what she was doing there. She wasn't sure that the person she came to see would have even buzzed her in.

She stashed the soggy newspaper in a small trash bin near the door and shook the water off her hands, trying to push aside memories of the last time she was here as she trudged up two flights of stairs. By the time she reached the third-floor landing, she felt the emotions in full force. She put her hand on the brass door knocker to apartment 3A. She'd been here before, during one of the worst experiences of her life, and had spent much of the past year trying desperately to forget this place and everything that had happened on the other side of this door.

This time is no different; only the circumstances are different. Instead of my life, it's Rosa's that's in danger. And I won't make the same mistakes again.

A violent clap of thunder boomed, shaking the building and rattling Claire. It reminded her of her darkest day so many years ago, when, as a child, she witnessed the defining moment of her life: her best friend, Amy, being kidnapped right in front of her, stolen from her forever. Claire had the same feeling of dread right now—that she would never see Rosa again.

But this time she would act before it was too late.

She grabbed the knocker and rapped twice. No sooner did she let go than she heard footsteps approaching. But they weren't the ones she expected to hear. These were softer. Lighter.

Female.

She heard the peephole cover slide back, then a sharp inhale from behind the door. As the locks clicked and turned, Claire expected to see the scared little girl she'd met just a year ago, maybe a little older.

But when the door opened, Claire was shocked to see a beautiful, smiling teenager standing before her. A young woman with silken brunette hair and piercing blue eyes she'd clearly inherited from her father. Those eyes were now staring at Claire as if she were a long lost family member.

"Claire," she said, throwing her arms around her.

Nick Lawler heard the name through the closed door of his bedroom and raised himself up on the bed in which he knew he was spending way too much time. He turned his head to check the clock on his bedside table but couldn't see it, and he realized he had to turn his head further now. The tunnel comprising what remained of his vision had closed even more in the last year, an abyss at the bottom of which he knew was no light at all.

His hearing, however, had never been better. When he first heard the name, he thought he was dreaming. But the continuing conversation convinced him that he was very much awake. And completely unpresentable.

He sprang out of bed and headed for his closet to put on some real clothes for the first time in days.

"My God, Jill, you're all grown up," was all Claire could get out as she returned the embrace, feeling her nervousness melt away.

"Last time I saw you we were running for our lives," Jill said.

Her childhood was stolen from her, Claire thought. *Just like mine.*

"Come in," Jill said, "before the dog gets out."

Claire walked in and looked around. Her visit the previous year had been short and frightening, and Claire had barely had time to even notice the place, except that it was unkempt and if not dirty, messy. Now she looked around and saw the fresh coat of ice blue paint, an entry wall from which hung family photos. A new, pristine-looking brown leather sofa/recliner in the living room, seats aimed at a flat-screen TV Claire estimated to be at least sixty inches.

But there was a woman's touch here as well. A vase with excellent quality fake forsythias sat on a round cherrywood table. It took a moment to realize the woman who'd done this was not a new addition to the family but the smiling teenager standing before her.

"How have you been?" Jill asked her. "Or should I ask, where have you been?"

Claire was surprised by this question and decided right then she would tell Jill nothing but the truth. "I took some time off," she admitted. And then she wondered why Jill had asked. "Why? Did you try to contact me?"

"Once. About six months ago," Jill replied. "I called the hospital but they said you weren't there anymore."

Claire felt bad she hadn't been there to get Jill's call.

"It was nothing, really. I just had a question to ask you," Jill continued, as if reading Claire's mind.

The jingle of a dog collar turned her attention to a friendly German shepherd approaching her for an introductory sniff.

"I don't remember you having a dog," Claire said.

"His name's Cisco," Jill told her. "He helps Dad get around."

Claire had feared this was coming. "So your father . . ."

"Pretty much completely blind at night," Jill confirmed.

"And during the day?" Claire asked.

"Not quite as bad," Jill said, "but not great. He can still read the paper, thank God. And it was his excuse for getting this monster of a TV."

"It's a big one," Claire agreed, thinking Jill neither talked like a teenager nor acted like one. "How's Katie?" she asked, referring to Jill's younger sister.

"Getting better. She took Nanna's death real hard—" Jill said, stopping when a slight shock crossed Claire's face.

"When did that happen?" asked Claire, beating herself up even more for not keeping in touch.

"You didn't know," Jill said, registering that her father and Claire hadn't spoken in months.

"I should have," Claire stammered. "Your father and I . . . we haven't talked in a while. I'm so sorry."

"Thanks," Jill said, a bit too much like the adult she shouldn't have to be yet. "It happened about a month after . . . everything." She looked into Claire's eyes, the two of them knowing Jill meant the insanity of last year. "Nanna felt some pain in her stomach and she was starting to lose it mentally. By the time Dad convinced her to go to the doctor it was too late. She had stage five pancreatic cancer."

"Three weeks later she was gone," came a familiar male voice from the hallway, as Nick Lawler emerged, comfortably dressed in a pair of jeans and a Mets T-shirt. His somber expression softened and he took Claire's hands in his.

"Detective Lawler," Claire said, smiling.

"Doctor Waters," he replied, clearly glad to see her—*or perhaps glad he can still see me*, Claire thought. "To what do we owe this pleasantly surprising visit?" he asked.

Claire didn't realize she was smiling until she remembered what they'd just been talking about, and then she changed her tone. "I'm terribly sorry for your loss."

"Thanks," Nick said. "At least it was quick. We put her right into hospice. They shot her up with morphine and she didn't feel a thing."

"That's good," Claire said, and then qualified, "If something like this can ever be good."

What a stupid thing to say, Claire thought. She'd played this scene in her head at least a dozen times on her way over, wondering how she'd feel seeing this man who not only saved her life, but also helped her bring closure to the horrible childhood event that defined her. She owed Nick so much that it had embarrassed her to stay in contact with him. She'd been sure he'd greet her with indifference because she'd just disappeared with no explanation. But as she stood before him, she realized Nick's grin wasn't the only thing on his face she didn't expect. He sported the beginnings of a beard; Claire estimated about a week's growth.

Wow, that really works for him. . . .

Nick was still as handsome as Claire remembered, only his piercing blue eyes crinkled more in the corners and his hair was tinged with a touch of silver she didn't remember being there last year. His lean, muscular build hadn't changed. Claire thought that he must still be hitting the gym every day.

She shut herself down before she could take in any more of him. She had never let attraction enter into their equation before.

Nick seemed to sense her discomfort. He turned to his daughter to break the charge between them.

"Homework done?" he asked.

"School's almost over, Dad," Jill said, sounding for the first time like the teenager she was in that "are you stupid?" way kids speak to their parents. But Jill got the message. "I'll leave you two alone," she said, smiling at Claire. "Don't let him get you into any trouble."

"I won't," said Claire, turning back to Nick, trying not to admit to herself his eyes held the same spark for her that she couldn't hide from him.

"She's all grown up," Claire said, breaking the silence.

"Both of them are, and way faster than I would have wanted," Nick replied, leading Claire into the living room and lowering himself into a comfortably worn brown leather chair that was a close match to the new couch. His face was turned slightly away toward the window. Claire thought he was trying to watch the raindrops against the panes while he still could.

Turning back to Claire, Nick spoke. "The girls loved their grandmother. She took good care of them. And then she died so fast they barely had time to say good-bye."

"They're stepping up to fill the void," said Claire. "It's common after the loss of a parent."

"They wouldn't have had to if their mother was still alive," he replied.

He's still blaming himself, Claire realized.

"They're lucky they have a strong father," she offered, trying to reassure him.

"A blind father," Nick reminded her. "At this point, I'm an insult to fatherhood."

"You're doing the best you can," said Claire, suppressing the urge to move toward him and trying not to sound like a shrink. "Their mother's death wasn't your fault."

Nick's smile was bittersweet. "Jill's the new mother around here. To Katie and, sadly, to me."

"That's not your fault either."

"I thought about you a lot while all this was going on."

Claire tried to cover her shock that he'd actually say something like that. She didn't remember this man as being a fountain of emotion.

"Jill said she tried to call me," was all she could think of. "I'm sorry I wasn't there for her. I would've been glad to help."

Nick brushed an imaginary bit of lint from his jeans. "You had your own shit to deal with. I thought I could handle mine. I don't need a shrink," he quipped, accenting the ongoing private joke between them. Claire smiled, feeling sorry for him and hoping it didn't show, knowing it was the last thing that would help him now. *He's depressed. He's lost so much and he's about to lose even more.*

"Are you keeping yourself busy?" she asked.

"Believe it or not, I'm still working," Nick replied.

"Not as a cop . . ." Claire blurted, at once regretting it. When they'd met a year earlier, Nick was a homicide detective in the New York City Police Department. He'd later admitted to her, and only her, that he suffered from retinitis pigmentosa, a degenerative and incurable genetic disorder that would eventually rob him of his vision. He'd gone to great lengths to hide his condition to avoid being forced to retire from the job he loved, though his pride and stubbornness almost killed not only him, but Claire and his daughters as well.

She made sure to tamp down her disbelief when she continued. "You still haven't told them?"

"Relax," Nick said. "I told my boss."

What a relief, thought Claire. "Lieutenant Wilkes?" she asked, referring to his former supervisor and protector, with whom she was more familiar than she ever wanted to be.

If Nick had a problem with this line of conversation, he didn't show it. "He's a deputy inspector now," he replied. "But yeah."

"Deputy inspector?" asked Claire, unfamiliar with the term.

"It's a rank in the job. Two up from where he was a year ago."

"I didn't know that was possible."

"He was the golden boy after last year."

"Is that why they let you stay?" Claire asked.

"Yep. Chief of detectives made a concession for the so-called hero cop," Nick said, almost embarrassed, though there was nothing "so-called" about it. "Put me on the 'Rubber Gun Squad.'"

"I don't understand," said Claire. "What kind of squad is that?"

Her naïveté made Nick laugh. "One that doesn't really exist," he said. "When they take your guns away, no matter where you're assigned, you're on the Rubber Gun Squad. Usually, it's a disgrace. In my case I get to keep working and feeding my kids."

"Where do they have you working?" Claire asked.

"Homicide Analysis Unit," Nick nodded. "All desk, all the time. At headquarters, in the chief of D's office. Where he can keep an eye on me," Nick said, his eyes narrowing as he smiled mischievously.

"That your idea or the chief of D's?"

"His," Nick admitted. "To save me from myself. Also his words. All of which is code for stopping me from doing anything resembling real police work. I spend my days putting virtual pins in virtual maps on a computer," he said, musing as if coming to terms with his fate. "Not my first choice, but it beats the hell outta taking my pension and sitting on my ass feeling sorry for myself."

He didn't feel himself lowering his eyes as one does in shame. But Claire knew that's exactly how he felt.

"I had the best job a cop could have—clearing murders," Nick said. "Speaking for the dead. And until my eyes started crapping out on me I was damn good at it."

"You were good at it even after," Claire reminded him. "We wouldn't be sitting here right now if you weren't, because I sure didn't know what I was doing."

"Don't sell yourself short," Nick replied, shaking his head in disagreement. "As I remember it, you were pretty good with that gun."

"Please, don't remind me of that," Claire begged him.

He looked up at her. "Are you just gonna stand there? Because I'm starting to get an inferiority complex. Like I got Freud himself hovering over me."

Claire hadn't realized how frozen in place she was. "Actually, you're right. Freud wouldn't have approved of my hovering," she said, taking a seat on the new sofa, its pillows a bit firmer than she preferred. She shifted, and her obvious discomfort reminded Nick that he hadn't asked her a single question. "You haven't told me how you're doing," he said.

"Better," Claire replied.

"So once again the shrink won't allow herself to be shrunk."

Touché, Claire thought. "That moment . . . with the gun. I think it's in one of the nightmares I keep having."

"You think?" Nick asked, eyebrows raised. "What does that mean?"

"I don't remember the details very well. Of the nightmares."

It was more than she wanted to say. But somehow being in Nick's presence made her comfortable in a way she hadn't felt in months. She found herself leaning against the arm of the sofa, starting to relax and wondering how she felt so at home.

"You know there's nothing to be afraid of anymore, right?" Nick tried to convince her, looking straight at her as if interrogating a suspect.

"I wish it were that simple. The feeling—the fear—stays with me even after I wake up."

"But those dreams aren't the only thing scaring you right now," he said, standing up as if satisfied he could read her mind. Claire shifted again, unsure how to broach the reason she was there, uncomfortable that Nick could sense what she was thinking. And then he did it again.

"Whatever it is you need my help for, you don't have to be afraid to ask," he said. "So go ahead. Ask away."

How does he know?

Claire stiffened. "I don't want to take advantage—" was all she could muster before Nick interrupted her.

"Ask," he ordered.

She dove into the story of what had happened to Rosa Sanchez that morning. She talked for ten minutes, with Nick asking only the occasional question. When she finished, he summed up the situation.

"You think the guy who cuffed her was impersonating a cop," he said.

"I've checked everywhere that made sense and called everyone I could think of," Claire said, not trying to hide her exasperation. "If she was arrested she would've turned up by now. The guy using Rosa's cell phone to call her mother clinched it for me."

"I'd be thinking the same thing," Nick said, the wheels in his head turning.

"Would it help if *you* called Missing Persons?" Claire asked, anxious for a solution.

"Problem is, for an adult they won't take a case until the person's been missing for forty-eight hours," Nick said. "And even I couldn't grease any wheels with them. They get calls like this all the time. They're not gonna add this one to their caseload on my say-so."

"Is there some unit in the police department that handles kidnappings?"

"Major Case Squad," said Nick. "But they need proof someone's actually been snatched, which you hardly have. And even then, they only move on order of the chief of detectives."

Claire thought her problem was solved. "You just said you work in the chief's office."

"If I went to him with this or he got wind I was looking into it, he'd string me up like a Chinatown window chicken."

As much as she wanted to find Rosa, Claire knew she couldn't do it at the expense of Nick's job.

"How about tracking Rosa's cell phone?" Claire suggested. "At least then we could see where she's been for the last twelve hours."

Nick looked at the ceiling thoughtfully. "Tough to do without a warrant."

"She's on probation, and the man on her phone claims she left the state. Doesn't that make her a fugitive?"

"Right. But Probation would have to declare her a fugitive," Nick answered, "and the warrant would have to come from them."

It was exactly what Claire didn't want to hear. "If Probation gets involved, it's out of my control," she told him. "She's a victim, not a perp."

"Unless you can prove that, no judge will let us go digging into someone's phone records."

"Okay," Claire said. She wasn't giving up. "You said it's tough to do without a warrant. So it's not impossible."

She said it as bait, but Nick wasn't taking it. "This isn't as easy as it looks on TV," he said with serious eyes, "and excuse me for being selfish here, but it's my ass we're talking about. If I try doing this without Rosa's permission, that's breaking the law. I wouldn't just be fired, I'd lose my pension and maybe go to jail. And we can't exactly get Rosa's permission, can we?"

He rose from the chair and took a few steps, looking exasperated. Claire realized why: he *wanted* to help her. His willingness triggered something in Claire's brain. "Does the permission have to come from the person who actually has the phone in their possession, or can it come from the person who holds the account?"

Nick stopped walking and looked at her; he hadn't thought of this. "Tricky legally, but is that the case here?" he asked.

"I don't know for sure. But I do know Rosa's mother. And I doubt any cell phone company would've taken a chance on a woman convicted of passing bad checks. Would you?"

"No way," Nick agreed, leaning on the chair he'd been sitting in. "That's why we spend so much time banging our heads against the wall trying to track disposable cells. It's the easiest way to reach out and touch someone without a credit rating or an income."

Claire was ready for this. "But that wasn't an option for Rosa, because she'd have to keep changing phone numbers. I made it a condition of her release from Rikers that she get a regular cell phone and be reachable at all hours of the day or night. It was more for Rosa's own safety than for me to keep tabs on her. I'll bet Rosa's mother has two phones on *her* account and one of them is Rosa's. And her mother would do anything for me."

Nick looked at her with those piercing blue eyes. "Even with the mother's permission, it's a huge risk if we're caught."

Though it came across as a warning, Claire could see that it was nothing more than a disclaimer. Nick was in. Determined. Hungry for the answer. And eager for the hunt he missed so badly.

"If Rosa was kidnapped," she said, "it's worth the risk. Isn't it?"

Nick considered. If Claire was right, there was someone out there in big trouble.

"No promises. And if anyone comes sniffing around I may have to stop. But I'll give it a shot," he said. "How's that?"

Claire stood. The Nick Lawler she knew, the one who wouldn't take no for an answer, was back.

"It's more than I have a right to ask," she said. "Thanks."

CHAPTER 5

It was just before seven the next morning when Nick Lawler emerged from the dark subway station under the old Municipal Building at the end of Chambers Street. He rubbed his eyes, trying to make them focus in the bright sunlight and oppressive humidity, and made his way toward the NYPD's monolithic headquarters about a hundred yards away.

The previous day's thunderstorms had done little to relieve the late spring heat wave scorching the Northeast. Nick carried his charcoal-gray suit jacket over his arm because as bad as it was above ground, stepping onto a subway platform in weather like this resembled stepping into a steam bath wearing a parka. Air-conditioning hadn't been an option when the city's subway stations were built. But until Nick's gun was taken away, neither was taking off his jacket in public.

Fortunately there was great air-conditioning on the new subway cars the city had purchased over the last decade, no doubt because the former three-term billionaire mayor himself rode the trains to work. Nick silently thanked him for his cool thirty-minute respite from the heat in a frigid subway car and hoped he could make it inside police headquarters before he started to sweat.

He looked up at the boxlike structure looming before him, a building most cops mockingly called the Puzzle Palace or, more derogatorily, the Porcelain Palace. To him, though, the building appeared less like a toilet than a kiln that would, in this hundred-degree heat, bake anyone who entered. Most cops would argue that could happen in this place on even the coldest day.

He'd just felt the first beads of sweat hitting the T-shirt he wore under his blue oxford dress shirt as he made it into the building, his police ID card already hanging from a strap around his neck, his detective's shield clipped to his belt. The only missing accessory was the nine-millimeter Glock, and without it he felt like an outsider. Every cop knew the gun and the authority to use it was the real badge of the job; the power to use it to save a life or take one was what separated them from every civilian. Especially a man like Nick, who'd been an expert marksman. A cop without a gun was like a man without balls. That he had to enter this place each day without his was just one constant reminder of his fate.

As he walked through the doors into the expansive lobby and swiped his ID card across the reader, Nick told himself as he did every day that his new assignment was both a blessing and a curse. He'd be able to support his daughters as long as he could still see, perhaps long enough to retire with nearly three-quarters of his pay and health insurance for the rest of his life. Maybe they'd even let him bring Cisco, his trained service dog, to work. Presently, Nick used Cisco at night to guide him on long walks through the city. Eventually, Nick mused, he'd need Cisco during the day too.

He joined the queue of people waiting for the next elevator and wondered how they'd react to Cisco guiding him around when that time came. The scene before him resembled similar scenes at this time of day in every office building in Manhattan: the coffee-cup-and-briefcase-holding masses heading for another day of work in an office or cubicle. The only difference here was the attire. The ID cards everyone wore identified them as either cops or civilian employees of the police department. Stripped of his gun, Nick felt more like a civilian these days.

As the rickety, forty-plus-year-old elevator doors opened, he determined to prove to himself and everyone else that, half blind or not, he was the real deal. The information Claire Waters had given him last night would open a path to his salvation.

The elevator car was already occupied with uniforms and suit-wearing cops lucky enough to rate a parking spot in the garage below the building. Most, if not all of these cops, also rated department-issued vehicles, and many of them drove great distances to get here. Nick knew he was lucky to have a short commute. He'd inherited his

rent-controlled apartment from his parents; it was the only way anyone could live in Manhattan on a cop's salary back when he came on
the job, and especially now.

He entered the battered, scratched metal car and was about to
press number thirteen when he noticed all the other buttons were
lit. He hoped otherwise every morning but was almost never pleasantly surprised. The "meat wagon" would once again stop on every
floor. Today, though, Nick smiled, thinking it would give him time to
think about last night. He'd thought about Claire a lot over the last
year. Seeing her was even better than he'd imagined. Then he forced
himself to think about Rosa Sanchez and the business at hand.

Before Claire had left Nick's apartment, she'd called Rosa's mother,
who told her that, yes, she paid for Rosa's cell phone as another
number on her own account. Maria gave her blessing to track Rosa's
cell, saying she'd sign whatever papers Claire needed.

But there would be no signature required for this transaction, for
officially it would never exist. Nick wasn't about to leave a paper trail.

As soon as Claire left, Nick had called Dave Banion, a detective
and old pal who worked in TARU, the department's Technical Assistance Response Unit. Banion assured him he'd have what Nick needed
when he showed up at work this morning and nobody would ever
know.

The elevator doors opened and Nick walked into the oak-paneled
suite of offices occupied by the chief of detectives and his large staff.
He nodded hello to Sergeant Patrick Young, the chief's sixty-year-old
secretary and gatekeeper, who was waiting out his time to retire here
at the reception desk. Nick walked through a second door into the
room that housed a large bull pen of more modern work areas on a
newly recarpeted floor, each cubicle occupied by a detective dressed
in business attire. The bland colors and ever-present fluorescent
lighting made Nick think that if the people in this room weren't
wearing guns, this could have been the office of any corporation.

As he reached his desk in the corner of the large room, Nick spotted a large, sealed, white envelope, labeled only with his name,
placed on the far right corner. He knew it was from Banion, who had
clearly covered his tracks by putting it in the early morning inter-
office mail so no one would know who sent it. Nick sat down and
picked up the envelope, knowing that by opening it he would be

committing his first act of betrayal against the chief. It was a breach of trust that, if discovered, would probably mean the loss of his job.

Especially if he—and Claire—were wrong and Rosa had violated her parole. But he was pretty confident that wouldn't be the case. It took Nick less than a minute to open the envelope, read its contents, and realize that once again, Claire was right. He had clear evidence that Rosa Sanchez was the victim of a kidnapping. He needed help. And he needed to keep this from the chief for as long as he could.

Nick stepped onto the elevator and, just as he noted that the button for the sixth floor had already been pushed, a hand appeared between the closing doors to force them open.

"Morning, Nicky," came the voice of Chief of Detectives Tim Dolan.

"Morning, Chief," he said.

His boss wore a bluish glen-plaid suit, red paisley tie, and black Johnston & Murphys. At six-foot-three, Dolan was known throughout the department as the Big Man, though his shaved head and natty clothes long ago earned him the nickname Kojak, after the seventies TV detective. Dolan made a show of waving off the nickname, but secretly he loved it.

Nearing sixty, Dolan had been a cop for thirty-nine years, all but the first four spent in the "Bureau," as cops called it. As its chief, he commanded an investigative force of five thousand that was second in size only to the FBI and, under the previous administration, had run circles around the "feebs" on almost every level when it came to antiterrorism. Respected by nearly all his troops, Dolan made no secret of his preference for the street and a good crime scene over office politics. He was known as a "cop's cop," a breed of boss most police officers thought was in danger of extinction.

Dolan hit the button for the garage level, noticing the lit-up sixth-floor indicator. "Where you headed, Nick?" he asked, knowing that Nick had no business being on a floor where active cases were being investigated.

"Down to IT," Nick replied without a hitch. "I wanted to discuss ordering new software." He hated lying to the chief but couldn't risk the truth.

Dolan looked at him. "IT is on the fourth floor," he said.

Nick feigned sheepishness. "My finger must've slipped," he said with a grin. The button on the panel for the fourth floor was just below that of the sixth.

Dolan grunted, seeming satisfied, and checked his watch.

"Everything okay, Boss?" asked Nick as he pressed the correct number.

"I got a helluva day with the mayor," answered the chief, who gave an exaggerated shudder, then relaxed. "How're the girls?" he asked with real concern as he straightened his tie. Nick appreciated the chief's interest, but was even more grateful that the elevator jolted to a stop on the fourth floor and the doors were opening.

Nick stepped off the car. "I need a crash course in surviving teenagers. Don't let Hizzoner double-talk you," he finished as the doors closed on a smiling Dolan. Nick breathed a sigh of relief and waited for the next elevator car up.

Arriving at the sixth floor, Nick walked a few yards down the hall to a door with a small placard labeled MAJOR CASE SQUAD. Ironically, this was the place Nick would have gone every day if not for his screwed-up eyes. Working behind that door was one of the most prestigious assignments a detective could get. But for Nick, the sign might as well have read "Do Not Enter," because of his vow to stay away from active cases.

Ignoring the vow, he opened the forbidden door and walked in without hesitation.

It was still early. The standard issue metal desks occupying the office were mostly empty except for the two guys Nick knew he would find there. One of them, his old friend Detective Sergeant Tony Savarese, jumped out of his seat like a bald jack-in-the-box before Nick could even close the door.

"Nicky, are you nuts?" Savarese said, giving him a punch on the shoulder. Savarese and Nick had met more than twenty years ago, and he wore the same blue blazer and red-and-blue-striped tie today as he did back then. "What are you doing down here?"

"I gotta talk to you and the boss," Nick replied, returning the punch.

"He's gonna shit a sofa when he sees you," Savarese said under his breath, escorting Nick to the squad commander's office.

They made it about halfway there when Deputy Inspector Brian

Wilkes stuck his head through the doorway. "You know, I thought I heard a voice," said Wilkes in his trademark gruff Brooklynese. "But I couldn't have, because that would mean someone was being a naughty boy."

A big, crooked smile appeared on Wilkes's round, freckled face topped with flaming red hair, giving him the appearance of an aging jack-o'-lantern.

"Get in here, you crazy-ass mother-forker," said Wilkes, hugging Nick, pulling him across the threshold into his office, waving Savarese in as well. Wilkes, always a straight shooter, thought the chief's edict was horseshit, though he'd actually brokered the deal in the first place. "How the hell are you, and what are you doing down here busting your parole?"

Nick glanced around the office, filled with nondescript furniture that was just a little less worn than the metal stuff out in the squad room. There was an old but clean sofa against the southern wall, below windows that presented an expansive view of the Brooklyn Bridge and Lower Manhattan. An aging but well-preserved wood desk faced the doorway, a computer monitor atop it in one corner. The wall and a matching credenza behind the desk were covered with awards and photos. One of those pictures was of Nick and Wilkes, both smiling.

Wilkes motioned Nick to a chair, and they sat together for the first time since that day nearly a year ago when he'd accepted his new position.

Nick glanced out the window. "Nice," he said to Wilkes. "Beats the view from your old office."

"Yeah, I sure got sick of looking at you sorry freaks," the inspector replied. "Now what are you doin' down here breakin' my balls and the chief's law?"

"I need your help." Nick launched into the story of Rosa Sanchez, getting as far as her rape at the hands of the corrections officer when Wilkes put his hand up.

"Whoa, whoa, hold the friggin' phone," Wilkes interrupted, remembering the case well. "She was one of *that* guy's play toys?"

"Yeah," Nick answered, not surprised that Wilkes would know of Jack Storm, despite the fact that the names of the Rikers sexual assault victims were never reported by the media.

Wilkes's shit detector was on full alert. "Didn't I read somewhere that those women were all released and put into counseling at Manhattan State?"

"Yes," Nick replied, shifting in his seat, knowing what was coming. Wilkes hadn't gotten to this position because he was an idiot.

"So this came from that crazy shrink, Waters," Wilkes said, referring to Claire. "And for her you risk coming here?"

"Worst that can happen is forced retirement and a pension, right?" Nick said.

"Yeah, for you maybe," Wilkes replied, sitting back in his chair as if resigned to his fate. There was never a question he'd help Nick, and both of them knew it. For Wilkes it was simple: he wouldn't be sitting in that chair if not for Nick Lawler.

"For me it'll be running some precinct in a Staten Island cornfield," Wilkes said. "This better be worth it."

"You're damn right it's worth it," Nick said a bit too harshly. "Whoever cuffed this woman was impersonating a cop so he could grab her in broad daylight—"

"Okay, okay, Nicky, take it easy," Wilkes interrupted, his hands up as if he were being arrested. "We're in. So let's calm down, huh?"

Nick took a breath, not expecting to blow like that. "Sorry, Boss. Pot finally boiled over."

"Forget it," Wilkes replied. "I knew it would have to be something good for you to risk coming here. Just tell me it ain't some fantasy the good doc dreamed up and you bought into after too much time riding a desk."

Nick reached into the breast pocket of his suit jacket and took out three sets of stapled papers. He gave one each to Wilkes and Savarese and kept one for himself. "You'll want to shred these when we're done," Nick said.

"Don't tell me that," Wilkes answered, his nose already in the papers. "Or where the hell you got these."

"These" were a series of street maps that tracked the location of Rosa Sanchez's cell phone throughout the previous day. The maps were color printouts with dots tracking her path with data beside each dot and a line drawn by computer from one dot to the next.

Banion had come through with flying colors.

"It's all legal," Nick offered.

But Wilkes's face turned to stone. "I don't care if the chief justice of the Supreme effin' Court signed the warrant himself," he said. "You're not supposed to be doing this shit, Nicky."

"There was no warrant," Nick said. "We're looking for her as a victim, not a perp."

Wilkes didn't budge. "She's a convict on probation who's in the wind. Which makes her a perp, which also makes her guilty until proven innocent. And that means we'd need a warrant," Wilkes said almost all in one breath, rapid-fire, realizing the huge jackpot of trouble Nick was putting them in.

"Seems kinda hinky, don't it though, Boss?" Savarese said, flipping a page of the maps. "Guy collars this woman, then takes her on some magical mystery tour through every borough?"

Wilkes looked up from the papers. "I never said he wasn't right, you idiot." He turned to Nick. "Please tell me you didn't have the service provider ping her phone."

Wilkes had good reason for asking. Pinging would have meant Rosa's cell service provider actively sent a signal to her phone requesting its Global Positioning System (GPS) coordinates, a routine procedure used by the police to track fugitives and other persons, usually after considerable resistance from the cell phone companies that didn't want to end up on the wrong end of an invasion of privacy lawsuit.

"Couldn't," Nick told them, "because her phone was turned off. Those maps were all done by triangulation."

Triangulation used calls made to or from a mobile phone to determine its location based on the strength of the phone's signal bouncing off towers within its range (usually, most mobile phones can hit at least three towers from any urban location). Unlike pinging, triangulation could be done using data from past calls and, though not as precise, could give the phone's approximate location.

Which, surprisingly enough, seemed to be in the middle of the East River.

Wilkes's features softened as he tried to find some reason for the seeming randomness of Rosa's movements. "Okay, so at ten-fourteen in the morning they're going over the Williamsburg Bridge, presumably into Brooklyn and heading north, because thirty-four minutes later they're at Vernon Boulevard and Forty-First Avenue in Astoria."

"Right by the Triborough," Savarese said, using the old moniker for the bridge linking three of the city's five boroughs. The bridge had been renamed several years earlier for assassinated former senator Robert Kennedy.

"Hey," Wilkes cut in, realization dawning, "all these calls were made to Rosa's phone from the same number. We know whose?"

"Claire Waters," Nick replied. "She tried Rosa every couple of hours."

"So the doc's next call wasn't until one-twenty in the afternoon," noted Savarese. "Rosa's phone was in the South Bronx, Mott Haven, most likely on Walton Avenue."

Wilkes took up the thread. "Then Ocean Avenue and Lincoln Road by Prospect Park in Brooklyn at two forty-two in the afternoon, and Battery Park at three fifty-six . . . What the fu—?" he finished, catching himself as he turned to the last page.

"This makes no sense," Savarese said, eyeing the final location, deep in the middle of what appeared to be a huge park at the southern end of Staten Island. "North Mount Loretto State Forest, six thirty-three p.m. Why there?"

Nick saw the concern on Wilkes's face and knew he'd convinced him. "To me it says desperation," he said with more confidence in his voice. "Guy kidnaps girl, guy looks for place to rape or kill girl, guy drives all over the five boroughs until he finds just the right spot. If you look at the maps, other than when she's on the Williamsburg Bridge, every one of these locations is near or next to a park."

"He'd have to be a moron to think he could hide a body in Battery Park," Wilkes muttered, his mind churning, his eyes never leaving the maps.

"Unless he thought he could take the Staten Island Ferry, which would make him a real moron or someone from out of town," Nick followed, alluding to the ferry's closure to vehicles since the terrorist attacks of 9/11. Wilkes poked the last map. "You think this is where he dumped her?"

"If this guy is the idiot we think he is," Nick said, "he threw Rosa's cell in the trunk of his car and forgot to turn it off. Claire said she tried Rosa again after seven and it went right to voice mail. Phone probably ran out of juice by then."

Wilkes was too good a cop not to admit something was out of whack here. "If your girl was legitimately collared by a real cop outside the hospital, she would've been brought to a precinct for booking, not dragged all over town."

Savarese placed his finger on the last page of the map. "Probably worth sending a radio car out there for a look-see, Boss."

"Radio car my ass," Wilkes growled. "All I need is Dolan asking why I sent patrol into the woods at the ass end of Staten Island looking for a ghost and, even better, where I got the tip. You and me, Tony, we're gonna have to do this. Ourselves."

He stood up, then eyed Nick. "Not a peep about this to anyone, *capisce*? No calls to me or Tony or anyone in the office, nothing. I'll text you from my personal cell phone when we figure out if this is anything, and not a moment before. You understand?"

Nick pursed his lips and gave an affirmative nod, but Wilkes wasn't done. "And one more thing. I don't want you telling Doctor Waters a goddamned thing. You don't call her, you don't even answer *her* calls until I say you can."

"Got it," Nick said, just glad Wilkes wasn't booting him out of the office.

"Right now I don't give a shit about you or Doctor Waters," Wilkes said. "I'm just covering my sorry ass and making sure you and I are talking the same language. So I'm asking you—are we clear, you sonuvabitch?"

"Crystal," answered Nick.

CHAPTER 6

It was just before two in the afternoon when Claire said good-bye to her last patient of the day and closed the door to her office. She grabbed her purse, pulled out her cell phone, and checked to see if Nick had called while she was in session.

One look at the display told her he hadn't.

What happened to him?

She considered the possibilities. Perhaps Nick hadn't gotten anywhere. Or maybe he had, but got caught by his superiors.

Or maybe he changed his mind.

Claire regretted involving Nick, but what choice did she have? She was certain that Rosa was in danger—if she wasn't already dead or badly hurt.

Claire stared at her phone, as if that would make Nick call her. She put the phone back in her purse, which she then set down beside her desk. Then she opened the door to her office, intending to walk down the now quiet hallway to get a glass of water.

She was about to close the door when she heard muffled ringing.

She nearly tripped as she hurried back to her desk, clumsily snatching her purse and rummaging through it until the phone was in her hand. She pushed the button to answer it. "Hello," she said, before the phone was to her ear.

"Doctor Waters?" came a frantic female voice from the other end of the line that Claire instantly recognized as Rosa's mother.

"Maria?" Claire said. "Is everything okay?"

"No," answered Maria, sniffling from crying. "Rosa doesn't answer her phone and she never called since yesterday morning. She wouldn't miss saying good night to the *niños*. . . ." She stopped, and Claire knew Maria feared the same thing she did when she saw Rosa being led away in handcuffs.

"Take a breath, Maria," Claire urged her patient's mother.

"Have you heard from her?" Maria asked. "And did you find out where her phone is?"

Claire silently cursed Nick for leaving her with nothing to tell this woman.

"I'm sorry," was all she could think to say. "But I'll ask my friend who was going to help me."

"Please," Maria begged. "The children miss their mama."

"I'll call you back as soon as I know something," Claire said, and hung up.

She'd already tried Nick's cell a few times, getting annoyed when he didn't pick up. Claire didn't want to pester him, but her need to know drove her to call.

She dialed Nick's number, and again listened to it ring.

Nick stared at his cell phone, vibrating on his desk, the display announcing it was Claire. Again. He couldn't blame her; he too was restless and unable to concentrate on his work. He checked his watch. It was almost two o'clock, nearly six hours since his meeting with Wilkes and Savarese. Waiting to hear from them was driving him nuts. He wanted to tell Claire to sit tight, that he was working on finding Rosa. But Wilkes's order for him not to speak to her forced Nick to let Claire's call go to voice mail.

What the hell could be taking them so long? Nick wondered. Wilkes had made it clear that he and Tony Savarese would leave headquarters for Staten Island after ten to avoid the morning rush hour. But that was four hours ago, Staten Island was a reverse commute in the morning, the weather was clear, and if traffic was heavy, Wilkes would have made Savarese (who always drove) flip on the lights and siren in Wilkes's unmarked Ford Crown Vic. They should have been there by noon at the latest.

Aggravated, Nick got up from his desk to stretch, wondering whether Wilkes and Savarese made the trip at all. He glanced at the carpeted, cubicle-filled room, its modern, updated furnishings a step up from the comparative squalor of a police precinct or even a prestigious unit like Major Case, where the furniture still looked like something out of a seventies period movie. Rank did have its privileges in the NYPD, and the recent renovation of the chief's office was one of those perks.

But Nick still thought of himself as a real cop, and real cops didn't belong in places like this. Here he was just another suit in just another quiet, sedate, boring office. A real cop's real office was the street or a busy unit like Major Case. He knew the reason he probably hadn't heard from Wilkes and Savarese was the job itself. Anything could have come up since this morning—a new case or a break in an old one—to turn them in another direction. Forbidden from calling them, Nick was at Wilkes's mercy. All he could do was try not to stare at his cell phone. And wait.

He headed over to the coffeemaker, passing his other deskbound, civilian-clothed detective colleagues. Most were there by choice, hoping an assignment in the chief of detectives' office would be a path to something better. But Nick knew that for him this was the end of the road. Each day in this place, he felt like a little piece of him died.

I'm just office furniture, he thought. Just like the file cabinets he now walked past.

He knew he was staying for a good cause, to make things easier for the girls and to save for their college educations. But at what cost? Was it worth spending the rest of his working days in this dead-end job?

No.

He poured himself a cup of coffee, headed back to his cubicle, and began to put together a plan for the future. He'd turn in his retirement papers with six months to go, take his remaining vacation time and terminal leave at full pay. He and the girls would be fine on his pension, and he'd help them look for financial aid for college. . . .

The sharp ring of his desk phone shook Nick out of his own head. Wilkes and Savarese knew better than to call him on a department line. And he didn't need to talk to anyone else.

Looking at the caller ID, he saw it was Patrick Young, the detective sergeant Nick had passed earlier on his way into the office. The desk of the chief's receptionist and gatekeeper sat no more than twenty yards away from his own. Nick picked up the receiver.

"Yes, Sergeant," Nick said in a faux-patronizing tone.

"Cut the horseshit," came Young's voice, which he could hear faintly even without the phone. "Grab your coat and meet the Big Man on the roof. Forthwith."

Nick was stunned. The only reason to go to the roof of One PP was to board a police helicopter on the building's landing pad.

"Where exactly am I going?" Nick asked, picking up his suit jacket.

"How should I know?" Young asked. "Your security clearance is higher than mine."

Electronic music blasted from speakers above Claire's head, competing for her attention against the pounding footsteps and rolling conveyor belts of the bank of treadmills. She was running on one of them as fast as she could, at her gym on East Thirty-Third, as if fleeing from her thoughts about Rosa. But the faster she ran, the faster her brain seemed to be sorting through the direst possibilities. Right now she pictured Rosa locked in a windowless room with a mattress on the floor, screaming for help. She blinked the thought out of her head, and all at once she saw Rosa trapped in a dark box—a coffin—gasping for air. But she was still alive. She tried to shake the thought from her head—and it was instantly replaced with a picture of Rosa buried in a shallow grave with dirt being shoveled on top of her. She couldn't breathe. . . . She was suffocating. . . . She needed help. . . .

Claire caught her breath and slowed down. She hadn't realized how fast she'd been running, as though someone was chasing her. Like she'd been chased in her dream.

She turned off the treadmill and grabbed her gym bag. She reached in and took out her cell phone. The only call was from her father. His voice mail told her he was heading back to Rochester but would see her next week. She dialed Nick again, but his phone went directly to voice mail.

What was going on? Why would Nick have turned off his cell?

It only made Claire more uneasy as she headed into the locker room, hoping a shower would calm her fears.

The engine of the Agusta A119 helicopter was revving up as Nick stepped onto the roof helipad, ignoring the magnificent views of Manhattan in every direction, and battled his way through the wind from the rotors to the chopper's open rear door. He had no time for sightseeing now. Something was going down and he was being invited to a table he thought he'd never eat at again.

He climbed aboard to find Chief Dolan already strapped in and wearing a headset. "Nicky," the chief shouted over the din. Nick closed the door, threw on a headset as he sat beside him, and buckled himself in. It was then he noticed Dolan faced straight ahead. He'd never once turned to look at Nick.

"Chief," Nick replied, covering his nerves and wondering exactly how much trouble he was in. "Mind if I ask where we're heading?"

"I think you know," he said, without emotion.

All at once, Nick realized the chief had his number. He assumed Dolan knew everything discussed that morning in Wilkes's office. And that's when Nick's fear for his own hide gave way to excitement. The chief of detectives wouldn't fly at taxpayer expense to Staten Island or anywhere else in a police helicopter without a good reason. And certainly not with a half-blind detective.

Unless that half-blind detective had struck gold. His presence here had to mean Wilkes and Savarese had found something. Wilkes, who hadn't gotten where he was without mastering department politics, had done the only thing he knew would save his own hide. He'd managed up and called the chief first.

As the chopper lifted off the pad, Nick wasn't sure if he was brought along for the ride because he was right, or because the chief wanted to bust his balls for breaking their deal. When Nick looked out the chopper's window, he saw the newly completed Freedom Tower, its exterior shining in the sunlight like a beacon, a symbol of the city's recovery from the darkest day in its history.

Maybe it was a good omen, he thought. A reprieve, if only temporary, from a fate over which he had zero control. A stay of execution for his career.

Not until they finished the ascent off the roof and swept southwest over the Brooklyn Bridge did the chief utter a word.

"First time?" he asked Nick. Dolan was still staring straight ahead, but his tone wasn't in any way accusatory. He was almost making small talk.

"In an Agusta, yeah," answered Nick. "I flew recon in Cobras during Gulf War One."

"Army?"

"Yes, sir. Special Forces."

The chief spoke through the headset to the pilot and his observer up front. "Guys, we need some privacy back here."

"Yessir," came the voice of the observer, who flipped a switch so he and Nick could talk confidentially.

"We had a deal," said the chief, his voice lacking any hint of malice or anger. His even tone unnerved Nick even more than if he'd shouted.

"I know, sir," was all Nick could say.

"You disobeyed direct orders. After I put my neck on the line for you."

"Yes, sir," Nick replied, wondering why the chief bothered to spare embarrassing him before the two guys up front if he was about to drop the hammer.

"I should bust you out," Dolan replied.

To Nick, that would almost have been a relief. "That's your call, Boss," he said, bracing for his punishment. "But for whatever it's worth, I did what I had to."

The chief stared out the window at Battery Park as the chopper passed over the tip of Lower Manhattan and out over the harbor. The headsets eliminated the need for Nick to read Dolan's lips, which was a good thing because he couldn't see them.

"You better be right about this," said the chief.

"I know," replied Nick.

He breathed a sigh of relief, entering his small basement apartment. He'd accomplished his mission. Perfectly. Every detail carried out as planned. He felt a serenity he hadn't felt in a long time, replaying in his head the many moments of his conquest. Savoring them.

He unpacked his knives. He'd dunked them in a bucket of bleach and the stainless steel blades gleamed. They'll need sharpening, *he thought.*

Ten minutes later, the chopper touched down in the empty parking lot of a church, just south of the massive wooded area where Rosa's cell phone was last tracked. Nick saw two men in suits standing beside two unmarked police cars, and he wondered where the rest of the cavalry was, because certainly they'd need more troops for the task ahead. A thorough search of that forest would require plenty of manpower.

They exited the chopper and were warmly greeted by one of the suited men. Lieutenant Mike Fitzsimmons, the commander of the local precinct detective squad, made small talk with the chief while they were escorted to the newer of the two unmarked cars, a dark brown Ford Taurus. Fitzsimmons handed Nick the keys.

"Try not to smack it up too bad," said Fitzsimmons. "Thing just came from Motor Transport last week."

"Hey, Nick, why don't you let me drive," said Chief Dolan. "I've been wanting to try one of these."

Nick handed Dolan the keys, grateful to his boss for not outing him. In the police department, no cop of Dolan's exalted rank ever drove—he or she was always driven. But never by a cop who was going blind.

"You know where you're going, Chief?" Nick heard Fitzsimmons ask Dolan as he buckled himself into the passenger's seat.

"Yeah. And don't worry, Mike, this is your turf and I'm not gonna cut you out. Just bear with me."

The chief raised the window, threw the new car into gear, and steered it out of the parking lot and onto Hylan Boulevard. "Only five people know what this is about," he said. "You, me, Wilkes, Savarese, and a detective from CSU. Understood?"

"Yes, sir," Nick answered, the adrenaline rush confirming his suspicions. That Wilkes had called the Crime Scene Unit meant he and Savarese had found something.

Barely a quarter mile down the road, a radio car sat parked at a corner, its roof lights flashing, its uniformed driver waving the chief to turn right.

They drove in silence down a residential street lined with well-kept blue-collar homes, mostly small Capes, split-levels, and the occasional high ranch, their lawns neatly trimmed. At the end of the street, Nick could see Wilkes's department-issued Ford and a CSU Sprinter van parked where the woods began.

People who lived closest to the forest were coming out of their houses. In a quiet, safe, suburban neighborhood like this one, the

Crime Scene van stood out like a pink elephant, a billboard announcing not just that the cops were here, but that something big was brewing. Nick wondered why the van was parked lengthwise across the asphalt, its left side facing oncoming traffic. As the car came to a stop, the radio car from the corner pulled up behind them and positioned itself a few feet in front of the van. Nick and Dolan got out of the Taurus and the chief walked to the open driver's side window of the radio car.

"Nobody goes past this car, including you two," he said to the cops inside. "Any bosses pull up and start giving you shit for not letting them in, I don't care if it's the borough commander himself, you tell them they're to stay out by order of the chief of detectives."

"Yes, Boss," Nick heard the cop in the driver's seat reply to Dolan, who now gestured to Nick. They strode around the CSU van to the side facing the forest where Wilkes, Savarese, and a CSU detective named Terry Aitken waited. Nick knew Aitken, a lean, muscular guy in his early thirties with a blond marine buzz cut. They'd worked together for a short time the previous year and Nick respected him for leaving no stone unturned looking for evidence at a crime scene.

It wasn't until Nick approached Aitken to shake his hand that he understood why Aitken's van was parked where it was—to block the neighborhood residents' view of the yellow crime-scene tape tied around two trees, restricting access to the dirt road that led into the woods.

"You're a piece of work, Nicky, you know that?" Wilkes said. "Good thing you were right, because if I had to drive all the way out to this shithole for nothing I would've kicked your ass myself."

It was Wilkes's trademark backhanded compliment, leaving Nick to wonder exactly what he was right about.

"What'd you guys find?" Chief Dolan asked.

"Tire impressions," Savarese answered, leading the group to the edge of the dirt road. "Gotta be fresh because it rained last night. Left the road nice and muddy."

Aitken, wearing a blue Crime Scene Unit collared polo shirt, kneeled down beside the tracks. "I took photos of these and ran them through the database," he said to the chief. "Treads are from Dunlop 235-55 HR 17s."

"Those tires specific to any particular car?" asked Wilkes.

"Yes, sir," Aitken answered, standing up and nodding toward the inspector's unmarked Crown Vic. "It's the high-performance tire of choice on Ford Crown Victoria Police Interceptors."

Savarese eyed Wilkes's car. "We had a whole fleet of those, didn't we?" he asked cryptically. Nick knew he didn't want to come out and say what they all feared: that a cop had abducted Rosa Sanchez and brought her out here to do god-only-knew what.

Wilkes, however, jumped in. "Every police department in the Tri-state has driven these cars since the late nineties. If a cop took Rosa Sanchez, he doesn't have to be one of ours."

"Or even a cop at all," Nick chimed in. "He could be an impersonator. Used police Crown Vics are easy to come by. Our perp could've bought one almost anywhere."

"Do we know what happened to this woman?" Chief Dolan asked.

"Yeah," Wilkes said, gesturing into the woods. "But based on what's up there, we're gonna have a helluva time proving it."

Claire sat on the sofa her patients usually occupied, trying to read a copy of *People* that someone had left at the gym and she'd somehow accidently put in her bag. But her mind wandered. She looked out her window over the Manhattan cityscape, wondering where Nick was. Had he found Rosa yet?

She forced herself to think of something else, anything to keep from seeing those terrible images of Rosa she'd conjured up before. She started to free-associate, thinking about the stifling heat. Then she thought about the sun, how children always drew it with a smiling face. But she never had. When she was a child her suns were red orange and angry. Now she thought of the sun as a burning ball of fire, sending unbearable heat to the city. *What will happen when the sun burns out?* she wondered. *What will people do? How will the world survive?*

The team walked around the trees strung with crime-scene tape and along the side of the road, careful not to disturb the tire tracks or any other potential evidence. They'd gone nearly a hundred yards from the paved street when they came to a small open area, shaded by the canopy of the surrounding tall red maple and oak trees. Aitken motioned for them to stop on a bed of dry leaves that appeared to be untouched since falling the previous autumn.

"This is as far as we should go," Aitken advised, "until we get a team in here to process all this."

He gestured to four large, black, metal pots sitting atop a cooking grate held up by large charred logs around its perimeter. A pile of ashes under the grate was what remained of a campfire.

"Looks like someone was doing a little cooking," Chief Dolan observed.

"And forgot to take his pots home," Savarese added.

"Anyone beside me smell bleach?" Nick said, detecting an odor that, as far as he knew, wasn't found in nature.

Wilkes shook his head. "Only thing I'm sniffin' is burnt wood."

"No, he's right. I smell it too," said Aitken. "And when we get closer I'll bet we'll find our guy used it to clean those pots."

Chief Dolan needed no prodding to say what they all suspected. "Only reason to clean with bleach is to remove any trace of human remains. Get rid of the DNA."

"He did more than clean," Aitken said, pointing to where the clearing and the tire tracks ended. "Look at the ground just past the end of the tire impressions. It's all unnaturally matted in a perfect square."

"He must've laid out a plastic tarp," Savarese suggested.

"A big one," Aitken said in agreement. "So that when he cut up the body he wouldn't leave anything behind."

Indeed, thought Nick, the spot in the woods looked completely out of place. Like it had been sterilized. A small piece of order that didn't belong in this chaos of nature.

"I don't know how you do that without leaving a shitload of blood," said Wilkes.

"If I had to guess, I'd say he drained the blood somewhere else," Aitken answered.

"So we're thinking this whack job cuffs our victim, kills her, *then* brings her out here and cooks her," mused Chief Dolan. "Why?"

"To get the meat off her bones," said Nick from a few yards behind them, farther into the woods, leaning against a maple tree. None of them noticed that Nick had wandered off.

"Nicky, you okay?" Savarese said, heading toward Nick, who appeared to be using the tree to hold himself up.

"You know how when you put a chicken in a pot to make soup, when the soup's done the meat just slides off the bones? That's what our guy did here," Nick said as Savarese reached him.

"You think whoever this sick bastard is cut this woman up, boiled her to get the meat off the bones, and made a meal out of her?" asked Savarese.

"No, he either threw the meat into the fire or disposed of it elsewhere."

"Nicky?" Wilkes asked as he approached with Aitken and Dolan.

"Fresh Kills is only a few miles from here," said Nick, the simmering anger in his voice apparent as he referred to the infamous, ironically named landfill on Staten Island's west shore. "But he couldn't get the fire to two-thousand degrees, which is what it takes to incinerate bones. . . ."

Savarese put a hand on Nick's shoulder. He turned to face the group, his complexion pale. "Jesus, Nicky, what the hell? You look like you just saw a ghost," said Savarese.

"I did," Nick replied, his voice shaking. "My father's."

"You're not making any sense," Wilkes said. "What does your father have to do with this?"

"He had a case just like it," answered Nick. "When I was ten. He told me all about it, much later. Sonuvabitch killed women and cooked them. Gave me nightmares for years." He looked at Savarese, who removed his hand from Nick's shoulder. "I'm okay, Tony."

"Here's what we're gonna do," the chief said to Aitken. "Call Captain Lumer," Dolan continued, referring to Aitken's boss, "and tell him I want as many teams as he thinks he can spare out here. Pull them in on overtime if necessary."

He turned to Wilkes. "I think Nick's right on the money. We're gonna proceed on the assumption that this lunatic snatched Rosa Sanchez off the street, killed her and drained her blood somewhere else, and possibly dismembered her. We're gonna get this scene photographed, picked up, and processed back at the lab as quick as possible, even if it takes us all night. But we're gonna do it on the down-low. If the media gets wind of this and we've got reporters all over the place asking questions, the whack job who did this is gonna know we're onto him. That's the last thing we want."

Wilkes spoke up. "All due respect, Chief; we bring a fleet of Crime Scene vans past those houses, we're not gonna keep this under wraps for too long."

Dolan had his smartphone out and was viewing a map on its screen. "Looks like the dirt road continues north and dead-ends in Amboy Avenue. Not a lot of houses up there, so we'll bring our personnel in that way. Tony, you'll supervise the operation," he said to Savarese.

"You got it, Chief," replied the detective sergeant.

"What about us?" asked Wilkes, including Nick in the package.

"We're flying back to headquarters," said Dolan to Nick. "And once we're there you're gonna tell us what your father was talking about."

CHAPTER 7

An hour and a silent, uncomfortable helicopter trip back to head-quarters later, Nick, Wilkes, and Dolan sat at the well-kept, walnut-stained conference table in the ornate, oak-paneled conference room adjacent to Dolan's private office. The room was a tribute to its predecessor, the old conference room in the previous, historic head-quarters building at 240 Centre Street. It was just the three of them. What had happened in those Staten Island woods and what was about to be discussed was for the ears of these men only. Nick took a silent but deep breath and began.

"Back in seventy-seven my father was working a sector car in the Six-nine," he said, referring to the police precinct covering the Ca-narsie section of Brooklyn. "He'd just started an eight-to-four tour and Central sends him on a nonemergency run to a two-family over on East Eightieth Street. When he gets there, the homeowner shows him a mound of dirt in his grass where someone had dug a hole dur-ing the night and then filled it back in."

Nick stopped, as if waiting for a response. Neither Dolan nor Wilkes had one, their faces signaling the only thing they wanted was more information.

"So," continued Nick, "Dad takes a look and tells the guy it seems like whoever did it buried something there, and asks if it's okay to dig it up again. The guy says sure, go ahead, but he doesn't have a shovel. So Dad calls the sergeant to bring a couple over from the precinct. Once Dad and his partner start digging, they get only about a foot down when they hit something hard. They clear away the dirt and see the top of a burlap sack. Dad reaches in and next thing he knows, he's got a human skull in his hands with a bullet hole in it. So while he goes out to the street and loses his breakfast, his partner and the sergeant call for help. Forensics and the medical examiner show up and get the bag outta the ground. When they look inside it's full of human bones."

Nick's eyes landed on Wilkes and Dolan, and it was clear he had their attention. Wilkes's face, though, was twisted into something quizzical, as if trying to squeeze from the sponge that was his brain a memory that didn't exist. "Why don't I remember this?" he asked. "I was on the job then."

"Because it happened on August first," Nick replied. "The day after David Berkowitz shot his last two victims over in Bath Beach. My father even said it to me later, that the bag of bones never made the papers 'cause all anyone gave a shit about back then was Son of Sam."

"Jesus," Dolan said, a pained expression crossing his face that Nick hadn't seen before on this man.

"You okay, Chief?" Nick asked.

"Just keep going," Dolan replied.

"Okay," said Nick, "so the ME checks out the bones and tells my father that by the size of the pelvic girdle, he could say the victim was a woman. Then, the next night, the exact same thing happens two blocks away. A bag of some poor woman's bones turns up buried on some other poor schmuck's front lawn. I'll never forget it. Dad came home and drank himself nearly into a coma. He started calling the perp 'the Butcherman.' Dad couldn't understand what kind of monster would kill someone, dismember them, and then boil them to get the meat off their bones. . . ."

"Wait a minute," Wilkes interjected. "The ME knew the bones were boiled?"

"Yeah, both victims. I don't remember how the ME knew," Nick replied. "We'll have to pull the files if we can find them. Thing is," Nick concluded, "every cop in town was looking for Berkowitz, so the bones cases got put on the back burner. The victims were never identified and no one ever collared the perp. And far as my father knew, it never happened again."

Chief Dolan's expression hadn't changed, and now he sat wearily back in his seat. As if he'd put two and two together and it added up to six.

"He was right," said the chief in a heavy voice. "It didn't happen again. But it happened before."

Nick and Wilkes locked eyes, both covering their shock in respect to their boss. "Uh, Chief," said Wilkes, "you mind telling us what you're talking about and when it happened?"

"About a month before what Lawler just told you," the chief said, straightening himself up. "I was a rookie in the One-Twelve in Forest Hills, and some dog dug up a bunch of bones in Flushing Meadows Park. They kept me on overtime to stand guard in the rain at the crime scene. I don't even know if the detectives looked into it. We were the only precinct in the city where Berkowitz struck twice. Nobody cared about anything else."

"Was that victim ever identified?" asked Nick.

"I don't think so, and as a rookie I knew better than to ask," Dolan answered. The comment sounded ironic, given his position now. "I don't remember if I ever knew about the bones in Brooklyn."

"Well, someone's gonna remember them," Wilkes warned.

The chief's ringing cell phone interrupted.

"Hold that thought—it's Savarese," said Dolan, answering. "Tony, I'm with Wilkes and Lawler and you're on speaker. What's going on out there?"

"Nothing good," came Savarese's voice through the crappy speaker. "Aitken says there isn't a trace of a dead body on any of these pots or around the campsite," he said.

"How can he know that so fast?" Wilkes growled.

"Because the cadaverine gas from the corpse would have attracted a shitload of flies and animals and there's no tracks or anything else to indicate they've been here. We're gonna keep looking, but if whoever left all this stuff really did cook some woman, he did a helluva job cleaning up."

"Let us know if anything changes," said Dolan, ending the call and looking down at the table.

"Okay, guys, what now?" he asked. "If a body's cooked in the forest and no one can find a trace of it, is the person really dead?" It was a rhetorical question. They all believed Rosa Sanchez was, in fact, a murder victim.

"Only way to know for sure is to find those bones," Nick said.

"And how are we gonna do that?" Wilkes asked.

"Assuming it's the same guy from thirty-five years ago," Nick postulated, "we should look where he left the other ones."

Dolan eyed him like he'd lost his mind. "If it *is* the same guy," he said, "you can't think he'd be that stupid."

But Nick was undeterred. "He was stupid enough to leave Rosa's cell phone on," Nick replied. "Meaning he wasn't stupid at all. He wanted us to find his campsite. That's why I think he wants us to find the bones too. I think it's worth a try."

They drove across Brooklyn to the Canarsie neighborhood where the last two bags of bones had been found.

Chief Dolan stayed in his car on the phone while Wilkes and Nick walked four blocks up East Eightieth Street looking for freshly dug-up ground. But it was apparent no bodies had been buried in the neighborhood. They saw a radio car from the 69th Precinct parked at the curb on the next block, the cops inside appearing to be writing up paperwork.

"This is nuts," Wilkes said to Nick, gesturing him to turn around before the cops spotted them. "Anyone sees the chief of detectives out here, they're gonna know something's up," he growled as they hurried back to their own car.

"Let's go to the next stop," Nick suggested.

"Screw that," said Wilkes as he removed his suit jacket, not caring about exposing the nine-millimeter Glock holstered on his belt. The heat was clearly getting to him. "I'm gonna recommend to the chief we send a radio car out to that spot in Flushing Meadows Park and see if anyone dug up the ground. We don't have to tell the cops why."

A short *whoop* from the siren on Chief Dolan's department-issued Chevy Tahoe cut him off. Wilkes and Nick ran the remaining block back to where the Tahoe was parked.

"What's up, Chief?" Wilkes panted as he climbed behind the wheel, breathless.

Dolan was busy shouting into the radio mic. "No, Central, have patrol seal off the street and wait for our arrival. No one goes into or out of that block before I get there."

"Ten-four," came the dispatcher's voice.

"Where we going?" asked Nick, barely in his seat before Wilkes threw the Tahoe in gear and stomped on the gas.

"South Bronx," the chief shouted over the din of the siren. "Coupla sanitation guys dumped a garbage can from a street corner and a bag full of bones fell into their truck."

CHAPTER 8

There was no easy way to get from Canarsie to Yankee Stadium. Wilkes chose surface streets to avoid the Belt Parkway's perennial construction backups. He maneuvered the Tahoe up Pennsylvania Avenue through Brownsville and East New York, still two of the most crime-ridden neighborhoods of the city. They were also the city's most neglected, pothole-ridden streets. Between the bumps, the blare of the siren, and the decrepit buildings passing by his tunnel vision, Nick found himself with a raging headache and almost got carsick.

The stop-and-go traffic didn't help; Brooklyn drivers rarely pulled over for a cop or fire truck on an emergency run to begin with. Add in air-conditioning and music at full blast with the windows closed, and most drivers wouldn't even hear the siren until it was right on top of them. If even then.

When they hit the Jackie Robinson Parkway, the pavement and the ride smoothed out and the traffic dissipated. Wilkes gunned the Tahoe onto the Grand Central Parkway, hitting eighty on the speedometer as they flew past Flushing Meadows Park, Citi Field, and LaGuardia Airport. They came to a dead stop on the RFK Bridge because of an accident, and Wilkes's cursing the hapless livery cab driver who'd changed lanes into a Toyota Camry didn't help Nick's headache. Neither did the fear that the crime scene to which they headed would be contaminated by the time they got there.

Nearly an hour had passed before they hit the Deegan Expressway in the city's northernmost borough. Only when he saw Yankee Stadium come into view did the throbbing in Nick's head begin to subside. Wilkes sped the chief's Tahoe down Walton Avenue, past the Bronx courthouse, and brought it to a stop in front of several radio cars parked at odd angles in front of 157th Street, closing it off to traffic.

As he sprung from the Tahoe with Wilkes and Dolan, Nick's earlier fears subsided as well. It was what wasn't there that soothed him: no medical examiner's van, no Crime Scene Unit vehicle. Chief Dolan's orders were being carried out to the letter. Only the garbage truck sat there, its two spooked sanitation workers standing with four uniformed police officers who made sure nobody crossed past their patrol cars.

Other than the fact that the street was closed off, no bystanders seemed to care. When anyone asked what was going on, the officers said what Dolan had instructed them: "Checking out a water main. No danger."

Nick pulled out the chain holding his detective's shield and hung it around his neck. It was the first time in almost a year he'd been to a crime scene, and though this was serious business, he suppressed a grin. He was back on the streets, back in the game. He followed Chief Dolan and Wilkes as they strode to the rear of the garbage truck and looked inside the hopper.

In front of them, atop a mound of garbage, was a large burlap sack. Human bones protruded from a tear on the side. It stank but Nick barely noticed. He'd smelled many a decomposing body in his time, and to him rotting garbage was a walk in the park.

Chief Dolan kept a poker face as he turned to the patrol cops, all young, all humbled, and perhaps even scared facing a commander of Dolan's rank.

"Who was first on the scene?" the chief asked.

Two of the uniforms raised their hands, and Dolan motioned them over. "Did you see what was in that truck?" he asked.

"Yessir," answered one of the cops, whose name plate read *Singh*.

"Did anyone else? Besides the two sanitation guys?"

"No, Chief," replied the other cop, Hammond. "Orders were not to let anyone near here. Even the sergeant didn't see it."

"Did you fill out sixty-ones?" asked the chief, referring to the standard police report form number.

"We were told to wait for you," said Officer Singh.

Dolan nodded, satisfied the cops had indeed done what he'd wanted. "Here's the deal," he began. "The sanitation guys told you what they thought they saw. You responded to the job on the radio and when you got here you took a look yourselves. You weren't sure what you were looking at, so you're impounding the vehicle. And by my order, the Detective Bureau will take over from here. We understand each other?"

"You got it, Chief," said Officer Hammond. Dolan pulled a notepad from his pocket. "I'm writing down your names and shield numbers," he said as he wrote. "Do like I say, keep this quiet, and I'll personally make sure you're taken care of."

Both officers knew what that meant: as long as they followed the chief's orders, he'd put them on his list for assignment to a detective squad. "Now," Dolan said, finishing, "we need this truck towed to the pound and the two sanitation guys brought downtown to my office. Tell your sergeant I asked you to do that yourselves, and if he has any questions he can talk to me directly."

"Sergeant's a she, sir, but we'll tell her," said Officer Singh, and the two of them gestured the shocked sanitation workers to follow as they headed off to their radio car to carry out the orders. When they were out of earshot, Dolan turned back to Wilkes. "We'll have Crime Scene come over in their unmarked van and get the garbage can," the chief said. "They can meet us at the pound along with the ME to empty the truck."

Nick gazed up and down the block of converted tenements, having to move his head and body more than he was used to so he could see everything. He felt an uneasiness coming over him that grew stronger by the second. "I don't get it," he said.

"Get what?" Wilkes asked.

"He could've scattered the bones in those woods on Staten Island and it would've taken weeks of grid searching to find them, if we ever did. Instead, he dumps them in a garbage can in broad daylight, on a street three blocks from Yankee Stadium in a neighborhood with more cameras than a busload of Japanese tourists."

Dolan turned his head as if to find the cameras of which Nick spoke, and three caught his eye. "He's got stones, whoever this psycho is," said the chief. "ME needs to rush the DNA."

"They gotta extract DNA from the bones first before they can process it," Wilkes replied glumly. "We're not gonna have a positive ID on those bones for a month."

"We don't have a month," Dolan shot back. "We have until someone leaks word that the bones are Rosa Sanchez's. Someone's gonna remember the cases from seventy-seven, the media's gonna get hold of it, and folks are gonna panic that a serial killer we didn't catch thirty years ago is back."

He turned to Nick. "Until we positively ID those bones as Rosa Sanchez's, not a word of this to your Doctor Waters. We clear?"

"Yes, sir," Nick answered.

"Good," Dolan said, sounding almost dismissive. "You've been a big help. Escort the two sanitation guys downtown in the radio car and up to Major Case. You don't need to ask them any questions. Inspector Wilkes'll have his guys take over from there."

"That's it?" Nick asked, unable to keep his disappointment to himself. He was being sidelined again.

But Dolan was done with Nick and turned to Wilkes. "MCS will handle this as a kidnap-murder," he said. "Choose five detectives you trust and set them up in a spare office. Tony Savarese will run them. We need to keep this as contained as possible."

Realizing Nick was still standing there, he grew cold. "You have your orders," the chief said, "and this time you'll obey them. I'll see you at your desk when I get back to the office."

Nick walked away before he said something he'd regret. He removed his shield from around his neck and climbed into the front seat of the radio car. The two sanitation workers were already settled in the rear. He couldn't understand why Dolan had humiliated him in front of Wilkes, but had no problem at all understanding why he'd been dismissed. Dolan valued loyalty and trust above all else. This was Nick's payback for breaking his deal with the chief.

The problem, though, was that Nick Lawler never started a job he didn't finish. As he tuned out the blaring siren and stared out the windshield while the radio car weaved through traffic, he vowed to himself he wouldn't let this be the first time.

And once again, that would require disobeying the chief's direct orders.

*   *   *

Claire sat in a booth in the back of the Chelsea Diner, a stainless-steel-clad structure that looked like a dining car of old, and sipped her black coffee, recoiling as it burned her tongue. She gazed out the window onto Tenth Avenue, now nearly empty of traffic at eleven o'clock at night, and wondered why Nick hadn't answered his phone all afternoon. He'd finally called back three hours ago, saying he couldn't talk where he was and arranging to meet at the diner. But all those hours with no news had left her in a downright panic about Rosa's well-being.

She took in the nearly empty diner as a waitress filled the salt shakers and ketchup bottles to prepare for the next day. Claire thought of the last time she and Nick were here together, glad that at least now it wasn't her life in danger but still aching to know what had happened to Rosa.

She was just reaching into her purse to pull out her phone when she heard the door squeak open. Looking up, she saw Nick enter, his face indicating he'd been through hell—and, if that weren't enough, he had his night-vision dog, Cisco, on a leash to guide him.

"Over here," Claire called.

Nick turned, his eyes still adjusting to the light. Cisco headed toward Claire, recognizing her scent from her visit to the apartment, his tail wagging happily as they approached her.

"Sorry I'm late," Nick said as he slipped into the seat across from her, eyeing the chipped brown china mug of black coffee Claire had the server pour for him at least ten minutes earlier.

"You may want to freshen that up," she said.

Nick lifted the cup and sipped. "It's fine," he said. "And look, I'm even sorrier I couldn't answer your calls. I'm under strict orders not to say a word to you about anything that went down today."

Claire sat back in the booth, crushed. *Was this all for nothing?*

But Nick wasn't finished. "Relax," he said. "Just because I got those orders doesn't mean I'm gonna follow them."

That's the Nick I know, Claire thought. "What happened?"

"Not so fast. I'm already in hot water with the chief of detectives for breaking our deal. He finds out I disobeyed him again, I'm on the street."

"Nobody else ever has to hear what you tell me."

Nick took a breath. "You need to prepare yourself, because it isn't pretty."

Claire was already prepared for the worst. "Rosa's dead," she said, a tear falling from her right eye.

"We're pretty sure," Nick began, launching into the day's insanity, leaving out only the two similar murders from thirty years ago. Claire tried her best to take what he said as clinically as possible, but when she heard Rosa's bones were dumped in a trash can her tears fell more rapidly.

"What about her family?" Claire asked, trying to compose herself. "Her mother needs to know."

Nick put a hand on Claire's. "She can't right now. And you can't tell her or anyone you know about this or I'm toast. I'm not even supposed to be on a case."

"So you're going to make Rosa's mother wait and hope that her daughter's alive," Claire said, pulling away. "That's cruel."

"All we have are bones, Claire," Nick said. "You only know this because you know me. In any other case we'd make a positive ID before we tell the family. Once we have that, Inspector Wilkes will make the notification."

"You're going to need a DNA sample from a family member."

A loud group of a dozen boisterous, laughing, drunk men and women in their twenties burst into the diner, almost drowning them out and annoying Nick as they sat too close for his comfort. Cisco, who'd been lying on the floor at Nick's feet, suddenly sat up, on guard, ready to protect his master.

"I can't ask Rosa's mother to give us one," Nick reminded her, as he lifted his mug and took another sip of his lukewarm coffee. "I'm officially out of the loop. It's gonna take a month to extract and profile the DNA from those bones. Until they have the results, they don't officially exist as far as the police department is concerned."

Claire knew Nick was holding back. "What aren't you saying?" she asked, controlling her temper.

Her eyes followed Nick's around the room, clearly checking out the diner's clientele. *He wants to tell me*, Claire realized. *But there are too many people here.*

As if reading her thoughts, Nick signaled their server for the check.

"Outside," he said.

They came through the door and walked down the street. A fresh, cool breeze blew from the Hudson River just a block away, bringing relief from the oppressive humidity of the day. Claire realized that with Cisco on his leash, she and Nick could easily be mistaken for a couple from the neighborhood out taking a late night stroll. When Nick was convinced there was no one nearby, he began.

"Fewer than ten people know what I'm about to tell you, and it has to stay that way," he said, and proceeded to relate the story of the two killings from 1977. When he was done, Claire looked at him, stunned.

"And you're thinking the same person killed Rosa?" she asked.

"Why not? He was never caught, and the victims were never identified."

"Well," Claire began, her mind racing at full speed, "if it's the same killer he'd be pretty old by now. And you know, a serial killer taking a nearly four-decade break between murders is unheard of, right?"

"But not impossible," said Nick, his mind churning as fast as hers. "He could've been doing time for a different crime and recently paroled—the guys'll have to check. Or it could be a copycat."

Claire was skeptical. "Copycats usually emulate a known criminal because they want to be like them or be better," she said. "And you have no idea who committed the original murders."

"Good point," Nick admitted. "I gotta believe our people are searching the evidence warehouse for the bones from the first two girls—if they weren't buried in Potter's Field years ago. If they can find the bones and extract their DNA, maybe we have a shot at finding out who the victims were. And besides," he said, a thought popping up in his brain, "who's to say there aren't more of this guy's victims in shallow graves all over the Tristate? Problem is, the two cold cases were barely investigated back then because of Son of Sam. We—I mean, *they*," he corrected himself, "don't even know where to start."

"They can start with Rosa Sanchez," she said as they waited for the traffic light at the corner of Twenty-Third Street, "and work their way backward. But all they seem to want to do is cover this up so nobody knows how badly they screwed up forty years ago."

The light changed. Claire started to cross the street at the same time Cisco pulled Nick off the curb, making him stumble and grab onto Claire's arm so he wouldn't fall.

"Sorry," said Nick, righting himself.

"It's okay," said Claire, an electric shock running through her from Nick's touch. A shock that wasn't unpleasant.

"This isn't political," said Nick. "They're not trying to cover anything up. They don't want the city in a panic and I don't blame them. But they can only hold back for as long as it takes to positively identify Rosa. Which gives them a month."

"Not if I can help it," Claire said.

"What does that mean?" Nick asked, worried that Claire would leak the news.

"I'm going to try to identify her sooner."

This scared Nick. "You're not even supposed to know she's dead. Don't throw me under the bus and make me sorry I told you."

Claire appreciated the risk he took for her.

"Let me put it another way," she said. "What would you say if I told you I might be able to ID Rosa sooner?"

"Does it involve breaking any laws?"

"Do you really want me to answer that?"

For the first time since their conversation began, Nick smiled. "Of course not," he replied, his tone making it clear she had his unofficial blessing. "And if anyone asks, I'll say that we never had this conversation."

Claire grinned back. "What conversation?"

CHAPTER 9

Claire walked quickly down the hallway to her office, but not so fast that she'd attract attention from the occasional custodian mopping the floor. It was after midnight, the wing of the hospital housing the doctors' offices was empty, and even though the sneakers she wore made little noise, Claire felt vulnerable walking alone under the glare of the ceiling lights.

Her goal was to ID Rosa and tell her family. That she was doing it late at night was no accident. The building teemed with patients and doctors during regular business hours. But at this hour the odds against getting caught rose in her favor. She knew well that what she was about to do could cost her the medical license for which she'd worked tirelessly, not to mention exposing herself and the hospital to a huge lawsuit.

She reached her office, quietly unlocking the door and purposely not turning on the light. She entered and closed the door behind her, plunging herself into darkness. She regretted having closed the blackout window shades before leaving that day as she made her way to her desk. All went well until she bumped her leg into the corner of her traditional, comfortable couch, which, though overstuffed, still hurt. She winced at the pain and thought about Nick. *Soon he'll be living in total darkness.*

She felt her way to the desk and switched on the lamp, which wouldn't bleed light through the crack under her door as much as the overhead fluorescents. Any doctor could find a reasonable explanation for working late. But if confronted, she'd need to talk fast to justify the next step. It would be the most dangerous part of tonight's mission, and it would unfold in another part of the hospital.

But only if she was right.

Claire unlocked her desk. The click of the lock reverberated through the room, reminding her that she had one last chance to turn back. But Rosa's memory drove her forward. She opened the bottom left-hand drawer, pulled out a thick folder, and flipped through, finding the section she was looking for, confirming she'd remembered correctly. She made a few notes, ripped the paper off the pad, and stashed it in her purse. Then she switched off the lamp and headed for the door, making it there without further mishap, confident she was doing the right thing.

And knowing, whether or not she succeeded, that it had to be done.

Nick welcomed the air conditioner's relief when he entered the aging building on First Avenue that housed the medical examiner's office. Though it was only eight in the morning, the city air was once again heavy with heat and humidity. On sweltering days like these Nick longed for the cool blast from the AC of the Impala he used to drive.

He reached into his pocket for his shield and ID to show to the security guard at the desk, but before he could open his wallet, the door buzzed. He looked up to see Lester, an old-timer with tufts of white hair springing from the sides of his otherwise bald head, behind the glass, waving him in. After so many years in homicide, Nick was hardly a stranger here. The doctors and staff were old friends.

He waved to Lester, pushed open the heavy metal door, and as always headed for the stairs to the basement, where the autopsy rooms were located. Today, however, was different. He wasn't supposed to be there. None of the bodies in the ME's refrigerators "belonged" to him.

A phone call from Claire, a little over an hour after they left the diner, had brought him here despite the warning from Chief Dolan to stay off the case. Their conversation had been brief. Claire told Nick what she needed and was about to tell him why when he cut her off.

"I don't need to know," he'd said. "I'll get it for you tomorrow."

Then he hung up.

Nick's problem now was that he didn't know who could give him what Claire needed.

He reached the basement and started down a tiled, brightly lit hallway lined with empty gurneys. He couldn't help but think it was a slow night in the "chop shop;" on a busy night those cots would be laden with body bags filled with New York's freshly dead. But the body he sought now wasn't that of a victim who'd been killed, it was that of a particular assistant ME named Pam. Pam of the killer body, who'd made it very clear she'd jump Nick's bones any time for the asking. But she had a face made for radio, so Nick had yet to take her up on the offer. He was about to turn down another hallway when he heard a male voice behind him:

"What, you don't love us anymore?"

Nick didn't have to turn around to know the voice.

"Who said I ever loved you?" he asked, turning to face Doctor Rich Ross, an assistant medical examiner whose thick mane of dark red hair and pointy features always reminded Nick of a fox. The comment was a joke between them; for years Nick had no love lost for this man, but was now indebted to Ross for providing him with the crucial lead to one of the biggest cases of Nick's career.

Ross walked over and the two men shook hands. "Thought we'd never see you back here," he said.

"You *don't* see me here," Nick replied. "I'm serious," he added when Ross gave him a quizzical look. "Anyone at the Puzzle Palace finds out, I'll be drawn and quartered."

"So the golden boy is in a jackpot again," said Ross, his voice thick with friendly sarcasm.

Nick stepped closer. "No, but I need your help."

"Oh, so you want to put *me* in a jackpot," Ross quipped. Then Ross lowered his voice. "Long as it has nothing to do with that bag of bones that *didn't* come in here yesterday."

Nick's expression told him otherwise.

"I was afraid you weren't gonna say that," Ross said.

"I saw the damn things in the back of a garbage truck," Nick said.

"Funny that you're not one of the three guys on the 'need to know' list."

"*Your* 'need to know' list? They gave this case to *you*?" Nick asked, incredulous at his good fortune.

"Yeah. Lucky me, huh?"

"Is the victim's name on the bones?" Nick asked.

"Nope," Ross said, reducing his voice to a conspiratorial near whisper. "They're logged in as belonging to a Jane Doe."

"Anything interesting about 'em?"

"Besides all the secrecy? I haven't checked them out yet. All I know is they came in late last night and the boss saved 'em for me. Remind me to thank him when this is over." He smiled at Nick, delivering the best news for last. "Oh, and it's a complete skeleton."

This was the piece of information Nick had hoped for. "Any chance you can get me some X-rays?"

Ross let out a cynical laugh. "You know, Nicky, if this job doesn't kill me, I'm pretty sure the trouble you're about to get me into will," he said. "You want those films before or after I send the bones to the lab for DNA extraction?"

"You may not have to extract anything if you get me those X-rays."

"Goddammit, you know who she is, don't you?"

"Yeah, and so do the three guys on that 'eyes only' list of yours. But I can't tell you, because if you slip and say her name they'll know who you got it from."

"Oh, so this cloak-and-dagger bullshit is for *my* benefit." Ross snickered. "Okay, sure, what the hell? Break a federal privacy law or two, that's no big deal, right?"

"Join the club," said Nick. "We have jackets."

"Jackets my ass. You mean those nice orange federal prison jumpsuits, don't you?"

Nick grinned, but didn't answer, exasperating Ross.

"What good's the X-ray if you have nothing to compare it to?" Ross asked.

"What makes you think I don't?"

"You sonuvabitch. Let me see it," said Ross.

"I don't have it," Nick answered.

"You just said you did."

"What I said was, I have something I can compare with the film."

"Okay, so stop jerking me off. Bring your something here, I'll do the comparison, and we'll give this woman a name," Ross said, fed up with Nick's runaround.

"I can't," Nick said.

"Why the hell not?" Ross demanded.

"Because of where I got it."

"Oh, that's what you meant when you said 'join the club.' We're *both* going to Club Fed."

"No one's going to prison if you do what I say."

Ross looked back skeptically, so Nick dove into his sales pitch. "We speak for the dead, right? Well, this woman deserves to be spoken for, her family deserves to know where she is, and the scumbag who chopped her up and boiled her bones deserves to be publicly dismembered himself, but I'll settle for putting him away for life. I don't see the downside here."

The expression on Ross's face confirmed that the last piece of information was news to him. "I'm sorry, but you did say *boiled*, right?"

"I shit you not," Nick continued. "And the sooner we ID this woman, the sooner we get this guy off the street before he does it again."

"How do you know that'll happen?" Ross asked.

"Because he's done it before," Nick said. "Thirty-five years ago. And I guarantee you, someone in this office is looking for those *two* sets of bones as we speak."

Nick knew he had Ross when the guy was finally speechless.

"There's this glassed-in coffee place outside the Alexandria, that new building next to Bellevue," Ross said. "Go grab a cup. Gimme half an hour and I'll bring you the damn films."

Inspector Wilkes appeared in the doorway of his office and stared into the Major Case Squad room, at the dozen or so detectives at their desks or moving around, all going about their business. Wilkes could keep a poker face as well as anyone, and though he smiled at one of his troops passing by, he silently fumed about how his day had so quickly gone to hell.

It started with a call from the chief of detectives at eight-thirty, asking if he knew why Nick Lawler was late for work and didn't bother to call. Wilkes wanted to answer that maybe if Dolan hadn't been such an asshole to Nick and dismissed him from the case the guy would've shown up on time. He'd put his own trust in Nick, who'd not only led them to the bones on Staten Island, but also linked them to the eerily similar 1977 murders. It was the second time Wilkes had taken a chance on Nick, who'd come through on both occasions. And gotten screwed both times as well.

But of course, Wilkes held his tongue with his boss, informing the chief that he'd last spoken to Nick yesterday when they were all together in the Bronx. It happened to be the truth, and it mollified Dolan enough to let it go.

Now Wilkes had a more difficult issue on his hands. Thirty minutes earlier, at 11:32 a.m., Assistant Medical Examiner Rich Ross had called him, saying he had "a matter of extreme importance that would be best to discuss privately." Before Wilkes could complain about driving uptown, Ross said he'd be at Police Plaza before noon and hung up before Wilkes could even answer.

When he was in a good mood, Wilkes liked to quip "I may be an idiot but I'm no fool." Right now, though, he felt like both. There were no dead bodies Doctor Ross needed to investigate at police headquarters. Wilkes knew of Ross's relationship with Nick, and he, like most seasoned detectives, didn't believe in coincidences.

At 11:45, when Ross strolled into the squad room with a large manila envelope, Wilkes couldn't help but feel the fine hand of Nick Lawler behind whatever was about to land on him.

"Doctor Ross," Wilkes said, smiling like the canary knowing he's about to be eaten by the cat.

"Thanks for seeing me, Inspector," Ross said as the two shook hands. Wilkes ushered him into his office and closed the door. "Sorry I was so abrupt on the phone but I wanted to get down here as quick as possible."

"You brought a little show-and-tell," Wilkes said, pointing to the manila envelope Ross laid on the desk. "I'm presuming this has to do with the bones from the Bronx."

"Yeah, and if you don't mind, I'd like to show-and-tell with the blinds closed," said Ross, referring to the faded venetian blinds hanging over the wall of windows separating the squad room from Wilkes's office.

"Sure, Doc," the inspector said, lowering the blinds so they had privacy. "I wouldn't have it any other way. Any other requests?"

"Mind if we use the lamp on your desk?" asked Ross.

"Knock yourself out," said Wilkes, taking a seat behind his desk.

Ross sat back down, flipped the switch on the lamp, and pulled out an X-ray. "Do you know what an occult fracture is, Inspector?" he asked.

"Sorry, I missed that class in medical school," Wilkes answered.

Ross ignored him and pressed on. "It's a break inside a bone that can only be seen through imaging. I didn't get your bones until this morning, but the first thing I did was x-ray the larger ones—skull, pelvis, extremities. Everything was clean except for your victim's right tibia, which is where I found the occult fracture."

Ross pointed to a mark on the X-ray of a leg bone.

"Are you gonna wait for me to ask or tell me what this is about?" the inspector growled.

"Sorry," Ross answered, pulling out a second film from the envelope. He showed it to Wilkes and pointed. "Here's the exact same fracture on a second film," he said, placing the first X-ray over the second. "The fractures on both films match up. Perfectly."

"I can see that, Doctor," Wilkes growled again. "And now you're gonna tell me these films weren't taken at the same time."

Ross admired Wilkes; the guy was smarter than he looked. "That's right, Inspector. The second film was taken at the infirmary on Rikers Island back in February when an inmate was injured during a sexual assault."

Wilkes was getting tired of this. "And the inmate's name?"

"Former inmate," Ross replied quickly, replacing the films in the envelope. "But her name is—or rather, was—Rosa Sanchez."

Wilkes was dumbstruck, but impressed nonetheless. "So you're telling me you can positively ID the victim as Rosa Sanchez by that one little mark?"

"Just to be sure, I had Doctor Wagner take a look," Ross said, referring to the city's chief medical examiner. "She signed off on it, so the answer is yes. And she sent me here to tell you personally."

Wilkes realized this wasn't just a revelation. He was being set up.

"Okay, Doc," he said, trying not to blow. "Just so I know this is all kosher, why don't you tell me how you magically got your hands on that film from Rikers. Or would you like *me* to tell *you* how you got it?"

"Well, Inspector, I was going to tell you I started under the assumption that the bones belonged to a homeless person who might've been in jail at some point, so I sent my X-ray to the Rikers infirmary and the doctor recognized it and found the matching one belonging to Ms. Sanchez."

"And when I call Doctor Wagner she'll back you up on that," Wilkes said.

"Yes, sir, she will," Ross answered.

The inspector cracked a smile, thinking Ross was a lousy actor but he sure knew how to cover his ass.

"I gotta hand it to you, Doc, that bullshit story you're slinging is as good as the best phony alibis I've ever heard."

He leaned over and got in Ross's face, unnerving the doctor so much he pushed his chair back. "But you and I both know that's not how it went down, don't we? What really happened was your buddy Nick Lawler got that X-ray from his pain-in-the-ass shrink friend, Claire Waters. Nick talked you into zapping those bones, and once the two films matched, you and him concocted this whole flippin' charade."

When Ross didn't answer, Wilkes knew he was right. He admired Ross for protecting the same guy he, Wilkes, was trying to protect. And Ross had also given him a card to play. Wilkes loosened up and headed behind his desk.

"Hey, c'mon," he said in a much friendlier, more conspiratorial tone as he sat down and relaxed in his chair. "I don't like this any more than you do. There's too much at stake here to get buried in political bullshit. Believe me, in this job I've got more than enough of that."

Ross couldn't tell if Wilkes was serious. "You're not yanking my chain, are you, Inspector?" he asked.

"Look," Wilkes began, "I may not like how he does it, but Nicky doesn't give up. By coming to me this way you've done both him and me a huge solid."

"I—we did you a favor?"

"Hell yeah. You guys gave me enough to take to my boss without having to out Nick."

Ross felt the tension leave him. "All Nick wanted was to get some justice for this poor woman," Ross blurted, relieved to drop the act. "But he was afraid your chief would blame *you* for his actions. Yeah, he brought me the X-ray from Doctor Waters. Calling Rikers and having my boss sign off on it, though? That was all me—"

Wilkes interrupted him by picking up the phone and dialing. "Yeah, it's Inspector Wilkes. Tell the chief I need to see him. Now." After a moment, Wilkes went on, "Okay, I'll be right up." He put the receiver down and looked up at Ross. "Thanks, Doc, you've been a huge help."

Ross was almost afraid to ask but did. "What are you going to tell your chief?"

Wilkes grabbed the X-rays and headed for the door. "What I should've told him yesterday," the inspector said, exiting.

The glare of the sun through Dolan's filthy windows nearly blinded Wilkes as he sat across from his boss. The chief of detectives stared at the X-rays, turning them in different directions like an adolescent looking at the centerfold of a nudie magazine. "We're sure about this?" he asked, looking up at Wilkes.

"The DNA will confirm it, but the ME says this is enough to ID the victim as Rosa Sanchez," Wilkes said. "They're leaving the announcement to us."

Dolan placed the films on his desk. "Let's not rush into anything," the chief said in that politician's voice that made Wilkes want to wince. "We'll give it forty-eight hours and see if your guys come up with anything on our perp," said Dolan. "Who do you trust enough to work this?"

This was where Wilkes had to be careful as he made his move. "Chief, I trust all my guys," he said. "But if you wanna keep this quiet and hold on to some deniability, the thing to do is give this one to Nick Lawler."

Dolan got up from his chair like he was uncomfortable. He stared out the window. "Nick Lawler's technically not a cop anymore," he said, his voice tight.

"All the more reason to use him," Wilkes pressed. "This isn't something where he's gonna have to run around town chasing down leads."

When Dolan didn't answer, Wilkes rose from his chair and joined his boss at the window so there would be no avoiding the issue. "I know he's your boy," Dolan said to Wilkes. "But Lawler's turning into a loose cannon."

"You know, Chief, I held back yesterday but now I'm gonna say it," Wilkes blurted. "We wouldn't know about any of this but for Nicky. He's the best, and he's being sidelined by his own bad fortune. You gave the guy a break once and he came through. Give him another one now and it'll work for all of us."

Dolan wouldn't look at him. "If anybody out there finds out, we're gonna have a shit storm on our hands," he said.

"That's the whole point," Wilkes said. "The more people know about this, the bigger the chances it'll leak. So we keep the circle small and the information contained. Nick works it from the inside, Tony Savarese does whatever shoe leather's necessary. If we need a third body I'll get involved myself. And I don't have to tell you that Nick'll keep his mouth shut."

Dolan eyed Wilkes, sensing there was more. "What else?" the chief asked. "Or maybe I should be asking *who* else?"

Wilkes knew this was the risky part, fearing any answer would incur the chief's wrath. But he couldn't back off the limb now. "We have two days to get out in front of this. Two murders barely anyone knows about that are three decades old. With an MO identical to Rosa Sanchez's murder. We've gotta assume they were done by the same perp, and we need to get out ahead of him and stop him from doing another woman."

Dolan knew where Wilkes was going. "You want to bring in some-one to profile the guy. And I'm guessing it's Doctor Claire Waters."

Wilkes was impressed; Dolan had his number. "Chief, I can't be-lieve I'm saying it myself. But Doctor Waters pulled our asses out of the fire last year. She and Nick work well together, and she's not gonna write a book about it or go on TV," Wilkes said. "If we bring in the FBI they'll leak it and that's the last thing either of us needs."

Dolan knew Wilkes was right. The police commissioner and the FBI were like oil and water. Asking the feds for help of any kind was practically verboten in the NYPD. Though he didn't like Wilkes's idea, he couldn't come up with anything better.

"Do it," Dolan said.

CHAPTER 10

Wilkes sat down on the plush sofa in Claire's office, trying hard not to feel like he was in enemy territory or, even worse, that he was about to have his head shrunk. Because his dislike of doctors was surpassed only by his outright hatred of hospitals, he was more than just a fish out of water. He shifted, trying to find a place that felt comfortable. Nick sat a foot away on the other end of the sofa and Claire faced him, sitting in her wing chair, waiting for him to speak. Wilkes wished he could have held this meeting in his own office, but that was out of the question.

"First of all, Doctor," he began, "I need your assurance that what we discuss stays in this room."

"I'm a psychiatrist, Inspector," Claire replied. "I know how to keep a secret."

"Okay," Wilkes said, choosing deference over his trademark sarcasm. "Here's the rest of it. Doc, you can't set foot in police head-quarters. Nicky, this is the last time you come to this hospital until we're done. And the two of you are not to be seen together in public."

"Why?" Nick asked.

"This town's full of loose lips. Some reporter sees you walking down some street, they'll put two and two together, and before we know it this whole thing is on the front page of the *Post*," Wilkes answered. "We've managed to keep this under the media's radar thus far and we have to keep it that way. Understood?"

"Yes, sir," Claire answered sincerely. Neither Nick nor Claire liked the conditions, but as the price of admission to the Big Show, they would live with it.

"What's next?" asked Nick.

"We have to find you two a home base," Wilkes continued. "It cannot be here, Doctor, and I can't put you in a police facility either."

"We'll work at my place," Nick interrupted, surprising Claire. "There's plenty of room and the building's quiet during the day. And selfishly, I can be there when the girls come home from school."

"It's not selfish," Claire assured him. "And that's fine with me."

"Me too," Wilkes agreed, surprised how easy this was turning out to be. "Nicky, your cover story's simple," the inspector said. "You're taking two weeks' vacation, which you won't be charged for. I'll have Tony Savarese bring the files on Rosa Sanchez and the two Jane Doe cases from seventy-seven over to your house. Tony is your go-between, our pipeline back and forth. Whatever paper you need he'll get you. Any shoe leather you need done, he'll do. Under no circumstances are either of you to do interviews, surveillance, or any other kind of street work. And here's the other thing—no electronic communications either. E-mails, texts, all verboten. We don't want a digital trail coming back at us if this thing blows up in our faces. Are we clear?"

"Yes, sir," Nick answered, "but how's Tony gonna feel about being our errand boy? We already have Ross at the ME's office."

Wilkes anticipated this. "Obviously Ross already knows you're involved, so I don't see the harm in you talking to him directly. But stay the hell out of that building," the inspector warned. "And we don't want too much communication between Ross and our office either; it'll look hinky if anyone checks. Tony's loyal. He's a good soldier, he knows what's at stake, and most importantly he's one of us. He'll do as he's told and take it to the grave with him. So he's our guy."

Wilkes looked squarely at Claire, but this time more like the colleague she was being asked to become. "Now you, Doc. No pressure or anything, but I put my balls on the chopping block to bring you into this. You don't work for me but if we're going to accomplish what we're setting out to do, I'm going to need your complete cooperation and assurance you'll follow orders. And I'm not asking you to do this in a vacuum. I have an assurance for you as well, and this comes straight from the chief of detectives. You'll not be asked to do anything that'll put your medical license or your position and standing at Manhattan State in jeopardy. Is that agreeable to you?"

Claire was impressed. This was not the Wilkes she'd come to know. His words made her feel even more secure in what was at best a proposition filled with insecurity. "Yes, Inspector," she said readily, "and thanks for looking out for me."

"Don't thank me so fast, Doc," Wilkes shot back in his more traditional bluster, "'cause I'm gonna put you through the wringer, starting right now. We need a profile as quickly as you can get us one, like yesterday or sooner. If the guy who did Rosa Sanchez is in fact the same perp who did the other two women back in the seventies, we have to believe Rosa isn't gonna be his last victim. So the first thing I'm having Tony Savarese do is check prison records. We're looking for someone who was put away for the last thirty-five years, possibly a serial rapist targeting women who looked like Rosa."

"We're gonna need a photo of her," Nick said.

"I'll send Tony to her mother's house," said Wilkes.

But Claire wasn't having it. "You will not."

Wilkes was dumbfounded; hadn't the shrink just agreed to all his conditions? "Doctor," he said, still deferential, "I can't risk —"

"Rosa's mother deserves to know what happened to her daughter," Claire interrupted. "You might think it's okay to hold back information but I can't let that woman suffer one second more than she has to."

"Telling her is a bad idea, Doc," said Wilkes.

Claire stood her ground. "I know her well. She'll do whatever I ask her to, including keep her mouth shut. I can guarantee it."

Wilkes knew he would lose this round. "I wanna order you not to, but I get the feeling that no matter what I say, you're not gonna listen."

"Not about this," Claire agreed. "I'm going right after we're done here. And I'm taking Nick with me."

This was news to Nick, and Wilkes shot him a harsh glance.

Claire went on. "Don't blame him, Inspector. He didn't know about it until it just came out of my mouth. It's my idea, not his. I want Rosa's mother to know the police are on this. It will help me convince her not to tell anyone."

Wilkes was cursing himself for bringing Claire into the fold but knew it was too late to back out. He didn't have time to find another shrink he could trust to keep their mission a secret. And down deep, he really *did* trust Claire. Involving her was a small risk to take for an investment that could pay big dividends.

"In that case, I won't argue with you, Doc," said Wilkes, standing up.

"We'll work as fast as we can, Inspector," Claire assured him.

Wilkes headed for the door. Nick followed him out and down the hallway, now bustling with people, forcing them to keep their voices low.

"She's a piece of work, Nicky," said Wilkes, exasperated but resigned.

"Yes, she is," replied Nick. "But she won't screw it up."

This Wilkes knew, or at least wanted to believe. "I'll have Tony bring those files to your place this afternoon," the inspector said.

"Thanks, Boss," Nick answered. This was now the third time Wilkes had resurrected his career. "For dealing me back in. Again."

Wilkes pressed the button for the elevator. "We're using you, Nicky, because we need to keep the lid on this, and because right now you're the Invisible Man. Hopefully the third time's the charm, right?"

The elevator doors opened and he stepped in. He turned to face Nick and gestured down the hallway toward Claire. "Keep her in check."

"I will," Nick said as the doors closed on his patron saint.

The door to the apartment opened, revealing Maria Lopez, much different from the cheery woman Claire had visited two days earlier. Maria had dark circles under her eyes, red from hours of crying. She looked first at Claire, then at Nick, and knew something bad was about to happen. Nick wasn't sure if Maria recognized him from all the press of last year's case or because she knew what his presence here meant.

"Maria," Claire said, taking her hand. "Are the children home?"

"No, they're at school," Maria said, making a visible effort to control her emotions. "Please, come in."

After they entered and she had closed the door, she turned to Nick. "You are the police, no?"

"Yes, ma'am," Nick said. "Detective Lawler."

Maria's eyes met Claire's, the sorrow behind them confirming her worst fears. "Oh, no," she cried, looking back at Nick. "Was it an accident?" she asked, not even wanting to say the word.

"I'm afraid not," he answered. "We're going to do everything we can to find the person who did this. . . ."

His voice trailed off as Maria sobbed, with such force that Nick held her lest she collapse onto the floor. With Claire's help, he led Maria to the living room sofa. Nick cleared a toy dump truck and a stuffed bear away so Claire could sit down with Maria. She held the grieving woman and stroked her hair as if Maria, a grandmother, was a little girl.

"I'm so sorry, Maria," Claire said as Nick lowered himself into a nearby chair. He'd made many death notifications over the course of his career; Maria's explosive sorrow was nothing new to him. Of the hundreds of murders he'd investigated, something bumped for him about Rosa Sanchez's. Something he couldn't put his finger on just yet.

Maria's sobs grew quiet, and after a few minutes she composed herself. "Please forgive me," she said, sniffling.

"No need to apologize," Nick said. "We're terribly sorry for your loss."

Maria wiped her eyes with a tissue. "Where should the funeral director go to pick my Rosa up?"

Claire began the conversation she'd dreaded since learning about her patient's murder. "Rosa's remains are at the medical examiner's office," she told Maria. "But you can't send anyone for her yet."

"I want to know what you mean by her 'remains,'" Maria said, knowing Claire was trying to spare her the details. But she wasn't having it.

"I'm not sure that's a good idea right now," Claire answered, struggling to maintain eye contact with Maria.

But the grieving woman was steadfast. "No, it has to be now," Maria said. "I have to know."

"I understand," Claire said, determined to abbreviate the story as much as possible. "We believe Rosa was kidnapped after she left my office the other day. When you gave me permission to track her cell phone, we traced it to some woods on Staten Island where we found evidence she was killed. And all we were able to recover were her bones."

That she neglected to tell Maria that Rosa's bones were discovered in the Bronx was part of the plan she and Nick had discussed before coming here. The fewer people who knew this detail, the better.

"Just her bones?" Maria asked, sounding like the breath had been knocked out of her. "Nothing else?"

"No," Claire said, wishing she could absorb some of Maria's pain. Maria sat staring into space. Claire wondered what horrible scenarios Maria was conjuring in her mind to explain what had happened to her daughter. After a minute, Maria blinked, like someone coming out of a trance. "If they're just bones, how can you be sure they're Rosa's?" she asked.

Claire explained to Maria how they matched an X-ray of the fracture Rosa sustained during the sexual assault in jail to the X-ray of the bone.

Maria's face turned to stone, taking in all the information.

She's shutting off her feelings. I can certainly understand that, Claire thought.

When Claire was finished, Maria looked up at her and Nick. "You said I can't put my baby to rest yet," Maria said, "and I need to know why."

Nick spoke before Claire could. "I know this will be very hard for you. But the longer nobody knows that Rosa is a victim, the better chance we have of catching the man who killed her."

"Someone who would do something so horrible is not a man, but a demon," Maria said with a bitterness that Claire and Nick had not heard before.

"You're absolutely right," Nick agreed. "And that's why we need you to keep what we've just told you to yourself. You can't even tell your grandchildren. And now I'll tell you why you can't bury Rosa yet," he said, launching briefly into the story of the two homicides from 1977. "We need to catch this demon before he hurts another woman. If he knows we're on his trail, he may leave the area."

Maria wiped away fresh tears. "Yes, I understand," she said. "I'll do whatever you say if it will bring me and my family justice for Rosa."

Claire and Nick got up and Claire embraced Maria. "You have my number. If there's anything you need, even if it's just a shoulder to cry on, call me and I'll come right over."

"Thank you," Maria said, "thank you for finding my little girl."

"It's okay, Cisco," Jill Lawler shouted to the dog barking behind the closed door of Nick's bedroom. She hurried to the entrance of their apartment, wondering what Claire was doing there so early. Just an hour before, her father had taken a phone call and left, saying that he had to meet someone. He said he'd be back in a few hours, before Claire showed up, but if for some reason he was late, Jill and her younger sister, Katie, shouldn't wait for him to have dinner.

Jill was surprised when she opened the door to find Claire holding several bags of groceries. "What's all this?" she asked as she took one of the sacks from Claire.

"Dinner," Claire answered, reshuffling the remaining two bags in her arms and laughing at her own clumsiness.

Jill led Claire into the small but workable galley kitchen that, like those in most rent-controlled apartments, hadn't been updated since the 1960s save for new appliances. The Formica countertops were in bad need of replacement and the wood cabinets had at least two coats of paint on them. There was a small table in one corner big enough for four people. Though only three had dined there for most of the last year, it would come in handy tonight.

"Dad said you weren't coming until after dinner," Jill said.

"He's not here?"

"He left a little while ago."

Claire glanced in the direction of the barking. "Without the dog?"

"He got a phone call and left. Said he'd be back before the sun went down."

Claire wondered where Nick had to go so suddenly but covered her concern. "Then he'll come back to a nice meal."

They unloaded the bags onto the table. "You don't have to do this, you know," Jill said, the adult in her rising to the surface. "I can handle it."

Claire was ready for this resistance. "I know you can," she said, "but tonight you get to take a break. And besides, it's been a long time since I had anyone to cook for."

Jill was about to reply when eleven-year-old Katie ran in, excited, wearing pink sweatpants and a yellow T-shirt, her auburn hair a mess. "What's going on?"

"Doctor Waters is making us dinner," Jill said, sounding more like a mother than a big sister.

"Please, both of you. Call me Claire."

"Dad may not like that," said Katie. "He says we should call adults *mister* or *missus*. Or *doctor*, I guess."

"I'll tell him that in my case, it's okay. It makes me feel more comfortable."

Katie eyed all the food being taken out of the bags. "What are we having?" she asked.

"Do you like chicken?" Claire asked.

"The dark meat grosses me out," Katie said. "But I like white meat."

"Well, then you're in luck, because I only brought white meat. I'm going to sauté it in a Dijon and garlic sauce. Do you know what haricots verts are?"

"Dad says that's a stupid name for green beans."

"Actually, it's French," Claire said with a chuckle. "I'm also going to make potatoes au gratin and a salad. How's that sound?"

"Better than what Jill makes us," Katie said, turning to her sister for a reaction that didn't come. Katie turned back to Claire. "Can I help?"

"You have homework," Jill said.

"You have homework too," said Katie, mimicking her older sister.

"Tell you what," Claire said. "Katie, you go do your homework and Jill will help me prepare everything. Then, when you're ready, Jill can do her homework and you can help me cook. Make sense?"

The gentle but firm authority got both girls' attention. "Sounds like a plan," Katie said. The girl raced out of the kitchen so fast that Claire and Jill could only laugh.

"You made that look so easy," Jill said.

"She's cute," Claire responded.

"She never does anything that easily when I tell her to," said Jill.

A pang of emotion hit Claire. "Katie's lucky to have you," she said, wishing she'd had someone like Jill, an older sister she could have turned to.

If Jill detected any of this she kept it to herself. "I can wash off the chicken breasts," she volunteered.

"Great, and I'll start on the potatoes," offered Claire, removing the spuds from a bag while watching Jill out of the corner of her eye take the chicken from its wrapper and expertly wash it. Clearly she'd done the same task dozens of times since the deaths of her mother and grandmother. Claire looked away, the emotion stirring inside her, wanting to mourn Jill's lost childhood.

"Are you okay?" Jill asked, after the kitchen had become quiet.

Claire realized she was just standing there with a potato in her hand. "Sorry, I was just thinking about something I have to do," she said, moving toward the sink where Jill stood.

They were standing beside each other, doing their separate tasks, yet somehow together. It seemed almost normal to Claire, comfortable, and she wasn't sure why.

"I know how that feels," Jill said, placing another chicken breast in a metal bowl. "Sometimes I daydream too."

Claire saw an opening. "You've got a lot on your plate these days," she said.

"I guess," Jill replied, trying to make light of it. "I never realized how much there was to do around here until Grandma got sick."

"You must miss her."

Jill stopped what she was doing, looking like she was about to cry. Claire was sorry she made the comment. But only a few seconds passed before the teenager resumed washing the chicken. Claire realized that this young woman was so much like her, especially when times got tough and the only way to survive was to bury your emotions and plow through.

And then, to Claire's surprise, Jill opened up, as if the water running on her hands was in some way therapeutic. "Yeah, I really do miss her."

"You were close," Claire offered, as she sliced the potatoes on a cutting board atop the counter to the left of the sink.

"We talked a lot. You know, about guys, the bitchy girls at school, stuff like that. It really helped after Mom . . . well, you know."

"I know," Claire said, trying not to revert into therapist mode, though clearly Jill could use one. "I'm sorry that happened to you," she said.

"I wasn't talking about when Mom killed herself," Jill replied so casually it almost seemed not to hurt. Not once since the discussion began had Jill turned away from the sink and directly faced Claire. "I mean like a year before, when she checked out mentally."

Claire realized that the girl's mother emotionally abandoned her long before she committed suicide. Claire put down her peeling knife and reached around Jill to shut off the water.

"What are you doing?" Jill asked.

Claire resisted every impulse to mother Jill, to take her in her arms and tell her it was all going to be okay. But Claire wasn't her mother. How could she or anyone else make that kind of guarantee?

What she could do, though, was give Jill a break from trying to be a mother to her own sister. "Why don't you let me finish?" Claire offered.

Jill looked at her blankly. "But you said—"

"When was the last time anyone cooked for you?" asked Claire. "I never get to make dinner for anyone. Let me do this. You get your homework done and then you can relax," she suggested.

But Jill seemed eager for the company. "Nah, I can do it later," Jill said. Claire could feel how starved the girl was for someone to talk to. She backed away, giving Jill enough room to turn around so they wouldn't be in each other's faces.

"I think it's great how you stepped up after all you've been through," said Claire. "And I know you want to take care of your dad and your sister. But you need to let yourself be taken care of too."

Jill dropped the piece of chicken in her hand. Still facing the sink, she could no longer control the pent-up emotion she'd held inside for so long. She cried silently, her shoulders moving up and down, half hoping Claire wouldn't notice, half hoping she would. Spasms of sorrow wracked the girl's body.

Claire moved up behind her and put her right hand on Jill's shoulder, then her left hand on the other. Jill reached up and grabbed both of Claire's hands, pulling them down so they'd wrap around her waist.

"I'm sorry," Jill uttered between sobs.

"It's okay," said Claire, her voice soothing. "You're allowed to cry. Let it out."

"It's just that I feel . . ." Jill said, unable to finish.

"Like you're all alone," Claire whispered in her ear.

"Yeah," Jill said. She turned around, facing Claire, putting her head on Claire's shoulder.

"Nobody knows what you have to deal with," Claire continued. "You don't want to burden anyone, especially your father and your sister. You want to be strong for them like your grandmother was and your mother couldn't be. And inside, you don't know where Jill went, what happened to her. Who she is."

"How do you know?" Jill asked, then laughed through her tears. "That was stupid," she said. "You're a psychiatrist."

"It wasn't stupid," Claire assured her, taking the teenager's hands in hers. "I know because I've been there. I look at you and I see myself. You've been through more pain than any fourteen-year-old should ever have to go through. Pretending it doesn't bother you just makes it worse."

"You've been through pain too. Dad told me what happened to you when you were a kid—how your best friend was kidnapped."

This surprised Claire, but she wasn't going to stop. "Yes, I've had some tough times, but I'm more than twice your age so I can handle it better," she said. "I want you to let me help you too."

"You mean, like a shrink?" Jill asked.

Claire laughed. "No, like a friend," she said. "Before I leave tonight, I'm giving you my cell phone number. Whenever you feel like you're about to explode, or if you just want to talk, or laugh, or cry, call me."

"Okay," Jill agreed.

Claire wasn't satisfied she'd convinced her of her sincerity. "I want to make sure you know this isn't an order or anything. If I'm stepping over the line you can tell me. In fact, you can tell me anything and I won't tell a soul."

"Not even my father?" asked Jill.

"Definitely not him," Claire assured her.

"No wonder my ears were burning," came Nick's voice from the kitchen door. Claire and Jill were so engaged in their conversation that they hadn't heard him come into the apartment and walk down the hallway. "Quite a feast you're cooking up here," he said, eyeing the chicken breasts, potatoes, and vegetables spread out on the table.

"Hi, Dad," Jill said as she went over to hug him.

He saw her red eyes. "Everything okay, sweetie?" he asked, kissing her on the head.

"Yeah, I'm fine," said Jill, enjoying her father's embrace. It made Claire think of her own father, and how safe his new presence in her life made her feel.

"You didn't reveal any family secrets, did you?" Nick asked his daughter, joking, but wondering what they had talked about.

Claire smiled. "Just a little girl talk," she said, exchanging a knowing look with Jill as Katie rushed in. "Homework done," she exclaimed, embracing her father.

Nick laughed. "What's all the excitement?" he asked.

"Claire made me a deal," Katie told her father. "I finish my homework and I can help her."

Nick's eyebrows went up. "You mean 'Doctor Waters,' don't you?"

"I told her it's okay," Claire assured him, bailing Katie out. "C'mon," she said to the tween, "let's get this dinner cooked and on the table."

Ninety minutes later, after Claire had made good on her promise to help Katie with her homework, the girls were in their rooms getting ready for bed. The low hum of an air conditioner and the snores of Cisco, lying at Nick's feet, created a homey background in the den, where Nick and Claire pored over the files from the two 1977 murder cases. Though the sun's final rays were fighting through a layer of city grime on the windows, you'd never know it was getting dark outside, as Nick had turned on enough lights in the room to perform surgery.

"I should put on my sunglasses," said Claire, half joking.

"Sorry," answered Nick. "Cisco helps me with a lot at night but reading isn't one of his stronger skills."

"You weren't kidding when you said there's not much here," Claire said, frustrated. "It doesn't look like the detectives back then even tried to find out who these two Jane Does were. I checked the

Internet last night and I couldn't find a newspaper article on either case."

"I know," said Nick as he lowered Rosa's medical file, which Claire had copied and smuggled out of the hospital. "And you don't get it 'cause you weren't even born yet. But it was all about Son of Sam back then. I was eight and I'll never forget it. David Berkowitz had the whole Tristate scared shitless. Nobody knew where or when the lunatic was gonna hit next. He terrorized the city for a whole year. The bones were found in Brooklyn the day after his last murder. Those cases were put on the back burner. End of story."

"I can see why," Claire said, reading from a medical examiner's report on the bones recovered from Canarsie. " 'No witnesses, no women reported missing. No evidence found except for bones.' Not a lot for the detectives to go on back then." She placed the two old case files on the floor beside her chair. "About the only useful piece of information in the ME's reports is that whoever chopped these women up did it with the skill of someone who knew anatomy."

"You mean, like a butcher or a surgeon."

"Yeah. And he didn't bother to remove all the muscle or cartilage back then."

"Probably because he didn't have to worry they'd be identified through DNA," Nick said.

Claire glanced over at the thin file in Nick's lap, containing the precious little they had on Rosa's murder. "Give me whatever you're not looking at," she said.

Nick passed it to her. "I've already been through it," he said.

"Good, than I can get up to speed."

She opened the red file, which contained photographs, vouchers for the evidence gathered out in the Staten Island woods, and one police report that Claire was about to read when Nick waved her off.

"Don't waste your time," Nick said. "All it says is that two garbage men found the bones when they dumped a trash receptacle into their truck."

But Claire's eyes grew wide with realization. "Oh my God," she gasped.

"What is it?" asked Nick, wondering what he could have missed.

Claire pointed to the report. "Did you talk to this man?" she asked, standing as she handed the report back to him and indicating a name on the paper. "Or say anything to him about whom the bones might belong to?"

"I didn't talk to either of the sanitation guys. The patrol cops got their statements," he answered. "Why's this guy so interesting?"

"Because," said Claire, "Franco Sanchez is Rosa's ex-husband."

Nick was stunned. "That couldn't be a coincidence."

"What did he look like?" Claire asked.

Nick gave her a brief description.

"That's him for sure," Claire confirmed.

Nick put the report on the battered mahogany coffee table in front of him and looked at her in amazement. "In any other case my first thought would be he's our best suspect."

"But you know he can't be," Claire said, on the same page with Nick, "because Franco would have either had to plant Rosa's bones in the trash can before he went to work, or carry them with him in the truck and throw them into the hopper right before his partner found them."

"And if Franco killed Rosa, he'd have to be a schmuck to set himself up to find his dead wife's bones, after going to all the trouble to make sure there was no evidence."

They looked at each other, both already having arrived at the only scenario that did make sense.

"Whoever this whacko is, he wanted her ex to find those bones," Nick said.

Claire barely could believe it herself. "That means he stalked Franco so he'd know *exactly* which trash can to dump the bones in."

She sank back into the sofa as she reached into Rosa's file, took out a large stack of photos, and flipped through them.

"It would explain why the bastard went all the way to the Bronx from Staten Island to dump her remains," continued Nick, picking up Claire's last thought as she gazed at the photos, a gallery of detritus from the garbage can. "What I don't understand is, why *that* particular can? There must be dozens of 'em in more secluded spots on Franco's route. Instead, this whackadoo chooses one in a 'hood with a ton of foot traffic and NYPD surveillance cameras all over the place."

"What is this?" Claire interrupted, showing him a photo of a discarded banana peel.

Nick laughed for the first time. "CSU got a little overzealous with the contents of the garbage can. Vouchered and photographed everything in the hopper of the sanitation truck they thought might've come out of it. Did you hear a word I said?"

"Every one," Claire answered, again going through the photos. "Can we get the video from those cameras?"

"Tony Savarese is working on it," Nick assured her, "and he'll make us copies. But unfortunately none of the cameras nearby were pointed in the direction of the trash can." Nick watched Claire thumb through the photos. "Why are you bothering to look through those pictures again?"

"Because they're here," Claire said, "and we don't have anything else to do."

"Then pass me a bunch," Nick said, "and let's get this over with so it doesn't take all night."

Claire gave him the bottom half of the stack and kept going. "CSU must have spent all night taking pictures of this shit," she said.

Her profanity made him look up from the photos at her. "Now, Doctor, you've been hanging around us foul-mouthed cops too long."

"I'm tired," Claire said. "Give me a break."

The hint of a grin appeared on Nick's face as he glanced up from a photo of an empty pack of cigarettes. "I used to sift through peoples' garbage all the time looking for evidence. Next to guarding dead bodies I think it's the most disgusting job a cop has to do."

"But you must find interesting stuff," Claire said.

"Sometimes, but mostly it's crap like this," Nick replied, holding up a shot of an empty milk carton. He held up the next photo, of an uncrumpled receipt. "And this," he said.

Claire leaned forward, as if struggling to see something on the receipt.

"It's from some bodega," Nick said.

"And somebody wrote something on top."

Nick looked at the handwritten words. "*Emigrant hasta?*" he read.

"What's that mean?" Claire asked, squinting.

"Who cares?" Nick shot back, flipping past more photos. "This is a waste of time," he grumbled. "Tomorrow I'll goose Savarese to get us the surveillance video. Maybe we'll get lucky and spot whoever dumped the bones."

"Let me see that photo again," Claire said.

Nick looked up from the pictures to see Claire staring at a photo in her hand. "Which one?"

"The receipt," she answered.

"Wait a minute," said Nick. "What are you looking at?"

Claire handed him the photo, putting the others down on the table and picking up the Rosa file. Nick eyed the photo, squinting, aiming it at the lamp behind him so he could see more clearly. He was looking at a paper coffee cup with the name El Primero Deli & Restaurant and its address—Jerome Avenue in the Bronx—stamped across the front.

"What about it?" he asked.

"Rosa wasn't a random victim. Whoever killed her stalked her first," said Claire.

"And you got that from a coffee cup?" Nick asked, bewildered.

"She had to inform Probation of any jobs she had. She was working there part time. I think one of her uncles owns it. That receipt is from the same place," she said.

She handed both photos to Nick, who stared at them like a winning lottery ticket. "Whoever this guy is, he's sloppy. First he forgets to turn off Rosa's phone, so we're able to track her movements to Staten Island. Then he dumps her bones in one of the busiest neighborhoods in the Bronx where her ex-husband the garbage man will find them. And if that's not enough, he leaves evidence that could help us identify her."

"If we hadn't ID'd her already," Claire said. "None of this was a mistake."

"How the hell do you know *that*?" asked Nick.

"Because someone who boils bones to remove all the meat is too meticulous to make mistakes. Whoever murdered Rosa left all this evidence for a reason."

"I'm lost," Nick admitted. "Why go to all that trouble to make a victim unidentifiable and then leave us a road map to her identity?"

"That's exactly what he's doing," Claire said. "I don't know why. But I can feel it."

She held up the photo of the deli receipt and pointed to the handwritten words at the top. "And when we find out what *emigrant hasta* means—*if* we find out—I'm pretty sure we'll know what Rosa's murder is all about."

CHAPTER 11

Deputy Inspector Wilkes paced his office the next morning, straightening up the items the cleaning crew had disturbed the night before. Though he liked things neat, order was the last thing on his mind right now. He was doing it because it beat sitting behind his desk and staring at the phone, waiting for it to ring.

It was now two days since Rosa Sanchez's bones had turned up in the Bronx. Nick Lawler's phone call to him at two a.m. this morning hadn't helped his perpetual insomnia. Nick had asked him permission to deliver a coffee cup and receipt found in the garbage can with Rosa's bones to the ME's office to test for DNA. Wilkes, dead tired at the time, said yes, not bothering to ask why before hanging up and turning over to go back to sleep.

Until his racing mind got the better of him and kept him up for the next four hours. He'd tried calling Nick back but the phone had gone straight to voice mail three times, frustrating Wilkes to no end. There were plenty of things he despised about being a cop. Not being able to reach a subordinate was near the top of that list.

At six a.m., Wilkes woke up Tony Savarese, ordering him to drive to the crime lab in Jamaica, Queens, some forty miles from his home out on Long Island, to retrieve the evidence, deliver it to Assistant Medical Examiner Ross, and wait there the few hours it would take the ME's DNA lab to recover and process the cells on the lip of the coffee cup for DNA. Best case scenario: Tony'd walk out of the chop shop with the identity of whoever used the cup.

He should be so lucky, Wilkes thought as he straightened a framed photo on the wall. Savarese hadn't called in yet. Now he wished he'd grilled Nick about the evidence, hoping his protégé wasn't going off half cocked. With each passing day more people were being added to the investigation, which always meant more chance of a leak. Make no mistake, he was grateful to Nick and Claire for coming up with their findings so quickly. But Wilkes knew if a word of this wound up in the media, his head was where the blame would land.

Always the political animal, Wilkes kept Chief of Detectives Dolan in the loop on every move, including this latest one. The chief had already called for an update that morning, asking whether the DNA had come back and what else, if anything, Nick and Claire had uncovered. During that call, Wilkes had grown some balls, "suggesting" to the chief that banning the duo from One Police Plaza had been, in hindsight, a bullshit move. After all, Nick worked in the building, and Doctor Waters could be there for any number of reasons easy enough to explain to a scoop-hungry reporter. The chief agreed, and Wilkes wasted no time summoning Nick and Claire to headquarters this morning.

As he straightened the coffee table in front of his beat-up nineties-era mint green sofa, he was staring at his phone. Where the hell were they?

He was just about to call Nick again when movement through the windows separating his office from the squad room caught his eye. The pair entered—with Tony Savarese. They all looked serious.

"I take it you're not coming from home," he said to Claire and Nick as they entered with Savarese, who closed the door.

"We met Tony at the ME's office," Nick informed him.

"Without my authorization?" said Wilkes, more exhausted than annoyed as he sat behind his desk.

Nick leaned against the sill of the window, the Brooklyn Bridge behind him. "You authorized me to talk to Ross, so I thought it wouldn't make a difference."

Wilkes realized it didn't matter and dropped the issue. "Tell me there was DNA on that cup," he said.

"There was, Boss," Savarese replied. "But there's a problem."

Claire, opposite Nick, spoke up before Wilkes could utter a word. "There wasn't enough of a sample for a hundred-percent match to anyone in the database."

"Shit," Wilkes said, closing his eyes and letting out a breath. "So now what?"

"We asked the lab to run the sample for a partial match," Claire continued, "so we could sort through whoever comes up in the database and see if they fit the profile."

"And how many thousands of people would that be?" Wilkes asked.

"Three," answered Nick.

"Three-*thousand*?"

"Three people," Nick replied, cracking a grin. "One of 'em's doing life in Dannemora for murder," Nick continued. "Another was paroled two years ago. He's wheelchair bound with multiple sclerosis. But we may have hit pay dirt with number three."

Savarese handed Wilkes the folder he was carrying, which the inspector opened. "His name's Jonah Welch," said Savarese. "Did a bid at Greenhaven for a home invasion in Sheepshead Bay. He raped the resident at gunpoint and beat the holy hell out of her."

"When?" demanded Wilkes.

"September of seventy-seven," Nick answered. "A little more than a month *after* the first two sets of bones turned up."

Wilkes perused Welch's mug shot, a photo of a handsome, dark-haired man in his twenties. "When'd this guy get paroled?"

"Ninety-seven," said Nick.

"So he's been out seventeen years." He turned to Claire. "Okay, Doc, why'd he wait so long to butcher Rosa Sanchez?"

"He wouldn't be the first," Claire reminded him. "The Grim Sleeper killer in California took his time between murders. If Welch is our guy, maybe he cooled off in prison and something happened recently that stoked his fire."

"Once a psychopath always a psychopath," Wilkes observed.

Nick leaned over the front of Wilkes's desk, reached into the folder, and pulled out a freeze-frame photo. "This was taken by security cameras at the deli where Rosa worked part time, two days before she disappeared. We confirmed with her uncle who owns the joint that she was working the register when this guy came in."

It was an enhanced, zoomed-in shot of an older guy, his hair streaked with silver. "Welch would be in his late fifties by now," said Savarese.

Wilkes put the mug shot beside the surveillance photo. "Yeah, he looks like shit but two decades in prison'll do that to you. He's the same guy."

"We need to pick him up," said Nick, "before he fillets another woman."

"*We* aren't going anywhere," Wilkes answered.

"Boss—"

"Don't *boss* me, Nick. You know better than to even ask. We're gonna do this right—with an arrest warrant and Emergency Services backing us up at two in the morning when the bastard's out cold and you can't see a goddamned thing. And even if we were gonna bust him at high noon I'm not crazy enough to send an unarmed man after a guy with a history of gunplay."

"I don't think you've made your case," retorted Nick in the wise-ass tone that signaled to Wilkes he wasn't going to argue the point any further.

"Okay, where does this guy live?" asked Wilkes.

"Bay Ridge," Nick answered.

"Take Simms, Frost, and Lynch," Wilkes ordered Savarese. "Get a couple of surveillance vehicles from Narcotics, go out to Brooklyn, and sit on this guy's place. I want him at night but if he tries to split before then, we'll take him any way we have to."

"Got it, Boss," said Savarese, who walked out of the office. Nick and Claire were about to follow when Wilkes stopped them. "I'm not done with you two yet."

"Do you need us for something else, Inspector?" asked Claire.

"Damn right I do," Wilkes said, looking into Nick's eyes, imagining what his former star detective was feeling. "I'm not cutting you out of this, Nicky. When the team brings this scumbag in you're gonna do the interrogation."

"I appreciate that, Boss," he said.

"Doc, you're in this too," the inspector said to Claire as he rose from his chair. "Both of you go over Welch's record. Come up with a strategy for Nick to use when he sweats this scumbag."

Nick couldn't help but think something was off as Wilkes walked around his desk, rubbing his palms on his cuffs and leaving streaks of sweat.

"All we've got on Welch is that surveillance photo from the deli and a partial DNA hit," Wilkes said. "Which means the DA's office will tell us we don't have dick on him. So unless you can get him to give it up, he could walk."

"Dolan okayed me doing this?" Nick asked, smelling a rat.

"He suggested it," Wilkes said, turning away.

Nick now realized who the rat was. "He wants a fall guy. And the blind cop is expendable."

Wilkes spun around, busted. "I'm not gonna lie to you. I owe you more than that," he said. "It's for the wrong reason, but it's still the right move. If anyone can get this sonuvabitch to spill, it's you."

Nick didn't care. If this was the price for getting back into the game, he was willing to pay it.

"Don't worry," Nick said. "I will."

"I don't get it," Claire said, without looking up from the piece of paper she was reading. It was after midnight and they were sitting alone in the Major Case Squad's windowless, utilitarian conference room on ugly metal chairs. The matching table, equally hideous, was littered with take-out cartons, paper plates, and coffee cups along with piles of papers and the red files. Nick sat at the head, Claire next to him on the right, unable to hold her tongue any longer.

"Get what?" he asked, putting a folder back in one of the cartons.

"How they can treat you like this after all you've done for them. And why you're not upset."

Nick rose from the hard chair in which he'd sat way too long and stretched. "I'm lucky they're letting me do this at all," he replied. "I'd rather be here, however they'll have me, than find something else to do and have to start all over again. Without being able to see."

"They have you over a barrel," said Claire.

"I've been over bigger ones," Nick said, sitting back down and leafing through papers to find a way to end the conversation. "At least this way I'm in control of what happens."

"How do you figure that?"

"I can get Welch to confess."

A yellowed DD-5, the form NYPD detectives used to document every step of every investigation, now caught Claire's attention. "According to this report, Jonah Welch wouldn't answer any questions the detectives asked him back in seventy-seven."

"That's because they had him cold," Nick replied. "Not only was the victim willing to testify, they also brought in a forensic dentist who matched a bite mark on her left breast to Welch's teeth. And his blood type matched the semen they found inside her. Before DNA profiling, that was as solid a case as you could have against a rapist."

But her look told him something was bugging her. "You're not convinced I can get him to spill?" he asked.

"It's not that," said Claire, not quite sure where to start. "Welch was nineteen in seventy-seven, when the two sets of bones were found in Brooklyn. But he didn't commit the rape until 1982."

"Doesn't mean he didn't do other rapes in between that never got reported."

"He's out of prison ten years," Claire answered. "Not once during that time was he even suspected of, or questioned by the police for, a sex crime. And no women disappeared right after his release."

"You're saying he doesn't fit the profile of someone who dismembers women and boils their bones," Nick said.

"I just don't see it," Claire answered. She spread her arms over the table at the sea of files and paper. "There's nothing in any of this to suggest his paraphilia is cutting up women. He never missed a meeting with his parole officer, never left New York State, worked seven days a week at two jobs, and is now fifty-seven years old."

"Two jobs?" asked Nick. "Where'd you see that?"

"On his latest sex offender registration form. He listed *dishwasher* at a lunch place down in the Financial District and *truck driver* for the *New York Ledger*."

"Delivering papers is a night job."

"Which means Welch might not be in his apartment when your team goes to arrest him."

"Or comes home from work, sees our guys waiting, runs, and we never see him again."

Nick pulled out his cell phone, but something stopped him from dialing.

"What is it?" asked Claire.

"Their phones'll be turned off," Nick said. "And their radios'll be tuned to a special band used for operations like this."

"Can you call them on that?" asked Claire.

"I can but I wouldn't. If someone has their radio turned up, I call and Welch is walking by the wrong place at the wrong time, I'd blow the operation. Or, even worse, he's in his apartment and hears a police radio out in his hallway. . . ."

"But we have to warn them," Claire said.

"Yes, we do," Nick said, rising. "Grab your things."

Two unmarked navy blue Dodge Sprinter vans slowly turned the corner off Lincoln Road and cut their lights as if on cue. The neighborhood, on the east side of Prospect Park and once one of Brooklyn's toniest, had fallen into the blight of drugs and crime back in the late seventies. Currently it was seeing the beginnings of the gentrification sweeping across the borough.

The vans stopped across from the Prospect Park subway station on an overpass from which a Q train emerged from underground, heading south to Coney Island, its roar reverberating off the prewar apartment buildings flanking both sides of the tracks.

On the same side of the block, closer to Flatbush Avenue, sat an unmarked Dodge Charger in which Wilkes, riding shotgun, was smiling, his hands raised like a maestro conducting the arrival of the vans and the screeching of the subway, the final movement of the great urban symphony he'd composed. Savarese sat in the back, watching Wilkes, wondering if his boss had finally qualified for a disability pension. Behind the wheel, a handsome, young, black detective named Billy Simms waited for orders.

"You gonna part the Red Sea, Boss?" Savarese said.

"Let me enjoy this flippin' moment, you idiot," Wilkes said. "I forgot the subway came above ground here."

"So what?" asked Savarese.

"Train runs right next to Welch's building," observed Wilkes. "We get everyone in position while the next one passes and he won't hear a goddamned thing."

Savarese checked his watch. "One fifty-eight," he said.

"We good with the super?" Wilkes asked.

"Should be waiting in the lobby right now to let us in. He shut off the elevator to the west side of the building too."

Wilkes opened his door. "Let's move."

*   *   *

The aging blue Chevy Impala sped down Flatbush Avenue, its crappy shocks doing little to cushion the ride over the pothole-ridden street.

"Take it easy," Nick said to Claire, who was driving like a cop, pedal to metal.

"We're running out of time," Claire retorted, dodging a dip in the road.

"We hit something, it's my ass," said Nick.

And indeed it would have been. As his impending blindness was a secret to all but a select few, Nick had grabbed the keys to one of Major Case's unmarked police cars.

He'd carefully driven it out of the garage underneath One PP, past the guard booths, raising no suspicion whatsoever. But he wasn't stupid either. Once far enough away from headquarters, he pulled over and switched places with Claire in a maneuver that would've been comical if they weren't in a hurry.

Still, if caught allowing a civilian to drive a police vehicle, especially at high speeds down city streets, Nick would be suspended at best and summarily fired at worst; the latter scenario being the more likely.

They were tearing south, down the stretch of Flatbush between Grand Army Plaza and the Prospect Park Zoo, approaching the traffic light at Ocean Avenue.

"Where do I go at the light?" Claire shouted.

Nick could just make out the green of the light ahead. "What's the sign say?"

"Eastern Parkway."

"Go right!" Nick exclaimed just in time.

Claire palmed the wheel and the beat-up car responded. She wasn't, however, expecting the immediate curve to the left that followed, and somehow managed not to sideswipe the line of parked cars on the right.

"Whoa!" she gasped, spinning the wheel back left.

"Slow the hell down," Nick commanded. "Lincoln Road's the next light."

"I see it," she said, looking ahead to the light, now turning yellow.

Nick saw it too. "Don't run it," he warned. "When it changes, go left and stop."

Claire brought the car to a stop at the intersection, another car stopping behind her waiting to make the same turn. Movement up Lincoln Road caught her eye.

"We're too late," she said.

"What do you see?" asked Nick.

"Your Emergency Service cops piling out of a van up the street."

Nick thought fast. "Nothing we can do," he said.

"You still want me to make the turn?" asked Claire.

"Yes, but pull into the first empty space you see."

"There's a hydrant about four car lengths up," Claire said, making the turn.

"That'll do. We're not going anywhere," Nick said.

Claire pulled the car into the spot without parallel parking. "We're sticking out," she said.

"It's Brooklyn. Nobody's gonna notice. Cut the engine."

"Now what?"

"We wait," said Nick, "until we see them bring Welch out. If he's there."

Wilkes, wearing his bulletproof vest, brought up the rear as his detail of heavily armed cops entered the ornate but dilapidated metal doors of the behemoth, 1920s-era, brick apartment building. He recoiled at the stench that hit him and the others as the superintendant opened the inner security door.

"Weed smoke and piss," he muttered. "Jesus."

They moved into the vast lobby, once a palace of marble columns and floors, now covered with inexpensive, ugly, filthy, red-and-white ceramic tile that had been badly installed. Ahead of him, also clad in body armor, were Simms, Savarese, and six ESU cops brandishing compact AR-15 assault rifles.

Wilkes could see the super pointing to the right. Wilkes had been in enough places like this to know the building had two separate sides, most likely with one small elevator for each side. He also knew no one in his party would be using an elevator. Tonight would be stairs only.

He followed the team to the right, up a few wide stairs and then left down a hallway, passing the elevator and gathering at the stair-well. It had no door and was wide open, all the way up and one floor down. The sergeant running the ESU detail, Tanner, raised a fisted, gloved hand signaling all to stop. Wilkes saw his chance.

He circumvented the cops in front of him to the head of the line.

"We should wait for the next train," he whispered to Sergeant Tanner.

"There hasn't been one in ten minutes," Tanner shot back. "The longer we sit here, the more risk some insomniac tenant takes his garbage out and spots us. Or your perp. Subway's running off peak now."

Wilkes was about to reconsider when he heard the low rumble he'd hoped for. He head-gestured Tanner. The train grew louder and the sergeant signaled his troops.

They raced up four flights of stairs, reaching the fifth floor in less than a minute and perfectly timed so the train noise was at its peak. Moving single file, they covered the last fifty feet until they were just outside the door to apartment 5H. Tanner readied a flash-bang grenade as one of the ESU cops raised a maul and swung it into the door at the lock, smashing it open.

"Police!" shouted the ESU sergeant, throwing the flash-bang in and closing the door. It went off a second later. Wilkes could hear people moving behind the doors of the other apartments on the floor, sliding locks and chains open.

"Police!" he screamed, his Glock in hand at his side. "Stay in your apartments!" He motioned Savarese and Simms to make sure no one came out. Then he heard voices screaming from inside Welch's apartment:

"Get down on the ground!"

"Face down, now!"

"Show me your hands!"

"No, no!" a female, Hispanic-accented voice cried. "Don't shoot!"

"Shit!" Wilkes exclaimed, knowing that voice didn't belong to Jonah Welch.

"Stand down!" Tanner shouted as Wilkes entered the apartment and saw the cops, their assault rifles already lowered, helping a young man and woman to their feet. The man held a boy Wilkes estimated to be four years old. The kid's frightened, tear-filled eyes met the inspector's. Wilkes, who generally dismissed religion as bullshit for weaklings, thanked God that this family wasn't lying dead in a pool of their own blood because a cop had mistakenly opened fire.

"You're not in any trouble," Wilkes said to the family, though he knew nothing he could say would prevent the media shit storm that was sure to follow. "But I have to ask, does Jonah Welch live here?"

"No, *señor*," said the man. "We've been here *tres años*."

Wilkes turned to Savarese and Simms. "We sure about the address?"

Savarese was scared too, mostly about the tongue lashing about to come from his boss. "Forty-two Lincoln Road, apartment five H," he said. "I checked it myself a dozen times on the computer before I did the warrant application."

"Get the super up here, show him a photo of Welch, and see if the sonuvabitch even lives in the building," Wilkes ordered. "And hope the guy says no, because if he heard us storming in here with our dicks sticking out of our pants, he's long gone and we're screwed."

Claire and Nick sat in the Chevy as patrol cars from the 71st Precinct flew past them toward the building, no doubt drawn there by frantic calls to 911 that a bomb had gone off at 42 Lincoln Road. It was three minutes since they heard the flash-bang. Claire peered through binoculars Nick brought along for her, waiting for the cops to emerge with Jonah Welch in cuffs.

"Nothing yet?" he asked.

"Don't you think I'd tell you?" she retorted. "What is taking so long?"

"They're probably securing the scene," he replied, his voice more calm than he felt. "Give it another minute and I'm sure they'll bring him out."

"What the—?" Claire stammered.

"What do you see?" asked Nick.

"Wilkes just came out with Savarese and Detective Simms."

"And Welch?"

"No. It looks like your boss is ripping them a new one. Maybe we were right and Welch wasn't there."

Nick frowned. "Wilkes wouldn't yell at the guys for that. But he would if *someone* screwed up on the address." He turned to Claire.

"The only screwup would be if Welch gave a bogus address on the sex offender registry."

"Wouldn't be the first time," mused Nick, more disappointed than pissed. "We might as well get back to headquarters before the boss knows we're here. Make a U-turn and go back the way we came."

Claire sat, staring straight ahead.

"You okay?" Nick asked.

"I wanted to see Welch in cuffs," Claire answered, turning the key and starting the Chevy. She was about to switch on the headlights when her eye caught a figure emerging from below the sidewalk and striding just a bit too quickly in their direction.

Nick sensed her hesitation. "What's wrong?"

"Someone just came out of the building's basement."

"Going where?"

"He's about to pass the car on your side."

"All I see are shadows," said Nick, "but is the guy hunched over?"

Sure enough, Claire now saw that the figure was wearing a base-ball cap and had his head down. A chill ran through her.

"It's Welch," she said to Nick.

"Are you sure?" he asked.

"I can see enough of his face to tell."

"Take out your phone and call nine-one-one," Nick said.

Claire was already opening the car door when Nick grabbed her arm. "Don't even think about it."

"I have to!" she said, and realized she said it too loud because Welch swung his head in her direction.

He was standing in the glow of a streetlamp, and Claire could see that the man was indeed Jonah Welch. He froze, perhaps trying to figure out whether she was a cop, whether she recognized him, whether the Chevy was too beat-up to be an unmarked cop car. Maybe all of the above. Then he bolted.

"He's running!" Claire yelled, starting the engine, gunning the car into a U-turn.

"Where's he going?" Nick asked, wishing he could see well enough to drive.

"Around the corner," Claire said, spinning the wheel to the left. The car was going so fast that the tires on the right side almost left the ground.

"It's a piece of crap!" Nick yelled. "Do that again and you'll roll it!"

Fortunately, Welch wasn't in good shape. Out of breath, he slowed down on the park side of Ocean Avenue, and Claire zoomed past him.

"I'm gonna cut him off!" she said, slowing down just enough, then making a sharp right between two parked cars onto the sidewalk. The car screeched to a stop and Nick could see a shadow he knew to be Welch running toward them. He jumped out, and Welch tried to run around Nick. But even with his limited vision Nick could see well enough to dive on him and bring him to the ground.

"Get off me!" Welch screamed.

"Jonah Welch, you're under arrest," Nick said, subduing the man and cuffing him.

"What the hell for?"

"Lying about your address as a registered sex offender," Nick said, dragging Welch to his feet, then bending him over the hood of the car to search him as Wilkes's unmarked Dodge raced up.

"Nick," Claire said, gesturing to the inspector getting out of his car.

"I see him," Nick said, not caring, feeling like a cop again. Wilkes could fire him right there and he wouldn't give a shit. At least he'd go out on top.

"What are you two doing here?" Wilkes asked.

"We got him," Nick said, pushing Welch toward his boss as if giving him a prize.

Wilkes, resisting the urge to take out his gun and shoot Nick and Claire, allowed a smile to cross his face. The sight of Nick Lawler, Night-Blind Detective, turning over a perp in cuffs, was so ridiculous that for once, he was speechless.

"What's the matter, Boss?" asked Nick. Wilkes's smile scared him.

"Nothing," Wilkes replied. "Nice collar, Nicky."

Chapter 12

Jonah Welch squirmed, trying to make himself comfortable in the government-issued metal chair. But there was no comfort to be found in the claustrophobic, beige gray cinderblock interview room where, as far as he was concerned, he'd already been held for too long. He rattled the cuffs attaching him to the metal table and pounded his free fist on it. The sound reverberated through speakers into the adjoining room where Claire and Nick watched his frustration on a monitor.

"He's getting jumpy," observed Claire.

"That's just how we want him," said Nick, turning down the volume. "Usually we'll put some perp in there, leave 'em for a while, and when we're ready to talk to them, they're snoring."

"You sure *you're* ready for this?" Claire asked.

"Yeah," he said. It was after four in the morning, nearly twenty-four hours since he slept. On top of that, arresting Welch was the first physical police work he'd done in a year. He couldn't remember feeling more pumped. "I'm fine."

She grinned. "That's the adrenaline talking."

"Let's hope it lasts," said Nick, tapping the folder in his left hand and heading toward the door into the room where Welch sat.

"Good luck," said Claire.

"I'll need it," he replied, opening the door and disappearing inside.

Claire turned her head toward the monitor and dialed up the volume in time to see Nick close the door to the interview room.

* * *

Welch looked up. "About time," he growled. "Now are you gonna tell me what I'm doing here?"

Nick pulled out the metal chair across from Welch and sat down, placing the folder on the table. "I already did. You lied about your address on the sex offender registry."

"Bullshit. You don't send cops with machine guns for that."

"We do when the perp's record says they were collared with one."

"That was thirty-five years ago. I haven't touched a gun since. And if I wrote down the wrong address by accident, so what?"

"It wasn't an accident, Jonah," Nick said. "Guy does that, it tells me he's hiding. Phony address buys you time to split if the cops get too close."

A bitter smile crossed Welch's face. "You wanna know the truth? Okay. I did it because it's none of anyone's goddamned business where I live."

"You're right. Screw the people in Albany who make the laws. You drive a ninety-eight Ford Crown Vic. Where is it?"

"That's none of your goddamned business either."

"Jonah, if you're as innocent as you say you are—"

Welch straightened up in his seat with his version of righteous indignation. "This is the United States of America. I have a right to my privacy."

"You gave up that right when the jury found you guilty of raping that girl."

"And I paid my debt. I didn't cause no trouble in prison. Never missed a meeting with my parole officer after I got out, haven't been without a job in ten years. I'm being a good boy, and you know why? Because I made a stupid mistake when I was twenty-four and paid for it with two decades of my life. I swore after the first ten years inside that if I made it out of Greenhaven with my life and a virgin asshole, I'd be a saint for whatever time I have left. I don't ever wanna go back."

Nick sat back in his chair and took a breath, as if emotionally stirred by Welch's speech. Then he burst into applause, stomped his feet. "Whoo-hoo! Bravo!" he yelled.

This, of course, shocked Welch and sucked away whatever mojo he had left. "Stop it! Shut the hell up!" he pleaded.

"No, really," Nick said, still clapping. "Were you in the prison drama club?"

Welch looked like he was about to cry. "Why do you have to torture me?"

It was the perfect opening. Nick removed photos from the folder and slapped them onto the table.

Bam. Bam. Bam.

"You know all about torture, don't you, Jonah," he said as fact.

Welch looked at the pictures—three skeletons laid out on metal slabs in the ME's office—and backed away as if they repulsed him. "What the hell are those?"

"Not only do you know what they are, you know *who* they are," Nick said. "And we're not leaving this room until you tell me."

"I don't know what you're talking about," Welch said, shaking uncontrollably.

"That's right, Jonah, you got plenty to be scared of," Nick pressed. "You kill someone, it's gonna catch up with you sooner or later."

"I swear, I never killed anyone in my miserable life," Welch stammered.

"Let me refresh your sick memory," Nick said, tapping his finger hard on the first two photos. "You murdered these two back in seventy-seven, boiled their bones to get the meat off them, and then buried them two blocks away from each other."

"Did you say I boiled . . . Are you crazy?" Welch cried.

"That girl you raped in eighty-two was lucky you got interrupted in the act," Nick continued, "or she would've been number three. And I'm sure you tried to suppress the urge when they let you out of prison ten years ago." He tapped the photo of Rosa's bones. "But when you saw her, you knew she was the one."

"You're insane!" Welch screamed. "I wouldn't even know how to do what you say I did!"

Nick bolted from his chair—mostly for effect—causing Welch to move back so fast the chain bolting him to the table went taut. "Don't hurt me," he whimpered.

"That would be too easy," said Nick as he reached for a television monitor hanging from the wall on a movable arm and pulled it toward the table. "Instead I'm gonna show you how you blew it."

He picked up a remote off another table beside the wall and switched on the monitor. Up came a frozen piece of video. "Look familiar?" Nick asked.

"What is this?" demanded Welch.

"Keep watching," said Nick, pressing the Play button. It was the surveillance video from the Hispanic deli in the Bronx. As soon as it started Welch saw himself come through the front door. He jumped up from his chair.

"I guess you remember now," said Nick.

"What does that have to do with anything?" Welch screamed.

Nick pointed to the screen as Rosa served him. "That girl's your latest victim, you sick bastard," he said.

"Because I walked into a deli?"

Nick laughed. "Pal, you wish that's all we had on you." He feigned excitement. "You haven't seen the best part yet."

Welch looked ready to spontaneously combust as, on screen, Rosa handed him his cup of coffee and the receipt. Nick paused the video. "See that cup?"

"So what?"

"We found it in the bag with her bones. Your DNA is on it."

Welch was almost apoplectic. "That's impossible!" he yelled, tears in his eyes. "I drank the coffee and threw the cup out!"

"Sure you did," Nick said as he moved back to the table and pulled another photo from the folder. "In the same burlap bag you shoved Rosa Sanchez's bones into."

He hit Play again, and this time the video was a wide, overhead shot of the street where Rosa's bones were found. "But it wasn't enough to dump what was left of her in some random place," he said, pointing to a figure on screen, his back to the camera, walking to the trash can on the corner. "You made sure her ex-husband the garbage man would be the one to find her!"

"What?" Welch bellowed. "I don't know any garbage men, or that girl!" He pointed to the screen. "I don't even know where it is!"

"It's two blocks from Yankee Stadium," said Nick. "We know you were in the hood that night because we have a charge on your credit card for tickets. Same as the day you went into that deli on Jerome Avenue and bought coffee from Rosa Sanchez."

The enormity of it hit Welch. He was speechless. Nick used the opportunity to drive his case home. "You saw Rosa. You stalked her. You kidnapped her outside Manhattan State University Hospital. You drove her all over the city in your ninety-eight Crown Vic, and finally out to Staten Island, where you boiled her bones in the woods."

"You're not even making sense! Why would anyone do that?"

Nick got in his face. "It wasn't anyone, Jonah; it was you. And you did it for the same reason you did it to those other poor girls thirty-five years ago—so in case they were ever found, nobody would ever know they were raped."

And then something happened Nick never would have expected. Jonah Welch burst out laughing, almost maniacally.

"You think there's something funny about this?" Nick asked.

"First of all, I can't even get it up anymore—ask my doctor—so I couldn't have raped this Rosa, or whatever her name is. And second of all, my car is parked three blocks away from my place in a vacant lot my friend owns, behind a wooden fence. I just saw it the other day and I haven't driven it in weeks."

"Bullshit!" Nick yelled. The car was his trump card and he was about to play it for all it was worth. He yanked another photo from the folder and shoved it in Welch's face. "Camera picked up your license plate going through the toll booths on the Staten Island side of the Verrazano, asshole!" he said. "On the day Rosa disappeared. So you can try talking yourself out of it all you want, but we show this stuff to a jury and they're gonna wonder how a smart guy like you could be so damn stupid. They're gonna put you away, Jonah, and this time it's for keeps."

Welch stared at the photo as if he was looking at the headstone on his own grave. Nick knew it was a bluff. All he had were tidbits of circumstantial evidence held together by the weakest thread. But he'd gotten murder suspects to spill their guts in the past with a lot less. Jonah needed just one more push.

"I'm gonna send our Crime Scene Unit out to get your car," Nick said in a quiet, confident tone, looking straight into Welch's eyes. "They're gonna flatbed it into their garage and go over every inch of it. They're gonna know whether the car was moved, and they're gonna find dirt on those tires or in the wheel wells that matches the exact spot in Staten Island where we found those bones. And that's when your ass is gonna be cooked, Jonah, like you cooked Rosa Sanchez. It's time to man up and stop the bullshit. I know you killed her, and so do you. You have to decide right now, right here, last chance. Are you gonna sit there and continue to play with yourself, or are you gonna tell me what really happened?"

Welch looked as if he didn't even know what hit him.

"I . . . I don't know," he stammered. "I don't know anything about any of this." Then, he seemed to gain some strength. "And I'm not saying another word."

"Fine," said Nick, gathering up the photos and shoving them back in the folder. He wanted to get out of the room before Welch asked for a lawyer. "I'm gonna leave you here alone for a while to think about it. You need to consider what's best for you, Jonah, now that you know what we have." He headed for the door. "I'll come back in a bit and we'll talk again. Hopefully you'll realize there's no way out of this. You can make this easy for everyone or not. It's your choice."

Before Welch could open his mouth, Nick was out the door.

Nick walked into the viewing room to find Claire with Savarese and Wilkes, who was pocketing his cell phone. "Just put out a call to the Seven-one," said the inspector, "telling them to check every vacant lot with a wood fence until they find that car."

"We should wait until they do before I go another round with him," replied Nick, glancing at Welch on the monitor. The suspect rested his elbows on the table and let his head sink into his hands.

"You got him going, Nicky," Savarese commented.

"The guy's either a schmuck or in denial," said Wilkes, "and I'm picking schmuck."

Nick glanced at Claire, who was transfixed on the monitor. Not only hadn't she uttered a word since his entrance, she wasn't even acknowledging his presence. And she had that look on her face, the one Nick knew well, the one that never led to anything good.

"I gotta get you to talk too?" he said to her.

"Something's out of whack," she replied evenly, her eyes glued to the screen.

"Another country heard from," said Wilkes, thick with sarcasm. "Don't hold back on us, Doc."

"He doesn't fit the profile of any serial killer I've ever heard of," she said.

"They come in all shapes, sizes, and personalities," Wilkes fired back, peering at the screen to see if he could pick up whatever Claire had latched onto. "This guy's all over the map emotionally because he didn't think we'd ever nail him."

"I don't think so, Inspector," Claire said, turning to him and making eye contact for emphasis. "A killer meticulous enough to butcher someone so precisely, to boil their bones, isn't just doing it to destroy the evidence, to cover his tracks. He's doing it to destroy the victim herself, to erase her from the planet. Like she never existed. Someone who believes he can do that thinks he's smarter than anybody. Than all of us put together. He'd keep up the facade, maybe even help us along if we couldn't figure something out, just to prove how smart he is. He'd be proud of his work."

She peered back at the monitor where Welch still sat, head in his hands.

"But Mr. Welch here? He's about to fall apart."

"He's pissed off. He's not the evil genius he thought he was," Wilkes argued.

"No, Inspector. He's lost. All he wants to know is how he got pulled into this. Why you're trying to pin these murders on him. He's looking for a way out of something he didn't do and that's why he can't find one. The person who murdered these three women wouldn't deny what he did. He'd shake your hand and slap you on the back to congratulate you for figuring it out."

Wilkes cursed himself for bringing Claire into the case. He looked at Nick for support. Nick shrugged.

"You said it yourself, Boss," he said. "It's a lot of nothing that looks like something when you put it all together. But even the DNA's only a partial match."

"We've put murderers away with less than what we have here," Wilkes said.

"I understand that, Inspector," said Claire. "But none of us wants to put away the wrong person. I'm pretty sure Mr. Welch didn't murder Rosa Sanchez."

Wilkes glanced at Nick, hoping what he was about to do wouldn't backfire on him. "Doc, I can't believe I'm saying this," he said. "But if you wanna take a shot at him, he's all yours. On the condition that you can be objective, since the late Ms. Sanchez was your patient."

"I want Rosa's killer more than you do, Inspector," Claire said. "Telling you Mr. Welch didn't dismember her is about the most objective thing I've ever had to do."

Welch's face remained buried in his hands as Claire opened the door.

"What'd you give me, five minutes?" he asked without raising his head.

When Claire walked toward the table, the sound of her heels brought Welch's gaze up. "So you *are* a cop," he said. In her jeans and loose-fitting top, she could easily have been mistaken for one.

"Actually, Mr. Welch, I'm a psychiatrist," Claire corrected.

"You work for them, though," said Welch, agitated. "If they think I'm gonna confess to some skirt headshrinker they can suck it, because I didn't do what they're accusing me of."

"How do you explain all this evidence they have against you?"

"How do you explain why they sent you in here?" he shot back.

"Rosa Sanchez was my patient," answered Claire. "They sent me in here because I told them you didn't kill her."

Welch laughed. "You're full of shit," he said. "They wanna string me up, not let me go."

"I answered your question, so I'd appreciate it if you would answer mine."

The authority in her voice wiped the smile off Welch's face. "You wanna know how I can explain all this so-called evidence? Either the cops made it up or someone's setting me up."

"For the sake of argument, let's rule out the cops. If they wanted to put this on you, they never would have let me in here. Can you think of anyone who'd go to this much trouble to set you up?"

He glanced up, as if he wanted to trust her. "How the hell do I know?" he asked pleadingly. "Just like I told them before, the things they say I did to this woman . . . I wouldn't even imagine how . . ." He trailed off, seeing the flat look on Claire's face.

"I believe you," she said.

"Bullshit!" Welch cried.

"If you give me a minute I'll prove it."

"How?"

"*Emigrant hasta.*"

"Huh? Emigrant what?"

"You heard me."

Welch pounded his fist on the table. "You trying to trick me here?"

"I want you to tell me what *emigrant hasta* means."

"It doesn't mean anything!" Welch cried. "I may be an ex-con but I'm not illiterate. It doesn't even make sense!"

Claire slapped a pad on the table, the words written on the top sheet. As forcefully as any cop in an interrogation, she shoved the paper across the table. "Dammit, you tell me what those words mean. Right now!"

Welch eyed the paper, terrified that if he answered incorrectly, this quiz would cost him the rest of his life in prison.

"Why are you doing this to me?"

Claire snatched the pad off the table. "Thank you, Mr. Welch," she said.

"Wait, where are you going?" Welch asked. "Thank you? What does that mean? You can't just leave me here. Tell them I want a lawyer."

She turned back and softened her demeanor. "You're not going to need a lawyer," she assured him.

"But she was your patient. You wanna see me fry like the rest of them."

"Only if you killed her, Mr. Welch," said Claire, opening the door. "And now I know for sure you didn't."

She closed the door and walked back to the viewing room, where she found Nick standing by himself. "Where'd everybody go?" she asked.

"Summoned to the chief of detectives' office," replied Nick.

Claire looked at her watch. "At five in the morning?"

"Chief's an early riser. And this isn't their only case."

"Are you satisfied?" Claire asked him.

"I've gotta believe that if he knew what those words meant he would've let on," he replied. "There would've been some recognition, even if the rest of his performance was just an act. Guy smooth enough to butcher three women would've wanted us to pay homage to his enormous ego and this douche bag barely has one. Am I close?"

"Right on target," she said.

Nick turned to the monitor, seeing Welch's face back in his hands, but this time wracking from spasms of sobbing. "I don't get it," he said. "The boss was right. The evidence was circumstantial. But the good kind of circumstantial."

"Maybe a little too good," Claire suggested.

"You're going all psych on me," chided Nick. "I thought you were the scientific one."

"I was," said Claire, walking away from the monitors. "I'm not sure what I am anymore."

His gaze followed her. "What does that mean?"

She stopped and closed her eyes for a moment. "I used to think the world made sense. That everything could be explained with facts and figures, in an empirical way. But lately there are a lot of things I can't explain."

"You mean like world hunger and war?"

She was about to answer him when Wilkes burst into the room.

"We've gotta go," he said. "You too, Doc."

"Wait, Inspector, you need to listen to me," she said. "Mr. Welch is innocent—"

"I know that, Doctor."

"How can you know?" Claire asked. "You weren't even here—"

"Patrol just found another freshly planted bag of bones out in Brooklyn," the inspector replied. "And we've had eyes on Mr. Welch for more than eighteen hours. It can't be him."

Claire and Nick followed Wilkes to the elevators.

"Are we just gonna leave Welch in there?" Claire asked.

"He just went from being our lead suspect to material witness," Wilkes said, hitting the elevator call button repeatedly. "If you're right and Welch was set up, he's got a bull's-eye on his back from the guy who's really doing all this killing."

"He keeps doing it, we're gonna have trouble keeping it under wraps," said Nick.

"Oh, it's not a secret anymore, Nicky," lamented Wilkes. "The sonuvabitch just unzipped his fly. Called Channel Three News and led 'em right to the scene."

* * *

The sun was just coming up as Savarese sped out of Manhattan in Wilkes's Charger, early enough to avoid rush hour on the Brooklyn-Queens Expressway and the Belt Parkway. Doing a modest eighty miles an hour with lights and siren, they made it to the still crime-ridden East New York section of the borough of Kings in less than half an hour.

Up ahead they could see a crowd of people being held back by a bunch of cops and yellow police tape strung across Linwood Avenue. Many of the onlookers wore pajamas, as if they'd been evacuated from their homes. TV news reporters and photographers moved among them, their "live" trucks with masts raised beaming video back to their stations.

"Just in time for the goddamned morning news," Wilkes complained. "That's no accident."

"Neither is the location," Savarese added as a patrol cop waved their car through the police line. "This guy's really shoving it up our asses this time."

"The location?" asked Claire, just as lost in Brooklyn as she'd be in Baghdad.

"Seven-five Precinct's a block and a half away," he said. "He's trying to prove his point."

Wilkes let out a sick laugh. "Yeah, that we're a bunch of morons. We can walk from here, Tony."

Savarese stopped the car behind a phalanx of police cars, fire trucks, the medical examiner's van, and the Crime Scene Unit's new mobile command post, a vehicle the size of a coach bus that contained a sophisticated laboratory.

Exiting the car, they saw the charred remnants of a two-story, tan brick apartment building. ME Ross emerged from its basement ahead of two attendants wheeling a gurney topped with a rubber body bag. Presumably, it contained the bones.

The normally unflappable pathologist looked as if he'd literally met a ghost. Nick had never seen Ross spooked before.

"You okay?" he asked Ross with real concern.

"Whoever this sicko is, he's getting on my nerves," Ross replied, uncharacteristically in no mood for jokes. He only briefly glanced at Claire, no doubt assuming she was another cop.

"Anything you can tell us, Doc?" Wilkes asked.

"Same shit, different day," Ross returned. "Once again dimensions of the pelvic girdle indicate the bones are female," Ross reported. "Length of the long bones confirms an adult. They're clean of any soft tissue, they're yellowish in color suggesting they were boiled like the first set, and they were dumped in the same kind of burlap bag *the others* were placed in by Yankee Stadium."

"Anything in there with 'em?" asked Wilkes. "You know, like another coffee cup, receipt, maybe a business card with the psycho's name and address?"

"Not this time," Ross lamented. "If you were him, would you make the same mistake twice?"

"It wasn't a mistake," Nick said. "He didn't have anyone else to pin it on."

"And Jonah Welch doesn't have a clue who he is," added Claire.

Wilkes turned to her. "Then maybe we should send you back to headquarters with Nicky so you can jog his memory some more."

"Are you asking me or telling me?" Claire replied, her voice tinged with annoyance.

"Asking," Wilkes admitted with respect. "You had him in the palm of your hand. If he's gonna open up, he'll do it with you. And we need him to, Doc. Because unless this guy left a sign leading us to him, which he's too smart to do, that poor slob Welch is our only shot."

CHAPTER 13

Claire and Nick entered the interview room at One Police Plaza less than an hour later to find Jonah Welch squirming in his chair. He would have been bouncing off the walls if he wasn't handcuffed to the table.

"What do I gotta do so you'll believe me?" he pleaded. "I swear on my parents' graves, I didn't kill anybody."

Nick went right up to Welch and stared down into his ruddy face. The prisoner recoiled, beads of sweat tumbling down his forehead from sparse tufts of gray, thinning hair sprouting from around his crown. He appeared to think Nick was about to hit him.

But instead, Nick removed a small key from his pocket and unlocked the handcuffs. That scared Welch even more.

"What's going on here?" he asked.

"You're no longer a suspect in this case," Nick told him as he looped the cuffs over his belt.

Welch sat in momentary disbelief. "Are you kidding me? This is some kind of huge mistake?"

"Yes, and it's our mistake, Mr. Welch," answered Claire. "But one we were meant to make."

Welch stood up, indignant. "What the hell does that mean?"

"It was just like you said. You were set up," Nick said, stepping up to block Welch in case he tried to move. He could feel the man's hot breath, which smelled like sauerkraut. Welch dropped back into his chair like a frightened child.

"Set up? Why? By who?"

"That's what we need your help with, genius," said Nick.

Gently, treating him like the victim he now was, Claire pulled another chair and sat facing him.

"I know you told me you couldn't think of anyone who'd want to hurt you this way," she said. "But we really need you to try. More specifically, *who* would want to hurt you?" she asked.

"I have no idea," Welch said.

Nick lowered himself into the remaining chair and took on a more empathetic tone. "Look, pal. Whoever this guy is, he's smart. So far he's been getting his jollies playing us for chumps. But nobody concocts an elaborate frame like this unless he wants the victim—that being you—to hang."

"Please understand," Claire continued. "Detective Lawler and I aren't trying to trick you into anything. He arrested you because the evidence was solid. The person who killed these three women may not stop at them."

"What . . . what do you mean?" Welch asked, not sure he wanted to hear the answer.

"We're putting you under protective custody," Nick explained. "Remember, this guy has it in for you. If he finds out he failed, that we didn't buy the setup, he's gonna try something else to get you one way or the other."

Now Welch was sitting at attention. "You're not gonna let that happen, right?"

"We're gonna put you up in a nice hotel with a protective detail twenty-four-seven. On the city's dime."

Welch relaxed only slightly. "Sounds like a good deal," he admitted.

"It beats your place in Flatbush and it sure as shit beats two decades in Greenhaven. But it's still a prison. Until we find this guy and neutralize him."

Welch put his head down again like there was no way to win. "I want to help you, I really do. But you can't get blood from a stone."

"We're not asking for blood," Claire assured him, "just a little sweat. And it's just as much in your interest as it is in ours." She stopped to let this sink in.

When Welch's head came back up, he looked back and forth between them. "What do you want me to do?" he asked.

"Just think," answered Claire. "As hard as you can."

"Who'd wanna see you fry?" Nick asked. "Someone threaten you in court after your trial? Maybe a family member of your victim? Or someone you did time with?"

"I . . . I don't know," Welch stammered, confused. Nick could almost see the thoughts tracking through Welch's brain as he struggled to remember all the run-ins he'd had, all the people he'd pissed off. Nick felt sorry for him.

"Does this mean I can go?" Welch asked Claire.

"Just sit tight, Jonah," Nick said. "Think some more. We'll leave the cuffs off and one of our detectives is gonna get you some chow. We'll set up the hotel as soon as I get back. But there's one thing we gotta check out first."

"What is that?" asked Welch.

"Your car," Nick said. "I asked you about it before and you said you haven't driven it in weeks. We just need to confirm you're telling the truth. The quicker you give me permission to search it, Jonah, the faster we get you out of this room."

Welch didn't hesitate. "Just give me something to sign," he said.

"Great. Now, you didn't hide the damn thing, did you?" Nick asked. "Because we've had the local precinct looking all night and they can't find it."

Nick finally asked Welch a question he could answer.

"There's a gas station at the corner of Empire Boulevard and Bedford Avenue," Welch said. "I pay the owner by the month to park it there."

In less than half an hour, Detective Simms drove Nick and Claire into Brooklyn and down Flatbush Avenue to Empire Boulevard. The gas station in question was a run-down old dump that hadn't actually sold gas in decades. But Nick wasn't leaving anything to chance. He'd asked a friend in the 71st Precinct detective squad to head over and confirm the car was there, and to guard it until he arrived. He did the same with the Crime Scene Unit, asking them to show up in an unmarked vehicle so as not to attract any attention. He also gave explicit instructions that no one touch the car until he got there.

When they pulled up, it was clear that they had honored Nick's requests. The detective from the 71st Precinct waved from the driver's seat of his own car and drove away as Nick, Claire, and Simms exited theirs and Crime Scene Detective Aitken approached.

"Thanks for the low profile," Nick said, grateful for the absence of yellow crime-scene tape.

"Figured it went with the stealth mobile," Aitken quipped, gesturing to the crappy, old, unmarked Chevy he'd driven over. "Your perp's ride beats the hell out of mine."

"So it was sitting here the whole time?" Simms asked.

Aitken led them to the far side of the gas station's building. "Yeah, but I can see why patrol didn't spot it. I had trouble finding it when I got here," he said. "Check it out."

They passed the garage bays and then they understood. Six battered vehicles sat parked in tandem beside the garage. Only a close look would have revealed Welch's black Crown Vic jammed against a fence behind a rusted, sixties-era bread truck.

"I asked the guy who owns the place," said Aitken. "He parked that bread truck there a week and a half ago and hasn't moved it since."

"Could've told you that just from the dirt," Nick observed, indicating the buildup of street muck around the truck's wheels. "Why don't you get a couple of shots before we slither in there?"

Aitken headed off, passing a fiftyish, silver-haired man heading toward them, wearing a mechanic's coveralls. He moved the two cars parked beside the bread truck and Welch's Ford.

"No question about it," Claire observed, getting a close look at the Crown Vic's tires. "This car's hasn't gone anywhere."

"We got the keys?" asked Simms.

Aitken held them up. "We got a warrant?" he asked.

"Better," replied Nick, holding up a piece of paper. "Written permission from the owner."

Aitken tossed him the keys. He pulled on a pair of gloves, unlocked the driver's door of the Ford, and took a look inside. The interior of the car, though worn, was remarkably clean. Aitken opened the rear driver's side door and inspected the backseat.

"I'll get it back to the lab so I can luma-light it for blood," he said, "but I don't see or smell anything that would indicate he had a dead body in here."

"We haven't opened the trunk yet," Nick reminded him. He clicked the auto-release inside the car, maneuvered his way to the back, and took a look. "Just as clean as the interior," he said.

"If a body had been in here, we'd know it," said Simms, joining him.

"Can't smell ammonia or cleaning solution," Nick said, lowering the lid of the trunk.

Claire thought about how Nick relied on his sense of smell ever since he'd begun to lose his eyesight.

Nick stopped, his hand on the trunk lid, staring at the back of it. "Terry, you got a magnifying glass in your bag of tricks?" he asked.

"What's wrong, Sherlock?" asked Claire, standing behind them.

"Sure," said Aitken, producing one and holding it out to Nick, who waved him off.

"No. Take a look at this plate and tell me what you see."

Aitken did as he was asked. A second later, he looked up. "Fresh marks around the screws," the CSU detective said. "You're right."

"Right about what?" asked Claire, baffled.

Nick stepped back to give Aitken working room and turned to Claire. "First thing we look for when we suspect a car's stolen is whether the license plates were changed. You check to see if the plates are cleaner or dirtier than the rest of the car, whether the screws are shiny, like someone used a screwdriver on them, or whether there are fresh marks on the plate from where the screws were recently turned."

Claire was amazed. "You're saying instead of taking the car, whoever murdered Rosa stole Jonah Welch's plates?"

"That's what he's saying," confirmed Aitken. "But I've never seen anyone do *this* before," he said.

"Do what?" asked Claire, bending down to take a closer look at the plate.

"Use Magic Markers the same color as the plates and screws to hide the marks he made taking them off the car and putting them back on," answered Nick. "He even smeared dirt around in the same pattern to hide it."

"But he didn't get it quite right, did he?" said Aiken, smiling.

"We'll find he did the same on the front," Simms offered. "It would explain why the camera at the Verrazano toll booth picked up Welch's plates."

Claire was astonished. She knew these were details she would have missed. She stood up and turned to Nick. "But that would mean—"

"That's right," said Nick, also somewhat amazed. "This guy had a real hard-on for Jonah Welch. Wanted to frame him so badly that he went out and bought his own ninety-eight Crown Vic, same color as Welch's, with the same make and model tires as Welch's, and threw Welch's plates on it to tighten the noose."

"And when he was done he put them back on," added Simms. "Both times probably at night, with that bread truck giving him all the cover he needed. Nobody would've seen him."

Nick turned to Aitken. "Let's flatbed this thing to your garage. Go over it, top to bottom. Maybe our smart guy left something."

"I doubt it," said Claire.

"Everyone makes mistakes," said Nick. "Even him. It's next to impossible not to transfer some piece of evidence by brushing against a seat or inadvertently coughing."

"Not this guy," Claire said. "You won't find anything more on this car, just like you won't find the actual car the killer used to dump Rosa's body. In fact, you won't even find a trace of that car, or where he bought the tires."

"How can you know that?" Nick asked.

"Because I'm starting to understand who we're dealing with. He's organized, meticulous to the point of obsession—because he thinks he can beat you. Beat us. He's smarter than everyone. The question is, what stirred him up after so many years?"

"I've got a different question," Simms interjected. "Someone thinks they're smarter than us cops, they usually wanna throw it in our faces, want us to know it's them. So why's this wacko trying to pin Rosa Sanchez on Welch?"

"He wants to have his cake and eat it too," said Nick, unconvinced by what he just said. "But there has to be some connection between Welch and the real killer. He didn't just choose him at random. We have to check."

"You can, but I'm betting that'll be a waste of time," said Claire.

"That's police work," said Nick, not understanding Claire's negativity. "That's what we do. We run down leads. We look at all the possibilities. It's never a waste of time if the wrong road eventually leads to the right place."

"Yes, and whoever's playing with us knows that, and wants to see us running in circles," said Claire.

Nick could tell he was making Claire uncomfortable by taking his frustration out on her, so he took a deep breath and calmed down.

"Okay, then. What about a connection between Rosa and her killer?" he asked.

Claire shook her head. "It doesn't jibe with what I saw from my window. If there were a connection between Rosa and the man who took her, if he was her probation officer, I would've expected to see some familiarity. But from where I was standing, it looked like she'd never seen him before."

"We need to talk to Rosa's mother again," said Nick.

"Why?" asked Claire.

"Because we haven't asked her if anyone came looking for Rosa around the day she disappeared."

Claire understood the need to do this. "Let me go ask her. Alone."

"Why?"

"She's fragile," Claire answered, walking toward the unmarked car. "I don't want to scare her, and we still need her to keep Rosa's death under wraps."

"All the more reason we should both go," said Nick, following her, getting testy again. "And just in case you forgot or didn't notice, I know how to be gentle with the families of my victims."

Claire stopped. "I don't think it's a good idea," she said.

"This is a police matter."

"Rosa was my patient."

"And now she's my victim," Nick exclaimed. "We go together or I go alone. Your choice."

Claire thought about going to see Maria behind Nick's back. But that would only lead to more arguing between them—and she realized that arguing with Nick made her uncomfortable.

What's going on with me around him?

"Fine. We'll do it your way," she said.

CHAPTER 14

It was past one in the afternoon when Maria Lopez opened the door to her apartment and, without a word, hugged Claire. "Hello, Detective," she said to Nick over Claire's shoulder, tears in her eyes.

"Mrs. Lopez," Nick said with warmth in his voice. She gestured them into the apartment and closed the door, leading them into the living room.

"How are the kids, Maria?" Claire asked, not wanting to stress the grieving woman by asking how she felt. It was clear just looking at her. Simple housedress, dark circles under her watery eyes, looking like she hadn't slept in a week. Clearly she was a wreck.

"They are missing their mama," Maria answered. "I am being very careful around them, but it's getting harder. Every time they ask about Rosa I almost tell them the truth and then catch myself. One of these days it's going to slip out."

But as much of a wreck as Maria was, Claire noticed the apartment was even neater than on her previous visit. The toys that had been lying around were now gone.

She also noticed the coffee table, on which was a makeshift shrine: a framed photo of Rosa, smiling, flanked by two candles. Maria saw Claire staring at it.

"I put it away when the children come home from school," she said.

"I'll call the medical examiner when we're done here, and try to find out when you can lay Rosa to rest," Nick said.

"Thank you, but the doctor called this morning to say he needed to keep Rosa for a while longer. So don't waste your time." Maria then stared straight at Nick. "Are you here with news for me?"

"I wish we had some," Claire said, walking to Maria's side. "You know that when we do, you'll be the first to hear." Claire took Maria's hand. "We came here today because we need your help."

"I told you I'd do anything you need," Maria said, gesturing them to sit. "But we have to hurry. The children will be done with school soon. I can't be late to pick them up."

"We want to ask you about the days and weeks before Rosa disappeared."

"Why is that important?" asked Maria.

"Because we're pretty sure whoever did this to Rosa either knew her, or was at least following her—maybe even stalking her," Claire answered, letting go of Maria's hand.

"*Dios mío*," muttered Maria. "You don't think the children are in danger, do you?"

Nick shook his head. "No, but if we ever do think that, your grandchildren will be escorted by police officers wherever they go, and you'll have a radio car stationed outside to protect you. I promise, if we even suspect there's a danger, that will happen instantly."

He turned toward Claire as if asking for her permission before he continued.

"What I need from you, Maria—is it okay if I call you Maria?" he asked.

"Of course, Detective," she answered.

"Maria," Nick replied. "We're going to spend many hours together, and I want you to be as comfortable with me as I am with you. So please call me Nick. Okay?"

Claire could see Maria begin to let her guard down. She knew what Nick was doing, which came from years of dealing with victims. It was one thing when a patient came to a psychiatrist like her seeking help. But it was quite another thing when a cop knocked on your door. Most people were afraid of the police, even victims.

He needs Maria to trust him. Just like he needed me to trust him when I was the victim.

"Yes . . . Nick," Maria said.

He took out his business card and a pen, and wrote. "I'm giving you my cell phone number," he said. "If you ever have any questions, anything you don't understand, anything you need me to help you with—and, of course, anything you think might help us find who took your daughter—you call me any time of the day or night. And I mean that. Even if it's just because you need to talk. Okay, Maria?"

A hint of a smile raised the corners of Maria's mouth. "Yes," she said, taking his hand as a gesture of thanks. "What is it you want to ask?"

Nick placed his other hand on top of hers. "Is there anything you can remember, in the days before Rosa disappeared, that seemed strange, a little 'off' to you?"

"Strange in what way?" asked Maria.

"In any way," answered Nick, leaning back. "Maybe you noticed someone suspicious outside the building, someone who didn't belong there, watching you or Rosa or the kids a little too closely. Or phone calls from wrong numbers, someone who called and hung up. Someone pressing the buzzer downstairs and then not answering when you asked who was there. A piece of mail that came to you from someone you don't know. Anything at all."

Maria didn't hesitate. "I've been thinking about this since the day Rosa left," she said. "Besides the phone call from the man who said Rosa went to Connecticut, there's nothing I can remember that seemed strange."

"Good," said Nick, staying positive even though he wished she had something to offer. "Now, how about Rosa? Did she mention anything to you about weird things happening in the days before she disappeared?"

"No, nothing," said Maria. "In fact, she was happy. Happier than I've seen her in a long time." She turned to Claire. "She said you helped her. She talked about you all the time, how much you meant to her."

Maria's chin quivered, and it took everything Claire had to stop hers from doing the same. She wanted to tell Maria how special Rosa was to her, everything she could without violating doctor-patient privilege. But all she did was nod.

Nick knew what he needed to ask next, but before he could get it out, Claire regained her voice and beat him to the punch.

"Maria," she said, "if it's okay with you, Nick and I would like to go through Rosa's belongings."

"Of course it's all right," Maria said. "But what are you looking for? I already went through her bedroom. I thought maybe there was a piece of paper, something to tell me where she might have gone. But I found nothing."

"That was good thinking, Maria," Nick said. "This is going to be hard to hear, but I'll always be honest with you. We have to consider the possibility that Rosa knew the man who took her. Something she had that means nothing to you may have some significance to us."

Something she had . . . Nick's words reminded Claire of the odd receipt they found with Rosa's bones.

"Maria," Claire said, "do the words *emigrant hasta* mean anything to you?"

"No," Maria answered. "Why do you ask?"

"Because we found those words written on a receipt from the deli where Rosa worked," Claire said. "The receipt was found along with her remains."

Maria's eyes widened. "Is her murderer sending us a message?"

"We don't know," Claire said as she stood, Nick following suit. "But if you think of any connection between those words and Rosa, please tell us."

Maria directed them down a short hallway to Rosa's bedroom. "Do whatever you have to do," she said. "Look anywhere in the apartment. Come back as many times as you need to. Just bring me justice for my little girl."

He picked up a black Magic Marker and faced his crossword puzzle.

Who's next? *he wondered, a smile spreading across his lips.*

He admired his work. The letters R-O-S-A-S-A-N-C-H-E-Z fit neatly into each square. He had rid the world of another parasite and it gave him a thrilling sense of complete control. He was the master of his universe and no one would be smart or clever enough to stop him from filling the grid with more names.

Nick and Claire entered Rosa's bedroom, which appeared to have changed little since she was a girl. Frilly pink curtains covered a pair of windows. A white, twin, four-poster bed faced a matching dresser. The furniture, though cheaply made, was in nearly perfect condition, her bookshelf filled with a neatly organized family of stuffed animals. She'd taken great care with all of her belongings.

"It's a beautiful apartment, Maria," Nick said.

"I've lived here a long time," Maria replied, "and I'm lucky I still can. Rent control."

"Me too," he said. "I live in the same rent-controlled apartment I grew up in."

"Rosa kept her room clean," Claire observed.

"As an adult, yes," Maria replied, standing in the doorway. "I kept it like this after she got married and moved in with Franco." A hint of a smile crossed her face. "It wasn't like this while she was growing up, believe me. But when she and the *niños* moved in here, she wanted to set a good example. That's why she put her *animales*—" She fought back tears. "I should leave you alone to do this."

"We won't take long," Nick promised.

Maria went down the hallway, back to the living room. Claire couldn't help but think how difficult it must be for her to live with the constant reminder of the child she lost. Claire knew the feeling well. She became anxious every time she visited her parents at her childhood home in Rochester, New York, every time she turned into the driveway from which her best friend, Amy, was kidnapped more than two decades ago. Claire could still see Amy's face through the rear window of her abductor's car, tears streaming down her cheeks.

A *thump* brought her back to the present. She looked up to see Nick lifting Rosa's mattress.

"What are you doing?" she asked.

He heaved the mattress on its side against the wall, exposing the box spring.

"Looking for Rosa's diary," he answered, surprised at the question. "If she had one. Little trick some shrink taught me last year."

Claire smiled, remembering the first case they worked on together. *If only she did have a diary*, Claire thought. She'd once asked Rosa to write down her thoughts and feelings. Rosa told her she didn't like to write, that she'd rather talk about her feelings with Claire.

"Wishful thinking," Nick said, letting the mattress fall back into place.

Claire was silent. Something was bothering her. She scanned the room: the stuffed animals, the frilly curtains, the childlike appearance of a home occupied by an adult. She realized it looked a lot like her own room as a child.

I grew up privileged, Rosa close to poverty. We're so different and yet so much alike.

She zeroed in on a framed photo on top of the bookshelf. Looking more closely, Claire could see it was Rosa and her son and daughter. She felt the room close in on her, spinning. Her heart was racing and she couldn't catch her breath. The children's smiling faces seemed to move out toward her, becoming the faces of eight-year-old Claire and Amy.

"Are you all right?" Nick asked. Claire realized his arm was around her shoulder, holding her because he thought she might faint.

"I need some air."

"Come on," Nick said, guiding her out of the room and down the hallway.

"Maria," he shouted, "we have to go. But we'll be back."

"I'm sorry, I'm in *el baño*," came Maria's voice from behind a door.

"It's okay," Nick returned. "We can let ourselves out."

Claire was relieved that Maria didn't see her like this.

He led her down the stairs and out the door to the building, where a wall of humidity hit them.

"I don't know how you're going to breathe out here," Nick said. He waved to Simms, who saw Nick holding Claire up.

"What happened?" Simms shouted, jumping out of his car.

"I don't know," said Claire, "but it's better out here. I can breathe."

Nick was still worried. "Bronx-Lebanon's the closest hospital," he said. It was more than a suggestion.

"I don't need a hospital. I work at one, remember?" Claire replied. "I can go later if there's a problem. I'm okay now."

But she knew she wasn't okay.

Claire walked down the hallway of MSU with a determination that surprised even her. Nick and Simms had just dropped her off, and during the mostly silent ride back to Manhattan State, she felt noticeably better. She breathed consciously and tried to work out in her head exactly what she was going to do.

Now, as she walked into Doctor Fairborn's outer office, Claire hoped to find her mentor and get her help.

"Claire," said Fairborn's assistant, Sara, a friendly African-American woman in her fifties who always wore bright reds and yellows that cheered Claire up. "Doctor Fairborn's been looking for you."

"I need to see her," Claire said, with more urgency than she wanted. "If she's available," she continued, pulling back her tone.

Sara wasn't used to seeing Claire in a state; she was always so calm and composed. She already had the phone in her hand and a concerned look on her face. "Doctor Waters is here," she said. The door to Fairborn's inner office opened and she appeared, wearing a dark blue suit that was as conservative as Claire had ever seen her dress.

"Come in, dear," said Fairborn.

"Thanks," said Claire, rushing inside and sitting in her favorite spot, a corner of the comfortable sofa. She was barely down when Fairborn closed the door and became uncharacteristically stern with her.

"You've been gone for days, cancelled patients, had your colleagues cover you on rounds," she said as she crossed the room and sat opposite Claire. "It's not at all like you. I need you to tell me what's going on."

Claire fidgeted. She would have been a fool not to expect this. She just didn't expect it to come this quickly.

"I've pulled Nick Lawler back into my life," she blurted before she could stop the words from leaving her lips.

Now it was Fairborn's turn to shift uncomfortably. "About Rosa Sanchez's case," she guessed.

"Yes," was all Claire could manage.

"After I told you not to get involved in her disappearance."

Claire wasn't going down without a fight. "I was concerned about her well-being, and I thought it was my duty to make sure she was okay," she explained. "And I was right," she said to Fairborn.

"Right about what?"

Claire knew she now had to go the distance. "I'm sorry I went against your wishes, Doctor. But I have to ask you to please not repeat what I'm about to tell you to anyone."

"But of course I won't, dear," came Fairborn's reply. "You know I can't tell anyone anything you confide to me about your patients."

Claire let out a deep, relieved breath. "Rosa was murdered," Claire said.

Fairborn grabbed the armrest of her chair with her hand. "Oh my God," she said. "What happened?"

"She was kidnapped, and I saw it happen." Claire told her mentor everything that had transpired the past few days. When she stopped talking more than twenty minutes later, Fairborn's hand was still clutching the armrest, so hard that had it been someone's neck they'd have been long dead.

"And your involvement in all this is with the knowledge of the police department this time?"

"They asked me to do it," Claire confirmed.

"You should've been honest with me, dear," Fairborn scolded.

"I know. But I was told I couldn't tell anyone."

"I understand, but I'm not just *anyone*," her mentor said.

Claire felt like a child caught swiping a candy bar from the store. She couldn't argue with Fairborn, who was right on every point.

"Still, you were acting in your patient's best interest," Fairborn said.

It sounded as if Fairborn was trying to find a way to let her slide.

"Doctor Fairborn," Claire said, "you've been nothing but understanding, and compassionate, and accommodating, and forgiving of my situation. I've asked more from you than I ever could've expected—"

"Stop," Fairborn said, putting up her hand for emphasis.

But Claire couldn't. "It's like I've been sucked back into the vortex of last year. Only this time there's a new twist. . . ." She stopped, the thoughts rushing through her head, then spoke with difficulty. "I . . . I should have told you I called Nick," she said.

"Claire. I know. It's okay."

This stopped Claire from further self-recriminations. "It is?" she asked.

"You went past the point where I would've stopped you," Fairborn continued, "but at the end of the day you were doing the job Paul Curtin trained you to do. If overzealously," she added.

"Are you going to ask me to stop?" Claire asked, dreading the answer.

"No," replied Fairborn, "because I know you need to do this, for yourself and for Rosa. But you've got to keep me in the loop. You've got to balance it with your work here. And if I get wind of you—let's call it 'misbehaving'—like you did last year, I'll have to change my mind."

"I didn't see it as 'misbehaving,'" Claire said, trying not to sound defensive.

"You cut your hair and changed its color to bait a serial killer," Fairborn reminded her. "That's for the police to do, not a psychiatrist. Forensic or otherwise."

"I promise I won't go over the edge," said Claire, though she had no idea if she'd be able to keep it. "But we've got a real puzzle on our hands, and not a lot of hope of being able to solve it."

"Maybe you need some fresh eyes on it," Fairborn said, her curiosity piqued.

Claire was not sure she knew the woman who was speaking to her. Was Fairborn so intrigued she wanted in on the investigation of Rosa's murder?

Claire tried to clarify. "What do you mean by 'fresh eyes'?"

"You're still teaching in Walter's class, aren't you?" Fairborn asked, referring to her professor boyfriend who taught a criminal forensic science seminar at Manhattan State University.

"Yes," Claire said. "In fact, I'm due there tomorrow morning."

"Then why don't you make it a class project?" asked Fairborn.

Claire tried to hide her surprise that Fairborn would suggest such a thing. And yet she saw the merit in it—after all, she and Nick were at something of a dead end.

"It's an interesting idea," Claire said, "but the police are so paranoid of leaks they'd never go for it. We wouldn't want the university being responsible for tainting the investigation."

"How so?" asked Fairborn, who, though an experienced psychiatrist, was new in the forensic end of the profession. It was no secret that she was looking forward to relinquishing the reins of the fellowship program as soon as the search committee found a suitable candidate to fill the late Paul Curtin's shoes.

"The police would argue they can't risk a group of students learning details of the cases that only the killer would know. It could create an evidence problem if and when the murderer goes to trial."

"You don't have to tell them everything, only what's been in the media," Fairborn suggested.

Which, of course, wouldn't work. "Except for the last murder, there hasn't been anything in the media—"

She stopped. Smiled.

"I know how I can make it work," Claire said.

CHAPTER 15

"No way," Nick argued. "I don't care how brilliant your students are. We can't involve them in an active investigation."

"They won't be," Claire retorted, sitting across from Nick at his worn Formica kitchen table. "At least, as far as they know."

She reached for her cup of coffee, which was embossed with an NYPD detective's shield. But instead of displaying Nick's shield number at the bottom, it sported the letters DEA, an acronym for the union to which Nick and every other city police detective belonged.

Claire took a sip and yawned. It was nearing midnight and Nick's daughters were long in bed. Yet neither she nor Nick seemed to want to go to sleep. As tired as she was, sitting here arguing with him beat the alternative of her sterile apartment, where she'd get into bed alone with thoughts of Rosa that would render her sleepless anyway.

"It's too much of a risk," said Nick.

"What else have we got?" Claire asked. "We've had no luck identifying the victim out in Brooklyn. We don't even know where to start."

In fact, she was understating their dilemma. All the residents of the fire-gutted building in East New York where the latest skeleton had been found were accounted for.

"We don't know where the victim lived, where she was taken from, how old she was—anything," she reminded him. "What have we got to lose?"

Nick said nothing, having already drawn his line in the sand. As he took a swig of coffee, Claire rubbed her right index finger along the tiny, nearly invisible scratches on the table's surface and thought about all the meals eaten around that table when Nick's wife and mother were alive.

"So as usual, now the ball's in my court," Nick said.

"A flat no isn't a viable option. We've gotta think outside the box," she replied.

Nick smiled. The two of them knew each other's tricks.

"Putting it on me isn't outside the box," he observed. "It's business as usual."

"So's being stubborn," Claire retorted.

She couldn't help but think they sounded like an old married couple. And this stalemate needed to be broken.

"Maybe you're right," she said. "Maybe it's too much of a risk."

Now it was Nick's turn to grin. "Don't do that," he said.

"Do what?" Claire asked.

"Manipulate me with the guilt trip. You don't think you're wrong. Stick to your guns."

Claire laughed and her hand grazed his. Nick felt drawn to her. He wanted to kiss her. Claire looked away. It wasn't the first time that had happened and it was getting more and more uncomfortable.

But not because he's overstepping. Because I want this. At least I think I do. . . .

"Okay," she now said, sitting up straight. "I wasn't trying to manipulate you, but I do think we should give my students a shot."

"You understand that if they come up with something, it would be by accident, right?"

"As long as it leads to the right place," Claire said, "what difference does it make?"

"Good morning," boomed Professor Walt McClure as he stood in front of the six master's degree candidates taking his seminar in criminal profiling. It was early the next morning, and the students were just settling at the conference table, shaking their umbrellas from the morning rainstorm, pulling out laptops, sipping coffees, grabbing muffins from the two boxes McClure brought with him each week.

At age fifty-five, thin, of average height, with his straight brown hair beginning to show some gray at the temples, McClure wore horn-rimmed glasses and a brown corduroy suit that gave him an air of the ultimate academic. In fact, he was anything but. After earning a master's and doctorate while rising to the rank of captain in the Philadelphia Police Department, the death of his wife of ovarian cancer prompted him to retire and move closer to his three grown children, who'd all wound up in New York City. He then built a solid reputation and bank account as a consultant, but was tiring of the constant travel just as Manhattan State approached him with an offer he couldn't refuse: they matched his income and guaranteed him tenure, which meant he had a job for life. What was at the time a no-brainer became a true gift as McClure found himself more fulfilled as a teacher than he'd ever felt as a cop.

To his left sat Claire in her work clothes, a burgundy suit, and an overdressed Nick: charcoal pin-stripe, white-and-royal-blue-striped shirt with French cuffs (held closed by NYPD cuff links in the shape of a detective's shield), perfectly matched paisley tie. Claire couldn't help but think he looked as bullish as any Wall Street investment banker.

"I saw you in the *Ledger*, Detective," Miguel Colon said, his head resting in hands held up by bent elbows on the table, stretching the dagger tattoo on his fully flexed right bicep into something more like a sword. "Like, what, a year and a half ago?"

"Yeah, probably," Nick said, trying to keep a poker face. The newspaper story to which Miguel referred had nothing to do with the case he and Claire had cracked. "That was right after my wife killed herself with my gun. The forensics came back inconclusive, so someone with a hair up his ass decided I must've murdered her. They investigated for half a year, but of course came up with nothing."

"Am I allowed to ask if you did it?" asked Cory Matthis, who looked like he'd gotten right out of bed and come to class.

As his classmates snickered and rolled their eyes, Nick turned to him. "Good for you," he said. "My answer is no, but beyond that I'm invoking my right to remain silent and I'm not answering any more questions without my lawyer."

He said it so seriously that the entire class, including Claire and McClure, cracked up, bringing a smile to Nick's face as well. This had been his intention, to break the ice with these students as quickly as possible.

Justine Yu, in jeans and sweats and no makeup, was sitting beside Cory and now crinkled her nose. "You just got laid, didn't you?" she said more than asked, as if it were fact.

Wes Phelps snickered. "How the hell would you know?" he asked Justine.

"She's more than familiar with the scent," quipped Miguel, which everyone in the room knew was a reference to her sexual preference for women.

Cory, for his part, turned redder than the acne on his face and said nothing as Professor McClure put up a hand. "Enough of this, and as Cory's attorney I'm invoking his Fifth Amendment right against self-incrimination." His eyes swept his students, some still smirking, to make sure they got the message. When he was sure they'd behave themselves, he continued. "Now, Doctor Waters has already told you about how she and Detective Lawler broke the case of those murdered women last year. She brought him here today for a different reason entirely."

"That's right," said Claire. "And though he didn't know it when he tried to get a confession out of Detective Lawler, Cory's question goes right to the heart of the subject, which we'll call *theory of the crime*. Anyone care to guess what that means?"

"It's not a trick question, is it?" asked Kara Wallace.

"No tricks here," Claire assured her.

"Then it's obviously what the person investigating thinks happened," Kara said.

"For the purposes of today's class, that's only *partially* correct," Nick confirmed. "Because it's not that simple."

To Claire's surprise, Nick rose and headed to a wall-mounted dry-erase board at one end of the room, picking up and opening a black marker. "I worked homicides for a long time," he said as he wrote *THEORY OF THE CRIME* in block letters near the top of the board, underlining it with a flourish before turning back to the class. "When you get to most murder scenes, you almost immediately know what we call the *cause of death*." Which he wrote under his heading as a bullet point as he spoke. "You know, gunshot, stabbing, blunt-force trauma, et cetera. Then," he continued, starting a new bullet point and writing, "we want the *manner of death*."

"Aren't they the same thing?" asked Leslie Carmichael, her long dreads tucked up into a wool cap this morning. Nick finished writing *manner of death* on the board and turned back to the class.

"He wouldn't be asking if they were the same," said Wes Phelps.

"You're right," said Nick. "The *manner of death* is more a legal term, and it can only be determined by a medical examiner. For example, say we're called to the scene where somebody washes up on the beach at Coney Island. What's the manner of death?"

He looked at the class. They looked at him. For the first time, not one voice spoke up. Claire couldn't help but grin, and when Nick noticed he did the same.

"How about it, Doctor Waters? You wanna tell them or should I?" he offered.

Claire eyed the students. "The answer is *it depends*. Because this time, Detective Lawler did ask you a trick question."

The students reacted, feeling a bit less dumb that none of them could answer. Nick saw his opportunity and continued.

"Why does it depend? Well, just because we find a person shot or cut or bludgeoned or drowned doesn't make it a homicide. Let's say some guy washes up on Rockaway Beach. If there's water in his lungs, we know what?"

"That's easy," said Kara. "He drowned."

"Then what's the manner of death?" Nick quizzed her.

"Is *accidental* a possibility?" the girl asked.

"Yes, it is," said Nick.

"Then I'd say accidental."

Miguel Colon shook his head.

"Dude with the blade on his bicep isn't buying it," said Nick.

"Nope," Miguel answered, "because we don't know *why* he drowned."

"Go on," Nick prompted him.

"Okay, so let's say the guy was on a boat. If he fell off, it's accidental. But if someone pushed him off, it could be murder but it would look the same."

"Exactly," confirmed Nick. "Now, here's another case, and this one is legendary. Happened back in the sixties. Woman's driving on the Belt Parkway. Just so happened a detective on his way to work was behind her. All of a sudden, this woman drifts from the left lane all the way over to the right, and keeps going onto the grass until she hits a tree. The detective pulls over. The driver, in her twenties, dead. Any guesses as to the manner of death?"

"Medical," said Wes Phelps. "She had a stroke or a heart attack, right?"

"And if that were the case, you'd be right," Nick answered. "Let me tell you, that's exactly what the detective thought. What if I told you that when the ME got her on the table down at the morgue, they found a small, bloodless bullet hole just behind her right ear?" He stopped, looked at the students. "So we now know the cause of death was a gunshot wound. What's the manner of death?"

Again, the students were stumped. Then, Justine Yu, who'd kept quiet until now, raised her hand. "It has to be a homicide, right?" she asked.

Nick closed the marker and put it back on the holder. "Tell me your theory of the crime."

"Someone knew she went that route every day, waited for her to pass the spot where the car started to drift, and shot her," Justine said.

"You're an idiot," Cory Matthis muttered.

"The name calling aside," Nick chided, "tell me why you said that."

"Because," began Cory, "no way in hell can someone get a shot off that perfect at a moving car."

"Lee Harvey Oswald did," retorted Justine. "Twice. Including a head shot."

"If you believe it," Cory said, waving his hand dismissively. "And assuming it's true, Kennedy's car was going, like, four miles an hour, wasn't it? And Oswald was trained to shoot in the marines, I think. This girl was on the Belt Parkway, so unless she was in slow traffic, the shooter would've had to be in a car going at exactly the same speed as the victim's or the physics of that shot make it impossible."

His classmates eyed Cory like he'd gone insane. Not Nick. Very slowly, he applauded five or six times, bringing a smile to Cory's face and shock to those of his classmates.

"He's right?" Justine asked, flummoxed.

"Even that detective who saw it thought like you did," Nick said. "But yes, your classmate is correct."

"But wait a minute," Justine interrupted, refusing to let go. "There must've been a bullet hole in the car, in one of the windows, no?"

Nick smiled again as he sat down; he was thoroughly enjoying this. "You'd think so. But that's just it. There were no bullet holes in the car and no shattered windows. Anyone wanna guess why?"

"The windows were open?" asked Wes Phelps.

"Not windows," said Nick. "Window. The right rear window. It's the only way the bullet could've entered."

Miguel Colon turned to Cory with newfound respect. "You nailed it, Holmes," he said, turning his eyes to Nick. "So this was a one-in-a-million shot?"

"Yep," Nick answered. "Now what's the manner of death?"

"Accidental," Miguel stated.

"In layman's terms, you'd be right," Nick told him. "But in legal terms, even back then the law prohibited firing guns anywhere in the city for any reason. The guy they eventually collared had fired the shot from a boat almost a mile offshore from where the girl was hit. He was testing an old rifle he found on board that he forgot he even had, to see if it would fire."

"And that's the shot that killed the girl?" asked Leslie in amazement.

"If the right rear window of her car had been closed, she'd be a grandmother now because the shot would've bounced right off it."

"Like how kids seem to be right in the path of stray bullets even though they're in their apartments and the shot comes from outside and manages to find them," said Miguel.

"Yeah," Nick said, moving again to the board and picking up the marker. "I've had more of those cases than I needed. But I don't wanna get off track. The point is, and again, I'll use murder as my example, *theory of the crime* is related to the manner of death but not the same thing. It's exactly that, a theory. The *why*, if you will. *Why* is a question, and the answer almost always begins with *because*." He wrote those two words on the board. "My job as a homicide detective was to figure out the why. Because the why almost always leads you in the direction of the who." He put the marker down. "In the case we just discussed, the answer to why the girl died is because some asshole in a boat fired his rifle in the wrong direction. And look how long it took us to get to that *because*. In this case, the theory of the crime changed several times because the evidence continued pointing those cops in new directions almost every day. Is everyone with me so far?"

The students answered by continuing to type on their laptops.

"I'll take that as a yes," said Nick, as one by one, the class finished their notes and looked up at him.

None of this was lost on Claire, who fought to hide her shock over Nick's teaching prowess. Whether he knew it or not, he was a natural.

"Let's try something more recent," Nick said, still in front of the board, as he chose a red marker from the assortment of available colors. "Anyone see the news yesterday or today?"

Claire's heart skipped. Like the skilled interrogator Nick was, he'd lulled these students into thinking this was just a class exercise. She knew this was the segue to the matter at hand.

"You mean, locally or, like, around the world?" asked Wes.

"Locally," Nick replied. "Out in Brooklyn yesterday morning."

"The fire where that body was found," Leslie guessed.

"That's it," answered Nick. "We're gonna do this one in real time, see how we can use what we've learned." A chorus of laptop typing and clicks indicated the students were bringing up whatever they could find on their screens. "What do we know about this so far?"

"Doesn't look like much," said Justine, who read from one article: "'Police are calling the fire that destroyed an East New York apartment building a case of arson, and may add murder to the list after the discovery of a body in the building's burned-out basement.'"

"Okay. What's the manner of death so far?" Nick quizzed.

"How can we tell from this?" Justine asked, frustrated. "All they're saying is that none of the people who lived there were missing. . . ."

She stopped, realizing perhaps she'd broken through her own attention barrier. "The dead person didn't live in the building," she realized.

"Excellent," Nick complimented her. "So what's the manner of death?"

"Still impossible to determine," Wes Phelps said. "For one thing, if the victim didn't live there, what was he or she doing there to begin with?"

"You're on the right track," Nick said. "Take that to the next step.

If you were me and you were on this case, what possibilities would you consider?"

"Well, that the victim either somehow wandered into the basement or was killed earlier and dumped there," Wes offered.

"That's a good start. Anyone else?"

"Wouldn't we have to know how badly the victim was burned?" Cory asked.

"Yes. And for the sake of argument, let's assume the body was burned to a crisp. No usable DNA to have even a hope of an ID, unless the medical examiner can find some viable cells in the skeleton."

"I might start by checking out whether there'd been any similar arsons in the area or even the city," Kara said.

"Yes, and that's a basic step we would take immediately in the investigation," he said, writing *similar arsons* on the board. "In fact, the arson investigators, both NYPD and the fire department, would be on the scene. They'd know instantly if a crime like this rang any bells. No pun intended. But remember, we're talking about the *why*. Why would this victim wander into this basement, if that's what happened?"

"I don't think that's how it went down," Miguel stated.

Nick put down the marker. "Tell me why," he said.

"Because there's no way somebody just happens to wander into a building's basement the same night some *match* lights the place up," Miguel said, using cop slang for *arsonist*.

"Just like there's no way some poor girl gets shot in the head while driving sixty miles an hour on the Belt Parkway because some asshole's in a boat. . . ."

Nick stopped, seeing Miguel get the point and shake his head "no," presumably at himself. "That was pretty dense of me, yo," he admitted.

"Don't beat yourself up," advised Nick. "Here's the deal, folks. This work ain't what you see on TV. Sometimes we find the perp in a day. Sometimes it takes forty years. And sometimes, as has happened, though fortunately not to yours truly, we collar the wrong person with the right evidence. And then we have to eat our own shit, pardon my expression, years later when we learn we screwed the pooch and put away an innocent person. You know when that's most likely to happen?"

It wasn't a rhetorical question. He looked at the students intently for an answer but none of them wanted to venture a guess.

"It's most likely to happen when you get too focused on the *who* instead of the *why*. As in why would this person I like for this murder want to kill my victim? Or, the flip side: why is it possible even with the evidence, the person you suspect may not have done the crime?"

"That's reasonable doubt," said Wes Phelps, the prosecutor wannabe.

"Yes it is," Nick said. "And reasonable doubt should begin with you as a cop, not with a jury, because by then it could be too late. But in a case like this one, you can never know the why without knowing who the victim is. So let's say the remains go to the medical examiner, who finds some viable cells for DNA, but can't come up with a full sequence. What's the next step?"

"I'd run it through the system anyway," said Leslie.

"Why?" asked Nick. "You'd get nothing back."

"Unless I ran it with a lower percentage match," she returned. "Maybe I'd get lucky and pick up a family member whose DNA is in the database, like a brother or mother, and that person could lead me to the victim. Like how they caught that Grim Sleeper dude in LA."

"Excellent idea," Nick said, writing *CHECK FAMILIAL DNA* on the board. "But what if we did that and still couldn't ID the victim?"

"Wait a minute," Cory said, staring at the board. "If we have DNA, we must know the sex of the victim, right?"

"Yes," Nick said, trying to move things along, "and let's assume it's a male. How does that help us?"

"Not much," Kara answered, "unless there's someone in the neighborhood who mysteriously vanished overnight."

Claire was bursting at the seams, wanting to join the conversation but holding her tongue. Nick could see this, which only added to his frustration.

"Okay," he said, about to go out on a limb from which he hoped not to be hung later. "We can't ID the victim, so let's assume the body was dumped by the same person who then started the fire."

"Wow," said Cory. "Some freakazoid who'd burn down a building full of innocent people just to cover up a murder?"

"It's happened before," Nick assured him. "The Jamaican drug gangs in South Ozone Park back in the eighties would kill anything that breathed to protect their businesses or send a message that they were not to be screwed with."

"But we're talking about seventy people living there," Cory pressed. "To me that adds up to a righteous psycho."

"If there could ever be such a thing," Justine whined, again intimating Cory was a moron.

"Okay," Nick prompted. "I'd probably think the same." He wrote *righteous psycho* on the board as Cory, empowered by his newfound bravado, took a swig of coffee. "If we're talking psycho, where would you turn next?"

"Honestly?" asked Wes Phelps. "I'd bring in the FBI."

"You wouldn't wanna close the case yourself?"

"Sure I would," Wes explained. "But the FBI has people who specialize in this stuff, the profiling. And if you've already exhausted your local resources—say, there's nothing in your databases with anything like this—then you take the next step, don't you?"

Nick turned to the board, shaking his head yes, and wrote *FBI/FEDS*. "This might not be our first choice, as the relationship between the NYPD and the FBI isn't the best," he said as he finished writing. "But your classmate is correct. Not pooling resources is what prevented us from possibly stopping the September eleventh attacks. If you have the information and you're at a dead end, you share it. It's a lot like life itself, folks. Whatever you put out there comes back to you, many times in ways you never expect."

He noticed Professor McClure giving him the high sign that it was time to wrap things up.

"Detective Lawler will be back next week with Doctor Waters," he said to the class. Then, to Nick and Claire, he asked, "Is there anything you'd like our friends here to do in preparation?"

"Yes," said Claire, now standing. "Cory, you asked who would risk more than seventy lives to cover up the murder of one person. I'd like you all to go with that scenario and write down what kind of person would do that, like a profile of sorts. As if you were the behavioral science folks at Quantico. Let your minds wander and jot down all your thoughts. Remember, there are no stupid or wrong ideas."

"Let's give it up for Detective Lawler," McClure said, and the class broke into enthusiastic and sincere, if abbreviated applause. "Thanks for waking us up, Nick."

As the students stood up loading laptops into backpacks, Claire glanced out the window. The rain had stopped and the sky was clear.

McClure walked up to her and Nick. "You're a natural up there," McClure said to Nick, "and they're always looking for adjuncts with your experience. Ever thought about teaching part time?"

Claire turned to Nick, anxious to hear his answer. Maybe this was a path he could take when his eyesight got worse. *And I wouldn't mind working with him*, she thought.

"I've done some classes at the academy in homicide investigation," Nick said, "but I'm not handing in my papers just yet. When I'm ready to take the plunge, though, you're my first call."

"Thanks for the great class," McClure said, shaking Nick's hand. He picked up his soft leather briefcase. "See you here next week. Same bat time, same bat channel," he quipped as he went through the door, leaving Claire and Nick alone.

"You did a great job," Claire said. But you'd never know it from the look on Nick's face. "What's wrong?"

"It was a waste of our time," he said.

"We got them going," she argued.

"Other than a half-assed part-time job offer, we got nothing. And we don't have time to wait for next week."

Claire wasn't so sure. "Maybe that kid Wes is right. We should go to the FBI."

Nick wheeled on her. "'We' already did."

"Is that right?" Claire said, a hint of anger in her tone.

"It's one of the first things we'd do in cases like this."

She looked away from him so he wouldn't see the anger on her face. He knew what fueled it.

"No, I don't tell you everything," he confirmed for her. "But Wilkes called a friend of his over at the New York field office and had him check. There's not a lot the behavioral science gang at Quantico hasn't seen in the way of serial killers. The one guy they collared for something similar is doing life in Leavenworth. And just for the record, I don't have to tell you everything and you're just gonna have to accept that."

Claire turned back, acceptance on her face. "I'm sorry," she said. "When I get like this it's not directed at you. I'm just thinking about Rosa."

Her words softened Nick. "Don't worry about it."

That afternoon they sat at the kitchen table in Nick's apartment, his laptop open as he typed furiously. "You're right, that class wasn't a waste of time," he said. "Seeing those students on their computers got me thinking."

"Are you going to clue me in at some point?" Claire asked him.

"Sure. I realized we didn't go far enough with the FBI and that there was a wider 'net' to be cast. The Internet," he said. "Just because this guy did it before and disappeared doesn't mean he was doing time here or even just evaded capture and lived happily ever after somewhere in Kansas like BTK."

"BTK was caught," Claire reminded him, referring to the infamous serial killer in Wichita who'd evaded arrest for years until finally being captured in 2005.

"He also took long breaks between murders," Nick observed. "One of them was almost eight years."

Claire came around the table and looked over his shoulder at the screen as he typed *human bones boiled* into Google's search engine and hit Enter. The results came up and Claire read them aloud. "I don't believe this. Instruction manuals for boiling human bones? The Church of Euthanasia? History of cannibalism?"

"Easy," exclaimed Nick. "We're only on the first page."

"Click to the next page," she said.

"Jesus," Nick muttered. "Give me a break." But he did it.

Claire's eye caught a line about halfway down the next page. She pointed and read. "Right there. 'Bones discovered on the beach were believed to be those of Martha Palmer. . . .' Click on that one."

"I am," Nick said, doing it.

Up on screen appeared a newspaper article from an English-language newspaper published in Costa Rica called the *Tico Times*, with a photo of a beautiful, middle-aged woman.

"It's from 2009," Nick observed. "Says here that the bones were found too far up on the beach to have washed ashore and were laid out as if someone put them there to dry in the sun."

"Does it say anything about boiling?"

"I'm getting there," Nick retorted. "Here we go. 'Police officials say the yellowish color to the bones indicate they may have been boiled prior to being placed on the beach.'"

Claire was getting discouraged. "One murder from '09 in another country does not a pattern make," she lamented.

"It's worth a call to the Costa Rican police," Nick replied.

"We may not need that," Claire said, her eyes a few lines further into the article than Nick's.

"What are you reading?" he asked.

"About why Martha Palmer's murder was such a big deal. Her husband, Victor Palmer, once was the owner of the resort."

Nick wasn't biting. "If my wife was found butchered on my property, I might sell it too," he observed. "Doesn't mean anything."

"But definitely worth making that call after all," urged Claire.

"We can do it from the office," Nick said, closing the laptop. "Instead of running up my phone bill."

"Let me hit the restroom first," Claire said.

She left the kitchen and walked down the hallway, past framed photos of Nick with his arms around Jill and Katie, several years younger. All were smiling broadly, standing in front of a cabin in what looked like the Adirondacks. She wondered if Jenny, Nick's wife who'd committed suicide in this very apartment two years earlier, had snapped the photo.

After completing her business in the small, rarely used powder room, Claire washed her hands in the sink and noticed the wallpaper, a faded sky blue studded with small silver stars. She realized that lately she'd been analyzing the apartment, looking for clues not only about Nick's preferences, but also to learn more about his mother, who'd lived here for forty years before recently passing away. Nick and the girls had lived with her for the two years after Jenny died, until her own sudden death.

Claire also noticed, when she turned off the faucet, that the toilet was still running. Her physicist father had taught her to be handy around the house. She knew how to unclog a drain, caulk a bathtub, and fix a running toilet.

When she lifted the porcelain lid off the tank, it was heavier than it should have been. One look underneath revealed why: a package, wrapped in dark plastic, was duct-taped to the underside. From its triangular shape she knew it held a gun.

Her anger rose to the surface. Nick had sworn to Wilkes he'd turned in all his guns. To be caught with this one would mean the end of his job for sure.

But what really angered her was that he'd left the weapon in an unsecured place. What if one of his daughters heard the toilet running, tried to fix it, and found the weapon?

Carefully, Claire removed the gun from the lid and slipped it into her purse. She was just replacing the tank lid when Nick's voice boomed from just outside the bathroom door, stunning her into nearly dropping it.

"You okay?" he called.

"Yeah, I'm coming," she shouted back, lowering the lid silently onto the tank. She looked in the mirror to make sure she hadn't dirtied or wet her suit. With everything in place including her poker face, she left the bathroom.

Chapter 16

A uniformed police officer in military body armor, AR-15 assault rifle strapped to his shoulder, waved the unmarked Impala through a security checkpoint outside the rear entrance to One Police Plaza's subterranean garage. Nick drove the car slowly to allow his eyes to adjust to the sudden plunge from sunlight into relative darkness. Focusing intently, he steered the big sedan down two ramps to the lowest level and into an empty space in which the letters MCS were stenciled in bright yellow on the concrete floor. He opened the door and placed the police parking plate on the dashboard as Claire got out of the passenger's side, forgetting what was in her purse as she yanked it from the center console with so much force that it nearly struck her.

"Whoa!" she cried.

Nick saw the whole thing. "What do you have in there, a bar of gold?"

Claire realized that taking her purse with the gun through metal detectors into police headquarters wasn't an option. "I wish," she replied, covering. "It's a paperweight. In case someone tries to mug me."

"Next time, try to remember it's in there or you're gonna hurt yourself," Nick said, giving her a wink.

Claire opened her purse, pulled out her wallet and cell phone before shoving the bag under the front seat.

"You can't leave it there," said Nick.

"Paperweight'll set off the metal detectors." Claire said, holding up her driver's license and her phone. "These are all I need."

"We don't go through the detectors from down here," Nick reminded her. "And we're done with this car. All we need is someone who knows the deal to see you driving on the street or me drive it here and we're both toast."

"Too bad," said Claire, grabbing the purse with respect for its heft and closing the car door. The Impala had been helpful for the two days they'd kept it. They didn't have to rely on subways or cabs to get everywhere, and as every cop knew, the police parking plate carried by all unmarked police cars was a license to park just about anywhere without fear of getting towed.

They passed through the doors into the downstairs elevator bank and made their way up to the MCS squad room, which was strangely empty for late morning. But for the administrative assistant, Wendy, covering the phones, there wasn't a detective in the place. Even Wilkes was gone.

"Something going on?" Nick asked Wendy.

"Boss is in a meeting upstairs and everyone else is out on jobs, I guess," Wendy replied.

"Good. That gives us some quiet to make the call," said Nick, sitting at his desk and firing up his desktop computer.

"Who exactly do you call in Costa Rica?" asked Claire.

"Their version of the FBI is called the OIJ, their Judicial Investigation Police," he said, pulling up the organization's Web site and dialing more than the usual amount of numbers on the keypad. "Hope someone there speaks English."

Twenty minutes later, Nick was scribbling furiously on a notepad. Claire stood over him trying to decipher his handwriting.

"You're sure about that?" he asked. "Thank you, thank you so much. If there's anything we can ever do for you here . . . You bet we will. *Muchas gracias, mi amigo.*"

He put the receiver down, glanced toward Wilkes's office. The inspector had come in a few minutes earlier, barely acknowledging Nick on the phone as he stormed into his lair and closed the door. "Antonio, my new best friend in Costa Rica, is going to e-mail me everything they have," he told her, not able to hide his excitement as he continued writing.

"Everything he has on what?" asked Claire as she sat in the chair beside his desk.

"Martha Palmer's murder. It wasn't the first bone-boiling homicide down there."

"When did they start?"

"You ready? Seventy-eight."

"Right after the bones were found out in Canarsie," Claire said in amazement. "How many victims in Costa Rica?"

Nick looked up from the notepad. "Twenty-two."

Claire was shocked. "How could we have missed this?"

"We weren't thinking outside the box. Our box being this country."

"But the only mention of bone boiling was with regard to Martha Palmer's murder. Where were the other bodies found?"

Nick clicked through his computer and brought up his departmental e-mail. "Not bodies, bones. Only bones. One homicide every year or two. Sometimes several in one year. The cops were stumped for most of that time because there was no clear pattern connecting the victims. They came from all walks of life, rich and poor, locals and tourists, found on beaches in different parts of the country on both coasts." Nick looked up at Claire to gauge her response. "And most importantly, Martha Palmer's murder was the last one with this MO."

"In 2009," said Claire, wrapping her head around it. "Four years ago. Was there ever a period that long with no similar killings between then and 1978?"

"No," Nick replied. "Antonio made a point of telling me that."

"So the Costa Rican police are going to help us?"

"They already have."

"I mean, checking their immigration records to see who's left the country since then and hasn't come back."

Nick clicked his mouse and typed again. "That won't be necessary," he said.

"Why not?"

He clicked the mouse again. "Because we already know the answer to that."

He pointed to the screen, and Claire gasped at what was there: a digital image of a New York State driver's license sporting the photo of a man, in his early sixties, a shock of white hair and a face that appeared to have either not aged or been reshaped by an excellent plastic surgeon.

"Oh, my God." Claire breathed. "He's here."

The name on the license was Victor Andrew Palmer.

"Since 2010," Nick confirmed. "Moved back after he sold his resort."

"Moved back?"

"He's a Brooklyn boy. Born and raised."

Holy shit. They sat there in silence.

"It can't be that simple," Nick said. "I mean, I get that maybe he
killed the women up here and down there. But why kill his own
wife?"

"Either he couldn't help himself, or she found out what her husband had been doing all those years and he murdered her to shut
her up. Then he comes back here, his impulses overwhelm him, and
he picks up where he left off in the seventies—butchering women
and boiling their bones."

"We've gotta tell Wilkes," Nick said, getting up.

Nick and Claire sat on the couch in Wilkes's office, Savarese in the
chair opposite them, the inspector at his desk as they recounted
what they'd learned about the murders in Costa Rica and Victor
Palmer.

Upon hearing Palmer's name, Wilkes stood up from his desk and
began to pace. It both amused and bothered Nick, for in all the years
he'd known Wilkes, he'd never seen his boss, his patron saint, do this
before.

"That's unbelievable," Savarese said after Nick and Claire finished.
"It makes perfect sense, but it's unbelievable. We know where this lunatic is right now?"

"Palmer got himself a driver's license when he came back. Address is on Seventy-Eighth. . . ."

"Between Riverside and West End," said Wilkes, dropping back
into his chair. "In a big-ass brownstone he bought with the proceeds
of selling his resort."

This statement brought silence to the room until Claire broke the
ice. "Inspector, how do you know where Palmer lives?"

"I've been there," he said, putting a hand to his head as if struck
by a sudden headache.

"To Palmer's house?" Nick asked, astonished.

"Commissioner dragged me to a party there about a year and a half ago," Wilkes replied. "They grew up down the block from each other in Flatbush. Palmer's tight with Hizzoner the Mayor too. Hell, I talked to the guy for a few minutes at that party. Told him I was planning a vacation; he gave me this whole sales pitch on Costa Rica and that resort he used to own."

His voice drifted off, and Nick knew what he was thinking. They were about to cause a category five political shit storm with Wilkes in its eye.

"Are you sure about all this?" Wilkes asked, turning to Nick. "Dead sure?"

"Yes, sir," said Nick. "What do you want us to do?"

Wilkes took a breath and stood up. Nick could see his old boss had returned.

"Not a damn thing until I say so," he said in the threatening voice Nick knew so well.

"Boss," Savarese said, "maybe we should get a couple of under-covers to sit on this prick in case he ventures out for another kill."

"Not a goddamed thing—did you hear me?" Wilkes said, raising his voice. Then, more quietly, he said, "Until I confab with Chief Dolan—which I'll do tonight—and he gives me the go-ahead, no-body's gonna do dick." He looked directly at Nick and Claire. "Which goes double for you two nobodies."

Nick watched the sun disappear behind the buildings on the far side of Central Park as he and Claire walked up the street to his brownstone. They stopped at the steps and he stared west as the light faded. Claire stood beside him, knowingly.

"Better enjoy this view while I can," he said.

He hadn't invited her in and she didn't feel like he wanted to. "I'm going out to the avenue and find a cab," she said.

Nick paused, never taking his eyes off the beautiful tableau. "Why don't you just take my car?" he said.

"We gave it back, remember?" Claire reminded him.

"No, not the police car. I have a car. Actually, right now a friend's kind of permanently using it because he has a free garage to park it in."

"Free parking? In this city?" Claire asked.

"His father died last year. He got the condo and the basement parking spot but the Mercedes went to his sister. I had no use for my piece of crap, so he took it off my hands until Jill gets her license," replied Nick. The sun gone now, he turned to her. "You wouldn't have to take a cab up here every day to get me, and Peter only drives the thing on weekends. Someone might as well get some use out of it for the insurance money I'm paying."

"Thanks, but unless your friend Peter lives near me and lets me keep it in his spot, I can't afford five hundred a month for a garage."

"You'll park a block from your building at the Midtown South Precinct, on the sidewalk where the cops who work there leave their personal cars."

"And not get towed?" she asked.

"I'll give you a permit to put on the dash and nobody'll touch it."

Claire felt awkward, and yet his generous offer was a relief. A car would provide them with cheap transportation and eliminate the need for Detective Simms to chauffeur them around on official business. More importantly, it would be a huge help if they needed to attend to any *unofficial* police business.

"If you think that'll work," Claire said by way of thanking him, "I'll just keep it until we're done with this case."

"Sure," was all Nick said. "Should we get it now?"

"Sure," Claire said, smiling.

She wasn't smiling, however, when she saw what Nick had referred to as a car: a 1989 red Jeep Cherokee, battered by years of street parking, that looked more like it belonged in a junkyard than in the spotless basement garage of a luxury condo building.

"Don't judge the book by the cover," Nick said, sensing her disdain. "It runs and only has forty-two thousand miles on it."

"And you let yourself be seen in this?" Claire asked.

"No payments. And in this city nobody gives a shit what anyone drives," he said. "If this thing was a safety hazard I wouldn't let you near it. Promise."

Claire stared him down as she got behind the wheel and turned the key in the ignition. Good to Nick's word, the interior was spotless and the engine hummed in a reassuring low roar.

"Thanks. I'm sorry I judged it before giving you a chance," she said. "Shall I drop you back at your place?"

"Nah, I could use the exercise," he said. "I'll walk. That permit is in the glove compartment. Just drive up Fifty-First Street past Third Avenue and find a space as close to Lexington as you can. And pick me up tomorrow at seven. We'll drive down to headquarters and park behind the building on Madison Street."

"Okay," she said, putting the Jeep into gear, pulling out of the spot, and driving up the ramp, watching Nick get smaller in the rearview mirror.

She turned out onto the street and drove the few feet until she had to stop for a red light at the corner. Realizing she hadn't adjusted her side-view mirrors, she did so, fixing the left one first and then the right. That's when she spotted Nick walking out of his friend's condo building and down the street.

He's going in the wrong direction, she realized. *Away from his building, not toward it.* Why would he say he was going home if he wasn't? Especially at night, without his dog Cisco?

An annoyed horn honked behind her, waking her up to the now green traffic light. She circled the block, hitting the gas when she saw Nick getting into a cab on the left side of the street and pulling up beside it on the right. Her window was open as was every window on the cab, allowing her to hear what Nick was saying to the driver.

"Seventy-Ninth and Broadway," he instructed.

"What for?" shouted Claire.

Nick turned and saw her. "Never mind," he told the driver, getting out and throwing him two bucks just for stopping. "I got a free ride."

He closed the door and circled around to the passenger's side of his Jeep.

"Going uptown?" he asked.

"I hadn't planned on it," she said. "What's at Seventy-Ninth and Broadway?"

"There's a bar up there I like," he said.

"Bullshit," Claire said. "You're going to sit on Victor Palmer's place. Despite direct orders from your boss."

"We can't wait for him to go to the chief of detectives," he said.

"He told us he would do it tonight." Claire worried about the repercussions if Wilkes found out that Nick had disobeyed his order—again.

"And if tonight's the night Palmer decides to cut up another woman?"

"What did you think you were gonna do by yourself? Tail him? In the dark, without your dog, when you can barely see your foot on the sidewalk?"

"I can see well enough," he muttered. "And I don't want another dead girl on my conscience, especially one I could've prevented from getting killed."

"Are you saying that to rope me in to your little plan?" Claire asked, the tension heating up between them.

"Rope *you* in? You're the one who roped me into that teaching thing."

"It wouldn't be a bad way to make a living, would it? Low pressure, decent money, on top of your pension. Or you could stay on the job and teach on the side."

"Stop planning my life!" Nick yelled, getting out of the car and storming down the street, against the one-way traffic. Claire threw the Jeep into reverse and backed up beside him.

"It's not just your life, it's your girls' lives," Claire said.

"You're not their mother!" Nick exclaimed.

Claire slammed on the brakes. "No, but you're their father," she shouted. "Have you thought about them at all? Because your future affects *theirs*. So if you don't want to plan your life after you retire from the police department, then at least plan for *them*."

It happened so fast that Claire didn't know what hit her. In an instant, Nick was in the car, leaning over, pulling her head toward his and kissing her. Claire was startled at first, uncomfortable. And then she realized this is what she'd wanted. She let herself kiss him back, get lost in it. At least a minute passed before she pulled away. Involuntarily. As if an unseen force had grabbed her collar and wouldn't let go.

"I'm . . . I'm sorry," said Nick, thinking he'd crossed the line.

"Don't apologize," said Claire. "It just . . . happened."

"I don't know why I . . ." Nick stopped, surprised by what had come over him.

"It's okay," Claire said. "But maybe we should keep things on a professional level."

"Right," Nick replied, opening the car door and getting out.

"You're not going to do anything stupid tonight, are you?" asked Claire.

"No, I'm not." He grinned.

Claire was skeptical. "Promise?"

"Cross my heart and hope to die."

And he crossed himself. Claire looked at him, framed against the darkening sky streaked with orange and red, thinking how handsome he was. "I'll call you when I'm here in the morning," she said.

Nick closed the door. Claire drove away, glancing into the rearview mirror at him, watching her. She wondered if he was thinking the same thing:

Why did I want him and then pull back?

Nick waited until the Jeep turned the corner. He felt embarrassed for kissing her. What had come over him? Still, she had kissed him back. He was sure she'd responded to him.

Or was she just too surprised to stop him?

He didn't want to think he was a jerk, taking advantage of the situation. When he got home, he knew he had to do something to make himself feel better.

"Hi, Dad," came the voice of his younger daughter, Katie.

"I'll be right in, girls," Nick shouted. He could hear that they were in the kitchen, putting plates on the table. But he had to make a stop first.

He veered off from the front doorway, down the hall and into the small bathroom. He closed the door, making sure to lock it. Then he turned on the cold water in the sink, though he had no intention of washing his hands. As quietly as possible, he removed the cover from the toilet tank and felt inside for what he knew would be there. . . .

Except it wasn't.

In a panic, he looked into the toilet tank.

The gun was gone!

Frantically, he retraced his steps. The damn thing was so much trouble to unwrap and then wrap up again that he hadn't checked it in months. At least not that he could remember. But was he forgetting something? Had he hidden it somewhere else?

Or worse, did one of the girls find it? Nah, they would've confronted me. . . .

"Dad! Everything okay in there?" came his daughter Jill's voice from the other side of the door.

"Yeah, everything's fine," Nick shouted back, replacing the lid on the tank.

He unlocked the door and opened it to find Jill standing there, worried. "What was all the banging about?" she asked.

"I had to give the toilet a jiggle this morning to stop it from running," he said. "Just wanted to make sure it wasn't about to flood the place."

If Jill had taken the gun, she didn't let on. "Well, dinner's almost ready," his daughter said, her voice brandishing the implied authority she now wielded as Woman of the House since Nick's mother had died.

"Smells like mystery meat," Nick quipped.

Katie threw her arms around him. "We're having your favorite— meat loaf. The way Grandma made it, with the bread crumbs."

"Well, not exactly the way Grandma made it," Jill corrected. "I think I actually got the recipe right."

"I'm sure you did," Nick said, as Cisco appeared at his feet, tail wagging. He sat and Nick petted him. "I can't wait to try it. Think Cisco needs a little air first, though." He registered the look on her face. "If that's okay."

"C'mon, Dad. It's hot. And it's on the table," Jill said.

Nick kissed his daughter on the cheek. "Guess I can go after we eat," he said.

He and Cisco followed Jill into the kitchen, where he forgot about anything else in his life but his two girls and the dinner they'd made. The meat loaf was even better than the one his late mother used to cook them. He savored a second bite.

"Something's different," he said.

"The sauce," Jill informed him. "I tried one with three cheeses in it."

"You mean instead of the ketchup Grandma used to use?" Nick said, taking another bite.

"Ketchup has too much sugar in it, Daddy," Katie said, like a mother scolding a child. "Grandma shouldn't have let you have so much."

"Grandmas from her time didn't really watch those kinds of things," Nick said. "But you're right."

Cisco jumped up against the table, the smell of meat and cheese too much for him to resist despite his training. They all laughed as Nick grabbed his collar and moved the pooch away from the food.

"No human food for you, my friend," he said.

Cisco sat, looked up at him with pleading eyes. Into which Nick now stared.

"That's not gonna work, today or ever," Nick assured the dog. "Now go wait by the door." Cisco shuffled out of the kitchen, tail between his legs as only a dog can show defeat.

The meat loaf wasn't the only improvement over Nick's mother's culinary skills. He bit into a steamed broccoli floret, marveling at its crispness, gratified that his daughters didn't cook like his mother, who never met a vegetable she couldn't boil to mush.

He relaxed, enjoying the one place where the outside world couldn't touch him. The feeling quickly passed, though, as Claire's words from before their spontaneous kiss—or, more accurately, his sudden move on her—came back to him. Was she right? Was he providing a safety net for his daughters?

Or was he so wrapped up in his return to real police work and his impending blindness that he was neglecting his duties as a father?

Nick stood up and kissed both of his daughters on the cheek, each of his arms on one of their shoulders. The girls, not used to such a display of affection from their dad, looked up at him, wondering if he'd lost his mind.

"What was that for?" asked Jill.

"You know how much I love you guys, right?"

"Sure we do, Dad," said Katie.

"I mean it," Nick said, detecting the concern in their voices. "I know it's been tough since Mom died. And I know I haven't been here—sometimes even when I *am* here."

"Dad, what's going on?" asked Jill.

"Just listen, okay? I'm going to make it up to you. We'll go on a vacation. Maybe to someplace like—"

"Hawaii?" asked Katie with excitement, starting to dance her version of a hula and singing her version of Hawaiian music. Nick had shown her pictures a few years ago of a trip he took before he married her mother, and Katie had been obsessed with the islands ever since.

"Sure, why not?" said Nick, a smile crossing his face to see Katie so happy. Those moments had been few and far between since their mother had died.

"Just the three of us?" Katie asked, making sure he was serious.

"Just us three," answered Nick, as he spied the hint of a smirk on his older daughter's face. "What?" he said to Jill.

"Why don't you take Cisco and get that drink you wanted," she said.

"Okay," Nick replied. "But I'm serious. We'll go during Christmas vacation."

"If you say so, Dad," replied Jill. "Just the three of us."

Claire sat behind the wheel of Nick's Jeep, parked beside the curb, staring down a side street. She'd gone home to change, her dress replaced with comfortable jeans and a dark blue cotton blouse. Now the only light came from the streetlamps above and cars whizzing by. She wished the passing headlights would hypnotize her. Anything to distract her from the turmoil in her head.

She replayed the kiss with Nick, wondering what made her want more of him and then back away as if she'd done something terribly wrong.

Why am I at war with myself? Did I bring him back into my life for more than just to help me find who murdered Rosa?

She thought of Amy, that day on her parents' driveway when her best friend was kidnapped. That day was the before and after of her life. After she lost Amy, she stopped feeling. She remembered telling her father that she wouldn't ever feel sad anymore and she made sure to keep that promise. Whenever something troubling happened, she turned her feelings off, shut them down. She had gotten so used to cloistering herself from the world to avoid pain that she forgot how to feel much of anything. And now, especially after tonight's experience with Nick, she so desperately wanted to feel. But could she?

Can I ever set myself free?

If she hadn't been staring down the side street she would have missed the sudden flash of green that broke her trance. It was too subtle and short to be from a changing traffic light.

She reached for a pair of binoculars, which she'd picked up at her apartment, and used them to see what she expected.

Nick. Holding Cisco's leash in one hand, his video camera, flashing a green light in night-vision mode, in the other. Pointing at Victor Palmer's brownstone.

It was the reason she'd parked here, at the corner of West End Avenue and Seventy-Eighth Street. Because she knew Nick's promise to stay away from Palmer was bullshit. And she was determined to save him from himself.

The video camera helped, Nick realized, even more than in the past, because of the extent to which his vision had deteriorated over the past year. The trip through the darkness was becoming more difficult, even with Cisco. He didn't want to appear he was using Cisco as his guide dog. He felt bad about lying to Claire, and was pretty sure she knew what he was doing. But he wasn't about to take any chances. Should this be the night Victor Palmer went out to kill again, Nick was going to stop him.

He settled on the sidewalk about twenty yards west of Broadway, where he felt Palmer wouldn't spot him. He turned the camera on, set it on night-vision mode, and zoomed in on Palmer's front door as a couple walked through the foreground of his shot, their hands locked as they headed up the street.

Am I falling in love with Claire?

He suppressed the thought as a man passed between the lens and Palmer's house.

Something about the man made Nick swing the camera right, toward the man, who was heading away from him toward West End Avenue, on the same side of the street as Palmer's home. The man moved quickly, carrying a heavy-looking duffel over his shoulder. Nick didn't remember seeing the man before the couple passed by him, which meant that he must have come from one of the brownstones on the block.

Was it Palmer?

He looked toward Palmer's brownstone. It was dark. Nick knew he had no choice but to find out. He headed toward the opposite end of the block, careful not to walk too fast so the man wouldn't see him and get suspicious.

The man reached the corner and crossed to Nick's side of the street, then headed across to the far side of West End.

Shit. If it's Palmer, I blew it.

He continued to the corner, stopping short and pointing his camera across the street. What he saw shocked and scared him:

The man was definitely Palmer, and he was talking to a woman on the sidewalk, standing beside a red Jeep Cherokee.

His Jeep Cherokee.

Claire had also seen the couple pass, and the man with the duffel appear seconds later. Though he moved at a fast clip and was across the street, Claire recognized him as Victor Palmer.

He's carrying a duffel bag. What's inside? More bones?

She lifted the binoculars to her eyes and pointed them toward Seventy-Eighth Street. No sign of Nick. She had to act.

Composing herself, she got out of the Jeep, went around to the back, and opened the rear hatch. She lifted the cover off the compartment that housed the spare tire, grabbed Nick's Glock, and had just wedged it in her pocket when a man's voice came from the direction of the sidewalk:

"Is everything okay, miss?"

Claire turned.

Palmer was standing right in front of her. Smiling. His vibrant white hair was impeccably trimmed and he wore a navy blue cashmere sweater, gray linen pants, and soft, tan leather loafers.

Somehow, she found the courage to smile back. "Thanks, everything's fine."

She hoped that Palmer would move on, but he stayed next to her.

"It's just that I saw you back here and you had the wheel well open and, well, it's nighttime and a lady as beautiful as you shouldn't have to change a flat tire alone."

Claire now understood how this man charmed his victims. *And if he's looking for another one, I'm making it easy for him.*

"I don't have a flat," she said, laughing so he wouldn't see she was scared to death. "And thanks for the lovely compliment. I keep some tools back here and I was just looking for a screwdriver. . . ." And then she decided to make sure. "I'm sorry, but I didn't get your name."

"Victor. What's yours, my dear?"

"Claire. And you're very nice to stop and see if I needed help."

"Excuse me, is everything okay here?" came Nick's voice from a few feet away. Claire had been so focused on Palmer that she failed to see Nick and Cisco crossing the street toward them. She decided to pretend that she didn't know Nick, but just as she was about to speak, Palmer went on the offensive.

"Yes, everything's fine, sir," he said to Nick.

"Do you know this woman?" Nick asked.

Palmer seemed confused. Why was this man who, judging from the presence of what was clearly a guide dog, couldn't see more than a few feet in front of him interrogating him?

"Yes, I do know her. Her name is Claire. Not that it's any of your business, though."

"Actually, sir, it *is* my business," said Nick, pulling his gold detective's shield from his pocket. "I live a couple of blocks away and we've had some complaints of break-ins in the neighborhood."

"Really?" Palmer asked, with suspicion.

"When I saw you over here with the duffel bag it just seemed strange to me, that's all," said Nick.

"Then you may want to call a cop who *can* see," suggested Palmer in an annoyed tone as he eyed Cisco and noted his service dog vest, "because I was locking up for the night when I saw a green glow coming from outside my window."

"Oh yeah?" asked Nick, covering.

"Like from a pair of night-vision goggles," said Palmer, "or from that camera you're holding."

Claire and Nick looked at the evidence in Nick's hand.

"You were pointing that camera at my house. And I live alone."

"I was pointing it around the *entire* neighborhood," said Nick.

Palmer pretended to relax but both Nick and Claire knew better. "I guess you have to protect the neighborhood from burglars, Detective," he said.

"That why you left the house with the bag?" Nick asked. "Afraid someone might steal your valuables?"

"Yes, because if someone was watching my house I'm not about to give them anything to look at. If you must know, I was going to stay at a friend's place."

"Great. Just tell me who the friend is and where he or she lives and we're done here."

It was as if Nick asked him the chemical formula for gasoline. "I . . . I don't think that's any of your business," stammered Palmer. Nick's detective brain knew he had him cornered. Palmer seemed to read his mind, however, trying something else. "I was actually going to ask my friend Claire here if she'd give me a ride over."

Palmer didn't look at Claire. But if he thought she was going to back up his bullshit story, he was sorely mistaken.

"Friends? We just met," she said, playing the part perfectly as she turned her gaze to Nick. "I was getting something out of the back of the car when he came up and started talking. And to be honest with you, Detective, I was a little scared."

Gotcha, thought Nick. "Sir, drop the bag and put both hands on the hood of the Jeep," Nick said.

Palmer did neither.

"You're not going to frisk me, are you?" he asked in mock surprise. "Because if it makes any difference, the police commissioner is a friend, and I have his cell on speed dial."

"Oh, there's not much the police commissioner can do to me," said Nick.

"He'll do plenty when he finds out about—"

Palmer never finished the sentence. In a flash, Nick grabbed him by the shoulders and threw him face first against the Jeep's hood.

"Shut up and don't move," he said.

Claire saw Palmer's right hand tighten around the bag and knew what was coming.

"Watch out!" she screamed.

Too late. Palmer jammed the bag into Nick's gut, catching him by surprise and propelling him backward until he fell, hitting his head on the sidewalk and passing out.

"Stop!" screamed Claire. Cisco lunged for Palmer but couldn't reach him because Nick lay atop the leash. In a flash, Palmer had the bag open and was reaching inside. When his hand came out it held a butcher knife.

"What are you doing?" Claire yelled.

Palmer approached Nick, the knife behind his back.

"I'll say it was self-defense," he said eerily, as if possessed. "I didn't know he was a cop."

"Drop the knife or I'll shoot!" Claire screamed.

Palmer turned to see her aiming Nick's gun at him.

"Back away from him!" Claire ordered.

"Don't be rash, Claire," Palmer said, letting the knife drop from his hand and clatter on the sidewalk. Claire kept the gun trained on him as she moved toward the knife and kicked it into the street.

Palmer was still on his feet, which Claire knew was a problem.

"Get down on your stomach, put your hands behind your back, and spread your legs!"

Palmer didn't move. Making her point, Claire unchecked the safety. If Palmer didn't think she meant business before, he did now, and lowered himself to his knees.

"You're making a mistake, Claire," he said, trying to convince her.

"There's no mistake," she replied, kneeling beside Nick, noticing a trickle of blood running from his head down to the sidewalk. She retrieved his handcuffs and detective's shield from his belt.

"On the ground, now!"

Several passers-by gathered around. Palmer knew he had no choice. Slowly, he lay prone on the sidewalk. Claire held the gun on him and straddled his legs as she cuffed him.

She looked up at the crowd.

"Somebody call nine-one-one!" she yelled. "Tell them there's a police officer down and we need an ambulance!"

CHAPTER 17

———✦———

"How is he?" Wilkes asked, heading toward Claire, who was leaving the treatment room of MSU Hospital's Emergency Department. The cluttered, crowded ER was more chaotic than usual at 10:35 p.m. on a weekday night as three pairs of paramedics wheeled trauma patients from a car accident past the usual suspects: people with the flu, lacerations from making snacks before bed, psychotics who talked animatedly to invisible foes.

"He's groggy but stable," replied Claire, knowing she was about to face the consequences for what she and Nick did tonight. "They're taking him up for a head CT to make sure there's no bleeding."

"Oh, there's gonna be blood, all right," said Wilkes, dispensing of all pretense. "After what you two pulled tonight."

"Inspector, I can explain—"

"The hell you can," he growled, taking Claire by the arm and leading her to a corner stashed with IV poles. "You know what Victor Palmer did the second after he was booked? He made his phone call," Wilkes said, stepping up to her and speaking right into her face. "He called his *personal* friend, the police commissioner, who immediately called me. On my goddamned cell phone. I told him I was just about to get an update on Lawler's condition and I'd call him right back. But I really got rid of the bastard because I didn't have shit to tell him."

Claire had never seen the inspector so angry. His face was reddish purple and sweat was pouring down his temples.

"So you'd better start talking, Doctor Waters, because when I call the PC back I gotta have something to say that's not gonna make him wanna bust me back into uniform running the motor pool."

"Tell him it's all my fault," said Claire.

Wilkes laughed in disbelief. "Don't play games with me, Doc, because this ain't the time."

"Blame me," Claire said. "It's the truth."

"You expect me to believe that this wasn't Nick's idea?"

"It wasn't. I brought him right home from your office. He told me to take his car. I made him promise he wouldn't go near Palmer and he agreed."

Wilkes paused. Then he pulled two metal chairs over and motioned for Claire to sit down.

"Okay, Doc, we'll do it your way," Wilkes said.

Claire sat down and Wilkes sat facing her, their knees touching.

"And then?" he asked. "After his alleged promise to you?"

"I went home. But we all know how Nick is about keeping his promises," Claire said, trying to inject some lightness.

"Yeah, and you too," Wilkes replied without any humor.

"I decided to drive by Palmer's myself," Claire said.

"Is that right?" he said, mocking her.

"Yes, sir. Just to see whether Nick was there." There was a tone of defiance in her voice that Wilkes detested.

"After I told both of you that wasn't an option," Wilkes said.

"Actually, you told *Nick* it wasn't an option. I just happened to be in the room. And with all due respect, Inspector, I don't work for you, so I'm not bound by your orders."

Claire's words enraged him. He leaned in close to her. "Listen carefully, *Doctor*," he said, with contempt in his voice. "As long as you're part of this investigation—which *you* wanted—and like I said from the outset when we brought you into this, you damn well better do what I say."

Claire knew she had to tread carefully, for Nick's sake.

"Now tell me the rest of it," Wilkes said, sitting back, giving Claire space.

"It got dark and I was sitting in Nick's car when Palmer comes out of his house and heads my way. So I got out and went around to open the trunk—"

"What the hell for?"

"To get the gun," Claire said.

"The gun," Wilkes repeated, afraid where this was going.

"From the spare tire compartment," Claire answered evenly.

Wilkes lowered his voice, but his tone betrayed his anger. "You're telling me that you knew Nick Lawler, the blind cop, who's forbidden to own firearms of any kind, kept a gun in the spare tire compartment?"

"No, Inspector," said Claire, knowing the lie she was about to tell had to be convincing. "The gun is mine."

"Really?" Wilkes said, suppressing a laugh. "Now you own a gun?"

"You can believe whatever you want," Claire said.

"And this gun you *allegedly* own . . . where did you *allegedly* get it? Wait, let me rephrase that. When, exactly, did Nick Lawler *give* it to you?"

"He didn't," said Claire.

"If Nicky didn't give it to you, who did?"

"My uncle Scott."

"Your uncle gave you a gun," Wilkes said, not believing a word of it. "For what, your birthday? Christmas?"

"Protection," said Claire. "After everything that happened last year."

Wilkes paused. It was the first thing she'd said that seemed plausible.

"Okay, Doc. Okay," he said in a tone suggesting she might have convinced him. "And you've been schlepping this cannon—which I'm assuming is unregistered—around New York City since then without—which I'm also assuming—a carry permit?"

"I don't have a permit, Inspector. My uncle gave it to me to keep in my apartment. I really don't know how to use it so I never take it outside."

"Then why'd you have it on you tonight?" Wilkes asked.

"It wasn't on me. It was in the wheel well of the car."

"Don't you split hairs with me, young lady," he warned. "I could lock your ass up right now if I had to. Why'd you bring the gun with you?"

"I can't explain it. I just thought I should have it with me."

"I see," said Wilkes, knowing everything coming from Claire's mouth was total bullshit. But he also realized that as long as she stuck to this story they might get away with it. He sighed and stood up.

"And if I need to corroborate your story about this mystery uncle?" he asked, assuming she had that base covered as well. "Because technically I could collar him too."

"I'll even give you his address," Claire said, "but arresting may be difficult. He currently resides at Mount Hood Cemetery upstate in Rochester. He died of cancer last January."

Wilkes smiled. "And this is what you'd have me tell the chief of detectives and police commissioner, am I correct?"

"Unless you'd like me to tell them myself, Inspector," Claire said, "which I'm more than happy to do."

Wilkes said nothing as he walked toward the exit. Claire followed him.

"Because here's what I'd tell them," she continued. "Nick went to Palmer's because he called several times and I didn't pick up. Knowing me, he assumed I'd gone to Palmer's on my own, and he wanted to make sure your orders were obeyed so someone as stupid and inept as me wouldn't screw up the case."

Wilkes considered her. "You're a whole lot of things, Doc," he said, "and *piece of work* is at the top of that list. But *stupid* and *inept* isn't even at the bottom of it."

Claire smiled back at him.

"Okay," Wilkes said, stepping with Claire through the electric doors to the outside ambulance bay. "Now that you've buried me in that huge heap of horseshit, I got some more for you to shovel on top of the pile."

"Hit me," said Claire, ready for whatever Wilkes was about to dish out.

"Here's the story: Palmer's a lying sack of shit. Not only didn't you hold a gun on him, that gun you never had—and I don't give a crap if it's something sentimental from your uncle—is gonna disappear."

"Inspector, bystanders saw me holding the gun on Palmer."

"I know you're new at this whole lying thing, Doctor," said Wilkes. "But when the crime lab folks find Lawler's fingerprints all over the cartridge and bullets, it's all over for him."

"That won't be a problem, Inspector," she said, keeping a straight face, "because the only prints you'll find anywhere on the gun or the ammo will be mine."

Wilkes shuffled his feet, amazed. Not only had Claire all but admitted to tampering with evidence—which of course he couldn't prove, not that he wanted to—but she had thought of everything. Right now, he was glad she was one of the good guys.

"Whatever you say, Doc," he said. "But we're still gonna disappear the gun. We don't want questions about why you were carrying an illegal firearm. Got it?"

"Got it."

"Fantastic. Now, Palmer's claiming he tried to stab Lawler in self-defense because he didn't believe Nicky's a cop anymore, which, in street terms anyway, he isn't. We've got twenty-four hours to arraign the sonuvabitch, and when it happens I don't want it to be for simple assault. I want to nail him for murder."

"Is that an order?" Claire asked.

"Damn right," he said, "not that you're good at taking them. We've got our work cut out for us. How are you at pulling all-nighters?"

"I made it through medical school and residency, Inspector. I can do them in my sleep."

"No pun intended," said Wilkes, suppressing the impulse to grin.

"Doctor Waters," came a voice from the entrance. It belonged to Trina Cates, the pretty, young, African-American, on-call neurologist with whom Claire was friendly.

"Trina. Is Nick okay?" Claire asked, walking over to her.

"A word, please," Trina said.

"Go ahead," said Wilkes.

Claire and Trina stepped aside. "What's up?" Claire asked.

"Your friend is conscious," she told Claire softly. "But there's a problem."

"Something show up on his CT?"

"There's nothing life threatening going on. But if this guy's a cop . . ." She hesitated. "He's a friend of yours, so I thought you'd want first crack at him."

"What's the deal?" asked Wilkes.

"Just a consult on another case," Claire said, the lie spilling effortlessly from her lips. "I'll be right back."

* * *

Nick was trying to sit up when Claire and Trina entered the treatment room.

"Welcome back," Claire said to him, relieved that he looked all right.

"How long was I out?" he asked, lying back down.

"About forty-five minutes, according to Doctor Waters," Trina said, checking his vitals on a monitor over the gurney. "You're lucky, Detective. Your CT shows no intracranial hemorrhaging."

"Then why was I out for so long?" Nick asked, thinking something must be wrong for him to be wired to monitors in the ER. "What aren't you telling me?"

"You have a concussion," Trina said, putting some authority into her voice. "Trauma to your brain caused you to lose consciousness—"

"I know what a concussion is, for chrissakes," Nick said.

"I'm admitting you so we can keep an eye on you overnight," replied Trina. "Just to make sure you're okay."

"She means you have to take it easy," said Claire, who stood across from Trina on the other side of the bed. Until her inquisition at the hands of Wilkes, she'd been with Nick from the moment the ambulance arrived at Seventy-Eighth Street and West End Avenue to scoop him up. Because Claire was a doctor, the paramedics allowed her to ride with him in the back. Though Roosevelt was the closest hospital, she requested they take Nick to MSU, where she had privileges and knew almost everyone who worked in the ER. And where she'd have some control over keeping Nick's secret.

"She knows, right?" he asked Claire, gesturing to Trina Cates.

"Yes, Mr. Lawler," Trina said. "I performed a thorough neuro exam, including looking at your retinas." Trina glanced over to Claire, then continued. "Since your preexisting condition has no bearing on your head trauma, I see no reason to include it in your chart."

"Thanks, Doc," said Nick.

Trina smiled. "No thanks needed."

Nick did his best to nod despite the throbbing pain in his head. "Can you give us a second alone?"

"I can give you more than that," Trina said. "Let me know right away if your vision changes, you feel dizzy, or you vomit," she said to Nick, and left the room.

"How are you feeling?" asked Claire.

Nick rubbed the spot on his head where he'd landed. "Like I got slammed with a baseball bat," he said.

"Whatever doesn't kill you makes you stronger," Claire responded.

"Remember that the next time we do something as stupid as we did tonight."

"We got Palmer, didn't we?" Claire said.

"Was there anything interesting in the duffel bag?" Nick asked, hoping that the case would be easily solved.

"Just the butcher knife and some clothes," Claire said. "Maybe he was heading out to find his next victim, brought along something to change into after the bloodbath."

"Where's the sonuvabitch now?" Nick asked.

"Inspector Wilkes told me he's down at headquarters."

The mention of Wilkes's name made Nick's headache go from bad to worse.

"Is Wilkes here?" asked Nick.

"In the ambulance bay, getting some air," Claire said.

Nick knew he had to bring up what he'd been thinking about since he regained consciousness.

"Guess it's a good thing you found my gun in the toilet," he said.

"You swore to me—and to them—that you turned in all your firearms."

"Only the registered ones. They didn't know about this one."

"They do now," Claire said, worrying how Nick would react. "Because they have it."

Nick thought he knew what this meant. "Then I'm toast."

"I don't think so," said Claire.

"My prints are all over the damn thing."

"Not anymore."

Nick paused, using his arms to hoist himself into a sitting position. "What did you do?" he asked.

"Wiped the entire thing down, including the clip and the bullets. Then reloaded and made sure I touched everything."

Nick shook his head. "I know you're trying to protect me. But it isn't gonna work. Wilkes is gonna throw a shit fit. And I'm gonna lose what's left of my job."

"I took care of the inspector," Claire said. "He's more concerned about protecting his own ass and this case than having his bosses think he's letting a blind cop keep a gun."

"What the hell kind of story did you tell him?"

Claire described the tale she wove for Wilkes, including the lie about her dead uncle giving her the gun. "As long as you stick to *my* facts," she said, "you're gonna be okay."

Nick was incredulous, which he showed by staring up at the ceiling. "You gave Wilkes a way outta this mess," he said.

"Not all of it," Claire replied, her hand brushing a wisp of his hair. "His way out is to get a confession from Victor Palmer. And it's our only way out too."

Nick swung his legs over the side of the gurney. "Then we've gotta get to it. Get these wires and tubes outta me so I can interrogate this scumbag," he said, trying to figure out how to make himself stand up.

But Claire stood in his way so he couldn't. "We will," she said, lifting his legs back into the bed. "But I'm not letting you sign yourself out of here against medical advice."

Nick grabbed her hand. "Wilkes, Savarese—they don't know this case like I do. Like we do."

"Maybe so. But we don't know Palmer. So we need to spend the night learning everything we can about him."

"That's why I need to be there," Nick exclaimed.

"In the morning," Claire replied. "Right now you need to let Doctor Cates make sure you're not going to keel over the moment your feet hit the floor."

Nick knew this was a battle he wasn't about to win. "Okay, Doctor," he conceded. "What do you want me to do?"

"Stay here and be a good boy," Claire said. "I'll go back to headquarters with the inspector and spend the night on the computer. In the morning I'll get you released. By then, we'll have as much dirt on Palmer as we need, or at least that we're going to get."

Nick wanted to be a part of this, fearing that if he didn't go now he'd be cut out of the action later. But he knew better than to argue with Claire—and he was still feeling like crap. Moreover, she had lied to save his ass and what remained of his job, so he owed her a solid.

"Okay," was all he said.

CHAPTER 18

Palmer was sitting at the table the following morning when Nick entered the interrogation room, carrying a folder and sporting a purple bruise the size of an egg over his right temple. Nick struggled to keep his balance as he pulled a chair opposite him and sat down.

"Looks like you took a nasty fall," Palmer said.

"Yes, sir, I did," Nick replied, his politeness part of his strategy.

"What you're doing to me is inhumane and probably illegal, Detective."

"You may believe that, Mr. Palmer, but it's not illegal. As for inhumane, I hardly think you have the right to make that kind of judgment."

"Detective, and whoever else is listening," he said, pointing at the one-way mirror, "I swear I thought you were impersonating a police officer. Why would I believe that you're a cop when you can barely see?"

Nick pulled the shield clipped to his belt and his ID card clipped to his shirt, tossing them on the table. "Because of these," he said, "which I showed you when I identified myself to you last night. You refused to accept the proof, which is why you're sitting in police headquarters."

"Yes, and speaking of that, is Commissioner Farrell in his office? I'm wondering if I can have a word with him. He's a personal friend, you know."

"Yes, you mentioned that last night," Nick said. In fact, he had prepared for this possibility. An hour earlier, right after he was discharged from the ER, he and Wilkes had met with the PC in his expansive office on the fifteenth floor of One Police Plaza. As his assistant served them coffee in NYPD mugs, they laid out everything they knew about Victor Palmer, which not only made Commissioner Farrell cringe, but also face reality.

"If it turns out you're right, I'll have to retire," Farrell had said, trying to joke. "Palmer's been to every major event I've hosted and there are dozens of pictures of us together."

How ironic, thought Nick. *Hours ago I thought my career was over, but now it's the commissioner's ass on the line.*

Nick leaned forward toward Palmer. Despite spending the night at headquarters, Palmer looked refreshed; his shirt was unwrinkled and his morning beard barely showed on his tanned face.

"The commissioner already knows you're here," Nick now informed him. "But he declined to join us. Friend or not, he's not real fond of anyone beating up on his cops."

Palmer tried to shrug it off. "I understand, of course. He's a busy man. He'll change his mind when he finds out this is all a tragic mistake."

"Tragic, yes. But I assure you, it's no mistake."

Palmer blinked—the first time he'd done so.

"I'm not sure what that means," Palmer said. "You can't possibly think I was robbing my own neighborhood. I've never even gotten a parking ticket."

"Our police department has a long memory, Mr. Palmer. You were arrested for first-degree assault in Queens in seventy-one."

Palmer stared into Nick's eyes—and then, burst out in laughter.

"Oh, come on, Detective. That was over forty years ago. I was a kid. The girl was a liar. It was nothing."

Nothing compared to the sick shit you've done since then.

Nick knew Palmer assumed he knew only of that one arrest, not the details. But in Claire's all-night search, the police computer spat out the ancient assault case, which Claire said fit Palmer's profile—a deep rage toward women.

"It was hardly nothing, Mr. Palmer," Nick said, opening his folder, "so let me refresh your memory. You slapped a teenage girl three times in the face, knocking out most of her teeth and fracturing her skull," Nick read from the file. "Cops who collared you said you were trying to pull her pants off."

If Nick's knowledge of the crime affected Palmer in any way, he didn't show it. "Please, Detective," implored Palmer, "if we're going to spend all this time in here over nothing, can't we at least be informal? Call me Victor."

Nick closed the folder. "I'd be glad to, Victor," he replied. "Unless you'd rather be called Vittorio."

He looked into Palmer's eyes to drive the point home. For the first time, the anger that Nick knew was boiling inside Palmer inched to the surface. This was all part of Claire's plan. Just before Nick entered the interrogation room, she'd laid out the strategy that they hoped would lure Palmer into a trap. Now she watched through the one-way mirror as Nick put the plan into action.

"Vittorio Palmieri died a long time ago," Palmer said, his words clipped. "And I'm not responsible for anything he did."

Spoken like a true psycho, Claire thought.

Nick paused, then seemed to relax in his chair. "You oughta be proud of at least some of what he did. Or at least his parents. I couldn't get enough of the food in their place."

This struck a chord with Palmer. "You've been there?"

"Are you kidding?" Nick said, a slight grin appearing. "I practically lived there when I was a kid. My dad was a cop in the Fifth Precinct for a while. My mom would bring me and my sister downtown to grab dinner with him when he worked four-to-twelves. They always wanted Chinese but I would beg for Palmieri's Pasta House and every coupla times they'd give in."

"When would that have been?" asked Palmer.

"Seventy-five, seventy-six or so. My dad went there a lot more than I did, though. Six-two, dark hair—"

"The place was always filled with cops," Palmer interrupted, his voice sharp, annoyed. Like Nick was wasting his time. "And back then I was working in the kitchen as a cook so I wouldn't have known your father."

"Sorry. Sounds like I hit a nerve," Nick said. "But I swear on my parents' graves the chicken parm there was still the best I've ever had."

At this, Palmer seemed to soften. "No, I'm the one who should apologize," he said. "I should be honored you have such fond memories of my work."

You don't know the half of it, thought Nick.

Claire knew this was part of the plan, to loosen Palmer up before pouncing. Part of her wished she could go in and shake Palmer up with a few more direct, pointed questions. But she knew Nick was a master at this.

Patience. He'll get there. His own way.

Nick seemed to sadden. "Shame there were no cops there when those Genovese guys beat the shit out of your father," he said.

A strange look crossed Palmer's face. "You remember that?" he asked.

"My dad told us that night when he got home," answered Nick. Claire couldn't help but wonder if it was true.

Palmer found himself sinking in the chair and sat up, scratched his temple. "It was morning," he said. "I was in school. He was setting up for lunch with my mother. I didn't find out till later."

"You mean that he was hurt or who did it?"

"Both," Palmer said. "But everyone knew what was going on. Mafia owned everything north of Canal Street between Lafayette and the Bowery back then, and there wasn't a restaurant owner in Little Italy who didn't pay protection money. It was the cost of doing business. I thought it was stupid of my father to refuse."

"Maybe," said Nick, "but don't you think going after that girl in revenge was a bit stupid too?" Nick asked.

"Not then and not now. My father walked with a limp for the rest of his life."

"Your father should've told you that you don't screw with the Mafia. It's like the rules of fighting a war, you know? Soldiers do battle but family's off limits."

"They broke the rules first," Palmer retorted. "And that was *my* family they hurt."

"They're the ones with the guns and no conscience," Nick said. "Did your father ever tell you how he knew they put a hit out on you?"

Palmer closed his eyes. *He took the bait*, Claire thought.

"Yeah," Palmer said, letting out his breath, "after the charges against me were dropped. Mom picked me up from the precinct in Queens, and I told her I was proud I paid them back and got away with it. Then she slapped me in the face, called me an idiot. She said they only wanted me out of jail so they could kill me."

"And that's why your dad had to pay them ninety percent of the restaurant's profits, isn't that right? To keep your ass above ground?"

Palmer shifted in his chair, the spell down memory lane broken.

"How is any of this relevant to what happened last night?"

"I'm just trying to get all the facts straight," Nick answered.

"Yes," Palmer said. "He paid for the rest of his miserable life. Since you already know all this, you probably know we lost the house in Bay Ridge and had to move into an apartment above the restaurant."

"So when your parents retired, they gave your brother the restaurant because you cost them their one true love," Nick said.

"No, because I didn't want it," Palmer snapped.

"I don't buy that," Nick said. "Not from the guy who had all that natural cooking talent, got the place a four-star Zagat rating when he was just seventeen."

"I got lucky," Palmer said. "A guy came in and ordered scaloppine. I was on sauces that night. I didn't know he was a critic. I'm flattered you read my bio."

"It was interesting reading. You're a fascinating guy, you know that? But you know what's not in there that I was wondering about?"

"Please, I'd love to hear," said Palmer, meaning exactly the opposite.

"Why you changed your name."

"I thought Victor Palmer sounded a little more worldly," he said.

"Maybe you would've thought differently if they had reality TV back then."

"Huh?" asked Palmer, clasping his hands in annoyance. "What does that have to do with anything?"

"Well," said Nick, "I have two girls. You know what they love to do? Sit around and watch cooking shows. So when I'm home, I watch with them. And all of a sudden I'm hearing names like Bobby Flay, Jamie Oliver, Mario Batali. And I'm looking at you and thinking to myself, Here's a guy who never even went to cooking school, makes it to the top of his profession, and changes his name? It's too bad. Victor Palmer, he could be anybody. But Vittorio Palmieri? Now, he sounds like one of those celebrity chefs on the Food Network, don'cha think?"

Palmer's eyes rolled skyward. He was getting tired of Nick's routine.

"I suppose I can't argue with that," he said.

Nick leaned in. "You know what I think? That you were so pissed off when your parents gave the restaurant to your brother that you changed your name to disown them."

To Nick's surprise, Palmer didn't even try to deny it.

"I was their firstborn. I put that place on the map. It was my birthright. You're damn right I was pissed."

"Not like you didn't make out, though," Nick followed, trying to keep Palmer on the positive side of off-balance. "I don't know a lotta guys who own brownstones in this city. Must've taken a lot of hard work to get there."

Palmer gave a flippant wave of his hand. "Another remarkable stroke of luck for me," he said. "When Guillermo Rodriguez came into the restaurant one night."

"Who's he?" asked Nick, though he knew.

"My godfather," Palmer replied, and let out a laugh that almost sounded like humility. "Like the Mafia, he literally made me an offer I couldn't refuse. Paid me a fortune to come down to his resort in Costa Rica and cook in his five-star restaurant."

"And you got the place when he died," Nick pretended to surmise.

Palmer smiled, and this time it was real.

"Guillermo had no children. He was like a father to me. He left me the resort in his will. I was as shocked as you can imagine. I had just turned forty. I still can't believe he would be so generous to me. Go figure."

"I hear Costa Rica's gorgeous. Always wanted to go."

"You should. While you still can—" He stopped.

"You were gonna say, 'While I still can see,' right?" asked Nick.

"Sorry, Detective," Palmer said.

"Please, call me Nick."

"Well, Nick, if you ever want to go, I'm on excellent terms with the folks I sold out to. On my say-so, they'll comp you for the hotel and meals. All you have to cover is the plane fare."

"Sounds like an offer *I* can't refuse," Nick said, smiling. "And I wish I didn't have to. My girls and I, we really need a vacation. Been a tough year for us."

"I'm sorry to hear that," Palmer said.

"Thanks. Two years ago they lost their mother, and my mother, who took care of them, passed this year."

Claire loved where Nick was taking this. *In another life, he'd make a great shrink*, she thought.

"I know what you're going through," Palmer said. "My wife died just before I moved back here."

"I'm sorry for your loss," said Nick, sounding as sincere as possible. "What was her name?"

"Martha," he said.

Nick played off the longing in Palmer's voice. "Fourteen years we were married," he said.

"What happened?" Palmer asked, sitting up with real interest. "Cancer?"

"Suicide," Nick said, surprised at how fast it came out.

"My God," Palmer blurted.

"Surprised you didn't read about it," said Nick. "It was all over the papers."

Palmer looked at him, a grin of realization crossing his face.

"Yes, I do remember now. They suspected you of murdering her," he said.

"Yeah, it sucked," Nick said, shifting in his seat. "Thought I was going to prison for a while there."

"How did you prove your innocence?" asked Palmer.

"It was more like the DA didn't have enough to charge me."

Now Palmer's interest was piqued. "Am I listening to a police officer confessing to murder?" he asked.

"Nah," Nick said, waving him off, though he wanted Palmer to believe they might have murder in common. "She shot herself with my gun. Automatically made me a suspect." He pretended he wanted to change the subject. "But what happened to your wife?"

"That's a good question," said Palmer, sitting back as if comfortable with the common ground they'd discovered. "She went out for a walk on the beach one night four years ago and never came back."

"Then how do you know she's dead?"

"The police found her bones on a beach on the other side of Costa Rica about two weeks later."

"Just her bones? That's all?"

Palmer looked down as if that would shake the memory away.

Nick knew he didn't want to talk about this anymore, and needed an out.

"It's okay. We can discuss something else," Nick said.

But Palmer's eyes grew distant. "I met her when she was four-teen," he said. "I was working in the kitchen at the hotel. She was a beauty. Long, brown hair, eyes like almonds that could look right through you. It was like we'd known each other all our lives the mo-ment we met."

"Was she from Costa Rica?" asked Nick, who just wanted to keep him talking.

"Chicago," said Palmer. "Her parents brought her and her brother down to the hotel every year on vacation."

"So you kept in touch," Nick surmised.

"Even after she got married," Palmer said.

"She was married before you?"

"To a lawyer from Detroit. They met in college at Michigan. They came to the hotel together. Nice guy. He died in a car accident. Very young. A tragedy."

"Yeah, that's horrible," said Nick, looking down and nodding in agreement. Palmer would've never suspected that not only did Nick already know this, he also knew the accident wasn't really an acci-dent. It was a hit-and-run that occurred when Martha's first husband, Bruce, stepped off a sidewalk outside his law office in Chicago's Loop. And it was still an open homicide case. Nick wondered if Palmer had somehow engineered this murder as well, but didn't want to steer him too far off track.

"Mind if I ask how you two finally got together?"

Palmer mused for a moment. "Martha's girlfriends brought her down to Costa Rica a few months after Bruce died. I was CEO of the hotel by then, and I made sure she had only the best. I put her in our Presidential Suite, and comped her entire stay, including meals. Her friends too."

"That's a helluva gesture," said Nick, sounding impressed.

Palmer wasn't even looking at Nick. "Apparently she thought so too, because she came down again a few months later. And that's when we . . . got together."

"It didn't seem like a . . . rebound thing?" Nick asked. "For her, I mean."

"We talked about that, but she said she'd been in love with me from the day we met."

"I'll bet you had a beautiful wedding."

Palmer smiled at the memory. "Five hundred guests, on the beach at the hotel. Even the president of Costa Rica was there," he said.

Nick needed to steer the conversation back to the matter at hand. "Do the police know what happened to her?" he asked.

"No," said Palmer. "They have no idea."

Finally, thought Nick. He'd caught Palmer in a lie he could actually prove.

"Victor," he said, "we both know that's not true."

Palmer's eyes darted up and right, the unavoidable sign of someone trying to create a story in his head. "What are you talking about?"

"The Costa Rican police say she was dismembered."

"Of course I know *that*," Palmer snapped, trying to cover himself. "I mean, they don't know who did it or why. And if you think discussing it is pleasant, then think again."

"I'm sorry," Nick said. "I didn't mean to upset you—"

"Why on earth would you talk to the Costa Rican police about me?" he interrupted.

"I didn't," Nick lied. "I just Googled you and the information came up."

This brought Palmer pause. Nick could see him breathing easier, placated. But he knew he had to work fast. It was time to begin Act Two of the play he'd scripted with Claire. He leaned back in his chair as if he was discussing the crappy weather.

"Victor," he said, "I just have to take care of a little piece of business before we continue talking. I need to tell you that you have the right to remain silent, and that if you give up that right, anything you say can be used against you. That you have the right to have an attorney here while I'm questioning you, and that the court will appoint one if you can't afford one. But we both know you can, don't we?"

Palmer smiled. "Of course. But only guilty people need attorneys, Nick."

"Then you understand your rights and you're waiving them?" Nick asked.

"I don't need a lawyer for this. I have nothing to hide. I've already told you I didn't believe you were a police officer when I hit you. And I'm sorry. I was scared and acted inappropriately."

"I'll need to get your signature on a form a little later."

"I'd be glad to do it as soon as you let me out of here," Palmer replied pleasantly, but with an undertone of impatience.

"We just have a few more things to talk about."

"What else could there possibly be to talk about?"

"Why you pulled a knife on me and that woman in the street."

"I told you. I was scared," he said, a tinge of the edge returning to his voice.

"Sorry. I mean, why were you carrying a knife in your bag?"

Palmer sighed. "You know I'm a chef."

"Yes," said Nick, "but you're not working as one now."

"When I saw that glow through my window and decided to get out, I thought of bringing one with me. If someone was watching me and wanted to attack me for some reason, I can certainly defend myself with a knife."

"Why do you think someone would want to attack you?"

"I don't know," Palmer retorted. "I have a lot of money. For all I know, you could've been someone trying to kidnap me for ransom."

Nick smiled. "But, Victor," he began, "if someone was gonna kidnap you, who'd pay the ransom?"

Palmer remained silent. Nick knew it was pure bravado. He had Palmer on the ropes, if only temporarily. It was the moment he'd been leading to, the climax of his second act, the knock now sounding on the door akin to the curtain rising on Act Three.

"What is it?" Nick shouted.

The door opened, and Claire strode in.

"Detective," she said, their prearranged greeting, her curt tone bringing Palmer's head up in shock.

"We're in the middle of something," Nick said, pretending to be offended by her presence. They both noticed Palmer avoiding her gaze.

"What's *she* doing here?" he said to Nick.

"I don't know," Nick answered. "She's not supposed to be."

Palmer still wouldn't acknowledge her.

"Who the hell is she?" he asked Nick.

"A shrink," said Nick, rolling his eyes in mock disgust.

"I'm a psychiatrist," said Claire, keeping her voice taut, suspecting Palmer didn't like women in positions of authority. "My name is Doctor Claire Waters. And if you have questions about me, then you can ask me, not Detective Lawler."

"Fine, *Doctor*," Palmer said with true contempt. "Why are you here?"

"Do you carry a lot of shame around with you, Mr. Palmer?"

"About what? And you didn't answer my question."

"Your wife's murder," said Claire. "And I'm the one who'll ask the questions. . . ."

Palmer's eyes turned angry. "You've been eavesdropping on us?" he interjected.

"Every word."

"You were outside my apartment with a gun!" Palmer exclaimed.

"That's not exactly true, is it?" Claire shot back. "And I want an answer to *my* question. Now, please."

Palmer glared at her. "Why would I be ashamed about the death of my wife?" he demanded.

"Because you didn't want anyone to know what you did to her."

Their eyes met—and that's when Claire saw it. That one fraction of a second, the recognition of knowing.

"You think *I* murdered her?" he asked with disbelief.

"Her bones were boiled. So all the meat would fall clean off them. Just like making chicken soup," Claire said.

"But the Costa Rican police cleared me!" Palmer exclaimed.

"Yes, they told us they questioned you. For five hours. That you were forthcoming, scared to death, and they concluded you weren't a suspect."

"Then why would you bring it up?" Palmer roared.

"Because you're a fascinating man, Mr. Palmer," Claire said as she leaned against the wall just feet away from him. "I read a lot about you since we met on the street last night. You know what I found most interesting?"

"I don't really care but I'm sure you're going to tell me."

"That so many years after you left the kitchen and began running the hotel, you'd still go every day to the farmers' markets in Santa Cruz or Tamarindo."

"I took a lot of pride in the food we served, and my talent in picking it," Palmer said. "I loved beginning my day that way. That this fascinates you makes me question your credentials."

He sounded off kilter, though, finishing his speech while Claire pulled a chair as close to him as she dared, turned it around, and sat straddling it, her arms crossed atop the back.

"Let me tell you why you so intrigue me," Claire said. "Because between 1978 and 2010, the bones of twenty-three women were found in various spots along the east and west coasts of Costa Rica. All of them were murdered, but the police don't know how or have an official cause of death for any of them—because the killer dismembered them and boiled their bones so the meat would slide right off. Don't you find that interesting?"

"Why?" Palmer spat out the word. "Because my wife was murdered the same way?"

"No. I think you're the killer because, except for your wife, all of those young women were last seen at either the Santa Cruz or Tamarindo farmers' markets. The same two you visited every day for the thirty-two years you lived in Costa Rica."

Palmer stared straight ahead, saying nothing.

"That was your hunting ground," Claire said. "Every serial killer has one. And you know how I know it's you? Because in that whole story you told Detective Lawler about your wife, Martha, you never once mentioned that you loved her. If you ever did."

"Of course I loved her!" exclaimed Palmer like the bad actor he was. "And why are we talking about crimes that happened in Costa Rica? You have no authority there."

"But we do in New York City," Nick said, opening the folder and sliding a photo across the table. "Because of this guy," he said. "Who exactly is he to you?"

Palmer stared at the mug shot of Jonah Welch and laughed. "Nobody," he said. "I've never seen him in my life."

"*Emigrant hasta*," Claire said in his face.

"What?" retorted Palmer, fear in his eyes for the first time.

"You heard me."

"*Emigrant hasta*? What the hell does *that* mean?"

"I think you know," Claire said.

"And I think you're both crazy!" Palmer shouted.

Claire pulled out more photos, slamming them down in front of Palmer one by one: *Boom!* Rosa Sanchez. *Boom!* Her bones. *Boom!* The bones from the basement of the burned-out building in Brooklyn. And finally, *boom boom!* The bones of the two victims from the seventies, to which she now pointed. "Until we found you, the police had no idea whose bones these are. Two victims, without names since 1977."

"Go to hell," Palmer hissed, refusing to meet her gaze.

"So we went back, did a little checking into your past," Claire said. "You had some problems in school, didn't you? Problems with girls. You liked to touch them. Inappropriately."

"You don't know what you're saying," Palmer exclaimed, his hands gripped around the chair's seat as if he were about to fall off.

"We didn't, for a while," Claire said. "But we do now. We got your school records. Six incidents of fondling girls' breasts. You slapped one of them when she wouldn't let you. Then you started cutting school. Transit police found you riding the subways, from borough to borough, when you weren't working at your parents' restaurant. Did it get you mad enough to kill two of those schoolgirls who didn't want you?"

Palmer said nothing. He just smiled.

"You remembered their names," Claire continued. "Even when they moved away. But you waited. And then you went after them. Celia Donato and Camille Panza."

If Palmer recognized the names, he gave no indication. Claire pressed on. "The police never found their identities because they both moved to Nassau County before you killed them and dumped their bones in Brooklyn. They were never reported missing here in the city. Their parents are dead. They'll never know after all these years that we found their daughters and their killer."

Palmer played with his fingers, cracking his knuckles. "I don't know what you're talking about."

Nick pointed to the photo of Rosa's bones, then pulled out the photo of the receipt and practically papered his face with it. "What does *emigrant hasta* mean?" Nick demanded.

But Palmer only stared at him. "For God's sake, that's not even my handwriting," he exclaimed, pointing at the two words. "And why would I write words in two different languages that have no meaning when they're put together? What is wrong with you people?"

Nick glanced at Claire and could tell they were both thinking the same thing: that however disingenuous the rest of Palmer's denials, this one was driven by pure fear and sounded real. Too real. So Nick went for it, banging his fist on the photos of the bones.

"Thirty-five years, twenty-four murders, all done the same way in places you were when they happened. I bring even this much to a jury, they'll see the pattern."

"I welcome you to try," Palmer said, as if it were a done deal. "But I have no idea why you're accusing me of such horrible crimes, including the murder of the wife I loved and cherished dearly. I've already admitted to hitting you, Detective, and told you why I did that. And yes, I'm ashamed of what I did and beg your forgiveness. But that's all."

Now his eyes moved back and forth between theirs like ping-pong balls flying across a table. As if making sure they'd hear what he was about to say loud and clear.

"As long as I live, I'll never, ever confess to anything I didn't do."

CHAPTER 19

Nick stood with Claire and Wilkes in front of a video monitor, its camera focused on Palmer, sitting at the table in the interrogation room. "What are we missing here?" Nick asked, frustrated.

"I don't know," grumbled Wilkes, "but the sonuvabitch is good, I'll give him that."

Nick and Claire had left Palmer after he'd laid down his gauntlet, agreeing only that he'd sign the form confirming he'd been read his rights and waived them. They expected a full tongue-lashing from Wilkes for not getting a confession.

"And so are you two," Wilkes said, surprising both Nick and Claire. "You stuck to the script and got him convinced that compared to us he's a shoe-in for Mensa."

"He chopped those women up," Claire said. "We just have to prove it."

"You've gotta be patient, Doc," Wilkes said. "This guy's been doing his dirty work for four decades and hasn't been nailed yet. I'm telling you, he knows we've got his number. The bastard is just gonna make us work for it."

"Then we'd better go back and look at the evidence again," Nick suggested. "Maybe there's something we're not seeing."

Claire's mind raced. "Okay, let me ask you this. All three of us saw the entire interview, from start to finish. At what point did Palmer get the most agitated?"

"Is this a quiz, Doc?" Wilkes asked. "Or don't you remember?"

"I know what I think," answered Claire. "I'm wondering whether you agree. And I don't want to say anything that'll influence your opinions."

"*Emigrant hasta*," Nick said. "That stirred him up."

"That's my vote," added Wilkes.

"Mine too," Claire confirmed. "He denied knowing what it meant and pointed out that it wasn't even his handwriting, something he knows we can prove."

"Wait," said Nick. "He said the words were written in two different languages. One, which happens to be in Spanish. Palmer lived in Costa Rica and he speaks it fluently."

"Meaning what?" asked Wilkes.

"Do you speak Spanish?" Nick asked.

"How many years you know me, Nicky?" Wilkes asked. "Hell, I have trouble with English."

"Okay, so when you're trying to communicate with someone who speaks only Spanish, how do you do it?"

"You mean, if I can't find a Spanish-speaking cop to translate for me?" A look of realization crept over his face. "I use the words I know and the ones I don't know I say in English."

"Just like anyone else in that situation would," Claire said.

"So you're saying that a guy who lived in a Spanish-speaking country for thirty-plus years wouldn't need to write the words in two different languages," Wilkes concluded.

"That's what's not clicking for me," said Nick.

"Are you saying he slipped up?" Wilkes asked.

"No," said Nick. "I'm saying he shouldn't have been so upset about a mistake he knows he didn't make. Especially if he's sure we won't be able to match his handwriting to the writing on the receipt."

Wilkes was rough and gruff, but you don't get to his position by being a moron. That didn't stop him from feeling like one at that moment.

"Doc," he said, "I'm having trouble wrapping my head around this. And you're the expert on heads, or at least what's inside them." He gestured to Palmer on the monitor. "What's inside *his*?"

For the first time since she'd met him, Claire felt a kinship with the inspector.

"Don't beat yourself up about it, because I don't know either," she assured him. "This is a tough one. Let's confirm that the writing on the receipt found with Rosa Sanchez's bones either is or isn't Palmer's."

"We'd better do it fast," said Wilkes, checking his watch. "Clock's running. And the bastard is right. If the only thing we can charge him with is assaulting Nicky, he's gonna make bail. No way can we let this scumbag take a walk."

Ninety minutes later, the handwriting expert on call to the NYPD only confused things even more.

"It's inconclusive," said Norma Rabin, a peroxide blonde whose age was estimated to be at least seventy, and whose heavy blue eye shadow reminded Nick of his own grandmother. She'd worked many times with Nick and Wilkes and had their complete trust as she pointed out similarities between the writing on the receipt and Palmer's writing on the Miranda form. "The pressure on the paper, the way the *T* is crossed, the *C* that looks a little like a *G* are all consistent. But there's a lot that isn't too."

Claire excused herself, leaving Wilkes and Nick to handle Norma. In her view, "inconclusive" meant they had to consider the possibility that, in fact, Palmer did write the words on the receipt. But even if true, it still wouldn't explain why he'd use two words in two different languages.

On the dry-erase board in Wilkes's office, she wrote the words. *HASTA EMIGRANT*. In bold letters. What did they mean?

She started with the first word's literal translation. In Spanish, *hasta* means *until*. *Emigrant*, of course, means someone who leaves one country to live in another. On the surface, Palmer was right, Claire thought. Together the words don't make sense.

What was going on in his mind?

Was this a message? That he'd left another body and was about to flee the country? A sort of farewell, *until* next time? *Hasta la vista, baby?*

Or was it something else completely?

Messages can be in code, or they can be scrambled. Is that what this is? Some kind of sick game he's playing on us? Is he trying to mix us up?

She stared at the two words. And all at once, it hit her.

Mix us up . . .

She quickly wrote on the board in big, black-marker block letters:

ANAGRAM

Was it possible? Was Palmer telling them something? Claire couldn't believe that the word *anagram* taken and rearranged from the letters in *hasta emigrant* could possibly be a coincidence. But that left six unused letters: HSTEIT. She focused on the letters and then wrote another word on the board next to *ANAGRAM*:

THEIST

She was just finishing when the door flew open and Nick entered, startling her so that she dropped the marker.

"Yikes, Nick—"

"Sorry I scared you," he said. Then he saw the writing on the board. "What's this?"

"I unscrambled the words and made two new words out of them," said Claire.

He stared at the words. "Any particular reason?"

Claire took him through her thought process.

"Okay, I know what an anagram is," Nick said when she was finished, "but what does *theist* mean?"

"A *theist* is someone who believes God is the creator," said Claire.

"Where the word *atheist* came from to describe someone who *doesn't*," Nick realized. "Hard to believe Palmer—or whoever wrote it if he didn't—believes in God or anything else that's sacred, you know, like human life. But I can't even guess what *anagram theist* means."

"Maybe he feels omnipotent," suggested Claire.

"Because he murdered all these women over three and a half decades and got away with it?"

"And now he's throwing it in our faces with word puzzles—"

She stopped, wondering if she was going too far with this, looking for an explanation for the unexplainable.

Nick sensed her doubt. "A theory is a theory is a theory," he said. "Like I said to the kids in your class, if one doesn't add up, let the evidence take you to another. We can check with the cops in Costa Rica to see if they found any cryptic message with the bodies down there. Meantime, come with me."

"Where to?" asked Claire.

"Crime lab. With Savarese and Wilkes. We're gonna go over the evidence, up close and personal, one more time. Maybe there's something one of us sees that doesn't pop in a photo."

If not for the fleet of Dodge Sprinter vans parked alongside the light-brick, four-story, converted apartment building beside the Long Island Railroad tracks, you'd never know it was the police department's state-of-the-art crime lab. Claire was surprised to see the building had no markings or signage, though the plethora of high-quality surveillance cameras on both corners of the building and the ID card reader at the door suggested more to the place than met the eye.

Upstairs, a lab technician, Renee Eckert, a stunner in her mid-forties with red hair pulled back in a bun and prominent cheekbones without a wrinkle, laid out on a table the scant evidence from Rosa Sanchez's murder, with labeled cards reading *Staten Island Woods* and *Trash Can Near Yankee Stadium*. On a second table sat even less evidence from the other two killings back in the seventies.

"That's all?" asked Wilkes. "Where's the stuff from the Brooklyn fire?"

"You mean that pile of ashes we've got three techs sifting through out at Floyd Bennett?" she asked, annoyed.

"Point taken," said Wilkes, chastened. "Gonna take weeks to find anything. If there's anything left to find."

"Only evidence not out is the bones," said Eckert, her thick accent betraying her Bronx roots. "Didn't think you'd need 'em."

Nick examined the large pots in which Rosa's bones were presumably boiled. "Not sure what looking at these again is gonna do for us," he said.

They spent half an hour poring over all that was on display, until they decided there was nothing to nail Palmer, or perhaps anyone else, as the killer.

"Guess this was something of a wasted trip," Wilkes said, summing up what they all felt as they waited for the elevator.

"Still worth a shot," said Nick, trying to make himself feel better.

That's when the doors opened and CSU Detective Terry Aitken emerged.

"Hey, you guys," he said. "Inspector," he added, affording Wilkes the deference due his rank. "What brings you all out from the Puzzle Palace to our oasis here in sunny Jamaica?"

"The 'bones' cases," Nick said. "Just wanted one more look at what you found."

"By the looks on your faces it wasn't enough," Aitken said.

"What swamp were you walking around in?" asked Savarese, looking down at Aitken's mud-covered boots.

"Alley Pond Park," said Aitken, referring to the easternmost park in Queens near the Nassau County border. "Just south of Northern Boulevard. Patrol in the One-Eleven responded to a nuisance call and found a dead guy right next to the dregs of Little Neck Bay."

"How'd he get dead?" asked Wilkes.

"We think it's a suicide," Aitken replied. "But it's a weird one. Guy cut himself open at the stomach and put a beach towel in to absorb the blood."

"Really?" asked Claire, her curiosity stoked.

Aitken was surprised by her reaction. "Pardon me for saying so, Doc, but you sure have a peculiar fondness for the macabre."

"Did you just use the words *peculiar* and *macabre* in the same sentence?" asked Wilkes, only half joking.

"Obviously you don't know your serial killer history, Inspector," Claire chided.

"An entire subject I wish I knew less about," Wilkes muttered.

But Nick caught Claire's spark. "You mean someone else tried that?" he asked.

"Not as a suicide," said Claire. "But back in the twenties, a sicko named William Edward Hickman kidnapped a little girl and dismembered her. *After* he cut her open and used a towel to soak up the blood."

She stopped, almost as if she was listening to a replay in her head of what she'd just said.

"Jeez, Doc, what is *that*?" Wilkes asked. "Required reading for Gore-ensic Shrinkology 101?"

When Claire looked at Aitken again, she was serious. "Are you sure it's a suicide?" she asked.

"Only footwear impressions in the mud are the victim's," Aitken said. "And he still had the knife in his hand."

"Wonder how rock bottom you must be to even consider doing yourself like that," Savarese said, as if Aitken's answer sealed it.

But Claire was on a mission. "Anything else on the guy?" she asked.

"No ID, if that's what you're asking. Just an almost empty pack of smokes and book of matches."

"And nothing else in the area?" Claire persisted.

"No offense, Doc, but you're beginning to make me feel like I missed something," Aitken said.

"Not at all, Detective," Claire assured him.

"What is it?" Nick asked Claire, wondering where she was going with this.

"I guess I'm just grasping at straws," Claire said to Nick, shrugging off her initial excitement. "Good luck with the case," she then said to Aitken.

"Thanks, but once we log in this evidence, I'm done until the trial, if there is one," Aitken replied. "But you know, while I have you all here, anybody know what *fornication cheeps* means?"

Wilkes laughed. "Sounds like a Craigslist ad for an illiterate hooker," he said. "Why?"

"Because my dead guy wrote that on the inside of his match-book—"

It was as far as Aitken got before Claire grabbed his arm.

"That actually hurts, Doc," the young detective said, "and now you're creeping me out."

"Where's the matchbook now?" she asked.

"My partner Joey just brought it in the lab," he said. "You wanna see it?"

It took them all less than a minute to rush back into the lab. Aitken donned gloves and looked through his case's evidence for the matchbook.

"You're thinking this is one of those anagrams," Nick assumed.

"Get me the receipt from Rosa's crime scene," was all she replied.

"Anagrams? What the hell's she talking about?" Wilkes asked Nick, who ran to retrieve the receipt as Aitken brought over the match-book, open in his gloved hand. He turned to Claire. "What *are* you talking about, Doc?"

Claire remembered Wilkes was unaware of her work on his dry-erase board a little more than an hour earlier. "Just go with me on this, Inspector," Claire said as she and Wilkes eyed the words inside, "and it'll explain itself."

"*Fornication cheeps*," read Wilkes. "What in the holy hell could it mean?"

"I don't think it means anything," she replied as Nick brought over the receipt in a clear evidence bag. "It's what's *inside* those words that may be important."

Wilkes was confused. "And what exactly does she mean by *that*?" he asked Nick.

But he and Claire were too busy comparing the handwriting on the receipt with the scrawl on the matchbook to answer.

"Hard to tell," Nick said to Claire. "The writing on the matches looks like it was done in a hurry, but the receipt seems more deliberate. We'll need Norma Rabin to take a look."

Claire's mind was elsewhere. "Is there a computer I can use?" she asked.

"Over here," Aitken said, indicating the terminal the field units used to log in evidence. He typed in his own password to give her access. "What do you need?"

"Just the Internet," said Claire, hurrying over and sitting down when Aitken was finished. She typed the words *anagram solver* into Google, bringing up a host of Web site choices. By the time Nick and Wilkes reached her, she was typing *fornication cheeps* into the search engine of one of the sites.

Nick looked over her shoulder, wanting to soften the blow he thought she might feel when this theory fell through. "There's no evidence this is even a homicide," he said. "It's in another borough. The victim is male, not female."

Claire only had eyes for the results of her search—literally thousands of them. She realized she couldn't do what she had to do sitting in the crime lab. There was something else that needed to be done first.

"Can you call the medical examiner and ask if we can come over?"

"Now?" asked Wilkes. "What for?"

"So we can go over the bones from all of the cases. Together."

Nick was hesitant. "He's gonna think *we* think he screwed up."

"Then tell him he couldn't have screwed up what he wasn't looking for," Claire fired back.

"What exactly *are* we looking for?" asked Wilkes.

"I'm not sure yet. But something's not right."

Wilkes wasn't satisfied. "You're gonna have to do better than that."

He never got to finish as Claire wheeled on him. "I'm sure you want to figure this out as much as I do, Inspector, maybe even more than I do. And if that's the case, please call Doctor Ross. I think the answer is in those bones."

Those bones—all four sets representing the four victims—were laid out on separate tables in an unused and old but clean autopsy room by the time Nick and Claire arrived with Wilkes and Savarese. They caught Assistant Medical Examiner Ross pacing between them as if the keeper of a high-tech crypt for the twenty-first century.

"This looks like the Spanish Inquisition," Ross quipped.

"This was her idea," Savarese said, pointing to Claire.

"Well, at least Doctor Waters and I speak the same language," said Ross.

"Don't give me so much credit," Claire warned him as she pulled on a pair of gloves. "I did my pathology rotation just like every other good little med student, but that doesn't make me an expert. I'm going to need your help."

"Your wish is my command," Ross said, sweeping his arm across his domain of death. "What are we looking for?"

"Anything that's different in these bones, from one set to the next. Did you do as I asked?"

"I did indeed," Ross answered. "You won't know which ones are from which crime until I tell you." He picked up two magnifying glasses, handed one to Claire. "Your glass, Holmes," he said.

The three cops stood back and watched as Claire pored over every bone from each skeleton. She shook her head after the first one, went on to the second. Spent a few moments. Nothing. But shortly after she began poring over the third skeleton, she stopped abruptly at the left shoulder.

"Here," she called to Ross. "Take a look at this."

He hurried over, peered through her glass. "See? On the inside of the glenohumeral joint?"

Ross moved over to the knee joint. "Here too. The same marks."

"You gonna let us in on the big doctor secret or make us stand here pissed off we were too dumb for med school?" asked Wilkes, as only he could.

Ross pointed to the bones on the other tables. "Those three victims—the two women from seventy-seven and the Jane Doe from the fire in Brooklyn the other day—were dismembered identically. With almost surgical precision. Expertly done, in such a way to suggest the killer had a working knowledge of anatomy."

He then moved to the bones Claire continued examining. "Rosa Sanchez, however, was a different story. The bones in every joint have almost invisible chips and gouges. Compared to the others, it's like Rosa was hacked apart by someone who didn't have nearly the finesse or anatomical knowledge."

"Or someone with a lot of anger, maybe in a rush," Nick said in an accusing tone, staring disapprovingly at Ross. "I wouldn't rule out either possibility."

"Don't put this one on me, Lawler," Ross said.

"He's right, Nick," agreed Claire. "Rosa's bones have plenty of other marks on them, probably from being knocked around in the perp's car. The mark I saw in the joint could easily have been mistaken for one of those."

She looked up at the men. "As for the perp being in a rush, Nick, I don't agree," she argued. "Rosa was dismembered in the middle of those woods on Staten Island. Nobody around literally for miles. Why would Palmer be in a rush out there?"

"Maybe he thought someone saw him," Savarese suggested. "He had to get out of there fast."

The wheels turned in Nick's head. And the answer came to him in a flash.

"Or it wasn't Palmer," he said.

"I think that's right," Claire confirmed.

Wilkes could've busted a gut right then. "You two built as bulletproof a circumstantial case against Palmer as I've ever seen. How could it *not* be him?"

Claire put the magnifying glass down on the table. "Put yourself in

Victor Palmer's shoes," she said. "Not a surgeon, but a chef, which means he knows how to expertly butcher a piece of meat. He's proud of his work. He murders the two women in Brooklyn in seventy-seven, two bodies who were forgotten because there was no evidence and every cop in the city was looking for Son of Sam. Then, he moves to Costa Rica and continues his killing spree. Call the police down there, Inspector, and I'll bet a week's pay their medical examiner will confirm every one of the bones on those twenty-two victims are pristine. Not a chip, a scratch, or a mark on them."

Wilkes turned to Savarese. "Make the call," he said, his eyes returning to Claire. "Go on, Doctor."

"Okay. Palmer murders his wife and moves back to New York. For all we know, he's killed more women we haven't found. But let's say he hasn't. And then, suddenly, he hears about an entire set of human bones found in a trash can three blocks from Yankee Stadium."

"Jesus, Doctor," Wilkes interrupted. "You're saying Palmer got all pissed off because he didn't murder Rosa Sanchez? Because someone copied his work?"

"That's exactly what she's saying," replied Nick, a grin of vindication spreading across his face. "It makes sense because Rosa's the only hack job here. Palmer took pride in his work. So he had to go out and murder Jane Doe here," he said, indicating the bones of the fire victim from Brooklyn, "because he's a perfectionist. Nobody does it like he does. He had to show everyone—"

"Hold on," Wilkes interjected, raising his hand. "There's only one problem. Rosa Sanchez still hasn't made the news. We kept the lid on it. How could Palmer know she was dead—?"

He stopped in midsentence off a look from Nick, who realized about a second before the inspector himself came up with it the answer to his own question.

"Palmer's friend. The police commissioner," Nick said in realization. "He must've told Palmer over dinner or something."

"That's why he said he'd have to resign if Palmer was the killer," Wilkes said. "Because if Palmer never knew about Rosa, Jane Doe might still be alive."

"Un-frickin' believable," said Ross.

"You breathe not a word of this to anyone," Wilkes said to Ross, "not even to your boss. We've got a few more questions to answer first." His head swiveled to Claire. "Like how you got all this from that other body out in Queens."

"Which one?" Ross asked.

"Bizarre suicide in Alley Pond Park," Nick informed him.

"You mean the guy who tried to cut himself in half?" Ross replied.

"It's most likely a homicide," Claire said. "A copycat too, of a horrible murder of a little girl back in the twenties. The connection is the words on that victim's matchbook and the receipt found with Rosa's bones."

Wilkes was trying to wrap his head around all this. "So we've got a nut job going around copycatting obscure serial killers and playing word games with us? Why?"

"Because, Inspector, like Palmer, our nut job is a perfectionist. And he wants to know if we're as perfect as he is," Claire answered.

Nick got it. "He's testing our collective IQs. To see if they're as big as his."

"Correct," said Claire. "And it's time we showed him."

She sat in front of the computer in the squad room of the Major Case Squad, back on the Anagram Solver's Web site. There was no longer a reason to sequester her in Wilkes's office, sneak her in and out of the building. In a short time it would all be out in the open, including her involvement.

Claire called Fairborn to fill her in, not wanting her to find out on the evening news, promising her it would all be over in a matter of days and asking her to please bear with her. Fairborn was circumspect, and Claire knew she was wearing her mentor's patience thin. She also knew, when all was said and done, Fairborn would have reason to be proud of her.

But Claire needed to be proud of herself too, and knowing the killer's motive wasn't enough. Nailing Victor Palmer wasn't enough either. She had to know what the words meant. She had to know who killed Rosa.

In the search engine she'd already typed *fornication cheeps*, bringing up hundreds of solutions. She pored over them, wondering when the obvious answer would pop out, when Nick appeared behind her, glancing over her shoulder. "How's it going?" he asked.

"Slow," said Claire. "How about on your end?"

"It's set. Seven o'clock tonight," he said. "They want to mention your name."

"They can. I got permission from Doctor Fairborn."

"You swore her to secrecy too, I hope," he said, pulling up a chair and sitting beside her.

"Yes," Claire replied, never taking her eyes off the screen. "And I didn't tell her everything, anyway."

"Claire," Nick said to her in a serious tone, getting her attention.

She swiveled in her chair to face Nick. "What's the matter?" she asked.

"They want you up there with us too."

Claire was flabbergasted. "Please tell me you didn't—"

"I don't have that kind of juice."

There was only one other possibility, and it stunned her. "Wilkes?"

"He told the chief of Ds, the PC, and the mayor that none of this would've been possible without you on board. Far as he's concerned, you're one of us. He said he'd pin a gold shield on you himself if he could."

When Claire didn't respond he realized she was lost in what was on the screen. "Did you hear a word I said?" he asked.

"Perfection," she said, staring at the screen. "It's about perfection."

Nick followed her eyes. In the list of anagrams of *fornication cheeps*, Claire was now looking at combinations of three words beginning with the word *perfection*.

"Perfection?"

And suddenly she saw it. What she'd been looking for. She wrote on a yellow pad beside her:

fornication cheeps = *PERFECTION IN CHAOS*

"What the hell are you two doing?" asked Wilkes, hurrying over. "We've—"

Then he saw what Claire had written on the yellow pad.

"Are you sure about this?" he asked her.

"As sure as I can be," Claire said. "And here's something else. I think he wants us to know who he is. Or at least who he thinks he is."

She wrote *ANAGRAM THEIST* on the yellow pad. "You said that *theist* means a belief in God. You still think this butcher believes in God?" asked Nick.

"Maybe he thinks he is God," Wilkes offered, only half joking.

"Almost," said Claire, rewriting the words *anagram theist* one more time. "If I take the first three letters of *theist*, that makes the word *the*. And if I take the last three letters, *ist*, and add them to the end of *anagram* . . . I get . . ."

Claire wrote the two words in bold block letters.

THE ANAGRAMIST.

"That's who he thinks he is," Claire said.

Wilkes shook his head in disbelief. "Maybe his friends Joker, Riddler, Penguin, or Catwoman can lead us to him," he quipped. "This case is screwier than a comic book."

"We've got to change the script, Inspector," Claire said. "Just a little."

"You wrote the damn thing," replied Wilkes, checking his watch. "So go do it. You've got an hour until showtime."

"Thank you all for coming today," said New York City mayor Mark Glassman into a forest of microphones atop the podium on the stage of the large first-floor auditorium at police headquarters. The room was packed with press and police brass as Hizzoner the Mayor said a few words, then introduced Police Commissioner Farrell, standing to his left, his suit and poker face perfect despite what he knew he had no choice but to do. Behind them stood Chief of Detectives Dolan and Inspector Wilkes and Claire, who was flanked by Nick and Tony Savarese, their shields hanging from the breast pockets of their suit jackets.

The snapping of camera shutters nearly drowned out Farrell as he said a few short words about retiring from the police department he so loved. Claire knew it was bullshit. Farrell was putting in his papers to avoid the scandal that would surely come if anyone ever found out what he'd told Victor Palmer. As his parting gift to the mayor, Farrell announced Palmer's arrest for the two 1977 murders and the murder of Jane Doe in East New York. That took about five minutes, during which Claire had to stand there, forcing the grim look she'd seen on the faces of participants at similar press conferences for years. This, too, was part of the script.

"Before I take questions, I'd like to bring up Inspector Brian

Wilkes, commander of the Major Case Squad, whose detectives investigated and broke this case."

As Wilkes stepped to the podium, Claire couldn't help but wonder if he could get through a sentence without dropping an F-bomb. But she hadn't seen the professional, polished police-department-politician Wilkes in action.

"Not to be the one to correct my bosses," Wilkes began, "but the arrest of Victor Palmer wouldn't have been possible without the invaluable assistance of Doctor Claire Waters of Manhattan State University Hospital. This is the second time Doctor Waters has worked with us, and this police department and city owe her a debt of gratitude. Doctor Waters will continue in her role as a special consultant in two other cases I'll tell you about now."

The cameras clicked and whirred—but now all of them were pointed at Claire, who continued to stand focused, staring straight ahead, nodding in acknowledgment of Wilkes's high praise, her face solemn as the inspector briefly went off the script Claire had written.

"The arrest of Mr. Palmer came as a result of the investigation of a homicide that occurred more than two weeks ago. In the press packets you'll all find handouts and photos of what I'm about to say. The victim of this brutal attack was Rosa Sanchez, twenty-four, of the Bronx. Her bones were found in a trash can three blocks from Yankee Stadium a day after she disappeared. At first, we suspected Mr. Palmer for the murder of Ms. Sanchez, as the modus operandi seemed to match the other cases for which Mr. Palmer was arrested. But new evidence has come to light convincing us Mr. Palmer cannot be responsible for Ms. Sanchez's murder. Thus, her homicide remains an open case, and bringing her killer to justice is the department's top priority. We're asking anyone who may have information about Ms. Sanchez to call us at the number on your screen. I'll take your questions now."

Claire unlocked her knees, trying not to show her tension. The most important moments of the press conference were yet to come.

"Do you have any leads or suspects?" asked a veteran TV reporter.

"C'mon, Louie, you know we can't give away the store here." This brought a wave of laughter from the press corps. It was classic Wilkes letting his hair down for the cameras. "But we believe Ms. Sanchez was chosen at random by a copycat killer."

"You mean someone copying the murders committed by Victor Palmer?" came another shouted question.

"And others," Wilkes answered. "There's another case we're working on that I can't tell you about right now, which may be linked to this one. Though I can tell you the MO is completely different from the Sanchez case, but similar in explicit detail to a murder from almost a century ago."

Another reporter, from the *Times*, cut in. "Can you tell us what exactly led you to believe Mr. Palmer did *not* kill Ms. Sanchez?"

"Not nearly as exactly as you'd want, Marissa," said Wilkes. "But I can tell you this—compared to Mr. Palmer's work, whoever tried to copy him did a terrible job."

"What do you mean *terrible*?" asked another reporter.

"Well, let's just say Palmer's copycat is sloppy, in that way you are when you don't do your research and prepare. For Palmer, murder was an art form. Compared to him, the work of this imposter is preschool finger painting. He's a rank amateur."

Claire tuned out the questions that continued to fly at Wilkes. Though the look on her face remained solemn, she felt more secure, satisfied she'd done her job. What Wilkes had just said was the most important part of the script she'd written. If Rosa's killer was all about chaos and words, words could also be his downfall.

He watched the news camera zoom in on Claire's face while the guy in charge of the investigation—he couldn't remember his name but it wasn't important—kept talking. It had started out with a beautiful gift, the news that after all these years, his work succeeded in smoking out Victor Palmer. That filled him with nothing less than sheer joy.

And then they shoved the knife in his gut. Describing Palmer as van Gogh, and him as an imposter whose work was no better than a nursery-schooler's finger painting? A hack? An amateur?

Who did these moronic cops think they were? Who did they think they were dealing with? Well, they were about to find out!

He picked up the antique porcelain lamp beside his bed and flung it across the room, shattering it into pieces. Then, he grabbed his alarm clock, the one his mother had bought him when he was seven, with the roman numerals, gold-plated casing, and twin bells on top. He threw it, with everything he had in him, all the anger, resentment, and jealousy that was overwhelming him. At the television.

At Claire Waters's face.

The screen shattered where her head was, the guts of the machine sparking as it grew dark until it was as dead as Rosa Sanchez.

Claire's presence there told him everything he needed to know. That idiot at the podium was just the vessel. He knew the words that left his mouth were put there by Claire. His beloved Claire. The object of both his undying love and his endless hatred.

Because she nailed it. She knew. Somehow, she'd figured it out. And that meant he was a failure. She was smarter than he was. . . .

Which meant he had to be smarter.

We'll see how smart she is, *he thought.* She's wrong about me. Just like the medical schools that wouldn't let me in were wrong too.

He could still show her. He'd show all of them.

He approached the large grid on his wall. Grabbed his marker, the sword he would use to slay the dragon lady, Claire. Furiously, he wrote words into the grid, above, below, and around the words already entered:

ROSA SANCHEZ

ROBERT NEWMAN

He saved a special space for the next words, in the center, hoping he wouldn't have to use them. But now, after all that had happened, after she'd threatened to ruin everything, he had no choice. With a red marker, he wrote:

KILL AGAIN

He stared at the blood red letters. Then a smile bloomed on his face. He wrote:

ALKALI GIN *under* KILL AGAIN. *Another perfect anagram made from the chaos of the world, he thought.*

He stepped back and admired his work. He'd left out the most important words of all, which he went back and wrote slowly and deliberately in the crossword grid:

CLAIRE WATERS

She would live to regret the day she dared to better him.

Because now, surpassing her wouldn't be enough.

CHAPTER 20

———◆———

The booming of a spring thunderstorm penetrated the brick walls of One Police Plaza, nearly drowning out Wilkes's words as he strode with Claire and Nick into the Major Case Squad's bustling office. Every desk was occupied, every detective on the phone. "If you wanted to piss Mr. Anagramist off, Doc, that should've done it," he said. "Great job. You even *looked* like one of us standing up there."

It was just before eight in the evening, and though Claire was exhausted, she could see Nick walking hunched over, ready to collapse from lack of sleep and still suffering the effects of his concussion. She wasn't the only one who saw it.

"*You*, on the other hand, look like dog crap," Wilkes said to him.

"I'm okay," Nick replied, trying to put on a good face.

"The hell you are," Wilkes said, in a friendlier tone. "You're going home."

Nick wanted to press on. "We've got work to do."

And then he nearly tripped over the leg of a chair. Claire grabbed his arm.

"I'm fine," he said, shaking her hand off him.

But Wilkes wasn't having it. "That's a direct order, Detective," he said, turning to Claire for backup.

"You need to rest," Claire said. "Or your brain won't heal properly."

Nick knew they were right but didn't want to admit it. "I'm not going anywhere until this is over," he said.

"It's over for you, for now," stated Wilkes. "You're not the only cop in this place. There's not much we can do anyway since we don't know who the hell Mr. Anagramist is. So we'll regroup in the morning."

"You sure?" Nick asked, knowing he was pushing it.

"I'm sure that if the doc here doesn't take you home, I'm gonna send you back to the hospital," Wilkes said, without raising his voice. "We just have to pray that this whacko doesn't go hunting tonight. Not that we'd be able to stop him, anyway." He turned to Savarese, who was on the phone. "We getting the word out, Tony?"

Savarese covered the receiver. "We're notifying every command that any death tonight that looks the least bit hinky should be reported to us right away. Me, Billy, and Vernon'll go to the mattresses to cover the phones," he finished, using *The Godfather* slang to describe the portable cots they'd pull into the squad room to sleep on.

"You see?" Wilkes assured Nick. "It's all taken care of. Doc, you have your stuff ready for tomorrow morning, *capisce?*"

"Yes, sir," answered Claire. "The Anagramist's profile will be ready."

"Good," said Wilkes, pointing Nick toward the door. "Now get this sorry sack of shit the hell home."

Claire fumbled through Nick's numerous keys until she found the one that unlocked the door to his apartment. "Surprised the perps can't hear you coming from a mile away with all that jingling," she said.

He'd handed her the ring of keys outside, after she'd parked his Jeep beside the hydrant in front of his building. The spot wasn't their first choice, even with the police parking plate on the dash. Nick had tried to convince her he was more than capable of walking to his door, but Claire could see he was fading fast. She barely had the door open when Cisco trotted over, tail wagging. Nick ignored the dog and used what little stamina he had left to make it to the living room sofa. He pushed aside some fashion magazines his daughters had left there and collapsed.

"Maybe you shouldn't come in tomorrow," Claire suggested, sitting on the matching love seat, leaving him the entire couch to stretch out. Which he did as Cisco did the same on the floor in front of his master.

"Not a chance," Cisco's master said, slurring his speech. Claire hoped it was from the exhaustion and not the concussion. She turned on a lamp next to the sofa where Nick sprawled and leaned over him.

"Open your eyes," she said.

Nick opened his eyes and Claire lowered her face so that it was inches from his. Then she shined the light from her phone into each of them.

"Ow," he cried from the sudden glare. "You wanna blind me faster?"

"I wanna make sure your pupils aren't blown," she said, feeling less anxious.

"Well?" he retorted. "What's the verdict?"

"In my business it's called a diagnosis," she answered. "You'll live."

"Daddy!" cried Jill, appearing in a nightshirt with the pop musician Adele's face emblazoned on it, as she ran over to kiss her father. She stopped short when she spotted the day-old gauze bandage on the back of his head. "Dad, are you okay?" she asked him. She turned to Claire. "What happened?"

"He got hit on the head arresting a killer," Claire said. "Your father's a hero again. But he doesn't know when to stop."

"That's because he's a stubborn mule," Jill said, caressing her father's hair.

"You're the hero," Nick muttered to Claire. "All I did was pass out. You had the gun on him."

Jill sensed there was something more between them than she'd seen before. "Will someone please tell me if he's gonna be okay?" she asked, breaking the short silence.

"I'm fine," said Nick.

"He will be if he gets some rest," Claire assured her.

"I'm right here. I can speak for myself," Nick grumbled, trying to get up.

Jill pushed him back down. "Easy, Big Guy," she said. "She's a doctor. Just listen to her. Listen to someone for once."

"I can stay if you want," Claire offered Jill, which brought Nick's head up.

"Thanks for asking." Jill answered, "I really appreciate it. But you must be exhausted too. I can take care of him."

"Where's Katie?" asked Nick.

"Sleeping," said Jill. "I told her you were on a big case. She didn't ask any questions."

Claire wanted to stay. She should have insisted he take it easy after being released from the hospital. But she knew he never would have listened to her. Just like he wouldn't let her care for him now.

"I'll go," she said. "But I'll be back first thing in the morning."

"You don't have to buzz yourself up," Nick said. "There's a set of house keys taped under the front seat of the car."

"The great detective has a mental block when it comes to finding his keys," Jill said to Claire.

"Call me if you need me," Claire told Jill. "You have my number."

Nick mustered what energy remained in him and sat up. "I'm walking you out," he said.

"Not outside, Dad," Jill ordered. "It's pouring."

"Yes, ma'am," Nick said with a mock salute. "Just to the hallway."

He managed to lift himself off the sofa and walk beside Claire toward the door. She resisted the urge to help him, steady him.

As Nick opened the door for her and hung onto it for support, she was all the more attracted to him, even in his weakened state. She had tried to convince herself she'd felt it for the first time when he kissed her in the car the other day. But she could no longer deny those feelings started longer ago than she cared to admit, and what bothered her was why she couldn't accept her emotions, embrace them. Was she drawn to him because he saved her life last year? Was it out of debt or gratitude? Was she attracted not just to him, but also to the thought of taking care of him and his daughters, of being part of a family?

"Thanks for bringing me home," said Nick, brushing her hair behind her ear and waking her up from her thoughts.

"You need to get into bed," said Claire. "And stay there."

"What does that mean?"

"It means that if you feel like crap you can't push yourself or you could end up with permanent brain damage—"

More gently than before, Nick bent down to kiss her. This time, she didn't hesitate, closing her eyes, losing herself in it, allowing herself to feel this kind of closeness for the first time since her fiancé's death. Their lips were locked for nearly a minute when Nick pulled away.

"Whoa," was all he said.

"I'm sorry," Claire stammered.

"Don't be. I'm the one who started it."

Claire picked up her purse, which she had dropped on the floor when Nick kissed her. "I'll see you in the morning," she said, and hurried toward the stairs.

The buzz stayed with her as she got in the Jeep and drove back to her East Side neighborhood, finding a rare open spot just around the corner from her building. Getting out, she realized that she didn't remember driving there.

She looked at herself in the reflection of the Jeep's passenger window, lit by a streetlamp. Her hair was a mess. She tried to think: was her father in the apartment tonight? She didn't want him to see her like this, nor did she want to answer the questions she knew he'd ask.

The ride up in the elevator gave her time to pull herself together and calm down to the point she looked forward to her father's visit, to speaking with him and hearing his calm, soothing voice. But once she opened the door to her apartment, it was clear he wasn't there. He always left the light on in the bathroom, and the flat was completely dark. She headed straight for her bedroom and lay down, fully clothed, giving in to the exhaustion building over the last two days. She'd barely kicked off her shoes when her eyes closed and she descended into a dreamless sleep that was interrupted by the ring of the phone on her nightstand.

She opened her eyes to blinding daylight and realized she'd fallen asleep fully clothed with the curtains open. She reached for the receiver, not bothering to check the caller ID. "Hello," she answered.

"Claire, honey," her mother said in a voice so tense it woke Claire up and made her glance at the number from which the call came. What she saw sent her into panic mode. "Mom, why are you at Rochester General?" she asked, afraid of the answer.

"Don't be scared, and don't jump on a plane."

"Mom!" she interrupted, darting out of bed, running to her closet as she spoke. "Just tell me. Is it Dad?"

"Yes, but they think he's going to be okay."

"What happened?" Claire demanded, fearing he'd suffered a heart attack or stroke.

She heard her mother take a deep breath on the other end of the line. "He was in a car accident this morning," she said.

Claire remembered her urge to speak to her father last night and wished she had called him. Then she shifted into clinical mode.

"Tell me exactly what the doctors are saying," she instructed her mother.

"It's Deb Hunter," came the answer, and Claire felt reassured. Deb was a family friend who also happened to be the hospital's chief of emergency medicine. "She ordered every scan under the sun, and she says your father's fine, that he's the luckiest man on the planet, given what happened."

"What *did* happen, Mom?"

"Well, you know how he goes to the gym at the butt crack of dawn."

Get to the point. "Mom, please—"

"He was on East Avenue at Culver Road and he had the green light—all the witnesses say so. But a city bus sped right through the red light on Culver and hit him broadside."

Claire was confused. "Witnesses? At five-thirty in the morning?"

"Thank God your father saw the thing coming at the last second and hit the gas so it only clipped him in the rear and he spun into a telephone pole."

Claire was having trouble understanding her mother. "Slow down, Mom, not all at once. Was the bus driver drunk or something?"

"They don't know who was driving," came her mother's answer.

"You're not making sense, Mom."

"None of this makes sense!" cried her mother through the phone. "All anyone's saying is that the bus was stolen."

"Wow," said Claire, pulling a small suitcase from the closet and throwing it on the bed. The thought of anything happening to her father was . . . well, unthinkable. But she had to keep it together for her mother's sake.

"Well, at least Dad's okay. Can I talk to him?"

"They're doing one last test, I think it's a CAT scan. As soon as he's back down here I'll have him call you. They don't let you use cell phones in here, you know."

Claire couldn't help but roll her eyes. "I know. I'm a doctor, Mom, remember?"

Her mother laughed nervously on the other end. "I'm sorry, honey," she said. "It's been a long morning."

"I can imagine," said Claire.

"What am I hearing in your voice?"

Claire was shocked her mother could detect the fear she felt. "It's just that . . . I had this really strong urge that I should call you and Dad last night."

"Why didn't you?"

"Because I was up for nearly two days straight and once I hit the bed I was out."

"Don't worry about it, dear," said her mother as soothingly as possible. "He'll be fine. Where will you be later?"

Claire eyed the still empty suitcase on her bed and made a decision. "At work, Mom," she said, omitting the fact that today work would be at One Police Plaza with Nick and the detectives. "And as long as you're swearing to me on a stack of Bibles that Dad's okay, I should get going. Just promise you'll put him on the phone with me as soon as he's back. I want to hear his voice."

"I promise."

"If I don't hear from you in two hours I'm calling you back."

"I swear on a stack of Bibles."

They said their good-byes and hung up. Claire threw the suitcase back into the closet, showered, dressed in dark blue slacks, tan blouse, gray blazer, and flats. Forgoing breakfast, she hurried downstairs and outside under overcast skies, around the corner to where she'd left Nick's Jeep the night before.

The Jeep was gone, a Volkswagen Beetle in its place.

Take a breath. You were exhausted last night. Are you sure this is where you parked it?

Her eyes scanned every direction until they landed on the streetlamp that had illuminated her image last night in the window of the Jeep. She pivoted around to check the parking signs for the block, confirming she'd parked legally and there was no reason for the Jeep to have been towed.

"Hey, lady!" came a male voice.

She wheeled around. A doorman from the nearest building was looking at her. "You lost or something?" the young man said.

"I think my car was stolen," Claire answered, pointing at the spot. "I mean, my friend's car. That's where I left it last night."

"What kind of car was it?"

"Red Jeep Cherokee. The old, boxy style, from the eighties."

"Can't say I saw it since I been here," said the doorman in thick Brooklynese. "Guess you better call the cops. Wish I could help you."

An idea popped into Claire's head. "Maybe you can," she said. "Does your building have any security cameras pointed at the sidewalk here?"

"Does it? You'd think the effin' CIA was in this place, all the cameras they got here. Wanna check out the video?"

"I probably sound like I'm insane, but please, yes."

The doorman, who introduced himself as Carl from Canarsie, said he'd show her as soon as he could get someone to cover for him. Claire called Nick, dreading telling him his car was gone, gratified when he told her not to worry about it.

"Just hang in," Nick said over the phone. "I'll grab a cab and get right over."

Right over turned out to be half an hour later because of traffic, which worked out fine because it took that long for Carl the doorman to find someone to spell him.

"At least I'm not crazy," said Claire, Nick beside her. Carl played the security video on a small monitor in a tiny room behind the apartment building's front desk.

"I never thought you were," Nick replied, feeling more like his old self today.

She suppressed the urge to ask how he was, knowing he'd only say he was fine. She turned her attention to the monitor, on which they could clearly see Claire check her reflection in the car window.

"You on your way to a date or something?" Nick asked with a grin.

Claire didn't even hear him. "Who's that?" she asked, staring at the screen, on which a man wearing dark colors and a wide-brimmed hat obscuring his face approached the Jeep. Without hesitation, the man produced a Slim Jim from inside his coat, slid it between the driver's window and the door, pulled it up, and popped the lock. He got in, reached under the dash, appeared to insert a key in the ignition, and pulled away with the headlights off. The whole thing took no more than twenty seconds.

"Jeez, the guy's a pro," said Carl.

Claire hit pause, freezing the image of the Jeep in the middle of the street. Nick turned dead serious. "Go get your boss, Carl. I need this DVD. It's evidence in a crime."

"Sure, Detective," said Carl, muttering, "Crime of the century, hot-wiring a beat-up piece of crap," as he left the room.

"Carl's closer to the truth than he thinks," Nick said.

"What are you talking about?" asked Claire. "I thought parts for old cars are worth a fortune in third-world countries."

"Not for my car, as far as I know," Nick replied. "He didn't hot-wire it either. He found the spare key I keep taped under the dash."

"To the car? You said you keep house keys under the seat."

"My house keys aren't the only ones I keep losing. I taped the car key to the steering column so I'd always have another one handy."

Claire gestured to the monitor. "This guy found it like he put it there himself."

A dark thought popped into Claire's head. "He showed up right after I left. Like he was waiting for me."

Nick already knew this. "I can't disagree with you," he said. "If that's the case, he'd have to know you were driving my car and tailed you."

"Or he's been watching my building," she said.

Neither option thrilled them. "Let's not jump off a bridge here," Nick cautioned. "We've got bigger fish on our plate."

"What do we do about this DVD?" asked Claire.

"I'll call the local precinct, have an Evidence Collection cop keep an eye on it here until the legalities are hammered out. In the mean-time, we need to get to the office."

"The commissioner would appreciate us collaring this sick sonuva-bitch sometime in the next two weeks, before he retires," Wilkes said to the roomful of detectives gathered around him in the Major Case Squad office. Now that the copycat murders were public knowledge, there was no need to keep the number of cops involved to a minimum. As of now, the force hunting the Anagramist (whose self-proclaimed moniker was withheld from the press) was nineteen detectives strong.

"Finding this whacko is priority one for the job," Wilkes contin-ued, "and that comes right from the fifteenth floor. We've been given the keys to the kingdom on this one. Unlimited resources. All we gotta do is ask and we shall receive," he said in his best princely manner, which for him was a stretch. "And we're gonna need all of it," Wilkes added, "because, unfortunately for us, the only physical evidence we have on this mook is the way he cut up Rosa Sanchez. Nothing whatsoever's been found to identify him—prints, DNA, not a goddamn thing. No car, no tracks, tire or otherwise, no nothing. This guy's not just lucky; he's good. And the fact that his MO keeps changing is just the gravy on this pile of dog crap, because we don't even know what we're looking for."

Behind the somber, attentive detectives stood Claire, her back against the wall. She was up next. And she was nervous. At least at the news conference she didn't have to speak.

"What we're looking for, people, is a ghost," Wilkes said, soldiering on. "We all know how hard it is to find ghosts. And now that we've exposed ourselves on television, he knows we're on to him. So make no mistake about it, we're playing catch-up here. It's time for us to pull ahead in this guy's sick little game."

He gave Claire the signal, and she walked to the front of the room. "I don't know how many of you have met Doctor Claire Waters, but she has been indispensable in this case, and she's working with us in an official capacity to help collar this maniac. She's worked up a profile for which the city isn't paying her a dime—not that she's asking. I give you Doctor Waters."

Claire reached the front of the room. She wasn't prepared for the spontaneous, thunderous applause that came from the detectives. She could feel her face flush with embarrassment and had no clue how to react. Wilkes saw her predicament and came to her rescue.

"All right, you morons," he yelled above the applause, "try not to make the doc here wet her pants." Over their laughter, he said to Claire, "You have some fans here and you've earned every one of them."

Claire squared her shoulders and took a deep breath. "Thank you, Inspector. I'm touched."

"So's he," came an unfamiliar voice from the back, which broke everyone up once again and relaxed Claire to the point that she felt ready to proceed in this roomful of seasoned cops.

"Okay," she said as the laughter died down. "Be glad you're laughing now, because I don't think our friend the Anagramist is going to be easy to catch."

She made eye contact around the room, and the looks she got back confirmed she had their attention. "Our killer is a student—of serial killers—and obscure ones at that. Other than myself, who studied William Edward Hickman in Serial Killers 101 (this drew a laugh), I doubt any of you ever heard of him. But to keep it short, Hickman murdered a little girl in Los Angeles back in the twenties and drained her blood," Claire said to the group. "Just like our killer tried to do to a man we haven't ID'd yet who was found dead in Queens after an attack similar to what Hickman did to that girl."

"What about Victor Palmer, Doc?" asked Savarese. "We didn't know he was dismembering women until recently, so how could the Anagramist know about him?"

"Unless he knew Palmer, there's no way he could have," Claire agreed. "Most likely, he just pulled up another grisly murder from the Internet. Got the information about the two killings from 1977 and copied them."

"And the murder of Rosa Sanchez put us back on the trail of Victor Palmer," Nick said, standing off to the side. "At first we thought Palmer killed Rosa, but then we realized that the Anagramist just made it *look* like Palmer's work. In a perverse way, we have the Anagramist to thank for helping us smoke out and nail Palmer."

"And don't forget that the Anagramist is a master copier. Not only does he copy old serial murders, he impersonates cops," Claire said. "It's how he lured Rosa Sanchez into going with him."

"Shit," Wilkes said. "Tony, put two guys on tracing whatever hunk of metal the Anagramist has that looks like a parole officer's shield. Any idiot calling themselves a collector can buy them off several Web sites. Let's get on that and the local police supply stores and manufacturers who make our shields."

He gestured to Claire, giving her back the room. "Now, as you might've seen last night, the inspector gave a great performance on television. But he stuck to the script we prepared for him. The script was designed to push our target's buttons and, we hope, cause him to make a mistake. It's probably too early to tell whether it worked. When the inspector called him an amateur, it was intended to go to the Anagramist's severe lack of self-esteem. He's looking for a way to feel good about himself, but he's having a tough time, especially now that we've called him out. He admires and copies the work of his pre-decessors, serial killers who came before him. I'm assuming he's picking the obscure ones because he can't think up his own meth-ods or anything more creative than what he's already seen. It's like plagiarism or art fraud. He's a wannabe. But he's probably congratu-lating himself on his brilliance by copying the unknown masters, thinking he can do it better."

"Has anyone done this before?" asked a female voice from the back.

"Not as a deliberate MO," said Claire. "As far as we can tell, anyway. There are plenty of murders where someone wants to get rid of their wife, girlfriend, or business partner, and kills in a way to make it look like the work of an active, current, serial killer. But I know of no cases like this."

"What about the word games?" asked Nick. "Why does he need them?"

"The fact that he's given himself a name—the Anagramist—sug-gests he wants more than just credit," Claire said. "He wants fame, the front page, the lead story on the six o'clock news, the top head-line of the Web site. A lot like David Berkowitz when the *Daily News* started calling him Son of Sam."

Wilkes shouted to Savarese, "Maybe our guy's a disciple of Berko-witz. Someone who did time with him in prison, got paroled, and de-cided he wanted to be more famous. Let's get two bodies up to Fallsburg and talk to Dave Berkowitz. He found God a long time ago, so he'll probably cooperate. Ask him if there's anyone who seemed to deify him a little too much. Go on, Doctor."

"I'm almost done, Inspector," Claire said. "One last thing about the word games, and this is perhaps the most important point. Peo-ple like our target often compensate for their poor self-image by con-vincing themselves that they're smarter than the rest of us. Please don't take what I'm about to say as an insult, but such an individual would believe a bunch of 'moronic cops'—and I'm using his words, not mine—would never be able to figure out his anagrams."

"Maybe he's right," Wilkes said, "because we didn't figure it out. You did."

Claire didn't want to end the briefing on such a note. "But you were smart enough to call *me*, Inspector," she said, getting the laugh she hoped for and turning Wilkes's face red. "Isn't that good enough?"

Wilkes wasn't too proud to be the butt of someone's well-timed joke. "The Doctor will be appearing at the Improv after we close this thing," he said. "You all have your assignments. We'll work two twelve-hour tours—midnight to noon and noon to midnight—with some flexibility for whatever may come up. Now let's get to it and collar this colossal pain in the city's ass."

Claire was glad there was no more applause before the briefing broke up. Most of the detectives shuffled out, but one stayed in his seat—Billy Simms. The handsome, young detective had been on the phone throughout the entire briefing. Only now did he hang up and give Wilkes the high sign.

"What is it, Billy?" Wilkes asked, hurrying over.

"We got an ID on the dude in Alley Pond Park, Boss," Simms said.

Wilkes summoned Nick and Claire over for Simms to fill them in. "His name's Robert Steven Newman, forty-three, of Spring Lake, New Jersey," he said as he pulled up Newman's driver's license on his computer. A handsome, dark-haired man in a gray suit and conservative red tie occupied the screen.

"Ain't that special," muttered Wilkes. "How'd he get from the shore to the swamps of Little Neck?"

"Good question, because the last time anyone saw him was three mornings ago, getting into his canary-yellow 2008 Porsche convertible outside Monmouth County Superior Court and driving away."

"Superior court?" asked Nick. "We know what for?"

"Jersey troopers say he's a personal injury lawyer and part-time public defender who was there to get one of his private cases adjourned. Newman's wife called the cops when he didn't show up at home that night. They had a statewide bulletin on him and his ride."

"Get that bulletin out to our troops, and all the cops on Long Island, including state," ordered Wilkes. "Canary yellow Porsche . . . we may actually have a shot someone'll spot it—"

"Someone already did," Simms said. "Yesterday, in the parking lot of the Atlantic City airport."

"And I'm gonna guess there's no record the poor bastard got on a plane or even bought a ticket," Wilkes said, his voice thick with sarcasm. "Fantastic. First person figures out how this poor slob got from

Atlantic City to a swamp in Queens without his car, I'll put 'em up for promotion." It was clear the case was getting to him. "Guess we'd better put a coupla bodies on Newman, see if anyone in his past or present figures into this."

"Cops in Jersey are on it," offered Simms.

"Well, I want our cops on it with them," Wilkes interrupted.

"Nick," shouted a detective named Stark from across the room. "Line three."

"Can you take a message?" Nick asked.

"It's your kid's school," said Detective Stark, "and it sounds urgent."

Nick found the nearest phone and yanked up the receiver. "This is Detective Lawler," he said.

"Hi, Detective, this is Dawn Frandon. I'm the assistant principal at—"

"I know who you are, Ms. Frandon," Nick said, remembering the woman from his daughter Jill's high school. She'd been very helpful in the weeks after his wife committed suicide. "Is everything okay with Jill?"

"Well, that's what I was calling to ask you," she said. "Because Jill's never cut a class, and when she didn't show up for her seventh-period history—"

"Do you know where she went?" asked Nick, the fear in his voice turning heads and bringing Claire to his side.

"No, but her friend Marnie told us Jill got a call from your younger daughter, Katie, and ran out of the building."

"I appreciate it," said Nick. "Please let me know if Jill comes back."

"Jill's gone?" asked Claire as Nick hung up.

"After Katie called her," said Nick, dropping the receiver, pulling his cell phone, and hitting *Jill* on his autodial. He ended the call after just a few seconds.

"Went right to voice mail," said Nick, hanging up and autodialing Katie's number. Again, he ended the call quickly, fear spreading across his face.

"What?" asked the inspector.

"Something with Nicky's kids," Simms answered.

Nick fumbled through his phone contacts for the number for Katie's school and speed-dialed it. "I.S. One-Thirty-Two," came a female voice on the line.

"Hi, this is Nick Lawler, Katie Lawler's father. Do you know which class Katie's in right now?"

"It's okay, Mr. Lawler," said the voice. "Everything's taken care of."

"What do you mean?" asked Nick.

"Well, we dismissed Katie with that detective you sent over."

"What?" Nick demanded. "I never sent any detective there to pick up my daughter."

This brought Wilkes flying over and detectives stopping whatever they were doing, rising from their seats. "What's going on?" the inspector demanded.

Claire just put up her hand, trying to eavesdrop on the voice coming from Nick's phone. She reached over and hit the button putting the female voice on speaker.

"Oh, we checked it out when he said he was a friend of yours and Katie said she didn't know him. But then he said you'd lent him your car to pick up Katie. We took her outside and she said it was your car, so we figured it was okay."

It's as far as she got before Nick dropped the receiver. "Mr. Lawler? Are you there? Mr. Lawler . . ."

Claire disconnected her. "It's him," she said to Wilkes.

Nick scanned the room. He knew that for his colleagues nothing else mattered now. He shot Claire a look of fear—the first time she'd ever seen him like that. She didn't know how to comfort him.

Wilkes bellowed commands. "Alarm out on Nick Lawler's personal vehicle," he said. "Red 1988 Jeep Cherokee, occupants likely two teenage girls and a man believed to be armed and dangerous and should be approached with caution. Amber Alert and Roadblocks at every tunnel and bridge on and off this rock. Cops on every subway train and platform just in case." He glanced at Nick to calm him. "We have to assume he has both of Nick's daughters," he said to the room. "I want every cop in this department to know it. Stark," he shouted, "you cover the phones. I want the graveyard shift in here forthwith on OT, everyone on the street, two to a car. We'll position you from the Battery to the Cloisters for immediate response *when* we find them." He emphasized the *when* to make a point, and turned to Nick. "That shithead's not leaving this island with those two girls. Now let's move!"

The entire room sprang into action. Claire moved over to Nick, who didn't resist when she put her hand on his shoulder. She said nothing, knowing nothing she could say would make any difference.

"You two," Wilkes barked at them, "let's go. I'm gonna need you."

"Where?" asked Nick, waking himself up.

"Katie's school," Wilkes shot back over his shoulder, already heading for the door. "I'm sending Crime Scene to dust anything this asshole might've touched."

Savarese drove Wilkes's Dodge Charger south on the FDR Drive, around the Battery and up West Street, lights and siren, as fast as traffic would let him. The familiar feeling eased Nick's paralysis of fear. For the first time since Wilkes took command of the situation, he spoke more than one word. To Claire.

"He *was* following you," he said. "Because he wanted *that* car. To get Katie out of school. He used the same shield on those idiots at the school that he used on Rosa Sanchez so she'd go with him."

"Then he used Katie to lure Jill in," said Claire.

"Car thirty-one, call your command," came a voice from the police radio.

Wilkes picked up the secure radio-phone in the car, which was linked to the chief of detectives' office. "Inspector Wilkes," he said.

For a few seconds he listened. "Ten-four," he finally said. "I want everyone moved to that location." He hung up the receiver and turned to Savarese. "Inwood. Payson and Dyckman Avenues," the inspector commanded.

Savarese obeyed, speeding the car up the West Side.

"What is it, Inspector?" asked Claire.

When Wilkes turned around to face them, he spoke with his jaw clenched. "Patrol found your car, Nicky. The girls are inside, alive, and the bastard didn't touch 'em." He paused, finding himself at a rare loss for words. "But it's not good."

CHAPTER 21

The car's siren and radios were off by the time Nick and Claire reached the police perimeter in the otherwise quiet Inwood neighborhood near the northernmost tip of Manhattan. Though the day was clear, the darkly tinted windows on Wilkes's Dodge made it difficult for Nick to see anything but the outline of his Jeep parked in the middle of an intersection a block away.

The picture became only slightly clearer when he got out of the car. He could make out two people in padded protective suits that made them look like supersized deep-sea divers. They were Bomb Squad detectives, he realized, and they were examining his Jeep.

His Jeep. In which he couldn't even see his two precious daughters he knew were trapped inside.

Wilkes had told them the story on the way uptown. The kidnapper, presumably the Anagramist, had stopped the car in the center of the intersection, just off Inwood Hill Park. He got out, displayed a remote control, and warned the girls that if they tried to escape through any door or window, the car would blow up. Then, according to what the girls told the first cops who arrived, he'd disappeared into the wooded park.

Nick headed for the yellow police tape.

"Where are you going?" Claire asked, alarmed.

Nick was just about to duck under the tape when Wilkes grabbed his arm. "Are you nuts?" he exclaimed. "You can't go down there."

Nick yanked his arm from his boss's grasp, but Wilkes grabbed him again. "Nicky, please. Let the bomb guys do their jobs," he pleaded.

"I'm their father," Nick said. "If they go up they're not going alone."

"That's just what this dickhead wants," Wilkes replied.

"You wanna stop me, you're gonna have to collar me," Nick said. His patron saint didn't want to let him go. But Wilkes knew he had no choice. He released Nick's arm. Nick nodded in thanks, then turned toward the Jeep, his walk turning into a trot, then a run.

Claire felt a wave of guilt for involving Nick in Rosa Sanchez's murder. Though of course she never imagined doing so would put him and his family in harm's way.

She couldn't change that now. But maybe she could mitigate the damage. She headed toward the yellow police tape and tried to duck under before anyone noticed. But Wilkes took her by the shoulder and pulled her back.

"Not a chance, Doctor."

"But I can calm them down," she begged him. "Please."

"I can't even justify Nick being down there. You're a civilian. I let you through and that thing goes off, forget what the department will do to me—I'll spend the rest of my life in a bottle of Johnnie Walker."

He handed her a pair of binoculars. She stood behind the yellow tape and put them to her eyes, watching as Nick reached the car. She imagined he felt even more powerless than she did as he saw his terrified daughters huddled together on the backseat, their arms clenched around each other, whimpering.

"Daddy!" screamed Katie.

"Don't move!" yelled one of the Bomb Squad detectives, turning slowly, like an astronaut walking on the moon, to see Nick wearing nothing more protective than his one-hundred-percent worsted wool, charcoal pin-striped suit. "Get outta here!" he yelled.

"They're my kids," Nick said, as if that explained everything.

He stopped a foot from the back passenger door of the Jeep, his straining eyes recording every detail. The first thing he noticed was that all four door windows were cracked open.

Thank God for small favors, he thought. *At least the sonuvabitch left them able to breathe.*

Nick leaned as close as he could to the door without touching it.

"I'm here, and I'm not leaving without you two," he said to the girls. "These guys are the best. Just stay calm and we'll get you out of there. I promise."

The girls were too scared to say anything. Nick turned to the Bomb Squad guys. "Where's the device?" he asked.

"Guy, I've gotta tell ya," said the Bomb Squad detective. "We've been over the car three times and we can't find anything—*outside,* that is."

Nick turned back to the rear door and spoke into the window. "Jill," he said, "do you see a device with wires anywhere in the Jeep?"

Jill looked around, never letting go of Katie, whose head rested in her lap.

"I don't see anything, Dad," Jill said.

"Okay, sweetheart," Nick said, his voice as calm as he could manage. "Tell me everything that happened, from when he picked you up until he got out of the car."

Jill summoned every detail she could remember. "I got in the car outside school. He said he was taking us to you. But then we started heading up the West Side Highway."

"Then what?" her father asked.

"He had one of those earpieces—you know, like the Secret Service guys wear. I asked him where he was taking us. He said you were waiting for us over in New Jersey. That's when I told him I was calling you. He pulled out a gun and made Katie and me give him our phones. I can't believe I was so stupid."

"You weren't stupid, you were smart," Nick reassured her. "Someone has a gun you do what they say. Tell me the rest."

"He was about to get on the George Washington Bridge. And then he suddenly kept going straight. We drove around for a while, like he was looking for something. And then he stopped right here and told us if we tried to get out of the car it would blow up."

"Did you see the remote? The one he said he used to set the explosive?"

"Yes," said Jill, trying hard not to shake too much.

"Can you describe it for me?" asked Nick.

"It looked like one of those electronic key things that opens a car door," Jill said.

Nick came to a decision. He hoped it was the right one, because the lives of his children—and therefore his own life—would depend on it.

"Here's what we're gonna do," he said to Jill and Katie as he waved the Bomb Squad detectives closer. Nick pulled out his memo book, wrote something down, and then showed it to everyone. "Nobody say a word, just nod an answer. Are we clear?" he asked.

The girls obeyed. Nick turned to the Bomb Squad detectives, who nodded as well.

Claire saw all this through the binoculars from behind the yellow tape. "I think they're gonna try something," she said to Wilkes.

"Start praying, Doc," came the inspector's response.

"I never stopped," Claire said.

A hundred yards away, Nick took a deep breath.

"Okay," he said. "On my count: One. Two. Three!"

He yanked open the rear door, grabbed Katie and ran as Jill scrambled out the other side and into the protective embrace of a Bomb Squad guy. They were fifty yards from the Jeep before anyone turned around.

Nothing. The Jeep was still there, intact.

Nick grabbed his daughters, pulling them close. Both were crying and shaking. The Bomb Squad detectives moved back toward the car, looking inside, under the seats, in the spare tire compartment, under the hood, at the undercarriage using mirrors.

"It's all clear," one of them yelled after a minute or two.

Claire and Wilkes bolted toward Nick and the girls, who stood huddled about halfway down the block between the yellow tape and the Jeep.

"What the hell was *that*?" Wilkes asked Nick, reaching the scene.

"This guy's a piece of work," Nick said, just starting to breathe again.

"You wrote something down and showed it to everyone," Claire said as she ran up.

Nick pulled out his memo book and showed them his written message:

IT'S BULLSHIT
ON 3 WE RUN FOR IT

"How'd you know?" Wilkes asked, amazed and relieved.

Nick recounted what Jill had told him. "Mr. Anagramist was making it up as he went along," he explained. "He must've had one of our police radio frequencies going into his earpiece. He heard Central order roadblocks on the bridge—that's why he swerved off the ramp. He took the first exit he could find and came up with plan B— the fake bomb—so he'd have time to get away."

Claire and the girls hugged each other.

"Are they okay?" Wilkes asked her.

"They're in shock," Claire replied, and indeed both girls were shivering despite the unusually hot and muggy spring day. "They should be checked at a hospital."

Wilkes agreed. "Why don't you take them over to the medics. Columbia-Pres is the closest ER," he said, referring to New York-Presbyterian/Columbia Medical Center. Wilkes then spoke to the girls. "We need your help here, ladies. You're the only people who've seen this guy's face. I'm gonna have an artist meet you at the hospital to get a description from you. That's okay, right?"

The girls, still unable to find their voices, simply nodded. Wilkes gestured to Claire, who put an arm around each of them and escorted them toward two approaching fire department ambulances.

"Boss . . ." exhaled Savarese, breathless from running down the block.

Wilkes wasn't interested. "When we get that sketch I want it out to every law enforcement agency within three hundred miles. This asshole finally screwed up and I don't care if it's in cuffs or a pine box, he's going down." His steely eyes focused on the Jeep. "Have Crime Scene flatbed this thing to the garage and tear it apart. Maybe he was dumb enough to leave prints and/or DNA too."

"Let me take a look first," said Nick. "I thought I noticed some damage that I don't remember being there."

He walked around the Jeep and sure enough, saw what appeared to be a fresh dent that left a swath of white paint on the red car. "Claire!" he shouted, waving her over.

Claire looked in his direction as two paramedics checked the girls' vital signs. "The paramedics will take you to the hospital and we'll meet you there," she told Jill and Katie. Then she hurried over to where Nick stood, looking down at the dent. "What is it?" she asked.

Nick knelt beside the car and gestured to the damage. "Do you remember this being here the other night when you parked the car?"

He stopped, hearing something in the distance from the direction of the park. A sound that, if not for his sensitive hearing, he might not have heard. Like the *pop* of a balloon bursting . . .

Claire felt his hand grab her arm, pulling just as the sharp pain, the burning in her right lower back, hit her like someone had branded her with a hot iron. Everything began to slow down and spin.

"Gun!" she heard Nick yell as she grabbed on to one of the Jeep's door handles, but it only broke her fall. She was too weak and in too much pain to hold on.

"Claire!" screamed Nick, rising to his feet to grab her but not fast enough.

Claire dropped to the ground, on her back, looking up at the blue sky, thinking it was a beautiful day. Wondering what tomorrow would be like. All the noise around her faded away. She was in her own bubble, and she wanted to sleep.

Like a vision in a dream, Inspector Wilkes appeared above her, his face massive.

"Get that bus over here, now!" she heard him say, referring to the ambulance parked nearby. It was strange, because his voice was only a whisper. Then she heard him say, "She's been shot . . . shot . . . shot. . . ." echoing over and over. She was aware of Nick's voice beside her but she just kept staring at the sky above. With those big fluffy clouds . . .

"Don't go out on us," Nick said. "We're gonna get you to the hospital."

She knew she had to fight as hard as she could to keep her eyes open.

But she couldn't.

CHAPTER 22

Claire heard the beeping first. She was in a fog. It took all her strength to force her eyelids open. Just a crack, but enough for the light to nearly blind her. She put it together—the collection of noises, the antiseptic smell, the rhythmic lines rolling across the screen of a monitor. She was in the hospital.

"She's awake," came a female voice she recognized but couldn't quite place. "Find out how far away her parents are."

Her pupils adjusted to the light, allowing her eyes to focus. She was in the post-op recovery room of MSU Hospital's surgical suite. She'd been there before, each time to observe a neurosurgical procedure. She couldn't remember why she now lay in a hospital bed.

"Claire."

The same female voice. She tilted her head to the left. Fairborn stood there, smiling, her face the picture of concern, her eyes red—from what? Crying?

Crying for me?

"Hi," Claire said, with a hoarse squeak.

"She's back," Fairborn said. She lowered her face close to Claire's. "Don't talk. They just took out your ET tube ten minutes ago. Just rest."

Back? Back from what? Where did I go?

Then Claire remembered. The bright, clear, blue sky. Wilkes standing over her.

"Nick," she whispered.

"He's here," Fairborn said. "It's like a police officer's convention in the waiting room."

"I was shot," she said, the memory emerging from her half-awake brain. "Where?"

"In your abdomen," said Fairborn, sounding like the doctor she was. "You lost a lot of blood, dear. Phil Mecklin had to open you up to stop the bleeding."

Claire remembered the burning in her back. Though she wasn't in pain and had never had surgery before, she felt a tightness she knew must be from the incision in her belly.

"A laparotomy?" she asked Fairborn. "Where was I bleeding?"

"The bullet hit your right renal artery and lodged in the renal pelvis of your kidney," said Fairborn with difficulty. "The damage was too extensive to save it. Phil had to take the kidney out."

Claire was so groggy from anesthesia that the news barely registered. "That's okay, I only need one," she said. "I'm really glad you're here."

Fairborn forced a smile. "Your parents will be here soon."

"Tell them it's not so bad, they don't have to come," she blurted, knowing Fairborn wouldn't stop them.

"Their plane already landed at Kennedy," Fairborn said. "The police department is flying them by helicopter here to the helipad on the roof. Same way you got here from uptown."

Claire was having trouble registering what her mentor was saying. "I was flown here?" she asked, her speech thick from the effects of the anesthesia.

"Courtesy of outgoing Commissioner Farrell," confirmed Fairborn. "He thought it was the least he could do."

Claire remembered Nick pulling her arm just as she felt the burning of the bullet.

"Nick tried to save me," Claire said. "Tell the commissioner he should do something for *him*. He's okay, right?"

She looked up at Fairborn. "Please, did something happen to him too?" Claire begged with the strongest voice she had in her.

Fairborn took her hand and stroked it. "There was a second shot. Nick was hit."

Claire registered this. "How bad?" she asked.

"He's lucky. He was turning to lift you into the ambulance when he was struck. The bullet chipped his left ulna."

"He'd have been killed," Claire said, her eyes welling up, stuck on the image of the bullet hitting Nick in his arm.

"No," said Fairborn, having to force the words out.

"What?" asked Claire.

Fairborn took a breath. "He was at the head of the gurney. His arm was directly in front of your left ear."

Somehow, in her fog, Claire realized what this meant. "I would have been shot in the head."

"But you weren't," said Fairborn. "You're here."

"Where are Jill and Katie?" Claire asked.

"Are those Nick's daughters?"

Claire nodded.

"I don't know, dear," said Fairborn. "But the police will. Inspector Wilkes says no one else was hurt."

Still, Claire could feel Fairborn's discomfort. As if her mentor was omitting some important information.

"You're not telling me something," Claire said.

Fairborn shook her head, amazed that Claire, in her present state, would detect her hesitance. "It's about your kidney. But I want to make sure you're awake enough to understand me, because it's important. . . ."

She stopped as the curtain parted and Claire's parents hurried in, accompanied by Inspector Wilkes.

"Oh, my God," cried her mother.

Claire tried to sit up but her father stopped her. "Don't," said Frank Waters, gently placing his hand on his daughter's shoulder.

Claire saw the bandage on her father's forehead and remembered his accident. "Does your head hurt?" she asked.

"Don't worry about me. It's time for you to stop taking care of everyone. And for us to take care of you."

She motioned Wilkes over to her. "I need to talk to the inspector, alone," she said.

"Your parents know everything," said Wilkes, in a soothing voice she'd never heard from him before. "I told them the whole story on the way over in the chopper."

That was exactly what Claire was afraid of. "Everything?" she asked.

"Even the stuff only us cops are supposed to know," Wilkes said. "And you."

Claire turned to her parents. "Was he able to make it through a sentence without swearing?" she asked.

Wilkes snorted a laugh and shook his head in amazement.

"Yes," said Frank, "and apparently he just got through two more curse-free sentences as well."

"Then I pronounce you cured," Claire said to Wilkes, drifting off into la-la land, prompting Fairborn to bring the visit to an end.

"We'll have a room for her shortly," she said, "and you can see her there. In the meantime, let's let her rest," Fairborn said to Wilkes, more an order than a suggestion.

It was the last thing Claire heard before she dozed off.

She saw Amy, being carried away by Mr. Winslow, the man who'd kidnapped her. Mr. Winslow shoved her best friend into his white BMW. Claire could not see her face until Amy turned to look out the rear window. But Claire didn't see Amy. Instead, she saw a girl with her own face, her freckles and her brown hair—Amy had blond hair. . . .

Who is this girl? Claire wondered. *Why does she look like me?*

Claire felt movement. She opened her eyes, squinting at the fluorescent lights passing above her, which hypnotized her. She realized that she was being wheeled to her room. Then sleep rescued her once again.

The next time Claire opened her eyes, the light was much dimmer. The head of the hospital bed was raised, and she was looking out a window, west, at the last vestiges of a pink and orange New York City sunset.

"It's beautiful, isn't it?" said Charlotte Waters, sitting at the side of the bed. Claire noticed that her mother's always fastidiously kept blond hair was disheveled.

She fell asleep. Sitting in that chair. Next to my bed.

"Yes," said Claire, her voice stronger. "It's gorgeous."

"How do you feel?" asked Charlotte.

"Grateful to be able to see the sunset."

She knew she was in the hospital tower, but the room she was in didn't look like any at MSU she'd seen before.

"Where am I?"

"You're in the hospital."

"I know, Mom. What part of the hospital?"

"The VIP floor," said Charlotte, a touch of pride in her voice. "Doctor Fairborn set it up. I better watch out for her before she takes my place."

"Nobody can take your place," Claire assured her mother.

"These people care about you," Charlotte said, looking around the room. "Treating you like this. Doctor Fairborn, that detective . . . inspector, whoever he is. Seems you're pretty important to them."

She said it as if she'd never realized how much her daughter had accomplished. Claire knew it was her mother's backhanded way of saying how proud she was. Charlotte Waters had always been the most emotionally shut down person Claire knew. Her mother tried to write it off as stoicism in contrast to her father's open, emotional personality. It was no mystery to Claire that, personality-wise, she was her mother.

She turned her head back to the window. "How long have I been here?" she asked.

Charlotte checked her watch. "They let me in just after three. And it's almost eight now. You've been asleep for most of it."

"I don't remember waking up in this room."

"You didn't, exactly," said Charlotte, brushing a wisp of her daughter's hair away from her face. "You were talking, though."

Oh shit, Claire thought. *What did I say?*

"You were calling for Amy," Charlotte continued, as if reading her daughter's thoughts. "Do you remember any of that?"

Claire remembered her dream, but she didn't want to talk about her childhood friend. She was shocked when Charlotte said, "Honey, you can tell me. I'm not afraid to hear anything you want to say."

There's so much I want to say to you, Mother. I'm not sure you're ready to listen. But what have I got to lose?

"I still blame myself for what happened to Amy," Claire said, staring straight ahead as the sun dipped below the buildings of midtown Manhattan. "But in my dream, Amy wasn't kidnapped. It was me, only I had blond hair just like Amy did."

When Charlotte didn't respond, Claire thought this would be another one of those times that her mother couldn't find the right words.

The sound of a sniffle turned her head toward Charlotte just as a tear dropped from her eye. Claire had never seen anything close to her mother crying and was surprised at how deeply this disturbed her.

"Mom?"

"Don't take care of me," Charlotte sniffled.

"I'm going to be okay."

"I know," her mother said, brushing the tears away as she stood up and slid her chair into a position where she could face her daughter.

"Then what is it?" asked Claire.

"While you were sleeping," she said as she sat back down, "Doctor Fairborn came in. Your father was here too, and she wanted to talk to us. *She* wanted to tell you what I'm about to, but I insisted that I be the one. And you know I can be very insistent."

Claire nodded—at least that much was true.

"Well, she told us that because you lost a kidney, they 'typed your tissues,' whatever that means, in case your other kidney fails and you need a transplant."

Claire couldn't understand why her mother needed to tell her this. "It's standard procedure, Mom," she said. "It's nothing to worry about."

"I'm not worried about your kidney—the doctors say it's fine." Charlotte stopped, not sure how to continue. Then she took a breath. "Doctor Fairborn came here an hour ago. And she told us that the DNA from your kidneys is different from the DNA in your blood."

It took more than a moment for what Charlotte said to sink in. Claire knew there could be only one explanation for such a phenomenon.

"I'm a chimera," she said, thinking back to her days in medical school when she studied embryology. She recalled that a chimera is formed when cells from one embryo are absorbed into another early in gestation. Claire knew the reason the DNA from her kidneys was different from the DNA in her blood was that the kidneys came from the cells of the twin she'd absorbed.

Claire turned toward her mother and could tell from the sorrow on her mother's face that there was more to this story.

"What is it, Mom?" Claire asked. "You look so sad." Then the rest of the story came to her. "You always knew, didn't you?" she asked.

"Yes," Charlotte said. "When I had an ultrasound early on in my pregnancy, there was evidence of twins. And then when I went back to the doctor the twin was gone."

Claire was stunned. *Does this explain why I always felt that something was missing inside me?*

Charlotte could see the pain in Claire's eyes. She took her daughter's hand in hers. "Ever since you could talk," Charlotte said, "you've been asking for the 'other girl.' Even though you never said it, I knew that you felt there was a part of you missing, someone you were reaching out for. And I knew what you were missing because I was missing that child too."

"Why didn't you tell me?" Claire asked.

"First, I didn't think you'd understand. Then I was afraid you'd think it was your fault your twin didn't survive."

"Mom, I'm a doctor. I know how these things work. It happens at the embryonic stage. There's no way it could be my fault, your fault. Anyone's fault."

"I never said my thoughts were always rational," Charlotte said. "After a while it just didn't seem important anymore. It didn't seem to affect your life when you got older."

If you only knew, Mom, how much it's affected everything in my life. How knowing would have helped me deal with the loss I've always felt.

"But I was wrong, wasn't I?" Charlotte continued. "Or I was just in denial about how it affected you."

It was as if her mother had just read her thoughts. Something Claire couldn't remember her ever having done before.

"What do you mean?" Claire asked, wondering what her mother saw that she didn't.

Charlotte's eyes met her daughter's. "Even after you found Amy's remains last year, you couldn't let go of what happened to her."

"I know it wasn't my fault, Mom," Claire said.

"Maybe logically you knew, but emotionally you never could come to terms with it, even now," Charlotte said. "But this—survivor's guilt, whatever it is you've been walking around with all these years—I think it started long before Amy."

Claire was still too groggy to register the shock she felt.

"Why do you think that?" she asked.

"Because, from the day you were born, you were unstoppable," Charlotte said, the tears flowing from her eyes. "You mastered every-thing you laid your hands or your eyes on. As if you were doing the work of two people. Or making up for something that was missing in your life—I don't know which. Maybe it's both. You're the shrink. . . ." She trailed off into quiet sobbing.

Claire found the button to raise the head of the bed and brought herself further up. "Mom, please."

Charlotte looked up at her. "I'm sorry. I didn't see it. . . ."

"How could you have?" Claire said, trying to comfort her mother. "You're right. I did feel something even before Amy was kidnapped. I'm the shrink and I didn't even realize what was going on until you just said it."

Charlotte found a tissue in her purse and wiped her eyes. "I wish I'd said it earlier."

"You can't say what you don't know," Claire reassured her.

"But I could've helped you," her guilt-ridden mother shot back.

The hint of a smile appeared on Claire's face. "You just did," she said.

Charlotte half laughed, half cried. "Better late than never, I guess."

"Does Dad know?"

"Yes, he found out when I did. He wanted to tell you for years. The only reason he didn't was because I wouldn't allow him to."

Claire knew that as devoted as her father was to her, he was staunchly loyal to his wife. As if on cue, Frank came through the door, carrying a cardboard tray that held two large cups and a white paper bag con-taining what smelled like burgers and fries.

"How're we doing?" her father asked.

Claire wondered if he was smiling because he was spared having to be there when her mother told her the news. "I know about the twin, Dad."

"Finally," said her father. "After what your Doctor Fairborn told us, I was going to throw your mother under the bus until she volun-teered to step in front of it."

"Good thing you didn't," Claire said. "You've suffered enough dam-age from a bus to last a lifetime."

She meant it to break the ice and end the discussion. The smiles she brought to her parents' faces confirmed her strategy had worked.

Frank turned to his wife. "I got you an iced tea and a hamburger with nothing on it," he said.

"I may have to ask you to eat it outside," said Claire. "I'm having trouble with the smell."

But her queasiness passed and she was okay. While her parents dove into their sparse meals, Claire used her segue about the bus to ask her father more about his car accident. "Did they ever find out what happened?" she asked.

"My God, we never got to tell you the rest," Frank said. "Apparently this wasn't just some kid climbing a fence and stealing a bus for a joyride. There was a murder involved."

"Who was killed?" Claire asked, suddenly more alert.

"The guard at the gate of the bus depot. Shot in the head at point-blank range. The cops have the whole thing on video."

"Do they know who did it?"

"No." said Frank. "The shooter knew enough to look away from the cameras. That's why the police think it was an inside job."

"But that doesn't make sense," Claire said, pushing as hard as she could through her groggy state. "Why kill someone to steal a bus?"

"Good question," he replied. "All the police know is that after the bus hit my car and crashed into that telephone pole, the guy driving it was caught on another security camera two blocks from the bus depot, where he got into a car and took off. He hit another car too, in his rush to get away. So at some point the police will find a red Jeep with white paint on it."

Claire would have sat up if she had the strength. "Are you sure it was a red Jeep?" Claire asked.

"It was all over the news. An old Jeep Cherokee, New York plates . . ."

He stopped when Claire threw the covers off and tried to get out of bed.

"What on earth are you doing?" he asked, taking her shoulder to stop her.

Agitated, Claire grabbed her father's hand. "I need my cell phone," she said.

"Who could you possibly have to call now?" asked her mother, rising from her chair and looking for the closet.

"Inspector Wilkes. I have to tell him what happened to Dad."

Claire's mother found her daughter's purse in the closet and rummaged through it.

"But, honey, it happened in Rochester," her father said. "Why would the police here need to know about it?"

"Because it wasn't an accident."

Claire saw her parents look at each other, convinced that the emotional and physical trauma she'd suffered was affecting her mind.

"That red Jeep belongs to Nick Lawler."

"Your detective friend," Frank remembered. "I'm sure he's not the only one in New York State or any other with a car like that."

"You don't understand," Claire said, trying to wake herself up. "I was driving that car last night. I left it around the corner from my building. This morning, it was gone, stolen. This afternoon, the man who stole it kidnapped Nick's daughters. I saw the car after Nick rescued them and it had a dent with fresh white paint on it. The man who stole it is the man who kidnapped the girls and shot me, the killer Nick and I have been looking for." She turned to Frank. "And he tried to kill you because you're my father."

She realized her parents thought she'd gone off the deep end.

"Should I call Doctor Fairborn?" her mother asked.

"I'm not crazy, Mom," Claire assured her. "Please. Just give me the phone."

It took less than an hour for Wilkes to arrive at Claire's bedside. Now wide awake, she was in pain from her incision, refusing to push the button that would release opiates into her veins, trading discomfort for clarity.

"You could have saved yourself an hour of agony if you told me this on the phone, Doc," Wilkes said after Claire told him the story. "We already know our guy drove Nick's Jeep to Rochester, and we've told the cops up there that we have it."

"But he had to *know* where he was going when he stole it," Claire said. "It's not a coincidence that he tried to kill my father."

"You're right," came a voice from the door, causing Claire to turn her head as Nick, wearing a fiberglass cast on his left arm, entered the room.

"Nick," was all Claire could think of to say as a smile spread across her face, his presence momentarily obliterating the pain. He came over and kissed her on the cheek.

"They told me it was just a chipped ulna," she said, touching his cast.

"And a hairline fracture from there to the other side," Nick informed her, "or however you say that in doctor-ese. On the positive side, it's another weapon."

Claire introduced him to her parents, who could see the relationship between them was more than just that of two injured colleagues.

"Okay," said Wilkes, finally growing impatient, "now that the reunion's over can we get back to business?"

"Yes, sir," Nick said to his boss as he turned to Claire. "The bastard was tailing you the night I gave you the Jeep. Apparently he thought it was the perfect vehicle—no pun intended—to use to hurt your father, then me and you."

Claire knew there wasn't much more to be said at this point. Whoever wanted to hurt her had done an excellent job.

"What about the girls?" she asked Nick.

"Protective custody," he replied.

"So they're safe," she exhaled with a sigh of relief.

"As safe as they could ever be," Wilkes assured her. "With my wife and three kids in our house out on Long Island, surrounded by a dozen Suffolk County cops and five of our own Emergency Service guys armed with automatic rifles. Just like the two we'll have standing outside your door, Doc, and the security detail your parents will have with them, whether it's here or back in Rochester, until we catch this lunatic."

Claire tried to hold back the tears she felt welling in her eyes. "You know that Nick was collateral damage."

"I was in the right place at the right time," he said.

"That makes your safety even more tenuous, Doctor," Wilkes said. "When the perp finds out you're still alive, we have to assume he'll try again. Your strategy of pissing him off at the news conference worked, maybe too well. I gotta believe that's why he's coming after you."

This was the last thing Claire's parents wanted to hear. "You've got to find him first," Frank told Wilkes.

"Doctor Waters, let me assure you that in addition to the two dozen detectives we have on it, there's not a cop in this city who *isn't* looking for him," said the inspector. "We've even got people coming in off duty and volunteering."

"Thank you," Frank said.

"I should be the one thanking you two," Wilkes said to Claire's parents, "along with the rest of the city. Your little girl here done you, and us, proud."

"Do you think you'll catch him?" asked Charlotte.

"Up until now, unfortunately, this guy's been a ghost," Nick told them, turning to Claire. "But now he's a ghost with fingerprints."

"What?" Claire exclaimed, the news filling her with hope.

"Mr. Smartass slipped up," Wilkes said. "We got his prints off a metal post he was leaning against at Nick's younger daughter's school. That's the good news. The bad news is, the prints don't match anyone in any database, including the FBI's. That means he was never arrested, and *that* means the chances of finding him aren't great. We have two detectives on a plane to Rochester with the slugs the surgeons dug outta your daughter and Detective Lawler, to compare with the ones found on the murder victim up there. But even if they're a match, all that'll tell us is it's our guy for sure. There's no way to trace the ammo."

"What else can you do?" Claire asked, closing her eyes as the pain returned.

"The girls gave our artist almost identical descriptions of the sonuvabitch," Nick said. "As soon as they're ready, the sketches are going out everywhere—cops, feds, media. He's on the FBI's Most Wanted list. We're hoping someone'll recognize him."

Claire gave in, pushing the button that would soon bring her relief from the intense pain in her back.

"I'll help you any way I can, Inspector—" she began, until Wilkes cut her off, laughing. "You think this is funny?" she demanded.

"Doc," he said, "you've given more than enough of your blood to this city and our job. More than most cops give in their whole careers." He turned serious. "You keep saying you don't work for me, but I'm giving you an order anyway, and you're going to obey it. I'm putting you on sick leave. When I'm satisfied you're better, and only then, I will bring you back into the fold. In the meantime, I don't want you anywhere near this. If you need information, call me. But we've got it from here. Are we clear?"

"Yes," she answered with reluctance. "But there's one more thing I need to ask you. Both of you," she said, looking at Nick, "and it's a favor."

"Go ahead."

"I want to be kept in the loop," she said. "Please."

Nick turned to Wilkes. "As long as neither you nor the information leaves this room," Wilkes said.

"Thanks, Inspector."

"Don't thank me until we have this guy," said Wilkes. "And we will get him. I don't know how, but we will."

Then Wilkes did something Nick had never seen his boss do except at a cop funeral. He stood at attention and gave Claire a sharp salute like the marine he once was. Then lowered his arm and kissed Claire's hand.

She looked up at him, tears in her eyes. And she could see water in his.

"Don't do that to me," Wilkes said, grasping her hand quickly, then wheeling and heading out the door.

The soothing relief of the opiates erasing her pain hit her full force, and she drifted off to sleep.

Bright colors flooded Claire's consciousness as her eyes opened. As she focused, she realized they were flowers; not real ones but the pattern on the tunic worn over white pants by an obese nurse whose name tag read Rita Grantz. "Hi there," Nurse Grantz said with a smile. "I'm Rita, and I'll be taking care of you tonight. How's the pain?"

Claire could feel the discomfort from her incision. "Not great," she said, reaching for the button that would give her another dose of morphine.

"Let me check your vitals before you give yourself another hit," Rita said, touching the button that inflated the mechanical blood pressure cuff on Claire's right arm while she checked the monitors above Claire's bed for her heart rate and pulse oxygen level.

"Where is everyone?" Claire asked.

"The police took your parents back to the hotel when visiting hours ended," said Nurse Rita.

"What time is it?"

"One twenty-five in the morning," Nurse Rita informed her as the BP cuff automatically deflated. "Everything's looking good. Anything I can get you?"

Claire felt parched. "Can I drink yet?"

"Ice chips only," the nurse said. "But Doctor Mecklin told me to get you on your feet."

"Now?" asked Claire, too out of it to even think about getting up.

"Yes, Doctor," Rita replied. "And you know why."

"We don't want any clots forming," said Claire. "Okay."

Nurse Rita lowered the side rail and helped Claire sit up.

"Ow," Claire exclaimed, grimacing at the pain from the incision.

Nurse Rita placed hospital slippers on Claire's feet. "Ready?" she asked.

"Ready as I'm gonna be," Claire responded.

With Nurse Rita's assistance, Claire's legs cooperated. She stood up, Rita's thick hands under her armpits, her heft blocking her view.

"Okay, honey, now grab the IV pole," the nurse said to her. Claire obeyed, holding the pole for dear life with her left hand as Rita moved to support her from her right, revealing the rest of the vast room that was only available on the VIP floor.

A man was curled up on what passed for a sofa against the opposite wall. He appeared to be out cold.

"Nick?" she asked, though she knew it was him from the cast on his left arm.

"Guess he's one of the cops protecting you," Nurse Rita said. "C'mon, just a few steps out to the hall if you can do it."

"I can do it," Claire said, commanding her legs to shuffle forward though her eyes were glued to Nick's sleeping figure on the couch. "How long has he been here?" she asked.

"He was here when I came on shift," Rita replied. "Two more outside the door, all armored up. Like they're expecting an invasion or something."

Claire saw them when she made it out the door. As Wilkes had assured her, each one carried an assault rifle in addition to a sidearm. They nodded to her, and Claire waved back at them, thinking she barely had the energy to walk. She made it halfway down the hall and back before telling Rita it was enough.

"You did great for your first outing," Rita said as they entered the room.

Nick was still sleeping, snoring a little. Seeing him lying there made Claire's truth clear: he wasn't just another cop protecting her, wasn't just a friend and colleague. He was the man she loved.

"Leave us alone. Please," Claire said as Rita helped her back into bed.

"You know where the call button is, Doctor," Rita reminded her as she left. "I'll be right outside."

Only when Rita was out the door did Claire's tears start to flow, the emotion of seeing him there, being there for her, overtaking her. "I'm sorry," she began, "for dragging you into all this." She began to sob. "I'm sorry your daughters had to see what happened, because no child should ever—"

"They're okay," came Nick's groggy voice from across the room.

As best as she could, she composed herself. "You should be with them," she stammered.

"No," he said, swinging his legs over the couch and standing. "Until we collar this guy, I should be as far away from them as possible." He crossed the room to her bed. "But they're okay, I promise you," he continued, pulling a tissue from a box on the nightstand and dabbing her tears. "They'll get some therapy—yeah, I said that," he admitted with a smile, "and all the love they need from Wilkes's wife."

Claire grinned. "She's not a pushover, married to a curmudgeon like him?"

Nick laughed. "Where do you think he learned to order us around? She makes him look like a girlie man."

He lowered the side rail of Claire's bed.

"I already took my maiden voyage," she said to him.

But that wasn't what he had in mind, she realized, as he sat on the mattress.

"The girls will be fine," he assured her, stroking her forehead. "Right now, this is where I belong."

He said the last sentence staring into her eyes. Grimacing, she slid over as far as she could and he lowered himself beside her. He held her free right hand while balancing the cast on his chest.

"How's the pain?" he asked.

"Better," she answered. "What do we do now?"

"Make him pay," he said, closing his eyes.

It was nighttime when he woke up. Still sleepy, he tossed the comforter to the side, slid his legs off the mattress and into his foam slippers, not liking the feel of his bare feet on the cold parquet floor.

He glanced at his watch. It was after two in the morning. He'd slept thirteen hours. After the exhaustion he'd built up over the last day, he knew there was more slumber ahead. But right now he had to find out. He had to know.

Shuffling across the floor, he reached the desk and hit a random key on his computer to wake it up. He sat down and scoured the news for any word of his quarry's fate.

It didn't take long for him to find it. Doctor Waters and Detective Lawler were both listed in "guarded" condition. The shooter had escaped. Police were keeping mum on the whereabouts of Detective Lawler's two daughters, but speculation was that they were in protective custody, lest their kidnapper try abducting them again.

He laughed. It was never the girls he wanted. In fact, it wasn't even their father he wanted. Yes, he'd aimed too low on the first shot, hitting her in the stomach. But if Lawler's arm hadn't been in front of the bitch's head when he fired his perfect second shot, the hollow-point bullet would have ripped right across her midbrain. She would've had just a split second at the end of her life to realize that he'd won. That she'd been beaten.

By someone much better than she. Much smarter.

But he was willing to keep the game going. In fact, maybe it was better this way. He'd see just how strong she was. Whether she could rise above the adversity he created. The stolen Jeep. Her father's near death. The kidnapping of Nick Lawler's daughters. Did she love them? Did she love the detective?

What if Nick died? Could she survive that?

He couldn't wait to see. He'd gone to so much trouble to find out, traveled so far. Taken so many risks himself, proving his own strength at every step of the way. He'd driven nearly eight hundred miles in twelve hours, to Rochester and back. He'd killed the slug at the bus depot who tried to stop him from taking that which was rightfully his. He'd missed killing the bitch's father but that couldn't be helped; the old man had good reflexes. And he'd done all his driving at night, just in case he was pulled over. For he was fully prepared to execute any parasitic state trooper who dared to interfere with his life's work.

Just as he was prepared to execute Lawler and his two rug rats. In fact, maybe that would be even better. To see that bitch Waters suffer before he finished her. But next time, he decided, it wouldn't be from a distance. Next time they met, she'd see his face when he plunged one of his knives into her chest, drowning her in her own blood like he'd done to Rosa Sanchez. Enjoying the sight of her in her final throes of agony.

He got up from the computer and moved to his masterpiece, his crossword puzzle. It was almost entirely filled in, and soon it would be complete. He knew, though, that he had to wait. He couldn't risk killing another subhuman right now. He'd see the bitch again soon enough, and as badly as he wanted to strike, he'd muster the patience to bide his time.

For patience required perhaps the most strength of all, did it not?

CHAPTER 23

"I got an A on my math test!" Katie Lawler screamed with joy as Nick escorted Claire through the door of the apartment, wheeling a suitcase behind him.

"I guess all that tutoring in the hospital helped," said Nick as the girl ran over to hug Claire.

"Thanks for teaching me how to divide fractions," Katie said.

"Thanks for being such a good student," answered Claire, smiling even though she still felt some pain.

"Easy on Claire," Nick chided his daughter, removing her arms from around Claire's abdomen. "She just got the staples out from the surgery this morning."

Katie looked like she was about to cry. "Did I hurt you?" she asked in alarm.

"Not at all," Claire assured her. "After three weeks of seeing you from a hospital bed, being here with you is the best medicine ever."

She kissed Katie on the head, meaning it, feeling lucky after what had turned out to be a rocky convalescence from the shooting. Three days after the surgery her fever had spiked, revealing an infection that cost Claire an additional week in the hospital to be pumped full of intravenous antibiotics. Her surgeon, Doctor Mecklin, would've kept her a fourth week had Nick not stepped in, offering her the spare room in his apartment to complete her recovery so she wouldn't be alone.

It was an offer Claire wanted to refuse, reluctant to be a burden to anyone. But Nick wouldn't allow it. His daughters, both of whom Claire had tutored in math while in the hospital, helped convince her.

"You've taken care of us," Jill had argued. "Now it's our turn."

Walking through that door to the welcome Katie had given her made Claire realize she'd made the right decision, as Jill came out from the kitchen, wearing a torso-length apron with the familiar Life Is Good character on it.

"Hi, sweetheart," Claire said as Jill embraced her.

"Your room is ready," Jill said, "and I'm working on dinner."

"Let me help you."

"Not a chance. You're gonna rest. It'll be ready in half an hour."

Jill smiled as she hurried back to the kitchen, leaving Claire alone with Nick in the hallway.

"They love you, you know," he said, his arm around her.

"The feeling's mutual," Claire replied without hesitation. "Everything okay at work?" she asked. For all the time she'd been in the hospital, there hadn't been a peep from the Anagramist.

"We're all walking on eggshells," Nick replied, guiding her down the hallway to the comfortable room that had been his mother's, being careful not to hit her with the cast still on his left arm. "Not just looking for that lunatic and waiting for him to surface, but what's gonna happen with the new commissioner. Rumor is Wilkes is gonna get jumped over everyone above him in the Bureau to chief of detectives," he said.

Claire knew this could be both good and bad news. "What would that mean for you?" she asked him.

Nick shrugged. "I don't know," he replied. "Wilkes said he'd take care of me as long as he could." He turned to her. "But maybe it doesn't matter anymore."

He took her hand, his fingers intertwined with hers. She thought she could feel her heart skip a beat, and it made her think about how, every second of every day for as long as she'd been alive, her own heart beat in the same rhythmical way. Steady. Predictable. No matter what she was doing or thinking, no matter that she was unaware of the dependable contracting of the muscle inside her chest, the life force within her kept flowing. Then she had another thought:

Is this my heart beating or is it my twin's?

Claire realized it didn't matter. Somehow just knowing the origin of her life, that she had shared the womb for a brief time with another being, gave her comfort.

Maybe enough comfort to enable her to share her life with some-one else.

Claire sat facing Doctor Fairborn in her mentor's office, feeling re-laxed for a change. Now she was at peace, which she found strange in light of what had happened to her and the shocking news about her missing twin.

"Your mother told me about the chimera," Fairborn said, breaking the silence. "How do you feel about that?"

"Sad, in a way," Claire said. "I wonder if it was a boy or a girl, what he or she would have looked like." Claire settled back into the brown, velour-covered chair. "All the DNA was there—the egg had the potential to grow into a human being . . . but then it didn't. I feel like I lost someone I know . . . but I don't."

"It's very hard to contemplate," Fairborn said. "To know that a part of you is different from the rest you—and that you literally ab-sorbed your twin."

"But it explains so much," Claire said. "That push and pull I've al-ways felt, not being able to make up my mind about things."

"Like how you feel about Nick?" Fairborn asked.

"Yes," Claire said. "But I know how I feel about him now." Claire closed her eyes, picturing his blue eyes drawing her to him. "Know-ing about my twin set me free. The battle inside me is over."

Claire opened her eyes and caught Fairborn's smile.

"You can come back to your patients just as soon as you feel up to it," Fairborn said. "Walt McClure is ready for you to resume teach-ing too."

"I'm ready," Claire said. "If I don't get back to work I'm going to go more insane than I already am."

"As long as it doesn't stress you out," Fairborn said.

"Not moving on with my life will stress me out even more," Claire answered.

"I think you're ready," Fairborn said.

"Thank you," Claire said, getting up, still feeling the tightness of her incision though she also felt lighter, like weight had been lifted from her shoulders. It was the weight of an entire lifetime.

*   *   *

The next morning, Claire was back in class beside Professor Mc-Clure, who was just as eager to hear about what had happened to her as his six students who sat forward, their phones and laptops out of sight.

"I can't tell you much more than was in the news," she said to them, "because the police want to conceal details that only he would know. In case someone who wants the notoriety decides to confess falsely. It's happened before."

She looked around the room at Cory, Kara, Miguel, Wesley, Justine, and Leslie. "But let me tell you," she said, "I hope none of you ever have to experience any of this. Ever. I'll answer whatever questions I can."

Every hand shot up except McClure's, and Cory didn't wait to be called on. "Why are the cops calling him the Anagramist?" he asked.

"That's one of the things I can't talk about," Claire replied. "But the reason for that'll become clear soon enough. And if you use your imaginations I'll bet you can come up with your own theories. Which of course I can neither confirm nor deny."

"Let's get some of this up on the board," suggested Professor Mc-Clure. Claire was about to stand when McClure put a hand on her shoulder. "Not you, Doctor, you're still in recovery mode." He scanned his students. "Kara, Wes, help us out."

The blond girl and the handsome young man rose as ordered and moved the few feet to the board, each picking up a marker from the holder. "Great," McClure said, determined to help Claire through her first day back. "We don't want you to work too hard, Doctor, so why don't you take us through the sequence of events you experienced?"

Claire, grateful, began by listing the timeline, which Kara wrote in purple marker: the stolen Jeep; the Anagramist murdering the guard at the bus depot in Rochester, stealing the bus, crashing it into her father's car, glancing off another car before he got away. Then, she moved on to the kidnapping of Jill and Katie from school, the bomb scare in the Jeep, and she and Nick being shot.

"Jesus," remarked Miguel when she was finished. "What a trip."

"It was almost my last one," said Claire. "I was lucky."

"Are you scared that he might still be after you?" asked Justine.

"The police aren't taking any chances, as you can see," she said as she pointed to the door. Its window was blocked by someone standing in front of it. "So my answer is, not as long as those two cops with the submachine guns are following me around."

The class erupted in laughter, bringing a smile to Claire's face.

"Why do you think he went after your father?" Leslie asked.

"Serial killers like to get into peoples' minds, especially the minds of the people hunting them down," answered Claire. "I guess this 'gentleman' thought hurting my father would hurt me. He kind of failed at both."

"I have a question," Professor McClure said. "When you were up there on stage at the first news conference, the one where the police went public about the serial nature of the killings, was that your idea? Or did the police want you up there?"

"It was both, actually," she said. "I wrote every word Inspector Wilkes said, and he wanted me up there."

"Did you want to be up there?" asked Wes Phelps from the board.

"Not at first, no," Claire admitted. "Then I got to thinking that maybe if I used myself as bait it would piss the guy off enough to make a mistake. Turns out I was right."

She stopped, realizing she was about to say too much. "Of course, I can't tell you what the mistake is," she said.

Kara's hand flew up. "Are you guys calling him the Anagramist because he's communicating with you through anagrams?"

Claire paused. It was a tough question that put her in a tough spot. If she answered yes, she risked poisoning the investigation, even though the killer's nickname had leaked just after she was shot. And if she said she couldn't say, it was just like saying yes.

"Fornication cheeps," Cory Matthis suddenly said.

"What?" retorted Claire, too surprised to hide her shock. "How could you possibly know that?"

"Maybe he's the killer," Justine Yu smirked. "He looks like one, doesn't he?"

"Shut up," Cory shot back, turning his laptop toward Claire so she could see the screen. "It's right here, on CrimeTime News-dot-com."

He slid the machine across to Claire, who read the story. It couldn't do much damage; it contained only one of the anagrams. Still, the story had been picked up by other news outlets, and she knew it would only be a matter of time before it was everywhere. She'd have to call Nick and let him know, if he didn't already.

But right now, what did she have to lose?

She looked at Wes Phelps standing at the board. "Wes, can you write those words up there?" she requested.

"Sure," Wes answered, turning to Cory. "Can you repeat them, bro?"

"Fornication cheeps," Cory said.

Wes wrote the first word and then stopped, confused. "I got the *fornication* part. But do you mean *cheaps* like in *cheapskate*, or like the noise a bird makes?"

"The bird one," Cory replied. "Double e."

Wes completed the second word with his black marker. "Do the cops know what it means?" Cory asked Claire.

"I don't know," replied Claire, "but more importantly, does that Web site know?"

"It's not in here," admitted Cory.

"Then I'm sticking to my story," Claire said with mock firmness.

"Maybe it's about some kinky sex thing with birds," offered Justine.

Miguel smirked. "Maybe they should put you on the payroll as a consultant about all that kinky shit," he sneered.

"Or maybe this guy works in a pet store," suggested Leslie.

"Why don't we try to solve the puzzle ourselves?" offered Kara.

"I see *fornication speech*," said Justine. "But he didn't sexually attack his victims and they were male and female."

"I can make *hencoop enfranchise*," said Cory, with a big smile. "But I don't have the slightest idea what that means."

Wes wrote both combinations on the board, checking each one to make sure the letters matched. "They both work," he confirmed.

"Anyone else?" Claire asked, halfway out of her chair when she felt woozy and sat back down heavily.

"You okay, Claire?" Professor McClure asked. Both Wes and Kara dropped their markers and hurried toward her.

"I think I just need some water," Claire said. "Maybe I'm pushing myself a little too hard."

McClure took the cue. "That's all for today," he said to the students. "We'll meet up again next week." As the class packed up and filed out, he turned back to Claire. "Do you need me to help you to your office?" he asked.

"No," Claire responded. "I'm sure it was a momentary thing. And my police escorts can help if I need it. Just give me a minute, and if I could get that water . . ."

"I'm on it," McClure said, nearly sprinting from the room. She was about to try standing again when she heard a squeaking beside her. She tightened in momentary fear until her head swiveled toward the board where Wes was erasing his and Kara's work.

"No, wait," Claire said, wanting to make sure she knew exactly what was said so she could tell Nick. "Keep it up there, will you? I'll write it all down and then I'll erase it myself."

"Sure thing, Doctor Waters," Wes said, grabbing his coat and backpack and leaving Claire alone. "Hope you feel better," he said as he left the room.

Claire resisted the urge to stand, knowing she'd best wait for McClure to return with the water before even trying. She also knew she had no business erasing the board, lest she pull one of the still-healing muscles around her incision.

So, instead of writing, she pulled out her iPhone and took several photos of the board.

I'll transcribe them later, she thought. *McClure can erase the board.*

Claire sat down to a bowl of tomato soup she'd warmed up in Nick's microwave. She wasn't hungry, but knew she should eat something. She had lost almost ten pounds since the shooting. With both of Nick's daughters at school and Nick at work, she had hours to herself, though they were hours she didn't really want. What she wanted was to be back in action. But Inspector Wilkes had laid down the law. She was barred from police headquarters until he felt she was ready to return.

She'd gone directly from McClure's class to her office to find Fairborn waiting for her. Naturally, McClure had snitched, informing her mentor of her episode in class. Fairborn, too, had instructed her to go home, offering to take Claire's patients for as long as was necessary for her to fully recover.

She pulled out her cell phone and listened to her voice messages—two from her dad and one from her mom, checking on her. Though her mother had rarely called her to chat prior to her surgery, mother and daughter now spoke at least once a day. To Claire's surprise, she enjoyed their conversations. But before she called either of them back, she wanted to make sure the photos she'd taken earlier of the dry-erase board in McClure's classroom were legible.

She brought up the photos on her phone and scrolled through them. The last one she'd snapped was a close-up of the Anagramist's words that had leaked to a true crime Web site.

Fornication cheeps

She stared at the words as if she'd never seen them before. Then, she scrolled back to the other, earlier photos. She was about to lock the phone when she went back and viewed that final picture one more time.

Fornication cheeps

What is it? What is it about those words that bother me?

It certainly wasn't what they scrambled into; she already knew it was an anagram for *perfection in chaos*. Was it the way they were arranged? The letters . . .

She used her thumb and forefinger to zoom in, so she could see each letter.

F-o-r-n-i-c-a-t-i-o-n c-h-e-e-p-s

She pored over the letters, one by one, close up. And a sickening feeling washed over her like a dirty puddle sprayed from the tire of a passing bus. . . .

Quickly, urgently, she dialed a number on her cell. It went directly to voice mail.

Shit.

With new energy, she bolted up from the kitchen table and made it to the front door, opening it to the surprise of the two Emergency Service cops standing guard.

"Everything okay, Doctor Waters?" one of them asked.

"We need to take a ride," Claire replied.

Nick sat at his desk in the Major Case Squad office, going through his notes. It had been more than three weeks now since the shooting, and there hadn't been a peep from the Anagramist.

What the hell is he waiting for? An invitation?

Not that Nick wanted another dead body to signal the bastard's return. But after twenty-one days of nearly around-the-clock work, one by one the task force had dwindled as detectives returned to other cases. Nick had put in the most work of all, often without putting in for overtime, and despite the fact that his exhaustion only made his deteriorating vision even worse.

His head turned as the door from the hallway opened and a figure in jeans and a sweatshirt entered. All he could tell was that it was a female. But when the faceless woman came toward him, he realized it was Claire and he bolted up from his chair.

"Are you out of your mind?" he exclaimed. "If Wilkes sees you—"

"I had to risk it," Claire said, pulling out her phone.

"You should've called me."

"I did. It went straight to voice mail. And no one answered the office phone."

"We were in a meeting."

Claire tapped on the screen of her phone. "I'm sending a photo to your work e-mail. I need you to print it," she ordered.

"You couldn't have done this from—"

"I couldn't take a chance. Please. Just do it and don't ask questions."

The urgency in her voice hit him. He leaned over his desk, brought up his e-mail on the computer, clicked on her message, and printed it. Then he walked over to the printer to retrieve the result. He slid it from the machine and perused it, the words stopping him in his tracks.

"Where was this taken?" he demanded.

"McClure's class this morning. It was on the dry-erase board."

"Someone wrote this on his board and left it for you to find?"

"No," said Claire, grabbing the paper from his hand. "Somehow it leaked to a true crime Web site and one of my students found it. But that's not important right now."

"I beg to differ," argued Nick.

"Just listen. It's what happened next that's important. Another student transcribed it onto the board. Take a look."

"I did," Nick said. "*Fornication cheeps*. What about it?"

Claire took a breath. "You know how sometimes when you write in cursive, you might throw in a letter that's in print or vice versa?" she asked, pointing to the words on the page. "Look at the *n* and the *p*. . . ."

"I can't see it well enough to get the point," Nick replied, frustrated.

Claire pulled a large binder off his desk, one with which she was all too familiar. She knew exactly where to find what she needed.

"Now look at . . . this," she said breathlessly, reaching the right page and pointing.

"The matchbook from the Newman crime scene in the swamp?"

"Just look, dammit!" Claire exclaimed.

Nick did. His head jerked up, his eyes meeting Claire's in realization.

"You're right," he said, his voice shaking in excitement. "Both *n's* have the same hump and the *p's* have two parts, a stick and a curve that don't connect."

"We'll need an expert to testify. . . ."

"We don't have time for an expert," retorted Nick, picking up the phone on his desk and dialing, looking like he was about to explode.

"Paddy," he shouted into the receiver, "I need Wilkes in here immediately. . . . It's an effin' emergency."

He stopped as Wilkes burst through the door like a Barcelona bull.

"What the hell are you doing here, Doctor?" he growled as Nick hung up the phone.

"We've got him, Inspector," Nick said.

"Got who? The Anagramist? Bullshit," he exploded.

"This time it's not," Claire shot back.

"Then what's the sonuvabitch's name?" the inspector demanded.

"Wesley Phelps," said Claire, incredulous. "He's one of my students."

Minutes later, they were in Wilkes's office, the inspector hanging up the phone. "Norma says the slant of the lines, the style, and the unusual way he makes the letter *p* suggest you two are right. Your student and the perp who wrote that jibberish on the matchbook we found on Robert Newman are the same person."

"Do we have enough evidence for a warrant?" Claire asked.

"Not with two letters, though it's gotta be him," Wilkes replied. "I need to know everything about him."

"I really don't know much," Claire said. "Other than he participates in class." She shook her head. "He was right there in front of me. I can't believe it."

"Well, believe this," Nick said, staring at Wilkes's computer screen. "The bastard was the only child of parents who died in an early morning fire three years ago when Wesley was still an undergraduate."

"Cause of the fire?" Wilkes asked.

"Inconclusive," Nick replied, reading from the screen. "Possibly faulty wiring in the basement, though paint thinner might have been used as an accelerant. Wesley was questioned by the police in his hometown of River Edge, New Jersey, and had a solid alibi—he was asleep in his college dorm, forty miles away."

"Or not," Claire said. "Wouldn't be hard to sneak out in the middle of the night, get back in bed before anyone woke up." She moved behind Nick, gazing over his shoulder. "Anything else come up?" Claire asked. "Trouble with the law when he was a kid? Complaints of cruelty to animals?"

"We don't need the triad to know this lunatic is a psycho," Wilkes said, nodding. "I bet the sonuvabitch tortured animals, set fires, AND wet his bed as a kid."

"Don't have that," Nick said, his eyes still on the screen, "but one more thing popped up. He applied to the NYPD to become a police officer, but then dropped out just prior to his interview with the background investigator and department psychologist."

"It doesn't *prove* he's a serial killer," Claire said, "but it's no coincidence. He must have thought better of risking that fire would put him on the department shrink's radar. He couldn't take the chance he'd be caught."

"He's our guy," Wilkes said, "and we're gonna collar him before he hurts anyone else." He pulled out his cell phone. "I know a judge who will give us a warrant on the down-low—but we gotta keep this close to the vest. No one can know anything about this unless I personally approve."

"I'll check Mr. Phelps's class schedule," Claire offered. "You can execute the warrant and search his place while he's in class."

"And I'll put someone on his tail to make sure he doesn't come back and interrupt us," added Nick.

"Tony and Simms'll sit on his apartment tonight," Wilkes said. "I'm gonna get some undercover narco guys to tail him on campus tomorrow until we can pick him up legally and hold him."

He turned to Claire and took her hand. "This time we're gonna get him," Wilkes promised. "Before he hurts another soul."

CHAPTER 24

Wesley Phelps emerged into the sunlight from his basement apartment on West Twenty-Fourth Street in Chelsea, his backpack slung over his shoulder, and headed west. It was a routine he followed nearly every morning, the short trek to the subway station at Eighth Avenue and Twenty-Third Street, where he'd catch a train uptown to school.

He noticed the traffic on his street, always busy this time of the morning, was at a dead stop today. Swiveling his head from west to east, he saw the reason: a Con Edison crew, just feet from his building near Sixth Avenue, working out of an open manhole, their truck and equipment blocking half the street and leaving barely enough pavement for cars or trucks to squeak by.

The blaring of a horn beside him made him jump. "Shut the hell up!" Wes screamed at the offender, a bald, heavy, middle-aged man behind the wheel of a gleaming, silver BMW. Smoke from the man's fat stogie wafted out his open windows. But the schmuck also had his sound system on, loud enough to annoy almost anyone and drowning Wes out.

Sometimes I wish I could just kill them all, he thought, moving past what he considered to be subhuman scum. Which, in truth, was his opinion of just about everyone but himself. He'd kill them again, and again, and again.

But he knew resisting his impulse to do just that was what made him different from all the others, the obscure ones who came before him. The ones who weren't as selective as he, who never had a plan.

Hickman and Palmer. Their names would forever be remembered now. Because of him.

As his would be as well. As soon as his life's work was complete.

Wes smiled, pleased with himself that he'd bided his time. Knowing it wouldn't be long before all this would be over. The pain of his existence would be extinguished.

Only then, finally, would he be able to rest.

"He's on the move," the Con Ed worker said quietly into a hidden microphone somewhere under the yellow vest he wore over his work clothes, as he peered over the lip of the manhole at the figure walking away from him.

"Did he make you?" came a gruff male voice through the earpiece in the man's ear.

As if on cue, the young man wheeled around, looking in the worker's direction. Then he turned back and continued on his way.

"He just looked in our direction but I don't think so," said the worker into the hidden mic. "He's back on his way toward Seventh Avenue."

"Roger that," came the voice in his ear. "Hold tight until I give the signal."

The worker twice clicked his mic, using a button hidden under his sleeve, to acknowledge his boss, who was as much his boss as he was a Con Ed maintenance crewman. In fact, he was an undercover operative with the Narcotics Division of the NYPD and had no idea what he was doing there. The only information he and his colleagues had been given was a photo of the subject and the surveillance location.

None of them were even told the name of the subject or the voice in their ears, the great Oz behind the curtain of the Con Ed step van parked two yards away.

"Where is he now?" Wilkes said into a radio mic as he hovered above a small desk in the rear of the Con Ed step van. Which didn't, of course, even belong to Con Ed. The van was one of many undercover surveillance vehicles owned and operated by the police department, and Wilkes had requested this one in particular because of the hidden cameras on the outside and bank of monitors, radios, and laptops on the inside.

"He just went down into the Eighth Avenue subway at Twenty-Third," came a female voice over the speaker.

Wilkes hit the Talk button on the mic. "Okay. Nobody moves until the bas—I mean *subject* is on a train."

He put the mic back on its hook and turned to Claire and Nick, who, like Wilkes, were decked out in Con Ed jumpsuits and work boots.

"Was this really necessary?" Claire asked.

"You wanted to walk the walk, Doc," Wilkes shot back. "This is how the pros do it. Now we just need Tony to show up with the warrant and we're good to go."

Tanisha Fuller, a pretty twenty-five-year-old African-American woman whose hair was secured in a bun, stood on the platform of the Eighth Avenue subway station, scanning the crowd. She was just about to turn toward the station's other entrance when she noticed a dark-haired young man in a blue oxford shirt and khakis come through the turnstile just as a northbound train roared in, its brakes squealing as it came to a stop.

Fuller watched as the young man boarded the train, and only when its doors were closed and wheels rolling did she glance at the photo on her cell phone to make sure she had the right person.

She grabbed the radio mic clipped to the epaulet of her shirt and raised it to her lips. "Transit Seven David, your boy is locked and loaded and headed north. Third car from the front."

"Ten-four," came Wilkes's voice in her ear.

Fuller clipped the mic back on her epaulet and walked toward the exit, shaking her head in amazement. She'd been planted here specifically for this purpose and went completely undetected by the dark-haired subject, whoever he was. Even she never thought she could work undercover hiding in plain sight wearing what she wore to work every day: the crisp new uniform of the rookie NYPD transit cop she was.

The rear doors of the Con Ed step van flew open, sending Wilkes, Nick, and Claire, in their coveralls and yellow hard hats, into the street. The inspector and Nick pulled their police shields, which hung by chains around their necks, out from under their shirts as they hurried up the stairs of Phelps's brownstone, where Nick banged his fist on the door.

"Police! Open up!" he shouted.

Claire heard pounding footsteps and turned toward Sixth Avenue, from which Savarese, in the same Con Ed costume, ran toward them with papers in his hand.

"Where the hell is he?" muttered Wilkes.

The door opened, revealing a thin, white-haired, African-American man Nick estimated to be around seventy years old.

"The hell is your problem?" said the man.

"Police," repeated Wilkes.

"Yeah, no shit," said the man. "What's all the ruckus?"

"Who manages this place?" asked Wilkes.

"Norbert Miller," said the man.

"Where can we find him?"

"You're lookin' at him, son," Miller replied.

Savarese, still breathless, handed Miller the paper. "This is a warrant to search the apartment of one Wesley Phelps, your tenant in the basement."

"Jesus H. Christ," Miller exclaimed, "you really gonna make me do this?"

"Yeah, and what's it to you?" Wilkes demanded.

"The guy's nuts, that's what," complained Miller. "I went in there to fix a leak two months ago after that big rainstorm and I thought he was gonna stab me to death."

"Look," Wilkes said, "we don't have time for this. We need into his place, and now."

"But he's got a clause in his lease requiring a day's notice," Miller pleaded.

"Now. Or I gotta collar you for obstruction," retorted Wilkes.

"Yeah, swell. You gonna stick around till the sonuvabitch comes home and deal with him, because I sure ain't."

"He ain't gonna be your problem after today," Wilkes assured him. "Now get the goddamned keys and let's do this."

*   *   *

Wes emerged from the subway station with the sea of humanity spilling from underground up onto Columbus Circle. He stopped at his favorite food cart and bought the same breakfast he ate every morning: a plain bagel with cream cheese and a cup of black coffee.

"Thanks, Samir," he said to the West Indian vendor, handing him a dollar more than his food cost as a tip and bringing a smile from Samir.

Wes felt good as he headed west on Fifty-Ninth Street. He sunk his teeth into the bagel, taking a bigger bite than usual, quickly chewing it as he hurried to make the green light on Columbus Avenue.

He was almost to the corner when he felt something vibrate in his pocket. He stopped, carefully placing his coffee and bagel on the roof of a parked car, and reached in his pocket for his phone.

He knew whatever this was couldn't be good. Because no one ever called Wesley Phelps. No one.

One glance at the screen on the phone confirmed his worst fears.

He removed the coffee and bagel from the car, flung them into a garbage can on the corner, and sprinted in the opposite direction on Fifty-Ninth Street, toward the subway station.

Norbert Miller turned the key in the dead bolt above the knob on the door to Wes Phelps's apartment. Or at least he tried to turn it.

"What's the problem?" Nick asked.

"You can see what the problem is," whined Miller. "I can't turn the key in the goddamn lock."

"Are you sure it's the right key?" asked Wilkes, ready to implode.

"Yeah, I'm sure," said Miller. "Son of a gun musta changed the lock." He smiled, exposing a mouthful of stained yellow teeth. "Finally, something I can evict him for. . . ."

"Stand back," Wilkes commanded him.

"You gonna bust it down like on TV?" the manager asked.

"Not if we don't have to," Nick said, pulling Miller aside, giving CSU detective Terry Aitken space to work his magic.

"How long's this gonna take?" Wilkes asked Aitken.

"Lock's nothing complicated," responded Aitken as he removed a lock pick set from his bag and pulled out a curved pick, which he expertly inserted into the keyhole and tapped with his long fingers. The lock clicked and Aitken opened the door.

"Nobody goes in without booties and gloves," Wilkes ordered. "Doctor, we got a shower cap for your hair too," he said. "I don't want this guy knowing we were here."

Wesley was breathing heavily as he reached the subway station, choosing the stairs over the escalator and descending two steps at a time, pulling his MetroCard from his pocket and trying not to go tumbling forward.

He reached the bottom of the stairs and glanced in every direction. Nothing to be worried about. Everyone seemed to be moving at a normal pace, nothing out of the ordinary.

He heard a noise behind him. From up the stairs. A woman yelling "Watch out, assholes!"

He wheeled. Two young men, around his age, backpacks on their backs, were flying down the stairs. Toward him. Their eyes on him. Their hands reaching under their shirts.

Wesley was prepared for this.

He slipped off his backpack, reached inside, and pulled out the nine-millimeter Browning he'd bought for just such an emergency. He grabbed a middle-aged commuter just about to pass him, his arm around her waist, and spun her in front of him.

His human shield. To protect him from what was about to happen.

"Police!" shouted the two young men on the stairs, their guns now in their hands. "Everybody down!" they screamed.

Wes began firing. Again and again and again. Hitting everyone between him and the two cops, who couldn't shoot at Wes lest they hit his hostage.

He smiled as they stumbled over the bodies below them on the stairs.

"Don't you move! Don't you move, asshole!" they both screamed at him.

Wes looked up at them, just feet away now, and shot each of them in the head.

His hostage screamed. "You monster! What's the matter, your mama didn't love you enough? Let me go! Let me go!"

Wes let her go, and before she could scream again, fired one right through her left eye, Moe Greene-style. "My mother put her cigarettes out on my back, bitch," he said to the woman as she dropped. He stuck the gun in his belt as he ran through the subway station and disappeared.

Booties, gloves, and shower cap on, Claire stepped inside Wesley Phelps's small, immaculate apartment.

What she saw took her breath away.

"My God," she said.

She was staring at a giant crossword puzzle, painted on the wall, each of Phelps's victim's names entered into the interlocking squares: *Nick. Jill. Katie. Rosa Sanchez. Robert Newman. Victor Palmer. Jonah Welch.* Though not a victim, the psychopath Phelps admired who drained the blood of his victim in the 1920s, William Edward Hickman, had his name up there too. Other words, such as *blood, corpse, disembody*, and *decapitate*, also filled the giant squares.

"There's only twelve blanks left," she said to nobody, stunned.

"Claire," Nick said from behind her.

She turned and gasped at what she saw on the opposite wall: the anagrams. Dozens of pairs of words, neatly printed in red, beginning with *infections poacher, octopi enfranchise,* and *Pinocchio fastener*. Above the list, the words *GATHER STAMINA* were written in yellow Magic Marker and outlined in brown. The bare bulb that lit the perfectly square room made the letters sparkle like gold.

Claire moved toward that wall, drawn to examine Wesley's intricate and precise work, almost mesmerized. "It's brilliant in its own way," she said.

"To you maybe, Doc," Wilkes said. "To me he's just another psycho."

Claire turned to Nick, as if waiting for his reaction. "He's obsessed with perfection and that's what he's going for," Claire said. "That's what this sick game is all about."

"*Gather stamina?* The hell does that mean?" asked Wilkes, just as horrified as Claire and Nick.

"Those letters rearranged spell *the Anagramist*," Claire replied.

Wilkes caught on, staring at the anagrams. "And those other words rearranged spell *perfection in chaos*?"

"Not all of them," Claire realized, the horror building as she focused on two pairs of words written in block letters and red marker: *ALKALI GIN* and *ARTERIES CLAW*.

Nick and Wilkes joined her, their faces grim, Nick's arm slipping around her. "*Alkali gin* rearranged spells *kill again*," he said.

His warmth gave Claire the strength to say the words. "*Arteries claw* is an anagram for my name."

"He is obsessed with you, Doc," said Aitken from across the room, approaching them holding a scrapbook in his gloved hands. "Check this out."

He opened the book and Claire gasped again. On the first page was a newspaper clipping. Photos of her and Nick, over a headline: DETECTIVE AND PSYCHIATRIST TEAM FINDS KILLER, the story underneath an account of the case that had brought them together a year and a half earlier. Claire felt sicker and sicker as Aitken turned the pages, filled with photos of her taken with a telephoto lens: On the street. Entering the hospital. Leaving her apartment. With Nick, outside *his* apartment.

"How did we miss seeing him?" she asked Nick.

"Speak for yourself," Nick replied. "At least I have an excuse."

"It's like he wanted to *be* me," Claire said, staring at a close-up of her face beside another newspaper article lauding her skill at solving her best friend, Amy's, murder. "But he was also obsessed with serial killers. He took the profiling course I coteach, not because he wanted to *catch* them, but because he wanted to *be* them."

"And then he took a left turn," Nick added. "The guy is all about perfection, and he found the perfect person to learn from. He fixated on you."

"You too, eventually," Claire said. "He had to prove to himself he was smarter than us, that he could involve me in his sick little game. That's why he went after Rosa."

"He had to beat you," said Nick. "That was his perfection in a chaotic world."

"Boss!" Savarese's voice boomed from outside the apartment. "Intelligence is calling a code at Columbus Circle!"

"Shit," exclaimed Wilkes, hurrying for the door as Claire turned to Nick.

"What now?" she asked.

"It means there's either been a valid terror threat or actual attack," said Nick, following Wilkes out to the street.

"What the hell, Tony?" demanded Wilkes.

"A dozen bodies in the Columbus Circle subway station," Savarese exhaled. "Transit says two of them were the narco guys we had on Phelps."

"Phelps is in class right now, goddamn it," bellowed Wilkes.

"I know he's supposed to be, Boss," blurted Savarese, "but the description headquarters has on the radio of the subway shooter sure as hell sounds like our boy."

"He knew we were here," Claire realized, running back into the apartment.

"Claire!" yelled Nick, going after her.

"You're contaminating the scene, Doctor!" screamed Wilkes, following them in to find Claire and Nick scanning the room. "The hell are you two looking for?"

"Cameras," said Claire, pointing to a tiny hole in the ceiling near one corner of the small apartment. "Get someone up there on a ladder, Inspector, and I'll bet there's one right there."

Aitken was checking the door. "There's something here too," he shouted.

Nick hurried over. "What is it?" he asked.

The CSU detective pointed to small, round pieces of metal imbedded in the side of the door and the doorway at the same height. "Contacts," he said. "He's got the place wired. I'll check the computer, but if I had to guess, he sets the alarm when he leaves and if someone opens the door he gets notified on his cell phone."

"And activates that camera," Wilkes said, glancing back at the tiny hole. "The bastard's streaming us on his phone."

He turned to Claire. "Okay, Doc. This is where the rubber meets the road. Where would he go?"

"He's not going anywhere, Inspector," she answered. "Until he finishes his puzzle."

"No way he's coming back here," declared Nick.

"It doesn't have to be here," retorted Claire. "He's gonna finish his masterwork no matter what."

Nick knew what that meant. "He's going after us. The girls—"

"Tony," shouted Wilkes. "Get ESU over to IS Twenty-seven and Stuyvesant High, full squads on each, and get Nicky's two girls outta there!"

"On it, Boss," Savarese bellowed, stepping out to the street.

"As for you two . . ." said Wilkes, turning to Nick and Claire.

"We need to get the scene processed," Nick protested, knowing what was coming.

"The hell you do," retorted Wilkes. "He knows you're here and we're not taking any chances. I'm having your protective details bring you both back to Nick's apartment."

"Inspector—" Claire began.

"Save it, Doc," Wilkes interrupted. "We're locking this place down and getting the hell outta here. ESU'll bring the girls home and that's where you're all staying until Phelps is either in jail or the morgue."

"If he murdered a dozen people including two cops, he's not gonna let us lock him up," Nick said.

"Whatever," Wilkes replied. "Dead or alive. I'll take him either way."

"They have Katie," Claire shouted, hanging up the landline phone in Nick's kitchen and heading out to the living room where he sat on the couch.

"How long before they're here?" he asked.

Claire sat next to him. "Tony says the Emergency Service team bringing her back is going to meet up with the team that got Jill from Stuyvesant. With traffic they're thinking a half hour to forty-five minutes."

"Sounds about right," Nick said, still bothered.

Claire rubbed his back. "Relax, Nick," she said, trying to comfort him. "They're surrounded by cops with machine guns. Nothing's going to happen to them."

"It's not that," Nick confessed. "The whole thing is just wrong. Phelps is out there and we're locked up here in our own prison."

"Let me make you some breakfast," Claire said, kissing him on the cheek and getting up.

Nick got up and followed her in to find her pulling an old cast iron skillet from a cabinet next to the stove.

"I can help you if you want," he offered.

Claire lifted her head out of the now open refrigerator. "You want to help me, go down to D'Agostino's and get me a dozen eggs."

"I'm not supposed to leave, remember?" Nick reminded her.

"Your boss isn't gonna suspend you for going to the supermarket," she chided. He glared at her. "As long as you take one of our machine-gun-toting soldiers with you."

The logic was hard for Nick to argue with. "I guess," he said, giving in.

"You won't regret it," Claire promised him. "If you're not back in twenty minutes, I'm calling the cops."

"Good luck with that," Nick said, heading for the door. "There's never a cop around when you need one."

The apartment was quiet but for the crackling sound of olive oil heating in the skillet on the stove. Claire put down the sharp knife she'd used to cut the fresh cloves of garlic she was about to sauté for the omelette she knew that Nick loved. She scattered the garlic into the heated oil, turned the burner down to medium, and took the remaining garlic back to the refrigerator.

She was about to open its door when she stopped to look at a photo of Nick with the girls, arm-in-arm ice-skating at Central Park's Wollman Rink, attached with a heart-shaped magnet that read *Happy Father's Day, Love, Jill & Katie*.

Father's Day, Claire thought. *I'd give anything to spend next Father's Day with Nick and the girls*.

"Beautiful family," a voice said behind her. She froze, knowing it wasn't Nick's voice. "Hello, Claire," the voice continued.

Claire wheeled. Wesley Phelps stood six feet away, a warm smile on his face and a very large gun in his hand. She fought to remain calm despite her terror.

"I didn't know we were on a first-name basis, Wesley," she said.

"Sure we are," Wes replied. "A girl doesn't go to a guy's place like you did and call him by his last name. That wouldn't be proper."

"There's two cops outside with machine guns, Wesley," Claire warned him.

"Not anymore there aren't," he said.

"There's no way you could've gotten past them," she said.

"Oh, Mrs. Kerner across the hall took care of them for me," he boasted. "She got them into her apartment and I took care of the rest. They never saw it coming."

"How did you get into Mrs. Kerner's—"

"She was a nice old lady. She let me right in the window when I came down the fire escape and said someone was chasing me. And then she went out and got the cops. Easy, peasy."

Claire felt herself starting to shake and did the best she could to suppress it. "I can help you, Wesley. I know a lot more about what must be going on with you emotionally now."

"So now you wanna help me?" he retorted. "After all those things you said about how sick and twisted I am? When you trespassed on *my* property? Went through *my* life?"

"Not before you invaded mine," Claire shot back. "I saw your little scrapbook."

"I'm offended, Claire," he said. "I thought you'd be flattered that someone was finally paying some attention to you. After what happened to your fiancé last year . . ."

"I have someone, Wesley," she declared.

"I know, but is that what you really want for yourself?" he asked. "I mean, come on. Why would you hook up with a guy who's not even gonna be able to enjoy the sight of you much longer?"

"He'll be back here any minute," Claire threatened.

"Oh, I know," snapped Phelps. "And the girls too. I'm counting on it."

She ran for the stove, grabbed the skillet, and flung it at him. The sizzling oil splashed him in the face, temporarily blinding him. He dropped the gun and grabbed his head in pain.

"You bitch!" he screamed, lunging for Claire, hooking his arm around her throat before she could grab the knife on the counter. He squeezed her neck with such force that she started losing consciousness.

"I don't have to complete my puzzle in order," he said as the life drained from her face. "I'll finish you and then Nicky and the girls when they get back."

Boom! A bullet ripped through Phelps's right calf. He released Claire and used that arm to grab onto the counter, screaming in agony.

Claire fell to the ground with him, facing the kitchen doorway where Nick stood with an AR-15 semiautomatic rifle.

"Every Tuesday at nine o'clock since I was a kid, Mrs. Kerner went to the hairdresser next to the supermarket. Never missed a day. But when I didn't see her in there today—"

"You shot me, you prick!" Wesley cried, holding his shattered leg.

"Devil's in the details, Wes," Nick said, advancing. He picked up Phelps's gun from the floor and pointed both weapons at him as Claire crawled past him.

"I didn't finish my puzzle!" he screamed.

"You screwed up, asshole," Nick said. "You're not the smartest guy in the room. You got beat by a woman and a cop. How's *that* feel?"

"I'm not beat yet," the killer cried, flinging something at Nick.

Boom! Nick fired, hitting him in the left shoulder but too late to stop him. The paring knife Phelps flung penetrated Nick's stomach.

"Nick!" Claire cried.

A fast-spreading bloodstain appeared on Nick's shirt around the protruding knife. He coughed, still on his feet but stunned, and dropped the assault rifle. Phelps launched himself toward the weapon.

"Who's the one who screwed up now, lover boy?" Phelps taunted him.

Crack! A bullet tore through Phelps's side. He started to cough up blood as he looked up to see Claire, her hands around Nick's right hand, pointing Wesley's own Browning at him. Her finger was still on the trigger.

And he smiled.

"Help him," Nick said to her.

Claire released her grip on his hand holding Phelps's gun. "But you're—"

"Blade isn't long enough to do any real damage," he said. "Don't let him die."

She scrambled to her feet, grabbed a dish towel, and knelt beside Phelps, now ashen, blood seeping from his wound. She tried to staunch the bleeding but he pushed her away with his last ounce of strength.

"You're strong," he gasped. "You're not a parasite. You're perfection in chaos."

Wesley closed his eyes.

CHAPTER 25

Claire had never kept a journal. She'd always resisted writing down her feelings because she didn't want to acknowledge them. Once she put them down on paper, they became real; they existed in black and white; they couldn't be ignored.

After Wesley Phelps died, Claire decided it was time to see her thoughts and feelings on the page, to commit them to paper as a way to work through her own trauma and understand this horribly disturbed young man. She found the perfect notebook at a small stationery store. It had blank pages (she didn't want lines; she preferred a white, open canvas) that were bound in exotic purple batik cloth, dotted with bursts of bright orange, hot yellow, and Day-Glo green. The cover reminded her of a brainbow—the multicolored imaging that used fluorescent dyes to highlight the brain's wiry neurons, which she made as a graduate student. She knew she'd feel comfortable writing down her thoughts in what she called her "brain book."

October 8—Entry Number One

Wesley Phelps.
Who was he?
Wesley was born January 5, 1986, in Morristown, New Jersey, to Ray and Ellen Phelps. An only child, he had no significant illnesses or hospitalizations and no criminal record. Parents are deceased (perished in a house fire while Wesley was in college). Only living relative is Susan Lantz, Wesley's maternal aunt and older sister of his mother. Ms. Lantz

reports that Wesley did not inherit any money after his parents' death because they were concerned about his "odd" behavior. When pressed, Ms. Lantz recalled that Wesley never could keep a pet—dogs and cats all "ran away." But Ray Phelps was putting in a vegetable garden several years ago and dug up dozens of animal bones. No one could prove they were Wesley's "lost" pets, but Ellen Phelps confided to her sister that she was concerned that Wesley may have also killed the neighbors' pets that had disappeared over the years.

Mr. and Mrs. Phelps placed their money for Wesley in a trust, with Ms. Lantz as the executor. They gave her explicit instructions that Wesley's college and graduate school tuition and expenses should be paid, and he was to receive a monthly stipend of $2,000. But under no circumstances was he to gain access to his sizable inheritance until he was thirty-five and had undergone a thorough psychiatric assessment attesting to his competence. If he was found to be mentally ill, or as Ms. Lantz put it, "a really sick puppy," the inheritance was to be donated to the Dumb Friends League.

Ms. Lantz reports that Wesley did not take this well, that his behavior scared her when the will was read. Instead of becoming angry, he giggled and stared at her, shaking his head. She hasn't seen him since.

She is devastated by her nephew's actions and blames herself for not seeing the "evil in his heart." She adds that she always thought Wesley was "a screwy kid," that he'd laugh inappropriately whenever someone got hurt. She suspects that Wesley tried to kill her after his parents died. She was in a terrible car accident two months later when the brakes failed on her new Honda.

Walt McClure, Wesley's professor, reports that his student "wanted to be the best." He told Professor McClure that he "admired" my accomplishments and hoped that he could do well enough in the master's program in forensic sciences to help him get into medical school. McClure also reports that when I started teaching his course, Wesley told him he wanted to become a forensic psychiatrist and hoped to "shadow me," and learn everything I could teach him.

Wesley admired serial killers to the extent that he copied their crimes in almost perfect detail. In a sense, I believe these killers are his alter egos. These psychopaths gained a massive amount of attention for their shocking crimes. Wesley craved that attention and modeled himself after them, but thought he'd go one better and never get caught. He believed that if he could stump me, and get away with these crimes, that he would find "perfection in chaos."

Perhaps Wesley suffered from schizophrenia. I don't know if he had auditory or visual hallucinations but he certainly appeared paranoid. His deep identification with other serial killers suggests he may have actually thought he was a famous serial killer like William Edward Hickman.

What was inside Wesley Phelps? Another person fighting to get out? To be heard? We'll never know.

In some ways, I think Wesley and I are alike. We have demons inside us.

It's like my own chimera.

I've had something inside me fighting to get out. And I've tried all my life to ignore the other voice. The voice of my twin.

I'm writing this now because I must listen to my own voice. And it tells me that I must be healing because I feel deep love for Nick and I want to take care of his daughters.

I want to be free to feel whatever life offers.

I want to get on with my life.

Claire went into Nick's bedroom, which was comfortably cool. It was just past seven and the sun was peeking through cloudy morning sky, dappling the room with light. She leaned over Nick and kissed his lips, then pulled the blanket up under his chin. He opened his eyes.

"Good morning, sunshine," he said with a smile.

"How do you feel today?" she asked.

"Not bad for a guy who got shot and skewered by the same guy in one month," he said. "Where were you last night?"

"I fell asleep on the couch, writing in my brain book," she admitted. "Do you want me to get the girls up for school?"

Nick threw the covers off and slid his legs over the side of the bed. "Nah, I've got 'em. You go to work," he said with a twinkle in his eye. "Sounds like you've got a big day, and someone's gotta bring home the bacon in this house."

She kissed him, slipped off her nightgown, and headed for the shower.

"You wanted to see me?" Claire asked Doctor Fairborn as she entered her mentor's office.

Fairborn had a serious look on her face. "How is Nick doing?" she asked.

"He's fine," said Claire. "He's going back to work tomorrow."

"And the girls?" Fairborn asked.

"They're doing okay. Still recovering from the bomb scare in the car, but they're not afraid of Phelps coming back to haunt them anymore."

Fairborn pointed to the velour sofa, beckoning Claire to sit down. Then she sat down next to her—which Fairborn had never done before.

"If you're going to take care of this family, then you're going to need a real job. I just wanted to tell you that you've got one here if you want it."

"But I haven't graduated from the fellowship yet," Claire said.

"There's nothing more I can teach you," Fairborn replied. "You're ready."

Claire was stunned. She had barely been back to work at the hospital seeing patients and certainly didn't expect this.

"But the search committee . . ." was all she could muster.

"Couldn't find a candidate who'd done in their whole career what you have in the last two years. They asked me to ask you."

"But how can I accept a position I'm not even qualified for?" Claire asked.

"You'll be qualified in December when you finish the fellowship program, and you can officially take the job then. Unofficially I want you to start now, preparing to take on this important role."

"I—I don't know what to say," Claire stammered.

"Say you'll accept the position," Fairborn urged. "Please. We need you."

Claire waited for the voice in her head to tell her what to do—or not to do, which had usually been the case all her life. But this time there was no voice. Her head was clear.

"Yes," she said confidently. "I accept."

She held out her hand for Fairborn to shake. Her mentor scowled.

"I hardly think that's appropriate," said Fairborn, standing up and embracing her star pupil. "You're the bravest, most stubborn and frustrating person I've ever had the pleasure of knowing. Other than Paul Curtin," she added. "And he'd be proud to know you're the one filling his shoes. If maybe a little surprised."

"Thank you, Doctor," Claire said. "I don't know what I would have done without you."

"You would have done just fine, dear," Fairborn said. "You don't need my help. You never really did."

Claire left Fairborn, musing over what she meant by that last comment. She went back to her office and sat at her desk, looking out the window.

Maybe she meant I shouldn't second-guess myself so much. That I should trust my gut instead of judging myself all the time. Stop living in the past and move forward.

Her eyes landed on a young woman standing outside, her brown hair pulled back into a ponytail. From behind, she looked exactly like Rosa Sanchez. Claire gasped.

The woman turned and seemed to look up at the window. Claire waved, fully expecting to see Rosa again, and the woman waved back. But of course it wasn't Rosa at all. And the woman wasn't even waving at Claire. A little girl appeared, and the woman held out her hands, grabbed hold of the girl, and spun her around and around. The little girl laughed with such pure joy that Claire laughed too.

It was the first time she'd experienced her own pure joy in longer than she could remember. And with that, Claire knew she would be all right.